# SHADOWS WE REMAIN

## BY MOSE J GINGERICH

Published by Greendiver Press

This book is a work of fiction. Names, characters, places, and incidents are either a product of the author's imagination or are composed in part by personal life experiences from the author's time living among the Amish.

Copyright © 2021 by Mose J Gingerich

All rights reserved. No part of this publication may be reproduced, distributed, or transmitted in any form or by any means, electronic or mechanical, including photocopying, recording, or by any information storage or retrieval system, without the prior written permission of Greendiver Press, except where permitted by law.

Book cover design and interior formatting by JD&J Design LLC. Photography by Angelique Hunter, www.photobyangel.com

ISBN: 978-1-5136-8782-7

For my daughter Ella, who's unwavering faith in her father's ability to write fiction is what made this work possible.

*We can't fail if we never give up on the dream—until then,
we are only honing our craft.*

By Mose J Gingerich

# PROLOGUE

The crime was possible because the community was too innocent and trusting of outsiders. When the midwife told the father that there were complications and he had to leave the room, he believed her. When the midwife told the mother that she needed anesthesia, the mother believed her. After all, the midwife was skilled with many years of experience in such matters. Or so the parents had been told.

A single oil-burning lamp lit the tiny bedroom. Standing next to the bed, the midwife's shoulders sagged under the burden of the injustice she was expected to commit. A single tear trickled down her cheek, clung for a moment to her quivering chin, then fell. It splashed onto the swollen belly, as if to mark the spot where the incision would be made.

The midwife hesitated. The crime was too bold. Surely someone would intervene.

But nobody came. Instead, a figure stirred in the corner, and a glint of something shiny caught the midwife's eye. The figure seemed to glide from the shadows, revealing a head full of long, flowing, silver hair.

His ominous presence had the desired effect. The midwife shuddered and bent over the swollen belly.

When the two had arrived earlier in the evening, the man's charming smiles and confident reassurances had easily put the Amish parents at ease.

The man was not smiling now.

With trembling fingers, the midwife made the incision.

An hour later she was finished. She cradled the new bundle in her arms, and tears of shame fell upon the red, upturned face.

## Prologue

She flinched as the man stepped from the shadows and held out his arms for the bundle.

When the first of the neighbors arrived the next morning, they found a proud new mother with a newborn at her breast, completely oblivious to the crime that had just taken place.

# CHAPTER ONE

The man who checked out of the hotel in Grafton, Illinois, had booked the reservation under a fake ID. The desk clerk wouldn't have found that small detail particularly strange. Nor would he have thought it strange had he learned that Carl Stanton wasn't the man's real name. The man who temporarily called himself Carl had dark hair with dark matching sideburns that extended exactly two inches below the temples of his reading glasses. The age on his ID showed thirty-three, which wasn't strange either, since that's almost exactly the age the desk clerk would have guessed Carl Stanton to be.

What the desk clerk might have found strange however, is that as soon as the man left the hotel, Carl Stanton disappeared. Forever.

The man who emerged from under the disguise looked to be barely half the age on the ID. After the wig and glasses came off, a thin-faced boy with blonde hair stared back from the rearview mirror of the vehicle.

The boy's real name was Sparrow. And that was the strangest thing of all.

Sparrow was frowning as he left the hotel. The mission was a simple one. So simple in fact, that it flirted dangerously close to boring. Nobody would ever check the hotel records to see who had stayed there. But orders were orders, and regardless how pointless the mission, records would show that Sparrow was never at the hotel.

It was Friday afternoon, and the time on his watch showed 4:25, which left exactly thirty-five minutes before he was to be in

## Chapter One

position. Sparrow turned north. He followed a winding road that overlooked the Mississippi River to his left, and twenty minutes after he departed the hotel, he reached the town of Caroline Creek. A side street led to the town's only gas station and Sparrow parked his car.

*Fifteen minutes.*

Sparrow powered on the battery-operated device and studied it with a scornful level of disinterest. He tested its weight and adjusted his grip.

*Much better.*

The new grip allowed him to operate the device with only one hand. *Useful information in case anything went wrong.*

Sparrow frowned again as he got out of the car. As if anything could go wrong in Caroline Creek, population less than three hundred people. *What was there to worry about? A stray dog chasing a cat?*

His destination was exactly two blocks from the gas station and Sparrow approached it from a side alley, careful to remain in the shadows. He scanned the parking lot. The blue SUV was still there alright, sitting in the middle of the parking lot, just like he knew it would be.

At the far end of the lot a steep embankment rose to meet the city park. A picnic table and bench sat at the top of the embankment, and Sparrow nodded his approval. *This spot will do quite nicely.*

*Five minutes.*

Sparrow decided to take a quick walk through the park. His trained eyes moved over the terrain, observing every angle, storing the details to his memory. A handful of trees were scattered about, their freshly fallen leaves covering the brown grass. At the far end of the park another embankment led down to the adjacent street.

*Two minutes.*

Sparrow walked to the picnic table and sat down with his back to the blue SUV. He held the device up to his face and, using it like a mirror, zoomed in on the back door to the building less than a hundred feet away. With a slight twist of his wrist, he panned the device across the parking lot until the SUV popped into the corner of the screen. A smooth flex of his wrist back in the opposite direction followed the exit route the SUV would take after the driver got in.

The instructions hadn't mentioned filming the vehicle after the man got in, but what the hell. *Since I'm here anyway, why not?*

Sparrow tapped the record button and zoomed in on the door. Then he slowly lowered the device until his face appeared in the bottom corner of the screen. The instructions rang loud in his head.

*Others have been sent on this exact mission, so it's crucial that you get your face into the shot to prove you aren't borrowing someone else's footage.*

It was a strange request all right, but what did it matter? It was going to be his last training mission before he was sent on to the big time. Once he moved on from training, his first real task, so he had been told, was to steal documents from a heavily-guarded government building. Of course, a task like that would require some formal combat training. But in this too, Sparrow felt quite comfortable.

At exactly five o' clock the door to the titling office opened and a man stepped outside. He carried a briefcase in one hand and a cell phone in the other. He stared down at the screen as he walked, his brow furrowed in concentration. It was Friday evening, and the man had already put his place of work out of his mind until Monday morning.

Sparrow's device recorded the man's progress as he walked. Just before the man reached his SUV, a commotion sounded at

## Chapter One

the exit end of the parking lot. The man glanced up and froze, the confused expression on his face turning to one of terror. He dropped his briefcase and started to run in the opposite direction. His path led him straight toward the embankment, and Sparrow.

Curious, Sparrow adjusted the device to see what the man was running from. A second vehicle popped onto the edge of the screen. The vehicle quickly closed the distance on the running man. Someone leaned out of the passenger window and the sun glinted off a shiny object. There was a muffled shot and the man stumbled and went to one knee. His fingers loosened their grip on his cell phone, and it clattered across the concrete.

"You're going to an awful lot of trouble for a simple training exercise," Sparrow muttered into the camera.

The scene had moved so close that it filled up the entire screen and Sparrow zoomed out.

The man was up and running again, dragging one leg behind him. He was almost to the grass when another shot sounded and a streak of blood burst from the man's chest.

It was the second bullet that finally convinced Sparrow that the innocent training exercise was something much more. His mind raced. Was this part of a higher level of training to prepare him for the unexpected?

The man didn't make it to the grass. At least not on his own. The front bumper of the approaching car caught him from behind, creating a loud popping noise as the tire crushed the man's leg. The impact tossed the man halfway up the embankment.

From less than twenty feet away Sparrow now stood, mouth frozen open, the device recording a patch of grass at his feet.

The car's passenger door flew open and a man with a gun jumped out. But he wasn't looking at Sparrow. His eyes were focused on the man on the grass.

Terrified, the wounded man looked up and saw Sparrow. He started to crawl. One arm and leg hung useless, so he dragged them along. His eyes pleaded for help and he tried to speak, but only the sound of blood gurgling from his mouth reached Sparrows ears.

Then the man with the gun was at the wounded man's side. He kicked him hard in the ribs. The man screamed.

"You know what we do to rats?" the man with the gun shouted. He leaned in close and grinned into the man's grimacing face, then put the barrel of his gun to the man's temple and fired twice. The man on the ground shuddered and went limp.

It was the grin on the man's face as he pulled the trigger that snapped Sparrow out of his trance, a grin so evil that Sparrow involuntarily shuddered and shrank back. In that moment he knew he was going to die if the man with the gun saw him. And that is exactly what happened. The man straightened and wiped the blood from his face, then his eyes locked on Sparrow. He scowled and raised the gun to eye level. "Who are you?" he hissed.

Sparrow opened his mouth to speak but was interrupted when the driver's door was flung open and the second man got out.

"You gotta kill him," the driver shouted. "He saw everything."

It was the interruption Sparrow needed. Functioning on an instinct born of desperate fear, he spun and leapt backward over the top of the picnic table. As he vaulted through the air, his hands closed on the edge of the table and upended it, forming a barrier. Then, crouching to keep the table between him and the men, Sparrow sprinted for the trees. Behind him wood splintered as bullets riddled the table. One of the bullets sliced through the wood and dirt kicked up in his path. His sunglasses shattered from his face, forcing him to stagger and alter his course.

He reached the first tree and realized he had a chance. Keeping the tree between himself and the men, Sparrow ran. When he reached the next tree, he changed direction and ran at right angles. Not far ahead was the adjacent street, and beyond that, thick woods. If he reached the cover of those woods, he would live.

## Chapter One

Just before he reached the street, tires screeched and a car flew into view. The car stopped on the side of the street and the driver got out. The driver's head was just visible above the top of the embankment, so Sparrow dropped to his hands and knees. The head disappeared below the embankment.

From somewhere behind came grunting and cursing as the first man tried to climb the embankment at the picnic table. Desperate, Sparrow scanned the woods. Men bookended him from the front and rear, and if he ran sideways, he would lose the protection of the trees.

But the men didn't know exactly where he was. At least not yet. What he needed right now was a break. Even the smallest break. And he had seen one during his earlier walk through the park. Seen it and forgotten it, his mind storing it away to be drawn up later. It was his only option now. If he was wrong, he was dead.

Thirty seconds later the rear man reached the other side of the park. He stopped when he saw the driver and the car.

"Anything?" the driver called.

"He beat you across the road," the man yelled back.

"Impossible. Nobody can run that fast."

"Well that is exactly what happened," the man with the gun yelled back. "I've followed his trail through these leaves, and it leads right past you."

From where they stood, the men scanned the park and the woods on the other side of the street. They cursed loudly. Then car doors slammed, and the car sped away.

Less than ten feet from where the man with the gun had stood, a pile of leaves rustled. From a small indention in the ground a figure emerged, brushing leaves from his hair. For Sparrow, it had been a close call. Maybe the closest yet. The thing that had saved him was the clear path of overturned leaves he had left for the man to follow—a path that led right past his hiding spot and stopped at the edge of the street only a few steps away.

———◆———

The men who gathered to watch the footage were skeptical. As well they should be. Shug, the man presenting the tape, was no better than the murderers he claimed to have caught on the film.

Judge Henry Majors III looked at the men seated on his side of the table. They were men he had worked with before, men he could trust. To his right was FBI Agent Rick Wright, and to his left was Castleton Chief of Police Calvin Westbritt, whose men had been the first at the scene of the murder.

On the other side of the table sat Charles Schlugen, or Shug, as he was called by most of his acquaintances. In his mid to late fifties, Shug had a thin face and long silvery-white hair that fell to his shoulders. Next to Shug sat someone the men of law were very interested in speaking with.

Judge Majors opened the conversation by addressing Shug. "Are you aware that anything we discuss will be admissible in my courtroom if there is a trial?"

"I am," Shug replied.

"How do you claim to have gotten the footage?" the judge asked.

"Call it… right place at right time sort of thing," Shug said.

"So, you're claiming you had no knowledge the murder was going to take place?" the judge asked.

"Of course not," Shug lied.

Judge Majors turned to the boy next to Shug. "Are you the person who happened to be 'in the right place at the right time?'" he asked.

"I am," the boy replied.

# Chapter One

"State your full name please."

"Sparrow."

"Sparrow?" Judge Majors asked. "What else?"

As instructed, Sparrow didn't answer. Instead, Shug cleared his throat. "For now," he said, "the name *Sparrow* is all you need to know."

"And when do we 'need to know' more?" Judge Majors asked.

"Once a deal has been reached."

"A deal?"

"A deal."

"Tell me about this uh, deal."

Shug ignored the request. Instead, he turned to FBI Agent Wright. "The dead man was your informant, right?"

The question caught Agent Wright off guard, and he pondered it carefully.

Shug didn't wait for a response. "Actually, your man has been snitching on the mob for almost a year," he continued. "And you still don't have anything that puts any of us away. Sound about right?"

"Get to the point," Agent Wright snapped, his face reddening.

"I'm going to save you a ton of time and paperwork," Shug replied. "This tape will hand you the men on a silver platter."

"The men?" Agent Wright asked.

"Number one *and* number two."

"And the deal?"

"You can have the old man and his son," Shug said. "But I walk away with a clean slate. Anything your snitch might have told you about me becomes inadmissible at the trial."

Agent Wright cringed. He weighed Shug's offer carefully, then said. "You and these boys go way back. What's your angle?"

"Power," Shug replied simply. "What else?"

"With the old man and his son out of the way, you're next in line to take over the top seat?" Agent Wright asked, already knowing the answer.

Shug nodded.

"Being the boss comes with a lot of risk."

"I'll take my chances."

Agent Wright tapped the table and considered. Finally, he said. "Let's see the footage before we make any deals."

"Fair enough," Shug said. He slid the device across the table, then sat back, arms folded.

Judge Majors carefully picked the device up between a thumb and forefinger, as if half-expecting the murderers to emerge from the device and continue their killing spree. He walked to a television set at the end of the room and plugged it in, then came back with a remote control in his hand.

The footage started, and Sparrow's face appeared in the bottom corner of the screen. The rear door of the building opened, and the man began to walk across the parking lot.

All eyes around the table were glued to the television set as a second vehicle moved onto the screen. They caught the glint as the gun barrel emerged from the passenger window and a puff of smoke rose from the barrel. A few seconds later came another puff.

Judge Majors paused the tape and hit the rewind button. He zoomed in on the victim's chest and replayed the scene in slow motion. He paused the tape at the exact moment where the second bullet hit the man. The terrified expression on the man's face, and the blood spurting from his chest, now frozen in midair on the judge's television, squelched any doubts of the tape's authenticity.

Nobody spoke, so Judge Majors hit the play button again.

Just as the bumper of the vehicle was about to hit the man, the footage began to get shaky. At the bottom of the screen Sparrow's face turned to confusion, then the scene disappeared. The screen filled with green grass and the toes of Sparrow's shoes.

Judge Majors thumbed the pause button again. His face was tight with tension. "Where's the rest of it?"

"That's pretty much it," Shug said. "Sparrow got scared and ran. The rest of the footage is all audio, well, except for a few seconds at the very end that you might find helpful."

Judge Majors frowned and rewound the tape. He played it again in slow motion. "No license plates," he said dryly. "Can't really see faces. Lots of circumstantial evidence here. Could've been anyone in that car."

Chief Calvin Westbritt cleared his throat and spoke for the first time. "From the sound of it, your boy here saw the murder. That correct?"

"That's correct."

"Could he identify the man from a lineup? I mean under pressure?"

All eyes turned to Sparrow, who sat pale-faced.

Sparrow nodded silently.

Judge Majors turned back to the monitor and hit the play button. For a while there was nothing but heavy breathing and a blur of grass and leaves. Then came complete silence, the only image on the TV screen the underside of a brown leaf.

"What's this?" Judge Majors asked.

"Sparrow hiding under a pile of leaves," Shug said, shrugging.

For almost a full minute the silence continued, the timer at the top of the screen the only indication that the footage was still playing.

*Four minutes fifty-four seconds.*

*Fifty-five.*

*Fifty-six.*

A twig snapped loudly and everyone around the table jumped. Leaves rustled near where Sparrow hid, then the sound of someone breathing heavily. When the man with the gun yelled to the man by the car, he sounded like he was standing almost on top of Sparrow and the recording device. The footsteps on leaves moved a few paces, then stopped again.

Silently, the leaf that was covering the front of the recording device, shifted. The footage on the TV screen panned upward, then stopped when the view reached the man's backside. The man was so close that the white knuckles that gripped his gun popped out on the screen like the cold twisted roots of a dead tree.

The man seemed to be scanning the trees and listening, his eyes prying for movement or sound.

The camera footage remained steady.

Finally, the man started down the embankment and disappeared.

The sound of the car started up, and then the footage ended.

Judge Majors' hand trembled as he hit the rewind button. He paused when he reached the backside of the man with the gun. "Does anyone recognize him?" he asked.

"That's Joey Trontelli," Shug stated confidently.

Judge Majors hesitated. "Anyone else?" he asked, glancing around the table.

"That's him all right," Chief Westbritt confirmed. "I recognize the voice."

"So, this footage puts *number two* in the area at the time of the murder," Judge Majors said. He turned back to Sparrow. "Besides that, we have an eye-witness who says he saw him pull the trigger."

Sparrow nodded.

Judge Majors turned to Agent Wright.

"Your call," Agent Wright said.

"Can it hold up in court?" Chief Westbritt asked.

"If the kid testifies, yes. We have a pretty strong case."

## Chapter One

Judge Majors removed a handkerchief from a coat pocket and wiped his forehead. He thumbed through his cell phone and checked his calendar. "Okay," he said. "Let's everyone meet in my office next Thursday at four o' clock. That's six days from now. I will have a court reporter and a state's attorney present, and we'll take a real deposition. Make it all official. At the deposition we will set a date for the trial."

"So, we have a deal?" Shug asked.

"We have a deal."

———•———

Shug's well-thought-out plan to become *number one* wasn't without flaws. The first indication that things were off to a shaky start occurred after they left the meeting and Sparrow finally voiced his concerns aloud. He, Sparrow, was now a snitch. So, who would protect him from meeting the same fate as the dead man?

Shug, unprepared for the question, handled it poorly. He began by addressing the bigger picture. He, Shug, would become the new head of the crime family, and for his unselfish sacrifices, Sparrow would be elevated in status to his right-hand man.

"Unless I'm dead," Sparrow stated.

Shug tried to defend his claims, but his voice held no conviction, and Sparrow realized the truth. A lifetime of loyalty to Shug, the only man he had ever answered to, could easily earn him a swift death as soon as he testified at the trial.

Late that night Sparrow made a difficult decision. He would do what it took to stay alive.

When Shug awoke on Saturday morning, Sparrow's room was empty. Gone also was the tape. And as the weight of Sparrow's betrayal hit Shug, he staggered at the consequences it might have.

Even before Shug glanced at his calendar to confirm the deposition date, now only five days away, he had already begun to assess the damages, and how best to remedy the situation. What was most obvious was that he needed both Sparrow *and* the tape for the trial to happen.

All day Saturday, Shug struggled with his decision. He had come way too far, and the stakes were way too high to fail now. But Sparrow was too well trained, and would never be caught, so, he would have to be replaced. Replaced with someone that could pass as Sparrow. And Shug knew of someone who could pass as exactly that person. Someone who lived off the grid, and who wouldn't really be missed all that much if things started to go wrong. The thing had to be done. Even if it meant risking everything.

Late Saturday afternoon, Shug picked up his phone and made a call. It was the phone call that would change everything.

## CHAPTER TWO

Bruce Ellsworth first heard about the murder in Caroline Creek on the way to his office on Monday morning. He had stopped at the usual café and ordered the usual breakfast, and it was while he was waiting for his coffee that he happened to glance up from his newspaper and see the headlines flashing silently across the screen of a small television mounted in a corner of the café.

Bruce frowned. *The name of the dead man is familiar, but why?*

Chief Westbritt appeared on the screen, no doubt talking about how the killer would be found and held accountable. Bruce's frown deepened. The chief handled himself well on camera, Bruce admitted to himself. Well, maybe not quite as well as he had when he was chief of police. But Chief Westbritt wasn't shabby. Not shabby at all.

Bruce kept one eye on the front door of the café. The client he was supposed to meet was already ten minutes late. He turned back to the story on the television, and the dead man's name clicked in his memory. He remembered it from a case he had worked on when he was Detective Bruce Ellsworth with the Castleton Police Department.

But too many years, too many cases had gone by to remember all the details just now. Bruce wrote the man's name on a paper napkin. He would connect the dots when he got to his office.

The front door opened, and the client entered.

Bruce nodded and the man sat down on the other side of the table, fidgeting nervously.

"Did you bring the money?" Bruce asked.

The man nodded, took a deep breath, then slowly slid an envelope across the table as if, in doing so, he was giving away a piece of his soul. This wasn't far from the truth, as he would soon learn.

Bruce thumbed through the hundred-dollar bills, then stuffed the envelope into his pocket. He slid a large manila envelope back across the table.

The man stared at it for a long minute, as if giving himself one last opportunity to change his mind and not look at what he would never be able to unsee. Finally, with trembling fingers, he pulled open the flap of the envelope. He glanced cautiously around the café, then removed several photos and placed them on the table.

Bruce's food arrived. There were four eggs, over medium, and six slices of wheat toast. Bruce spread grape jelly onto a piece of toast, dipped it into some egg yolk, and put it into his mouth. He savored the combination of sweet and sour on his tongue before swallowing.

The man's chin began to quiver, then he started to cry. He held his hand to the side of his face to hide the large salty drops that fell upon the contents of the envelope. Embarrassed, he rose quickly, stuffed the photos back into the envelope and turned to go. He glanced at Bruce as if expecting some sort of sympathy hug.

"I'm sorry about your situation," Bruce said without much conviction.

The man nodded without making eye contact.

Not many of them did.

"When?" the man asked.

"Two nights ago," Bruce said. "There is a detailed account of her entire weekend. Credit card expenses. Hotel room receipts. It's all there."

The man nodded, thanked Bruce half-heartedly, then walked out the door.

## Chapter Two

Bruce turned back to his food. He probably wouldn't see the man again. He would never learn what became of his marriage, or the once-prosperous business that was now on the brink of bankruptcy. That was okay with Bruce. He had done the job he was hired to do. He had followed, and documented, the cheating spouse. The gig hadn't paid enough to allow the man to cry on his shoulder. Sure, it was a far cry from his old days as chief of police, but it paid the bills.

Bruce's cell phone rang, and he answered on the second ring. The voice on the other end was Susan Finch, his office secretary.

"You have visitors," Susan said in a subdued voice.

"Who?"

"I think they are Amish," Susan replied. She pronounced *Amish* with the long "*A*" sound, typical of someone who isn't familiar with the word.

"Did they give you a name?" Bruce asked, his breakfast suddenly forgotten.

"Andy and Ruth Reader," Susan replied.

For the second time that morning Bruce's mind flashed back in time. But this time he knew exactly when and where he remembered the names from.

"Tell them I will be at the office in twenty minutes," he said, tossing a twenty-dollar bill onto the table as he left the café.

The drive from the café to his office should have taken less than ten minutes, but the twenty-two traffic lights almost tripled that time. The lights had long been a source of frustration for Bruce, but for once he didn't seem to notice. For him, the routine drive to work had turned into a morning of nostalgia.

Some years ago, he had worked a case for the Reader family. Ruth was a young mother who had given birth at home. When complications followed the birth, she was admitted to a hospital in St. Louis. There, the hospital staff learned that someone had attempted to perform a C-section at the Reader home. The matter was reported, which was how the Castleton Police Department had gotten involved. The midwife was never was located, and other cases quickly took priority.

Bruce was still reminiscing when he pulled up to the curb outside his office at 1311 East Fennimore Street.

# CHAPTER THREE

The Readers were sitting in the waiting room. There were three of them, and they looked up expectantly when Bruce entered.

Andy Reader sat in the middle with a woman on each side. Bruce had to look twice before he could discern which one was the mother and which was the daughter. He decided the nearer one had to be the daughter because she looked to be in her mid-teens. A black shawl was draped around her shoulders, and a black bonnet covered all but the front of her face. Her green dress protruded from the bottom of a shawl that reached almost to the floor.

Ruth sat on the far side, and Bruce caught his breath. The face hadn't aged much. And there was something about the innocent brown eyes that caught Bruce off guard every time.

"Andy and Ruth Reader," Bruce laughed. "I thought I recognized you. And who is this young one?" he asked, nodding at the teenager.

Andy Reader rose, unsmiling, and shook Bruce's hand. The women remained seated and silent. A closer look at their solemn faces, and Bruce quickly realized that the Readers were not in the mood for pleasantries.

"You've met my wife, Ruth," Andy said curtly. "And this is our daughter, Maria."

Bruce nodded at Maria, who returned a warm smile. Bruce did some quick math. Maria would be just about old enough to attend the Singens—the gathering of unmarried Amish teens on Sunday evenings—and no doubt her natural beauty was drawing the attention of more than a few boys in the community.

The pained expression on Ruth's face told him part of the tale. The bubbly charm that had warmed him to her years ago was gone. There were dark circles under her eyes that might have been concealed, had she chosen to wear makeup.

Andy Reader stepped closer, the motion drawing Bruce's focus away from his wife. Beneath his wide-brimmed black wool hat, his face was pale and drawn.

"Can we talk in private?" he asked, glancing nervously in Susan's direction.

"Certainly," Bruce said. "We can go upstairs to my office. Come on, follow me."

From her chair Susan watched the proceedings, trying to act like a visit from an Amish family was perfectly normal. She grasped her cup of coffee in both hands and took a long and deliberate sip. Over the top of the cup she watched the Readers follow Bruce toward the stairs.

Andy Reader wore a pair of faded blue corduroy pants held up by a pair of black suspenders. He wore a white button-down shirt and a pair of barn boots, which he had not taken the time to wash, because small clumps of animal manure dislodged and left a trail on the floor as he walked.

Susan jolted from her trance at the last minute.

"Do you want me to take your shawls and bonnets?" she asked, quickly rising and pointing toward the clothes hooks inside the front door.

The procession paused at the foot of the stairs and Susan watched as mother and daughter waited for Andy to make the decision for them. Andy considered the request. He seemed to reach a decision, because he nodded his permission.

The two women removed their shawls and bonnets and handed them to Susan, who hung them up, and then retreated to her chair. The cup of coffee went back to its original position in front of her face.

## Chapter Three

Ruth was a petite woman. Susan guessed her to be in her mid-thirties. A navy-blue dress reached to her ankles, and a white apron hung down the front, its strings tied neatly behind her back. A white cap on her head covered all but a few wisps of brown hair.

Susan wondered why Ruth wore a white cap, but her daughter's cap was black? She decided she would ask Bruce later.

Maria noticed Susan's curiosity and gave her a weak, sideways smile, then followed her mother.

Upstairs, Bruce moved a few chairs into a half circle in the middle of the room, then turned his own chair to face them. The smell of tobacco smoke hung in the air, and he quickly walked to the only window in the room and opened it.

"All right," he said, sitting back down. "What brings you in today?"

"Go ahead, tell him," Andy said, nodding to his wife.

"Our Eli… has run away." Ruth choked out the words as if they carried great weight. She rocked back in her chair and wrung her hands.

"Eli is your son?" Bruce asked, following along slowly.

"Yes, he is," Ruth responded. The words began to rush out in a confused scatter. "He seemed so happy, and he had so many friends, and we just never thought it would be him and… and… well here. He left this note." Ruth handed a folded yellow piece of paper to Bruce.

Bruce read the words slowly.

*I can't live this life any longer. I am going to a place that's far away from here. Do not come looking for me. I will write pretty soon.*

The bottom of the page was signed only: *Eli*

"How old is Eli?" Bruce asked.

"Fifteen. He will turn sixteen in a few weeks," Ruth answered.

"So, he's a minor," Bruce stated.

He received blank stares.

"Start from the beginning," Bruce said. "Was Eli having problems at home? Anything that makes you think he would run away?"

"No," Ruth responded. "Eli is a good boy. Really shy. He has never made any trouble for the church."

Ruth turned to her daughter. "You were the last to see him," she said. "Tell Bruce what you know."

"Yesterday morning after Eli and I finished the chores, I went in to help with breakfast, and Eli stayed behind to feed the chickens. When he didn't come in for breakfast, we got worried. We searched the barn and found the note in the milk house."

Maria's English, Bruce noted, was much better than her mother's.

Out of habit, Bruce reached for a pad and began to scribble notes.

"Would Eli have told you if he had plans to run away?" Bruce asked.

Maria nodded. "Eli and I talk a lot. We tell each other everything. He would have told me."

"So, you think there is more to this than a runaway brother?"

Maria nodded. "And there is something else. It's possible that it isn't anything, but we haven't seen our dog. We think he might have gone with Eli."

Bruce made a note of the missing dog. Below that he also noted that Andy had not voiced an opinion on his missing son. Instead, Andy sat with slumped shoulders and stared at a button on Bruce's shirt. He tugged at his scraggly black beard and tried to maneuver a thin tuft into the corner of his mouth, but it wouldn't quite reach.

"May I keep this note?" Bruce asked, holding Eli's note by a corner.

"Of course," Ruth replied. "But what will you do with it?"

## Chapter Three

"I think I'll have a forensic analyst look it over," Bruce said. "See if there are any strange fingerprints. There are other things they can look for as well. Like whether the person who wrote it was under any sort of stress."

The three looked puzzled but nodded their consent.

Bruce made a copy of the note and handed it to Ruth. He put the original in his desk drawer.

"I would also like to take each of your fingerprints," Bruce said.

"Why?" Andy Reader suddenly straightened, his black eyes suspicious.

"Elimination," Bruce explained. "I need to get your fingerprints on file so I can eliminate you as suspects."

"Such a thing goes against our religion," Andy Reader snapped. "The church would never allow it."

"Just trying to help," Bruce said, a little taken aback by Andy's sudden defiance.

The atmosphere in the room had suddenly turned tense, and Bruce thought he would try and change the subject.

"So how in the world did you guys find me?" he asked.

"We went to the Castleton Police Department first," Ruth replied. "They filed a missing child report, and..."

"And they told you they have to wait for forty-eight hours before they can open an investigation on a runaway teen," Bruce finished for her.

"Yes, they said that," Ruth replied. "So, we asked for you and they said you no longer worked there. They gave us this address. Our driver found the place with his phone."

"Well I'm not sure how much I can do," Bruce said slowly. "It won't take long to analyze this note. Once I have the results, I'll come out to your place and let you know what we found."

Ruth's lower lip quivered. "Our Eli is not ready for the world," she said.

"Well as I said before, Eli is still a minor," Bruce said. "Whoever is helping him will be in a world of legal trouble."

"We just have two children," Ruth continued. "Maria and Eli."

Bruce thought he caught a twinkle in her eyes.

Ruth nodded in Maria's direction. "I would not have guessed Eli would be the one to run away. Already this one is making trouble for the church."

Maria rolled her eyes and glared at her mother. "You don't have to tell strangers my secrets," she said.

Bruce rose and stretched. "Do you still live at the same address?" he asked.

"We do," Ruth said, breaking into a full smile.

And there it finally was—that charming smile that could easily have been mistaken for mild flirtation. The mood in the room lightened instantly.

Andy Reader sensed the change and got to his feet. He clenched his fist at no one in particular as he opened his mouth to speak.

"The world is full of demons and sinners," he said in a thin voice that complemented his pale face and sunken features. "Give Satan your little finger and before you know it, he has your whole body. That's what happened to Eli. He started to play with fire, and now Satan got him."

Andy was small in stature, and his attempt at an authoritative tone fell flat. Bruce studied him with a puzzled expression on his face, while Ruth and Maria shifted uncomfortably, their eyes on the floor.

Andy took a handkerchief from the pocket of his pants. The handkerchief was yellow with age and looked like it hadn't been washed recently. Andy removed his wool hat. His black hair was thin and greasy and sweat dribbled and ran into his eyes from the exertion of his words. He mopped his brow and put the handkerchief back into his pocket.

## Chapter Three

"Find Eli before Satan finishes him, and it is eternally too late!" He turned shakily and started for the stairs. Ruth and Maria rose and followed.

Bruce held the door as they filed out of the room, then followed them down the stairs. The women put their shawls and bonnets on in silence, then without a backward glance, followed Andy out the door. They crossed the street and got into a parked van.

"May I ask what that was all about?" Susan asked, interrupting his thoughts. "Are Amish people always that intense?"

"Their son disappeared," Bruce said. "They want me to help find him."

"You think he ran away?" Susan mused.

"Possible. But too early to tell."

"I noticed the mother was wearing a white cap, but the daughter's was black. Any idea why?" Susan asked.

"It's how you can tell who is married," Bruce said, still distracted. "Married Amish women wear white caps, unmarried wear black. It's the same reason married Amish men have beards, and unmarried men are cleanshaven."

"But why is that information important?" Susan asked curiously. "Out here in the world if we want to know if someone is married, we simply ask."

"Maybe it's for when they visit a new community where they don't know each other," Bruce replied. "That way they can save themselves the embarrassment of asking a married member on a date."

Susan pondered this for a bit, then seemed satisfied with the answer. She changed topics. "You and her. I noticed how you looked at each other. Is there something you need to tell me?"

"Who?" Bruce asked, avoiding Susan's eyes.

"The mother, of course. Don't play dumb with me." Susan's eyes begged for details.

The van pulled away from the curb and disappeared around the corner.

"You know, Susan," Bruce said as he started for the stairs, "some days you can be downright nosy."

As Bruce was pouring his fourth cup of coffee, his cell phone rang again. He smiled when he heard the familiar voice on the other end.

"Stan Prater, you ugly bastard," he said. "It's been too long. How the hell did you know I was about to call you?"

# CHAPTER FOUR

The Thirsty Toad sits a mile outside the city limits in Collinsville, Illinois. It is far enough off the main highway that it attracts mostly local customers, which is what makes it a favorite of the boys from the precinct.

Bruce backed his Explorer into a parking spot next to an old wooden fence in the gravel parking lot behind the Toad. For a few minutes he watched the entrance from the street. He did a quick count of the vehicles in the parking lot. There were seventeen. Three or four of the cars belonged to employees. That left thirteen—if half of them brought a passenger, the math came to about twenty customers inside.

*Haven't worn the uniform in years,* Bruce thought. *Why am I still cautious? Old habits, huh?*

Bruce turned up the collar of his gray winter coat and pulled his Cardinals baseball cap down low. The wind blew in gusts, and a pile of leaves stirred between the fence and a dumpster in the corner of the lot.

Bruce ducked as he entered the Toad. Roger Eberling looked up from the sink behind the counter and waved a wet washrag.

"Good afternoon partner. The usual?"

"You got it," Bruce said.

Jen, the plump, rosy-cheeked waitress, shot a smile in Bruce's direction. "I'll bring your coffee in a jiffy."

Bruce nodded and made his way to the rear of the diner. He glanced around the room and counted eighteen customers. Through the swinging doors that led to the bar area in back came the clack of the cue-ball as it hit its mark.

A middle-aged couple with two toddlers sat at a window booth, each of them using one hand to shove food into their mouth and the other to hold their cell phone to their face, all the while ignoring their noisy children.

Across the room two lawyer-types in dark suits hunched over a table. Recently-loosened ties hung like nooses from their necks as they discussed cases.

In one corner, a college-aged girl with a black ponytail stared at her laptop screen and sipped from a coffee cup.

Stan Prater was waiting in a corner booth, and he was on his fourth glass of whiskey. He looked up and frowned when Bruce sat down.

"And hello to you too," Bruce said, a hint of annoyance in his voice. "I see Alcoholics Anonymous has once again been a smashing success."

His ex-partner was in street clothes, and a bit thicker around the waist than Bruce remembered. The bald spot in the middle of his close-cropped red hair had expanded a little farther in every direction, but mostly backward. Apparently Stan was even more self-conscious about it than before, because he kept his head tilted upward, as if to reveal the entirety of the dreadful damage to the wall behind him—a wall with a framed glass photo that perfectly mirrored the bald spot back to the diner, should anyone care to look. The red-and-white checkered tablecloth reflected in Stan's dirty wire-rimmed spectacles and Bruce thought he could have passed for a rodeo clown.

"Did you run into any trouble getting the files?" Bruce asked, nodding at the briefcase under the table.

"Like you'd care if I got into trouble helping you," Stan replied dryly. "Three years you don't call, don't check up on me."

"You're right," Bruce replied, trying to hide a wry smile. "I don't care about you. Except when I need something."

## Chapter Four

Stan ignored the jab. He leaned across the table, suddenly seeming to forget the bald spot on top of his head. "Your favor could cost me my job. What's this all about, Bruce?"

"You go first," Bruce said. "Did you find anything unusual about the note Eli Reader left behind?"

Stan paused, no doubt calculating how much suspense he should spin into his narrative. Possibly it was the alcohol, because he gave up quickly. "So, get a load of this," he said, talking fast. "The Amish kid may not be as innocent as his family believes."

"Tell me more."

Stan leaned in closer and lowered his voice. "Multiple sets of fingerprints on the note. There were your prints of course, but besides yours there is a second set of fingerprints."

Stan paused to allow the weighted statement to sink in. Bruce ignored him. Instead, he picked up a menu and began to study it carefully.

"The second set of prints is already in the system," Stan volunteered.

Stan watched Bruce's face carefully, hoping for some drastic change in expression.

Bruce flipped a page in the menu and yawned. It was a tactic he had used often. Give Stan enough time and he would volunteer every detail without any prodding. Then, if Bruce didn't stop him, he would begin to come up with his own theories.

Bruce decided not to stop him.

"The prints belong to a girl that dances down at *Stripper Mall*," Stan continued.

"You don't say," Bruce replied, feigning disinterest.

"Her stage name is *Summer*, and she dances at the one called the Dark Angel. Remember it?"

Bruce nodded. "I remember it."

"In the past, we have booked Summer for doing some after-hours side business, if you know what I mean. Which is how her prints are in the system."

"Okay," Bruce said slowly. "So, our innocent Amish kid has a crush on a stripper. That doesn't prove anything. The most likely explanation is that he ran off with her."

Stan stared at Bruce, enthusiasm draining from his face. "Then why did you ask me to go to all that trouble to sneak out the old files?" he blurted.

Bruce answered the question with one of his own. "Let me guess," he said. "I bet you were about to tell me the Dark Angel is still owned by the Trontelli Crime Family. And you figured the reason I asked for the files is because I see a connection between the mob and the missing Amish kid. That sound about right?"

Stan drained his glass and set it down hard on the table. "God I've missed you, you ornery old goat," he laughed. "You haven't lost a step."

Bruce didn't smile. "But I'm not buying your theory," he continued. "And I'll tell you why. The whole connection seems a bit far-fetched. A stripper with mob connections is hanging out with an Amish kid. C'mon, Stan. Am I missing something?"

"Only one thing," Stan said, his face reddening.

Bruce waited.

"The man who was murdered in Caroline Creek on Friday evening was an informant for the FBI. *And*, he was murdered less than five miles from where the Amish kid lived."

Bruce nodded thoughtfully. He had always been impressed with how well Stan could articulate for a man who was often half-drunk. But Bruce remembered something else. Regardless of how wasted Stan got, he would be one of the first to arrive at the precinct the following morning, and he always showed up well-dressed and clear-eyed. Not that any excuses could be made

## Chapter Four

for Stan's addiction. In fact, the reason Stan was familiar with Alcoholics Anonymous was because Bruce had sent him there himself. The decision had been part of a compromise that kept Stan on at the precinct.

Stan licked his lips and scanned the room, searching for Jen. "It hasn't been the same since you left," he continued. "I really hate the new chief. The paperwork this guy is shoving down our throats. I tell you. And his phantom priorities..." Stan's voice trailed off as Jen appeared with Bruce's coffee.

"Another drink, hon?" Jen asked, glancing at Stan's empty glass.

"Yeah. For sure," Stan replied, sitting a little straighter. "And bring one for my old buddy here."

"What'll it be, Bruce?"

"I'll have one beer," Bruce replied.

"One beer comin' up," Jen smiled.

"Hoppin' for a Tuesday night, eh?" Bruce asked.

"All the farmers are coming in," Jen said. "Harvest is over, and they got money in their pockets. The tips are bigger, at least for a while." She winked at Bruce and left to get his drink.

"Thanks for getting me the files," Bruce said after Jen left. "Question though?"

"Yeah?" Stan asked.

"The guy who was murdered Friday night?"

Stan nodded. "I was one of the first to the murder scene."

"It was a mob hit, right?"

"It was."

"You're sure?"

Stan glanced around the room and lowered his voice. "Rumor has it that Joey Trontelli was in the area around the time of the murder."

"Whose rumor?"

"Chief Westbritt himself."

"And how would he already have that information?"

"Because he got called into a private meeting. A deal is being made, Bruce."

"With who?"

"He wouldn't say. Top secret stuff."

"Who else was at the meeting?"

"A judge. I think the feds sent one of theirs too."

"Sounds like a serious deal," Bruce said. "See what else you can find out. I'd like to know who is getting the good end of this one."

Stan nodded. "Will do, boss."

"The fingerprints bring up an interesting point," Bruce continued.

"They do?"

"Well, for now we have to assume the Amish kid is holed up in a hotel room with a stripper," Bruce said.

"So, if you are convinced there is no connection between the murder and Eli Reader's disappearance, what do you want with the files?" Stan repeated the question he had asked earlier.

"Call it a hunch," Bruce replied.

"You don't do hunches," Stan said dryly.

"I also don't do coincidences," Bruce said. "And for now, that's all this is, a simple coincidence. But because we have a mob hit, a stripper, and a runaway Amish kid, all in one weekend, I am going to approach this one a little differently."

"Differently?" Stan asked.

"I'm going to approach this thing from the angle that everything is connected, then I'm going to work backward to prove myself wrong."

Stan took another long swig from his glass and made a half-hearted attempt at following Bruce's logic. He failed miserably. "Let me know how I can help," he said.

"Sure," Bruce replied. "I think I'll take a trip out to the Reader farm, snoop around a bit. Care to join me?"

## Chapter Four

"Afraid I'll have to pass," Stan said, his words beginning to slur. "My oldest son is neck deep in baseball. You should come to a game sometime."

"I'll do that," Bruce replied.

Stan gripped the edge of the table for balance, then stood. "I'm going to go play a game of pool. Wanna join me?"

"Not tonight," Bruce replied. He waved a hand toward the briefcase under the table. "Gotta find a missing Amish kid."

Stan saluted Bruce, a clownish grin on his face. Then he turned and disappeared through the swinging doors and into the back.

Jen stopped by to pick up Stan's empty glass and Bruce handed her a fifty-dollar bill.

"I'll be back with the change," Jen said.

"Actually," Bruce said, nodding toward the seat that had held Stan a few minutes earlier. "Use what you need to make sure Stan gets home safely. Keep the rest."

Bruce walked to the swinging doors and watched the crowd in the back. A few old ranchers sat at the bar, and someone was putting money into the jukebox. Stan leaned heavily against the pool table and tried to put quarters in the slots. Bruce thought about joining him, but the weight of the briefcase reminded him that he had more important things to do.

The front of the restaurant was almost empty, and Bruce scanned the booths as he walked toward the door. The college girl with the black ponytail was still in the corner and Bruce hesitated. The time on his watch showed a few minutes after eleven o' clock. He thought it curious that a female student would still be out studying. Especially at a restaurant that was now turned into a bar. And somehow, he picked up a faint vibe that the girl had been watching him. He thought of introducing himself, but the girl seemed absorbed in her work, so he walked on. He filed the image of the girl in the back of his memory. It would remain there, alongside about a million other faces that hadn't quite fit. If he ever saw the girl again, he would remember her. He would piece together the exact place and time their paths had crossed. Some called it paranoia. Others thought of it as a curse. Bruce Ellsworth used it to stay alive.

---

The girl with the black ponytail waited until the lights from the investigator's vehicle disappeared into the dark. She glanced around the room. Nobody was paying attention, so she slid into the corner booth where the two men had sat. Her hand moved beneath the table and traced the outlines of the digital recorder she had placed there earlier. The device disappeared into her computer case.

When Jen came out of the kitchen a few minutes later, the restaurant section of the Thirsty Toad was empty.

---

Long after the rest of Florissant, Missouri slept, the upstairs lights at 1311 East Fennimore Street remained on. Bruce Ellsworth sat at his desk, his broad shoulders and tall frame hunched over the Trontelli files. A pipe hung from the corner of his mouth, and smoke drifted up in circles, giving the room a hazy gloom.

The Trontelli crime family had been around since the early 1900's. Their headquarters were in Chicago, but they owned a string of night clubs and casinos that stretched to St. Louis, Memphis, and all the way to Dallas. Bruce had long suspected that their entities were used as a front for laundering money and possibly even trafficking drugs.

For much of his time as a detective with the Castleton Police Department, Bruce had worked on the Trontelli files. At one time,

## Chapter Four

he had known the name of every member of the family. He had even personally known most of their top guys.

But things had changed. Guys had gotten killed off. Or been transferred to other cities. The top guys remained, but beneath them, the lines of who belonged where, were grey.

It had been while working on the Trontelli case that Bruce was promoted to chief of police. The added responsibilities had left less time to work the case, and it was shelved.

Now, while Bruce re-familiarized himself with the files, his mind went back to the woman, and the affair. She had been an employee of the precinct, and she was the reason he was now a private investigator instead of chief of police. She had loved him, or so she said. At the time it hadn't seemed like such a bad trade—his job for someone he would spend the rest of his life with.

But they hadn't spent the rest of their lives together. In fact, Bruce reminded himself, their problems had started almost as soon as he lost his job, and not for the first time Bruce wondered if she had truly loved him, or simply been infatuated by his status as chief.

Bruce refilled his pipe, lit the fresh tobacco, and inhaled deeply. He blew the smoke out through his nose and leaned back in his chair. He forced his mind back to the present. His failure to put away a single member of the Trontelli crime family had long hung over him like a gloomy asterisk. But if Stan Prater's information was to be trusted, and a deal was being made, inserting himself back into the center of things might be just the boost his private career needed. Digging into the Trontelli files would be off the record. He would not get paid for his time and efforts, but the recent murder in Caroline Creek had brought up old unsettled scores. It would not be the first time he had worked multiple cases at the same time, and besides, the missing Amish kid really didn't pose much of a challenge.

Bruce scribbled notes and entered data into his computer. The clutter that was his *Crazy Wall* of evidence began to expand and make sense. The *Crazy Wall* had been so named because of the numerous scattered post-it notes, the dividing borders made of color-coded yarn—held in place by scotch tape, and about a million random scribblings that were unreadable to anyone but Bruce.

One half of the wall was made of a magnetic dry-erase whiteboard, and Bruce cleared a space, the Trontelli Case taking priority over the mystery of a missing land deed that had been on the board.

At the very top of the wall, Bruce pinned a black-and-white photo of Ralphie Trontelli—crime boss, and as of the last documented report on file—head of the family.

Below Ralphie, and forming the beginnings of a triangle, Bruce placed a photo of Ralphi's only son. Joey Trontelli had recently been released from prison after serving only eighteen of a forty-five-year sentence. Joey had been out for less than a year, but according to Stan Prater, was now the prime suspect in the recent murder in Caroline Creek.

Bruce studied the order of power from the top of the triangle. If a deal was being made that would put away both Ralphie and Joey Trontelli, or number one and number two, as they had long been referred to, who was the next man in the line of power? Who had the most to gain by making a deal?

The face almost jumped from the wall, and Bruce wondered why he hadn't seen it sooner. The name was Charles Schlugen, better known as Shug.

Shug headed the St. Louis end of the Trontelli operations, while Old Man Trontelli and his son Joey watched from a distant Chicago. Shug had never even once been convicted of a crime, yet he was always there. Shug was not loud and splashy like most members of the Trontelli family. Rather, he was more of an undercurrent that lurked just beneath the mightier forces.

## Chapter Four

The color photo of Shug stared back from the *Crazy Wall*. Wavy, silver hair fell below his shoulders, and his piercing blue eyes seemed to pin Bruce to the opposite wall.

*You're playing a dangerous game,* Bruce said to the photo. *Do you really think you can betray the family, and nobody will come after you?*

The more he thought about it, the more sense it made. Finally, Bruce removed the photo of Joey Trontelli from the second spot and replaced it with the photo of Shug. The new order of power made more sense.

With a black dry-erase marker, Bruce drew a line down the center of the *Crazy Wall*. The left side would be for the Trontelli crime family, and the right side of the line would be reserved for Eli Reader.

Bruce didn't have much to add to the right side, so he sketched a crude drawing of Summer, the girl who danced at the Dark Angel, and whose fingerprints had been found at the Reader farm. Next to Summer Bruce drew another sketch of Eli Reader. He connected Eli and Summer's sketches with a red piece of yarn, then let the end hang loosely to the floor. He would come back to it later. Almost as an afterthought, he drew a sketch of a dog at the bottom of the *Crazy Wall*. The Reader's missing dog.

Bruce decided a visit to the Dark Angel was now inevitable. He would just drop in. Ask a few pointed questions. Like why the fingerprints of one of their girls had been found at an Amish farm at a time that coincided with the disappearance of an Amish teen. He rubbed his eyes and yawned. The time was 4:36 a.m., and Detective Bruce Ellsworth, the legend, was back.

Susan arrived for work forty-five minutes late, which wasn't unusual. She sang out in her usual over-loud and bubbly voice, but the man upstairs didn't stir in his chair. His large frame was sprawled across a disorganized stack of paperwork on his desk, the pipe that hung from the corner of his mouth long burned out.

## CHAPTER FIVE

Maria Reader squeezed the last few drops of milk from Betsy's udder and hung the milk stool on the wall. A dozen cats appeared, their tails sticking straight up, mouse-hunting forgotten. They rubbed against Maria's bare legs to show appreciation for the milk she was about to pour into their pan.

Maria stuck her index finger and thumb under her tongue and whistled. Barnie did not come. For a week, the dog hadn't come, but she would keep calling all the same.

Since Eli's disappearance, the barnyard animals had been subjected to many heartfelt conversations from Maria. This morning however, there was a bounce to Maria's step as she bustled about the chores. She hummed as she scraped the manure from under the cows and spread fresh straw.

Today was the quilting, and Maria couldn't wait to get away from the farm.

Trish stomped her hooves impatiently as if reading Maria's mind.

"Just a minute, you impatient animal," Maria said as she fondly stroked Trish's nose. "You'll be out of this barn soon enough."

She ran the currycomb down Trish's side and across her flanks, just the way Eli had taught her. Trish munched her oats, indifferent as to whom the attention was coming from.

When Maria came into the kitchen, Ruth was bustling between stove and the table. The smell of eggs and pancakes filled the air.

## Chapter Five

Maria set the bucket of milk on a shelf in the pantry, then took a dipper from the water bucket and dipped cold water into the wash basin. She washed her face and hands and dried them on a clean cloth.

"Mam," Maria said, calling her mother by the German nickname that is common in many Amish homes. "You haven't changed into your good clothes. Aren't you going to the quilting with me?"

"I've decided to stay home today," Ruth said, avoiding Maria's eyes. "Someone needs to be here in case news comes about Eli. And Maria, I really don't think it is a good idea that you go today."

Maria thought she caught a hint of worry in her mother's voice, but before she could ask about it, something else caught her attention. The table had been set for three.

"Andy is home?" she asked, referring to her father by his actual name, a mutual agreement they had reached many years ago.

Andy Reader had avoided all conversation on the way back from St. Louis on Monday, and after dropping his wife and daughter off at home, had left again with the English driver. He had not been home since.

Ruth smiled patiently. "It is for Eli," she said.

"Mam," Maria said, her voice choking. "Why are you setting Eli's place? You know he isn't going to be here."

Ruth nodded. "You are probably right," she agreed. "But maybe it will help draw him back."

Maria had heard stories of Amish parents who set the table for their wayward children for many years after they left the community—the idea being that if they set the table, they were not giving up hope that the lost soul would return. She remembered hearing something else, and as the memory was registering, it began to play out. Ruth walked to the front door, opened it and began to call Eli's name, her voice choked with grief and passion.

"No, Mam… Please don't," Maria cried.

"Eli," Ruth called. "Eli. Breakfast is ready. *Eli.*"

Maria's appetite vanished. "Mam, he can't hear you. Please stop," she pleaded.

The calling continued.

Maria swallowed a sob, then rushed up the stairs to her room. Below, the calling continued.

Maria changed into her best dress and tied her bonnet beneath her chin. She dabbed at her eyes with her apron.

*Mam can mourn all she wants*, Maria thought, as she hitched Trish to the buggy. She got in and guided Trish down the driveway, *but I'm going to have fun at the quilting, and her old-fashioned beliefs will not ruin my day.*

Her mother's words rang in her ears as she turned north onto Caroline Creek Road. *Maria*, her mother had said, *I really don't think it is a good idea that you go today.*

A few minutes later she turned onto a gravel road and headed west. She did not have far to go. The Reader's and Troyer's were next-door neighbors, with the back of their farms touching.

The Troyers had moved to Caroline Creek three years earlier. Of the ten children, Marvin was the oldest, and Edna came next. Edna had arrived with an aloof air that often becomes one that moves in from a more liberal community, and it had taken a while for her and Maria to hit it off. The girls first met in school, but by the time they graduated from the eighth grade the following spring, they had become best friends.

Edna was waiting on the front porch, and her face shone from under her blonde curls as she watched the buggy come up the driveway. She held her bonnet in one hand and waved bashfully with the other. "Why I almost thought you went to the quilting without me," she teased.

## Chapter Five

"Oh, climb on up here, you slowpoke," Maria laughed. "Besides, I don't even know how to quilt anyway, so you will have to show me."

Edna climbed into the buggy and sat down next to Maria. Maria slapped Trish's reins and the buggy lurched around the circle drive and back out onto the road.

"First things first," Edna began. "I have something to ask you. Well... *I* don't." Edna tugged at the black shawl wrapped around her thin shoulders. "I'm asking for Marvin," she said with a mischievous grin.

Maria's heart raced and her face flushed. "What is it?" she asked quickly.

"Oh, I forgot already," Edna said, turning her face so Maria couldn't see her laughing.

"You better ask me now," Maria said. She elbowed Edna hard.

"Much fun you are!" Edna said as she rubbed a sore rib. "Well, he wants me to ask if you would go on a second date."

Maria almost dropped Trish's reins. The request was not entirely unexpected. The Amish tradition is for two people to wait for four weeks after the first date, before considering a second date. For four long weeks Maria had waited impatiently for the second proposal from Marvin. Of course, she had known the question would not come directly from Marvin. The Amish tradition is that a close and trusted friend is the go-between, and Maria had thought it would probably be Edna again.

For four weeks she had suffered through the tortured emotions and the helpless feelings that come with wanting and waiting. The first date had been at the Reader house on a Sunday evening, and at the time it had seemed like Marvin enjoyed her company as much as she enjoyed his. But now, Maria was almost convinced he had forgotten all about her. At the Singens, she imagined he was smiling at every other girl except her. Desperately, she had wanted to send him a secret letter, or try smiling at him in church or the Singen, maybe even confiding in Edna that she was definitely interested in a second date. Because a second date would practically guarantee they were a steady couple.

Maria tried to hide her eagerness but did a shameful job of it. Edna was her best friend, and they kept no secrets, but now Maria was glad she had waited for Marvin to make the next move.

"Of course, I'll do it," Maria replied softly. She removed her bonnet and tossed it on the buggy seat between them. The wind blew her black cap from her head and it fluttered from her shoulders by two strings. Dark curls brushed her face, and her eyes danced with joy. "Marvin and Maria, Maria and Marvin, I can see it on the wedding invitations already," she sang.

Edna smiled and squeezed Maria's arm. "Marvin doesn't say much, but I know he is happy too," she said.

"And what is bothering you?" Maria asked, studying Edna's face. "I know you got baptized last Sunday and all, but you can still feel happy for me, you know, even if I didn't." Maria continued, "Besides, it's too late for me to join baptism classes this year anyway. I told you I am not ready to become a member of the church yet."

"It's not that." Edna's voice quivered. "It's about Eli. Have you heard anything from him yet?"

Maria sobered. As eighth graders, they had secretly discussed the matchmaking of Marvin and Maria, Eli and Edna. She put her cap back on and tied the strings loosely beneath her chin.

"Nothing," she said. "Edna, I am so sorry! I feel so dumb right now. I have no right to celebrate about Marvin. I lost my brother and you... Well, I know how you feel about Eli." Edna squeezed Maria's hand.

Trish trotted along at a brisk pace, neck arched, nostrils flaring, her breath turning into frosty steam in the chill morning air.

## Chapter Five

Edna continued. "Have they spoken to anyone in Missouri? Suppose he made it to Columbia?" She uttered the words in a whisper, as if she couldn't bear to hear the truth.

Maria shuddered. Columbia Missouri was about two hundred miles to the west, but to the Amish in Caroline Creek, it was a faraway place where Amish runaways disappeared to, never to return. It was said that drugs, alcohol, and women ran rampant there. Countless sermons are preached in Amish homes across the country, with much focus on the many sins of the ex-Amish that end up there. In comparison, if a teen ran away and got a local farm job, there was some hope of a return, but many a teary-eyed parent had been brought to their knees in prayer at the very mention of Columbia Missouri.

Maria clenched her teeth and took a deep breath. For the second time that morning, she willed herself not to cry. They were getting close to the quilting, and she *would* show up dry-eyed.

They arrived at the end of the driveway at the same time as Sadie Byler and her mother. Sadie smiled and waved at the girls. They waved back. The three girls saw each other almost every Sunday night at the Singens, but the time between sometimes seemed like an eternity.

Edna, still trying to recover from the earlier conversation, made a beeline for the outhouse half-hidden among the trees in the back yard, and Maria waited under the trees for her. More buggies arrived; horses were unhitched and led to the barn.

One buggy tilted dangerously, and the large rear end of Mattie Borntrager backed slowly out, feeling for the step with her foot. For just a second her thick, hairy leg showed before her dress fell back to her ankles. Mattie looked to be in her mid-fifties, and she walked with ease for a woman of her size. Her sharp eyes protruded from under bushy brown eyebrows. She didn't miss a thing as she took in the yard, the outhouse, and Maria.

Mattie had a reputation for being the gossipingest woman in Caroline Creek. She never missed a chance to attend a public event: weddings, funerals, horse sales, farm auctions, barn-raisings and quiltings. Mattie even had a way of snooping around at ice-skating events that were meant to be attended by only the Youngie—that is to say, Amish youth between the ages of sixteen and marriage. Mattie Borntrager talked and talked. It seemed like she only stopped talking if someone else had gossip that was juicier than her latest fabrication, which wasn't often. Mattie knew everyone in Caroline Creek, and she knew all their relatives—even those living in other communities. And somehow people kept talking to Mattie Borntrager, often confiding secrets they wouldn't tell a best friend. Maria wondered, but didn't ask, if Mattie stopped talking when she closed her eyes at night?

As if being the gossipingest woman in the community wasn't bad enough all on its own, Mattie was also in charge of writing the Caroline Creek section of *The Budget*—an Amish diary-style newspaper that finds its way into almost every Amish home. The role fit Mattie perfectly, but her loud and boisterous articles made her even more unpopular among the Youngie.

"Ptuh, ptuh," Mattie spat as she made her way toward Maria. "I do say, I am not ready for winter yet. I do say, but it is right a' comin' along and will be here before you know ut."

Before Maria could respond Mattie continued.

"Ptuh, ptuh, child. What is it that you are doing out here? Ptuh, ptuh." Mattie turned her head sideways as she spat into the grass beside the walkway. Maria had watched closely many times, and she was quite certain that nothing came out with each 'ptuh'.

The old farm dog ambled suspiciously behind Mattie and eyed this new development with his head half-cocked but careful to stay a safe distance behind. With each "ptuh," he jumped and tucked his tail, as if to avoid being hit by flying bullets of dry spit.

## Chapter Five

"I say, is your mam in the outhouse? If so, I say, no use in waiting outside. You can be of more use in the house."

"I... I... it is not that," Maria stammered. "My mam is not here today. Edna is here. I... I'm waiting on her."

"Oh, come along now," Mattie said with a wave of her hand. "She knows where the door to the house is. Come along then. There is much work to do I say. Ptuh, ptuh." Mattie brushed past Maria, half-spinning her around as she made her way along the walkway.

Maria swallowed hard and followed the very large and bobbing rear end. She took one last look in the direction of the outhouse. A few women had gathered outside and were waiting their turn. Having no choice in the matter, Maria followed Mattie into the house.

There was a steady bustle of dresses and shawls as the women gathered around the wood stove and held their hands to the heat for warmth. Two large pots sat on top of the stove. One held coffee and the other tea. The rising steam from the two mingled in the air, giving off a pleasant aroma.

A large addition had been built onto the east side of their two-story farmhouse for just such purposes as a quilting. In the middle of the room the first quilt was spread out on a wooden frame that was roughly fourteen feet square. Bright-colored squares adorned the borders of the quilt. Inside the cloth borders, and outlined with a lead pencil, was an array of lilac bushes with a handful of bluebirds resting in the branches. Chairs lined two sides of the quilt, and already a few women were seated.

Sadie Byler poured two cups of tea and handed one to Maria. A bubbly, freckle-faced girl, Sadie was a bit plumper around the middle than Maria. She wore her cap pulled forward on her face, completely covering her hair, and her dark brown dress modestly reached below her ankles. Sadie was two years older than Maria and Edna, and had been dating steady for several years. A marriage was expected late in the fall or early spring. Of course, any such plans were guarded with the utmost secrecy until the bishop made the announcement before the church.

Sadie tried to make small talk, but Maria was having none of it. "Have you and John set a date already?" she whispered.

"Shh." Sadie turned red and glanced around, lowering her voice. "You know I couldn't tell you so soon."

The two girls walked to the quilt and sat side by side. Maria left an empty chair for Edna, then began the painstaking process of trying to thread her needle. Her mind quickly moved to other activities she would rather be doing than quilting. An image came of her guiding a wagon pulled by two horses while Eli stacked the loose hay behind her. She smiled.

The memory was interrupted when Edna sat down. For a moment she watched Maria fumble with the needle and thread. "May I?" she asked, holding out her hand.

Edna placed the tip of the thread into her mouth to wet the end, then she seemed to bite down on it.

The trick worked. Maria watched as Edna effortlessly guided the flattened end of the thread through the hole in the needle, then handed it back to Maria.

On the other side of the quilt, Mattie Borntrager warmed up for a go at the latest gossip. The thimble on her finger bobbed and weaved and her needle dipped and glided along the outlined sketch of the bluebird.

At home, every father and son would hold their breath for several days after the quilting, because any rumor, regardless how far-fetched, would be picked apart with a fine-tooth comb and re-assembled according to the mood and temperament of the quilting group on that particular day.

The pendulum on the grandfather clock swung back and forth, as if trying to keep rhythm with a dozen needles as they moved through the fabric. The rectangular shape of the quilt got

## Chapter Five

narrower and narrower. Every so often, the clamps that held the wooden frame were removed and the finished sides of the quilt were rolled up further on the frame.

Maria bent over her section and tried to keep up, but her fingers were stiff and clumsy. Edna's needle slid gracefully through the fabric and in minutes her leaf was finished. She leaned in and began at the top of Maria's leaf. Maria smiled. "Thank you," she mouthed.

Across the corner Mattie's thick, calloused fingers flew and her mouth flew faster. "Over in Bowling Green, Missouri, they now are allowing the tractors for field work. They say it's okay as long as they take off the rubber tires and put on steel wheels."

Maria wasn't even remotely interested in tractors or the types of wheels that were allowed. Her mind drifted to Marvin and she smiled. Sunday night on their date he would ask her to go steady. She would become Mrs. Marvin Troyer before she reached the age of twenty. Her mind raced and she hardly noticed when the clock chimed at half past two and it was time for the mid-afternoon snacks.

Maria felt as if she were floating on clouds as she walked to the outhouse. Edna skipped beside her and did her best Mattie Borntrager impersonation. "Ptuh, ptuh," she mocked, head tilted back. "I say, I say child, if my rear end wasn't sticking out so far, I might fall flat on my big nose." The girls giggled all the way to the outhouse.

They were still giggling when they came back into the kitchen a few minutes later. Mattie was babbling as she wiped her hands on a washrag. Her words caught Maria's attention, and her ears suddenly burned hot. "If you ask me, it all starts with the parents. Spare the rod and spoil the child, I say."

*Was Mattie actually talking about the Reader family in front of everyone?*

The next sentence confirmed what Maria already knew, and suddenly her mother's words made perfect sense. *Maria, I really don't think it is a good idea that you go today.*

Mattie rambled on. "And when the man of the house is never home, who is supposed to wield that rod?"

Maria stood in the doorway to the kitchen, mouth open, shock written all over her face. Mattie's back was turned as she poured coffee.

"And how can one expect him to turn out good, coming from that family? I bet right now he is drinking and partying with some loose English woman. And look at Ruth—sending her daughter to a quilting all by herself, and her not even a member of the church yet."

Several of the women saw Maria in the doorway and shot her sympathetic glances. Sadie's face was red, but she remained silent.

Mattie noticed the silence and turned around. Her eyes locked on to Maria and she paused, realizing her mistake. "I thought you were…" she began.

A deep, burning resentment flooded through Maria, and shame and embarrassment flushed her face crimson. A week of confusion and frustration boiled over in one red-hot surge. She opened her mouth, but no words came.

"Now go back to your quilt, child," Mattie said. "Go on. Much work to do."

Maria didn't move. Finally, the words came. Hesitantly at first, then louder as the injustice overwhelmed her.

"I will not."

Her words cut the silence in the kitchen. "This is not your house and you are not my mother. You are… you are nothin' but a big, fat, stinkin' sow!"

The outburst was met with shocked silence. A needle dropped from somebody's grasp and tinkled across the tiled kitchen floor.

## Chapter Five

For once, Mattie had no words. She stood frozen, arm outstretched. The fingers that clasped the handle of the coffee pot turned white with tension. A growing stain of sweat stretched from her armpit halfway to her waist. The only thing in the kitchen that moved was the steam rising from the spout of the coffee pot.

Edna's fingers dug into Maria's elbow as she tried to pull her back from the doorway, but Maria refused to move. Finally, Mattie found her voice.

"Maria, I will ask you to leave. You…"

"I won't do it," Maria interrupted. "Eli is my brother and he is not bad. You don't know that he is bad."

Edna pulled harder on her arm. "Maria, let's go, please," she begged. Maria yanked her arm away. Her dark brown curls bounced from under her cap and her eyes flashed with anger and defiance.

Mattie's hand shook as she set the pot back on the stove. "If you were my child, I would spank you right here in front of everybody."

"Well I'm not your child," Maria snapped. "And you are a stinkin' hypocrite."

In that moment Maria realized she had said too much. A sob caught in her throat, and she spun and stumbled blindly toward the front door. When she reached the front yard, she began to run. Shame and guilt burned her face and fueled her steps as she fled Mattie Borntrager and the quilting. She ran for almost a mile before her lungs began to burn. She glanced back to make sure nobody was following, then waded through the ditch and sat down under a tree near the side of the road.

For a long time, she sat with her head in her hands. Hot tears of shame and frustration ran down her cheeks and fell into her lap. She almost didn't hear the clip-clop of Trish's hooves. The horse and buggy stopped at the edge of the road.

"Care for a ride?" Edna asked, avoiding Maria's eyes.

Maria wiped her eyes and climbed in beside Edna. "Thank you for remembering my shawl and bonnet," she said.

"You should've seen Mattie's face when you called her a fat sow," Edna laughed. "She looked like she wished she was in another country somewhere."

Maria smiled wearily. "Well she does look like a fat sow," she insisted. "I hate her for saying all those things. I wanted to stick her full of quilting needles."

The girls laughed, but the laugh was framed with worry. The punishment for Maria's words would be severe.

As the Troyer farm came into sight, Maria asked the question. "What do you think they will do to me?"

Edna tried to mask the concern on her face. "Well you know Mattie is the deacon's sister."

Those were the last words Maria would hear from her best friend for a very long time.

## CHAPTER SIX

At about the same time as Maria was arriving home from the quilting, somewhere in the mountains far to the west, a completely different scene was unfolding. In cold waters beneath the shadows of a rocky ledge, for the first time in over four days, a lone figure stirred.

With each ripple of water the head moved, then as the water receded, the head sank back down until the chin rested upon the chest. The water lapped gently against two cheeks, but otherwise the figure didn't stir. Presently a larger ripple came along. It covered the entire head, splashed cold water across the face, and filled the nose and mouth.

The first sound Eli Reader heard was a gurgle coming from deep down and rising all the way to his lips, and then coughing water spurting from his mouth and nostrils. For several seconds he remained still, waiting for the dream to pass, for the world around him to take form, and the usual sounds of the morning to come. But there was only darkness. He tried rubbing his eyes to make the darkness go away, but only his right arm moved.

A thought came to Eli then. He must be in his bed. He must be dreaming. He would simply kick off the covers and stand up. But when he tried this maneuver, his body was sluggish and unresponsive. His senses came back to him then. Not a little at a time, but all at once; a huge tidal wave washing over him, overwhelming him, drowning him. He really was in water, and wherever he was, it was very dark, and this was not a dream.

Eli stifled a scream. With all the willpower he could muster, he forced himself to remain calm. Gradually he became aware of a distant sound. He listened carefully. The sound resembled someone he had once watched in an office somewhere; someone tapping a keyboard.

A low moan escaped Eli's lips and echoed back into his throbbing skull. Then he became aware of a sharp pain in his left shoulder. The pain crept down his arm, through his wrist, and completed the circuit at the tips of his fingers. He tried to lift the arm, but a second bolt of pain shot through his shoulder. He stifled another scream.

"Don't you dare panic," his brain, numb with cold and shock, seemed to tell him. "Don't you dare panic, or it will all be over soon."

Another voice, soft and soothing, crept into his head. The second voice contradicted the first.

"It's okay. You can go back to sleep now. You deserve a deep and comforting sleep."

Eli's head snapped up, and he shook it wildly from side to side to try and clear the fog.

"Am I going to die? Is this the end of the world?" The words escaped from between his chattering teeth. "Am I going to drown in this dark place? Am I...?" His voice trailed off and his head sank slowly back down until his chin rested comfortably on his chest once again. The darkness came back.

The second voice picked him up and gently rocked him. The pain in his shoulder was not so bad now.

"Sleep," the voice said. "Sleep and it will all be over soon."

A sharp crackle sounded, and his head snapped back. Frantically, his eyes searched the darkness. Somewhere in front of him he thought he saw green eyes. They peered from the darkness, shimmering and bobbing, rising and sinking.

*A person tapping a keyboard. Green eyes. They were coming from the same place.*

## Chapter Six

The fog in his head was back. The pain in his shoulder was now stabbing through his entire left side, making him dizzy.

"It can't be real. I... I must be going blind," he stammered.

A crackling voice startled him. It was a man's voice, and it was speaking in a language Eli didn't recognize. It had a thin, mechanical sound, and it too, was coming from the direction of the green eyes.

"Help. *Help.* Can someone please help me?" Eli's voice echoed hollowly into the darkness in front of him.

There was silence, then the voice crackled back again, still in the strange language.

"I... I don't understand. Can you help me?" The words sounded strange coming from his own lips. The green eyes flickered and made a hissing sound.

This time Eli couldn't stifle the scream. The scream came from lips that had turned purple from the cold water. But the sound fell flat only a few feet in front of him, like a rock landing in a mud puddle.

Eli leaned his back against something hard and pushed upward with his legs until he was standing. A sharp object dug into one of his bare feet. He fixed his gaze on the twinkling green eyes. They seemed further away now. He moved forward. He seemed to be in some sort of aisle with seats on either side, because his shoulders kept bumping into hard objects.

He had to make it to the green eyes. There were dozens of them now, and as Eli approached, they transformed into tiny green lights. There was a whole dash panel full of them, and they cast an eerie hue across the water, forming sparkling shadows that danced and rippled across his path.

An object blocked his way and Eli staggered backwards, unprepared. The object was heavy, and it was floating on the surface of the water, but it moved when Eli bumped into it. Carefully he squeezed past. The floor beneath shifted and Eli stumbled. Panicking, he reached out and grabbed at the object to steady himself. His fingers closed on something cold and clammy. *Fingers. Cold, wet, dead fingers.* Another scream escaped his lips and Eli lurched away.

The mechanical voice came from the somewhere in front, drawing him forward.

"Must get to the green lights. Must..."

The cold fingers brushed against his cheek. Then long wet hair brushed against his neck, curling around the front of his throat like strands of a soft unwoven rope. *Hair that was too long to be that of a man.* Then the body bumped into his back and sent him lurching forward. He struggled to regain his balance. The sudden motion caused the floor to shift beneath his feet once again. The green lights dipped beneath the surface of the water. They faded, blinked twice, and then disappeared. The mechanical voice crackled, turned static, and then, it too was silent.

Eli waited for the voice to come back, but only the faint sound of water lapping somewhere against a wall reached his ears. For a while then, he stood still and tried to piece together some logical thought, but his mind remained blank.

From where he stood, the top of his head almost brushed against a ceiling. Here, the water reached to his armpits, giving him a pocket of air to breathe from. He seemed to be trapped inside some sort of round metal container. The container was balanced on the floor of a shallow body of water, and when he had lurched forward, he had shifted the weight of the container.

*But why is it so dark? Shouldn't there be windows that let in daylight?*

*Door. Even an enclosed container has to have a door.*

But which direction to turn?

*Door. Where the green lights were. Get to door. Push door open. Then daylight...*

## Chapter Six

Eli bumped into the place where the lights had been, then stopped and listened for the voice. He listened for the person tapping on the keyboard. Both were gone. The keyboard, he realized suddenly, was only his chattering teeth.

His entire body began to shake. The dizziness came back. He had to move fast or drown.

*Door on left side. Of course. In any large machines with a center aisle, there is always a door on the front left side.*

Eli moved sideways into a seat and sat down hard. He came up snorting water and gasping for air.

*Door must be here. But the bad shoulder. It's the only way out.*

Eli gritted his teeth for impact and threw the entire weight of his bad shoulder into the door. Pain numbed his left side, and he gulped a large mouthful of water. The door gave easily. Too easily. He barreled into open water.

But there was no daylight. Only more darkness. Deep and thick darkness. And here the water reached to his shoulders. Eli's knees wobbled, and his feet sank into soft mud. He began to trudge forward, pulling his bare feet from the sticky mud. His eyes filled with tears of pain, and his world began to spin and shift, as if bouncing him back and forth between two giant balloons. The balloons were laughing at him, and one was speaking.

"Sleep my child. Sleep and it will..."

He had to find a place where he could lie down. His chest bumped into a hard surface and his fingers closed on something sharp and jagged. It felt like a rock ledge or shelf, but it was too high to climb up to. Eli followed it uncertainly, his cold, trembling hand tracing the sharp edges, searching for a flat spot where he could lie down and rest.

The mud was gone, replaced by the soft, soothing sensation of a million grains of sand that sifted between his toes. Finally, he found a spot on the rocky ledge that was low enough to crawl up onto. And it was flat, and Eli leaned forward and placed a knee upon the jagged edge so he could roll his weight forward onto the ledge.

His shoulder hit with the full force of his weight and a bolt of pain shot from his neck down to his toes. He fought to remain conscious, but his eyelids fluttered.

Just before they closed, there came a faint sliver of light. Eli squinted at the sleek body of a large metal object. The object had a giant hole torn in its side, and from the jagged hole protruded a long flat wing. The wing had been half-torn from the sleek body, and it now bobbed freely on top of the water.

*Maybe it was just a dream after all.* He had never been in an airplane in his life, so it must be a dream.

*"Sleep,"* the voice encouraged him.

A heavy layer of cold enveloped the trembling form on the rocky shelf, and then Eli's world went dark.

## CHAPTER SEVEN

Maria set the laundry basket on the grass and reached for a pair of denim pants. She took two clothespins from her apron pocket and pinned the pants to the clothesline. Drops of water dripped from the pant legs onto the grass beneath, and a gentle breeze blew across Maria's face and ruffled the loose strings that hung from her head covering. Lately, the nights were becoming brisker, but so far, the days of autumn were warm and sunny. Maria found her mind returning to the events at the quilting the day before, and she shuddered. Her daydreaming was interrupted by a distant voice.

"Giddap. Molly, Pete, yeah."

Maria studied the corn field to the west of the Reader farm, trying to place the sound. A team of horses pulled a wagon along the edge of the field. The horses came to a stop, and a second later came the delayed echo.

"Whoa."

Marvin Troyer's voice was followed by dull thuds as ears of corn sailed into the wagon and hit the opposite wall, then fell into the bottom. A minute later the horses moved. They walked three paces before Marvin's voice sounded.

"Hyea. Molly, Pete." And again, "Whoa."

Maria smiled as her heart skipped at the thought of life with Marvin. In a few years she and Marvin would be husking corn on their own farm.

The wagon reached the end of the field, and Marvin climbed aboard and guided the horses along the end of the field, then turned and started down the other side. The tall rows of corn blocked Maria's view, and the distance was now too great to hear Marvin's voice, so she went back to the monotonous task of hanging the freshly washed clothes on the line.

Ever since she had graduated from the eighth grade four years earlier, life at home had been a steady routine of boring work. Every morning she helped Eli with the chores in the barn. After breakfast, Eli went out to the fields. Sometimes he needed help, and Maria was always happy to volunteer.

That had changed when Maria turned seventeen. Attending the Singens had given her something to look forward to, and with her quick wit and outgoing personality, it hadn't taken Maria long to become a favorite among the Youngie.

Then Marvin Troyer had smiled at her from across the table at the Singen. On that night, Maria felt a flame ignite on the inside that she didn't know existed. When Marvin proposed a date several weeks later, Maria accepted eagerly.

The turmoil and confusion she had often felt as an Amish teenager quickly vanished, and after only one date, spending the rest of her life in Caroline Creek suddenly made perfect sense. Gone were the endless hours of daydreaming of a life in the outside world. Life with Marvin would mean a life of bliss, with many children running around tugging at her apron strings.

And then yesterday had happened. The confrontation with Mattie Borntrager had suddenly shifted everything into uncertainty.

"Daydreaming again?"

Mam walked from the basement with a fresh basket of clothes. She gave her daughter a patient smile. "What is it that weighs on your mind today, Maria?"

"Mattie Borntrager," Maria said, anger quickly flaming. "She is so bossy. Who does she think she is, anyhow? Why, yesterday at the quilting she was talking about our family as if she is

## Chapter Seven

God herself. Mam, you should have heard her. She said very bad things about Eli and I... I..." Maria stopped to catch her breath.

Mam nodded. "I heard about it this morning already while you were in the barn doing chores. Alma Stutzman stopped by on her way to town and we talked. It is all everyone is talking about."

"Well, Mattie got what she deserved," Maria said defensively. "She needs to mind her own business anyhow."

"Maria," her mother said patiently. "You know that that is not how the ministers will see it. I can't fault you for standing up for Eli, but you must understand that Eli is not Mattie's son, nor have any of Mattie's children ever run away from home, so she can't possibly understand what you were feeling."

"All the same," Maria said, "I am not sorry, and I never will be. She had it coming, and you know it."

Mam nodded slowly. There was a catch in her throat as she spoke. "Maria, I expect the ministers will come and visit tonight. Let us pray that they show mercy."

"Let them decide what they want," Maria said shortly. "What can they do? I am not baptized, so they can't ex-communicate me. In fact, one of the main reasons I chose not to become baptized is the manipulation and control they use on the baptized ones."

"You know I would never force you to be baptized," Mam replied. "But surely you know that your stance made you unpopular with the preachers."

"I don't care," Maria spat. "If they make it too hard for me here, I will just marry Marvin and we will move to another community. Let Mattie have her judging and her gossip and her drama. I want no part of it."

"They want it a certain way, you know," Ruth said. "Deacon Koblenz and his sister Mattie and their families were the first to move in and start this community. As it so often goes, they feel like this is their community and their rules." Mam caught herself, suddenly remembering that the community forbade baptized members from discussing sensitive church matters with non-baptized members.

Maria cherished the moments when it was just her and Mam. She knew that most Amish mothers would never defend their daughters in the face of defying an elder of the church. To do so would mean that the parent was not raising her child in the strict manner that was expected and would almost certainly lead to a severe reprimand against both parent and child.

The screen door slammed, startling them both. Andy Reader walked out onto the deck and scowled at the two women. Mam's smile disappeared, and her face became expressionless. She quickly bent to pick up the next piece of clothing from her basket.

Andy routinely came home on Saturday night just in time to make an appearance in church on Sunday. Maria wondered if he had been drinking again; She thought he probably had. It would explain why he was home early. He had probably spent what little money he had and was now broke and hungry.

Andy leaned his gaunt frame on the railing of the deck. His unsmiling face was more pale than usual under his black hat and unshaven stubble.

"When will supper be ready?" he asked, making no effort to hide his annoyance that his wife did not have a warm meal waiting for him just in case he came home on this particular evening.

Mam stooped and picked up her empty basket. "I will go start it right now," she said.

Andy opened his mouth but stopped suddenly. His eyes were focused on a commotion in the distance.

"What in the world?" he said, squinting.

Two of the younger Troyer boys were running toward them, their straw hats waving wildly in their hands as they approached the barbed-wire fence that separated the two farms.

"What is it?" Andy Reader asked impatiently.

## Chapter Seven

Dannie, the oldest, stopped to catch his breath. "Why... why," he stammered. "We found your dog in the corn field. He... he's dead."

"Dead?" Andy Reader asked coldly. "What do you mean, he's dead?"

"It's true," said Milt, the younger of the two. "After we got home from school, we went out to the field to help Marvin husk corn. We found Barnie lying in the field. He is shot full of bullet holes."

The words hung in the air, thick with the suddenness of it all. A gasp escaped Maria's lips as the words sank in. *Eli's dog. Shot full of bullet holes. Is this somebody's idea of a sick joke?*

"Throw him into the pond," Andy Reader said evenly. "Let the fish be done with him." His eyes were cold, his face expressionless. He gave a dismissive shrug and turned to his wife. "I'm hungry. Let's go."

Mam hurried toward the house, the empty basket swinging from her hand. Her face was ghastly pale, and as she passed Maria, their eyes met. The fleeting moment of silent communication that passed between them was instantly clear. It spoke of a heart struck with terror, knowing only to submit entirely to her husband, to obediently follow him and do his bidding.

The Troyer boys turned and ran back toward the corn field.

Maria stood unmoving, trying to make sense of it. The loud mooing of Betsy, waiting patiently to be milked, brought her out of her trance. Maria dropped her empty basket on the floor inside the basement door, then ran to the barn. It was the one place on the farm where she could think clearly and make sense of the confusions of life.

# CHAPTER EIGHT

Bruce Ellsworth locked the front door of his office on East Fennimore Street. He crossed the street and got into his Explorer. Traffic was moving well, and he made good progress. He turned north and crossed the Clark Bridge over the Missouri River. A few minutes later he crossed the Mississippi River at Alton, Illinois, and turned onto Highway 3. The sun dipped low in the west, its glare reflected off the river, splashing the tall grain elevators in crimson colors laced in a golden hue.

It was dark by the time Bruce turned off the highway and started down the gravel road. The headlights on his Explorer projected dull yellow beams along the dusty road. He wasn't sure how fast a tired horse pulling a buggy moved, so he shifted into a lower gear just to be safe.

Most of the houses were dark, but every so often a single yellow light gleamed from the window of a house or barn.

There were no streetlights along this stretch of gravel road, and Bruce strained to see the potholes. Somewhere along here, he thought, there should be a row of trees running parallel with the road. Several hundred yards after would be the intersection of County Road 387 and Caroline Creek Road.

The road curved to the left, and a sign indicated the intersection a few hundred yards ahead. Directly across the intersection was Caroline Creek, a small ripple of water about thirty feet across. Beyond it rose the rock wall that made the east embankment of the creek.

Over the years, the Castleton Police Department had been called out to the community for a few small incidents, and as

## Chapter Eight

Bruce approached the intersection, an almost-forgotten scene flashed into his memory.

The buggy had been dimly lit, with only one oil-burning lantern. The driver of the truck hadn't seen them in the dark. Had he stopped at the intersection, the accident might have been avoided, but he hadn't stopped.

Images came of the helicopter circling overhead. Then there was the wreckage of the horse and buggy in the creek, and the husband and wife being flown to a hospital in St. Louis.

Bruce shuddered and tried to shrug away the memories. He turned north and rolled down his window so he could better see the Reader mailbox in the dark.

———◆———

The sun was low behind her when Maria closed the barn door and started for the house. Her shadow stretched across the driveway, and the milk bucket sloshed as it swung from her hand. She didn't hear the crunch of gravel beneath the steel wheels, and almost walked into the horse that pulled the buggy. Her head snapped up and her mouth went dry. Deacon Rudy Koblenz stared formidably down at her from the buggy, and next to him sat his sister Mattie.

Maria's reaction was what any Amish teen's reaction would be if their world had just collided with the two most powerful people in the community. The shock was even greater because those same two people had specifically driven to the Reader farm to deliver the assessment of her actions from the previous day.

Maria mumbled, "Sorry, didn't see you," then fled toward the house, milk splashing from the bucket as she ran. Everything she had thought she would say to the ministers, vanished at the sight of Mattie Borntrager. She raced up the stairs and threw herself onto her bed.

Ten minutes passed, but when no immediate footsteps arrived, Maria slowly slid out of bed and tiptoed to the window overlooking the front yard. Very carefully, she nudged the curtain to reveal a tiny sliver of light.

Two more buggies had joined the first one, and they formed a small row of solemn black boxes in front of the hitching post. A small group of people was gathered on the grassy hill between the buggies and the barn. Ruth and Andy Reader stood side by side, portraying the appearance of a unified couple. Facing them were Deacon Koblenz, Mattie Borntrager, and preacher Alvin Keim. The fourth person had his back turned, but Maria thought he looked like Samuel Mullet, the third preacher on the bench.

Maria ran the process through her mind. Andy would not be the one that came to deliver the preachers' decision. Andy preferred to fight his battles with people weaker than himself. Like Mam. Or Eli. But in the battle of wills between father and daughter, Maria had won a long time ago.

No, Andy would stay with the ministers and send his wife to deliver the message. Had Maria been a baptized member of the church, she would have been required to stand and face the ministers herself, but she was not baptized, so it would be Mam who came. Mam with her kind and gentle manner of persuasion. If the punishment wasn't too severe, Maria thought she might agree to the terms.

Just as she had expected, her mother abruptly turned from the circle and started for the house. But she did not come alone. Mattie stepped from the group and followed close behind. In that instant, Maria knew that the punishment was one she could never accept. There was only one reason why Mattie would need to see her, and Maria's heart hardened.

The two sets of footsteps stopped in the living room below, but only one set came up the stairs. Maria was waiting when Mam entered the room. Her face was pale and her eyes begged

## Chapter Eight

Maria's forgiveness before she spoke. She kept her voice to a whisper to avoid Mattie's prying ears below.

"You have to go downstairs and apologize to Mattie for what you said at the quilting yesterday." Mam spoke softly, but firmly.

"I won't do it!" Maria snapped defiantly.

Mam lowered her eyes and swallowed hard. "It is best for everyone if you get it over with now. You simply must do it."

"Is that all?" Maria demanded.

Mam shook her head weakly. "No," she said, her voice weary with defeat. "You are grounded for one month. You are not to attend any social functions. No Singens, quiltings or barn-raisings. The only place you can go is church."

"Why church?" Maria asked, her voice rising.

"They think it best if you continue to hear God's word," Mam replied.

Maria deliberated for only a second, then made her decision. "I won't do any of it," she snapped, intentionally raising her voice so Mattie could hear. "The church doesn't own me, and the preachers and Mattie aren't my boss."

Mam sat down on the bed. "Oh Maria," she said. "You have to do it, or it will go bad for you."

Maria's eyes flashed angrily. The words kept coming. "The only thing I did was stand up for Eli, and I would do it all over again. If this is what the Amish and their churches are about, I want no part of it."

Mam's shoulders shook and tears filled her eyes. "Maria," she sobbed. "I have lost Eli. I can't lose you too."

"Then for once go and stand up to them," Maria snapped. "Because if they ban me from the Singens, I will miss my date with Marvin. If that happens, this community will never see me again."

Mam drew a deep breath and straightened her shoulders. Then she patted a spot on the bed. Maria hesitated and, reluctantly sat down.

For a while Mam sat in silence, dabbing at her eyes with a corner of her apron. Finally, she spoke. "Maria. I have made many mistakes in my life. Mistakes that you don't know anything about. Not many people do. I thought I could hide them forever, but now God is punishing my children for my sins."

"Mam, don't say that. You know it isn't so."

Mam continued. "I was going to wait for a few more years before I told you, but..."

From the living room below came a loud and deliberate cough, a sharp reminder to move things along.

Maria wavered. She had been certain that she wouldn't budge an inch, but her mother's heartfelt words affected her, as they always did.

It was at this crucial moment, a battle of wills raging, and Maria, much weakened and badly outnumbered by seasoned veterans who had crushed many a willful child that came before, that fate stepped in.

There was a commotion in the yard below, and the dull thud of a slamming truck door. A loud voice boomed into the calm evening

"Good evening, gentlemen."

As one, mother and daughter rose and moved to the window. Daylight had disappeared, and the moon splashed silvery light upon the group in the yard. Bruce Ellsworth stepped from the shadows and began to shake hands.

Mam sprang for the stairs, everything else forgotten. "*Eli*," she cried.

Maria did not move. Mattie was downstairs, and there was unfinished business.

A moment later the front door opened, and her mother raced across the yard toward the men. Mattie followed more slowly, her large rear end bobbing from side to side.

Maria pried the window up several inches, then sat on the floor and pressed an ear to the opening to listen. Here, hidden

## Chapter Eight

from view, she managed to make out most of the conversation.

"You're telling me that you found the dog dead and you didn't think that's important enough to call me about?" Bruce's voice rose clearly above the chatter.

There was a confusion of voices defending Andy's claim, but Bruce's was the only one that came through clearly.

"There is some funny business going on here," he said. "I will find Eli. And when I do, he is not coming back here until *I* decide it's safe."

Deacon Koblenz spoke up. "If he has been taken, it is God's will, and..."

Bruce interrupted, his voice sharp. "You can forget 'God's will.' I enforced the law for almost twenty years, and I witnessed more murders than I can count. Where is 'God's will' when innocent children are dying of cancer? Or teenagers are bleeding to death in a back alley, because their parents couldn't afford to move to a good neighborhood? Why don't you talk to those families and see how they feel about 'God's will'?"

There was a shuffling of feet, but nobody spoke.

"You know what stops criminals?" Bruce continued. "I'll tell you what does. Good detective work stops criminals."

Deacon Koblenz recognized a stronger personality when he saw it, and he quickly shrank back and shut up.

Bruce walked to his vehicle and came back with a small briefcase and a headlamp that he was strapping to his head. He stopped to address Andy and Ruth Reader. "With your permission, I'd like to make a pass through your barn and milkhouse. See if I can lift any new fingerprints, anything else suspicious."

Andy and Ruth must have consented because Bruce moved toward the barn. The rest stayed behind. Maria tried to listen to the conversation until she was convinced there was no news on Eli. She closed and locked the window, then undressed and crawled beneath the quilt. The conversation below would go on for a while, but for now, the meeting with Mattie Borntrager had been avoided. Tomorrow her mother would tell her everything that had been said.

———◆———

It was almost midnight when Bruce maneuvered his Explorer onto Caroline Creek Road and started back toward St. Louis. He did not find it particularly strange that the elders of the community had been gathered at the Reader farm. Nor did he have any way of knowing that his visit had saved Maria Reader from a miserable evening.

# CHAPTER NINE

The buildings squatted low and flat and numbered eight in all. They resembled a cluster of old, faded matchboxes. New, the buildings had been painted in bright colors of pink, purple, yellow and red, but now the paint was faded.

The buildings were owned by the Trontelli crime family and were referred to as *Stripper Mall*. But the Trontellis hadn't set foot in the buildings in years. Instead, Old Man Trontelli and his son Joey watched from their multi-million-dollar homes in Chicago as Shug, their man in St. Louis, made all the money and shipped it to them at the end of every month.

Recent flooding had left a darker tinge around the bottom half of the buildings, but nobody had been hired to repaint the damaged areas. And why should the buildings be repainted? No doubt the Trontellis had made an important discovery—that as long as there were women willing to get naked and dance, there were men lining up to throw cash at them, regardless of the outside appearance of the building.

The flood had left behind a large weathered log that sprawled across the far end of the parking lot. Bruce maneuvered around it and parked.

The Dark Angel was the second building from the left, and a strong wave of cigarette smoke hit him when he opened the door. He found himself inside a small cubicle with a glass window to his right. A bouncer in a sweaty tank top greeted him from behind the window. The bouncer addressed him with a weird backwoods drawl that Bruce couldn't quite identify, but was pretty sure it wasn't from the St. Louis area.

"Fifteen-dollar cover charge," the bouncer said.

"I'm here on official business," Bruce said.

"Identification."

Bruce removed his driver's license from his wallet and placed it against the window.

The bouncer leaned in close and squinted. "You the law?" he asked suspiciously.

"Not exactly," Bruce replied. "A bit more low-key than that. I'm here to see one of your girls."

"Who?"

"Summer."

The bouncer made no attempt to hide his surprise. He placed a thick, tattooed arm on the window ledge and leaned close. He picked up a Styrofoam cup and spit a stream of tobacco juice, then seemed to reach some sort of decision, because he turned around and scribbled something on a piece of paper.

"Well it simply ain't yer night," he said, turning back to Bruce.

"It ain't?" Bruce asked.

"Nope. It ain't," the bouncer replied. "We ain't seen Summer around this joint in some time."

The news did not come as a surprise, but Bruce was careful to not show any expression. "Has anyone tried calling the police?" he asked.

"The cops? Naw," the bouncer said.

"Why wouldn't you report a missing dancer?" Bruce pushed.

The bouncer shrugged. "Strippers come and go. We can't control 'em. Summer was one of our best, but if she decides she don't want to dance no more, nothin' we can do about that."

"Well I'd like to speak to a few of the other dancers," Bruce replied.

## Chapter Nine

"Suit yourself," the bouncer replied. "But it'll still cost you fifteen bucks."

Bruce counted out the bills and passed them through the slot at the bottom of the window.

The bouncer took them, taking extra pains to flex his biceps in the process. "Jus' so we're clear," he drawled. "Ye make any trouble for any of our girls, and I'll personally throw ya out. Ya hear? I don't care what branch of the law you're hiding under."

"No trouble," Bruce replied. "Just a few questions."

"Your phone," the bouncer said, holding out his hand.

"Excuse me?" Bruce said.

"Club rules," the bouncer said. "Can't have customers filming our girls and posting the videos on social media, you know."

Bruce stalled, trying to think of an easier way to ask a few simple questions. He couldn't think of one, so he reluctantly handed his cell phone through the slot in the window. A buzzer sounded and the inside door opened. Bruce stepped through and the door closed and clicked behind him.

As soon as Bruce was through the door, the bouncer reached for a phone hanging on the wall.

"Hey Shug," he said.

"Don't use my name over the phone," Shug said firmly.

"Oh yeah, sorry boss."

"What is it?" Shug asked.

"Someone just got here, and he is asking about Summer," the bouncer said. "I called you right away, jus' like you asked."

In the basement of his house, Shug paused the baseball game on TV. He took a deep breath and smiled. "This man," he said. "What is his name?"

The bouncer squinted at his scribbles on the dirty piece of paper. "Bruce Ells… worth," he said, sounding out the last name.

Shug frowned as he tried to recall where he had heard the name. Then it came to him and his smile widened.

"Former chief of police of Castleton," he said. "I believe he started his own investigative business a few years ago. The question is, who in the world yanked his chain?"

"What?" the bouncer asked, confused.

"This Bruce guy," Shug said. "What is he driving?"

"Hold on."

The bouncer placed the receiver on the desk and walked to the window. He scanned the parking lot. It was dusk, and he could barely make out the vehicle at the far end of the lot. But it was the only vehicle in the parking area he didn't recognize. He walked back to the desk and picked up the receiver.

"He is driving a brown Ford Explorer," he said. "You can't miss it. It's at the far end of the lot, parked next to the dead log."

"I need for you to keep him busy for about twenty minutes," Shug said. "It'll take my guy fifteen to get there."

The bouncer hesitated. "What am I supposed to do if he tries to leave?" he asked.

"It's a strip bar," Shug said. "Surely he can be entertained for twenty minutes."

"Okay. You got it, boss," the bouncer said.

The sound of a baseball game began, and the connection went dead.

———◆———

*Dance clubs never really change,* Bruce thought as he scanned the room. The ceilings were still low and dark. The smells still consisted of sweat, mixed with a variety of body fresheners, hair spray, and stale cigarette smoke.

Bruce picked a dark booth in the far corner and sat down with his back to the wall.

## Chapter Nine

The song ended and Bruce glanced at the stage. A girl in nothing but leather riding chaps was crawling around on all fours. She gathered a few green bills into a pile at the far end of the stage, climbed down, clasping the bills, and disappeared through a door. There were four customers scattered around the stage, and they watched the door expectantly, waiting for the next girl to come out.

Bruce didn't think he had long to wait, and he was correct. The girl in the leather chaps appeared again. She walked toward his booth, smiled, and slid into the seat next to him.

"I'm Passion," she said, extending her hand.

"Bruce Ellsworth," Bruce said, seeing no reason to hide his real name.

"Did you enjoy my dance?"

"I missed it," Bruce replied. "I just got here."

The girl smiled again. "I know. I saw you come in. So did all the other girls. You are new here, right?"

"Right."

"Wanna buy me a drink?"

"A drink?"

"Well yes, cowboy," Passion said in a teasing voice. "A gentleman should always buy a lady a drink, right?"

"I guess so," Bruce said.

Passion leaned in closer and Bruce caught the faint aroma of something that resembled watermelon. "Perhaps after the drink we can go to one of the private rooms…"

"I didn't come here for a lap dance," Bruce interrupted.

Passion shrank away.

"You're a cop, aren't you?" she asked, a guarded expression obvious on her face.

"Not exactly," Bruce replied. "Investigator."

"Who are you investigating?"

Instead of answering the question right away, Bruce surveyed his surroundings. There had to be a better spot to ask his questions. A quieter spot. He had long ago come to terms with the fact that the dancers were only trying to make a living, and for many, the job was strictly professional. Sure, for some of the dancers the money made was used to support a drug habit. But for many, the dancing paid for a college degree. And the folks back home would never learn about their secret stint in a questionable area of East St. Louis. And then there were the young mothers—the breadwinners of their households, whose dancing careers made the mortgage payments while the boyfriend or husband sat on the couch at home and got fat and lazy, all the while bitching about the sketchy career choice of his partner.

Bruce turned back to Passion. "It's too crowded here. Can we talk somewhere else?"

"Like where?" Passion asked, glancing around the dark room.

"What time do you get off work?" Bruce asked.

Passion rose quickly and took a step back. "Not gonna happen cowboy," she said. "I'm not that kind of girl."

"That's not what I meant," Bruce said. "I wanna talk about…"

But Passion had already turned and was walking quickly toward the dressing room.

Bruce sighed. He sat back and waited. Another girl would be by soon. It was part of their routine. Maybe he would have better luck getting answers from her.

The door to the bouncer's booth opened and the bouncer in the sweaty tank top moved across the floor and followed Passion into the dressing room.

Bruce waited.

Then Passion was back. And her smile had returned. The leather chaps had been replaced with a pair of blue jeans and a white T-shirt. When she reached his table, she stopped and motioned for him to stand. "Follow me," she said.

"Where to?" Bruce asked, suddenly suspicious.

## Chapter Nine

"I think I misunderstood you," Passion said. "I have a place where we can talk in private. Completely professional."

Bruce rose and followed.

Passion led the way toward the back door. Once outside, she stopped and pointed down a dark alley. The alley ended at a quiet street, and directly across the street was a small diner. "Buy me coffee?" she asked.

They walked to the diner and picked out a booth. Bruce ordered two cups of coffee and Passion ordered hot cakes with a side order of warm strawberries.

"So, who are you investigating?" Passion repeated.

"Summer."

"You came here about Summer?"

Bruce nodded.

Passion studied his face for a few seconds, trying to get a read on him. "Why do you want to know about Summer?" she finally asked. "Is she in trouble?"

"Depends."

The coffee arrived and Bruce took a sip from his mug. "I'm working a different case and Summer's name came up, that's all."

Passion seemed to reach a decision, because she breathed easier. She gripped her coffee cup in both hands, as if seeking warmth from the liquid inside the cup.

"Summer and I share an apartment," she said finally.

"When did you last see her?"

"Here at the club on Saturday night."

"She wasn't at the apartment over the weekend?"

Passion shook her head. "Said she was going out of town, but I thought she would be back at the club for her shift on Monday night."

"But she wasn't?"

Passion shook her head again. The laughter was gone from her eyes, replaced by lines of worry.

"Did she say where she was going?"

Passion paused and seemed to be in deep thought. "Said she was needed to convince someone. A 'soft touch' I think she said."

"Eli Reader," Bruce said under his breath.

"What?" Passion asked curiously.

"Nothing," Bruce said. "Can you remember anything else?"

"That's it," Passion said. "I've tried calling her a dozen times. Straight to voicemail."

"Did Summer say who was sending her to do the convincing?" Bruce asked.

Passion shook her head. "Summer gets used a lot," she said. "She's very gullible. Coulda been anyone."

The pancakes arrived. Passion poured the strawberries evenly over the top, then using her fork, cut a small wedge from one side and placed it on her tongue. She closed her eyes, savoring the taste.

Bruce's mind raced with possibilities. *If Summer had been sent to see Eli Reader, who had sent her? And why? Had Eli somehow witnessed the murder? It seemed unlikely. Besides, if he had, why would the murderers kidnap him? If Stan Prater's theory was correct, and the murder was a mob hit, and Eli Reader had witnessed it, they would simply kill him to make a statement. No reason to go to the extra trouble of kidnapping him, right?*

Out loud Bruce said. "It was the bouncer, wasn't it?"

"The bouncer?"

"When you thought I was making a move on you, you got mad and left the table. But then you came back. It was the bouncer that made you, right?"

Passion nodded sheepishly.

"What reason did he give you?"

"None. Just told me I needed to talk to you for a while. Two-hundred extra dollars."

Bruce frowned, then rose to go.

## Chapter Nine

From the shadows in the alley behind the dance club, a figure watched the meeting in the diner across the street. His instincts told him the investigator could be trusted, but if he was wrong, things could go very badly. Besides, he couldn't take a chance at being recognized. Not by the investigator, and not by anyone connected to the dance club.

A minute later Bruce stepped out of the diner. Passion stayed behind and continued to pick at her food. Bruce was lost in thought as he crossed the street and headed down the dark alley. He had only to collect his cell phone from the bouncer. It would be another late night at the office, but based on the conversation with Passion, he thought he had a few important additions to add to his *Crazy Wall*.

A middle-aged man appeared from the shadows and walked in stride with Bruce. Bruce noted the dark hair and glasses. The man walked with a slight limp, which forced him to hurry to keep stride with Bruce. He was much shorter than Bruce's six feet, four inches, so he didn't really pose a threat. They arrived at the back door to the club together, and Bruce held the door. The man ducked under his arm and passed inside. As he did, his coat brushed against Bruce. Then the man turned and disappeared into the bathroom.

Something about the encounter seemed strange, out of place. As if the man had been waiting for him. For the second time in less than a week, Bruce felt like he was being followed. No, more like he was being watched. The first time had been at the Thirsty Toad with the college girl with the black ponytail.

Bruce pondered the coincidence as he walked to his Explorer, but by the time he turned the key in the ignition, he had put the thought out of his mind.

He turned north on Highway 3, and a few minutes later merged into freeway traffic. He headed west on 270, took the off ramp down into Florissant, and a few turns later, parked outside his office and entered the front door. His mind was completely absorbed in thoughts of Passion, Summer, and Eli Reader. Questions about the mob slowly shifted to the back of his mind and Shug moved forward to replace them.

While Bruce stood before his *Crazy Wall* and began to re-arrange in order of importance, a vehicle pulled up to the curb outside and parked behind his Explorer. The man inside the vehicle opened an electronic device and plugged in a set of headphones. He powered the device on and leaned back in his seat, then waited for Bruce to use his cell phone so he could make sure the transmitter was working.

The phone call came an hour later. The screen on the man's device lit up in pale blue. The man held his breath and waited. A phone number flashed across the screen. After two rings, someone on the other end picked up.

"Hey Stan," came Bruce's voice.

"Yeah. What did you find out?"

"They haven't seen Summer in almost a week."

"So, she disappeared with Eli?"

"That's my guess. Any ideas?"

"You still think they're holed up in some hotel doing the hanky-panky?"

"Doesn't quite add up, but it's the best I can do right now."

"If you think Eli was kidnapped, you gotta bring the Feds on board, right?"

"Guess I don't have a choice."

"Mind if I stop by your office after work tomorrow, discuss in person?"

"I was hoping you would say that," came Bruce's voice.

The phone number on the screen went away.

The man listening to the conversation clicked on a file. He renamed the file *Stan Prater 10/24*. Then he typed in Shug's email address and hit "send". The process took less than three seconds.

## Chapter Nine

He waited for confirmation that the file had been sent, then powered down the device. Outside Bruce's office the street grew dark as the vehicle's taillights disappeared into the night.

## CHAPTER TEN

The Amish community of Caroline Creek lies thirty miles north of St. Louis and is tucked away in the river bottoms between the Mississippi and the Illinois Rivers. It was established in 1984 by Rudy Koblenz, a man who was then in his mid-thirties.

The church grew slowly, hovering just below thirty families. Thirty is an important number, because once a community reaches that milestone, it is time to divide the church into two parts in order to fit everyone into the traditional farmhouses where services are held. For various reasons, every time Caroline Creek was on the verge of expanding into two churches, a few families had become restless and moved to other communities.

One week after Eli Reader disappeared, the community gathered for church services. The married folk arrived first. From every direction they came in their black double buggies, some with a team of horses pulling two-seaters, and some with only a single horse hitched between two shafts.

The men guided the buggies up the gravel driveway and stopped at the end of the dirt path in front of the two-story farmhouse. The women and children got off the buggies and filed into the house where the services would be held.

The men gathered in front of the barn. They formed two lines, facing each other, and as more buggies arrived, the lines grew longer. The school-aged boys stood next to their fathers and listened in silence as the men discussed the day's topics: the Yoder's farm auction the following Saturday, and speculation that they were

## Chapter Ten

moving soon. Much was made of the barn fire at the Schwartz farm, and how they would have to start all over, and so on.

The women gathered inside the house and started with the usual subjects. Unlike the boisterous gossip that ruled the quiltings, Sunday conversations were somber.

Fifteen minutes after the last of the married folk were in place, the Youngie began to arrive. Unlike the married folk who drove old, slow horses, the Singen boys competed to see who had the fastest and finest. One by one the Standard-Bred horses pranced up the driveway, necks arched, freshly combed manes and tails flowing in the wind.

Having the Youngie arrive after the married folks had its disadvantages, in the opinion of some, because it meant the married men had plenty of opportunity to inspect the horse, and the boy leading it, as they made their way between the two rows of men and into the barn.

If a young lad had decided to leave his shirt collar open, or turn the sides of his black wool hat up a bit too far, cowboy-style, the path of inspection on their way to the barn was where it was noted. The lad would then be paid a visit by Deacon Rudy Koblenz the following week. If the problem was fixed, the transgression was forgiven. If the problem was corrected, the transgression was forgiven. If the problem persisted, the young lad would soon enough find himself on the front bench before the members of the church, begging forgiveness.

The same was true for the Singen-aged girls. Mattie Borntrager had a front row seat at the kitchen window, and she inspected each girl as they stepped off the buggy and made her way up the front walk.

For many years Mattie had held her spot at the kitchen windows on Sunday morning. Since Mattie's brother was the deacon, he leaned heavily on Mattie for updates on who was crowding the rules.

In this manner, Caroline Creek kept a tight leash on their Youngie. That leash loosened slightly when someone became baptized. The hold loosened even more when the baptized became married. Possibly it is for this reason then, that many of the unruliest of the Youngie, once married and with less hovering eyes watching them, quickly turned into the hoverers themselves. The adjustment was rough for the Youngie, for only very recently, these same do-gooders had stood by their side and frowned at the superiority flexed by the married folks.

Nobody could remember for sure when the authoritative oppression of the Youngie in the Amish communities began. For that matter, nobody could really recall when the divide between the married folks and the Youngie began either. A few of the members held a theory, but since the Amish didn't document their history, and the internet wasn't easily available for research, only a handful of the older members could recall stories that had been handed down through generations.

Perhaps, they theorized, the oppression had started as far back as when Jacob Ammon, the founder of the Amish church, broke away from Catholicism in the mid-1600s. Had Jacob recognized even then, in those early years when the Amish were being persecuted for their newfound faith, that strict rules would need to be implemented if the movement was to be preserved? Had Jacob recognized that a life separate from the outside world was crucial? That without harsh discipline and strict rules, the Amish church would lose their youth to the world, and the cause he had worked so hard for would wither away after only a few generations?

Whatever the case, by the time the community of Caroline Creek was established four hundred years later, the oppression of the youth was so engrained into the fabric of the Amish churches that nobody bothered to question it. And standing in front of the kitchen window on that Sunday morning, Mattie Borntrager did

## Chapter Ten

more than her part to help fulfill the generations-old belief that the Youngie are to be monitored and micro-managed down to the minutest detail.

For about a year, Mattie had paid careful attention as Eli Reader dropped off his sister Maria. She had watched closely as Maria made her entrance, striding through the group of women in the kitchen and up the stairs to join the other unmarried girls.

Mattie was convinced Maria had shortened her dress at least an inch. And while her head covering was supposed to be large enough to cover all of her hair, it seemed with each Sunday that a few more curls snuck out from under the covering.

Mattie hardly noticed the other girls as they walked between the married women and their fussing babies. Maria Reader was forefront in her mind, and the time for discipline was now. Maria had refused to become baptized, so she could not be ex-communicated. That meant other means must be taken. Mattie was not sure what method the ministers would take, but in her judgmental heart, she felt a strong calling from the Holy Spirit to do her part in getting the wheels of justice turning.

A few more buggies trickled in and Mattie felt her impatience rise. *Maria usually arrives with Eli, but since Eli isn't coming today, who will bring Maria? Her parents?* Mattie doubted that.

A silence descended upon the kitchen. The last of the buggies had arrived. Mattie knew what the silence meant, and the truth hit her hard. Years of practice had made it a natural thing to keep a solemn expression on her face on the Lord's Sabbath, but Mattie silently rejoiced. Maria Reader was not coming to church today.

"I say, I say, is your Maria sick today?" Mattie leaned in close and whispered to Ruth Reader. She tried to feign concern, but the act was not lost on Ruth.

Ruth turned to stare at the woman who had caused so much trouble for her daughter. Little spiderwebs of red veins crisscrossed the whites of her eyes, and Mattie thought she looked every bit the part of a mother who had lost both of her children in so many weeks.

"I could not make her come to church today," Ruth whispered back.

"Ptuh. Ptuh. Well then we must pray harder for that child," Mattie replied solemnly. She turned her face so Ruth couldn't see the smile playing at the corner of her lips.

But Mattie had no intentions of praying. The punishment for Maria would be swift and severe. Maria would be used as an example, while the other Youngie watched from a safe distance. Respect for the elders would be regained soon enough. Mattie smiled again. She had seen it many times—a young rebellious girl who tried to defy the elders. But Maria had no idea who she was messing with. Perhaps a strong dose of solitude was just the ticket to molding her into shape.

The rest of the women milled about the kitchen, their black dresses, white aprons and white caps closely resembling so many penguins on an iceberg.

Upstairs, the unmarried girls gathered and waited for the services to begin. They spoke in whispers; nobody smiled. The absence of Maria hung over them like an ominous storm cloud.

Edna Troyer slipped in beside Sadie Byler and nudged her elbow. "Sadie," she whispered. "Do you think they have already punished Maria and that is why she isn't here?"

Sadie shook her head slowly. "Even if they already decided on the punishment, they would never ban her from the church," she whispered back.

Maria's two friends whispered softly, because they did not want to be overheard. Mattie had granddaughters among the Youngie, and they knew that was where Mattie got much of her information.

## Chapter Ten

At nine thirty, Bishop Reuben Mast started for the house and the other ministers followed. Deacon Rudy Koblenz brought up the rear. From her spot at the window, Mattie watched them come. She was one of the oldest in Caroline Creek, and it was her duty to lead the women to their benches in the dining room.

The last of the married women were already seated when the ministers entered the house. Bishop Mast led the way past the women and into the living room.

Five minutes after the ministers were seated, the rest of the married men entered. The oldest sat on the front bench and, descending in age, the younger married women sat behind them. The children were divided equally between parents, with the boys usually sitting with their fathers and the girls with their mothers.

The bench against the back wall would hold the Singen girls, and the one in front of them, the boys. In the dining room, the married women faced the men through the open doorway. In the same manner, the oldest women sat in front and descending in order by age, younger married women sat behind them. The children were divided equally between parents, with the boys usually sitting with their fathers and the girls with their mothers.

From the minister's bench, Deacon Koblenz watched the girls file in. He paid particular interest to the end of the line. Since Maria was one of the youngest of the Singen girls, she would be one of the last to come in.

Deacon Koblenz thought he must have missed her. He scanned the bench again. His bald head bobbed, and his thick neck craned. He leaned first to the left, then to the right as scanned the congregation. She was not there. Deacon Rudy swallowed hard and a thick vein popped out on the side of his temple. *The nerve! Well, I will have something to say about that. Believe me.*

Jacob Stutzman, one of the elders, called out the page number to the Loblied—a German hymn that is sung every Sunday in every Amish church. There is a longstanding tradition that every baptized male—pretty much every man above the age of seventeen, takes their turn in leading the Loblied. Today it fell to John Schrock, the oldest of the Singen boys.

The Loblied, like all German songs, is a slow melody. It took John about ten seconds to finish the first word, and he felt relief when the rest of the congregation joined in. From the dining room came the women's voices.

At the beginning of the second line, Bishop Mast rose and led the way up the stairs to the Obrod.

The Obrod is a private counseling session where the ministers meet to discuss issues within the community. Normally the time is spent deciding who is to preach that day, and where church will be held the following Sunday. Sufficient time is set aside to discuss which members are misbehaving, and what punishments would suffice in order to help that member reverse their waywardness.

Today's topic quickly shifted to the Reader family, and more specifically, Maria. Deacon Koblenz opened the conversation with a loud cough. "By now everyone here is aware that Maria has refused to apologize for her recent disrespect to an elder—a respected member of this congregation."

The other ministers nodded.

Deacon Koblenz continued. "I also noted Maria's absence on the girls' bench."

Deacon Koblenz was sure that none of the other ministers had noticed Maria's absence, so he paused to allow his words to have the maximum effect. He continued.

"Since Maria has refused to be baptized, we can't discipline her in accordance with the rules of this church, so today we must discuss what actions are to be taken that will re-direct her to the correct path."

## Chapter Ten

Deacon Koblenz wiped his mouth, then nudged the minister to his left to let him know it was his turn to have his say.

At thirty-three years old, Alvin Keim was the youngest of the group. He was a stocky man with thick eyebrows and a full, reddish-brown beard. Alvin's voice was low and husky, and he motioned with his hands when he spoke.

"We all know that if one apple begins to rot, it is best to quickly cast out that apple, before it contaminates the rest of the barrel." Alvin made a circular motion with his hands, outlining the shape of a barrel. "I vote we deal with Maria now, before her disobedience spreads to the rest of the Youngie."

Raymond Byler was next. Raymond had three teenagers of Singen age, and Sadie, the oldest, was a close friend to Maria. Raymond paused and considered his words carefully.

"I think we should go easy on Maria," he said. "She comes from a broken home. We all know the trouble her father makes for us. Now she has lost her only sibling. It is possible that the issue is not a matter of rebellion, but a child who is acting out in grief. I believe with time Maria will find her own way back into the church."

Raymond Byler knew his opinion would not be favorably received, but somewhere in the depths of his heart, he felt a tinge of sympathy for the Reader girl. Before he could continue, however, Samuel Mullet, the third and the oldest of the three preachers shuffled his feet to indicate he had something to say.

Samuel was by nature a shy man and humble man. The struggle of getting up to preach to a house full of people was very real. When the church had voted him into the lot of eligible candidates for the next minister, Samuel had fervently prayed that the book drawn from the lot would not fall to him. But it had. He had desperately tried to convince the other ministers that it was all a mistake. But his claims had been met with fierce pressure from the ministers and the rest of the congregation. After all, he had been chosen by God himself, thereby foregoing any choice in the matter. After ten years on the bench, Samuel had overcome most of his fears, but it was commonly known among the Youngie that he was a weak man who yielded in the direction from which the wind was blowing the hardest.

Samuel was pretty sure he recognized from which direction the wind was blowing today. Deacon Koblenz had set the tone; in his ten years on the bench, Samuel had never seen the deacon's will seriously tested.

"I do sympathize with Maria and the struggles she is going through," Samuel began. "But as Alvin said, one rotten apple can ruin the whole barrel. We have to set strict guidelines for our Youngie, or others will follow Maria's example, and we will begin to begin to lose our youth."

Samuel coughed, and beads of sweat formed on his forehead. He hesitated for a long moment, perhaps to assure himself that the direction of the wind hadn't shifted. It had not, so he continued. "I vote that we ban Maria from attending the Singens until she apologizes for her sins."

The ministers waited respectfully for Bishop Mast to speak. Around them, the room filled with the smell of foul morning breath from those who hadn't taken the time to eat breakfast or brush their teeth.

Mast was a quiet man who seldom spoke his mind in the Obrod. When he did, his voice was soft, and his words carefully chosen. This left a mystique about him that explained why, unlike the bishops in most Amish communities, Bishop Mast was a well-liked leader.

After an uncomfortably long silence, Bishop Mast spoke. "I agree with Raymond Byler. I vote not to punish Maria."

The comment caught everyone off guard. Deacon Koblenz's head snapped back like he had been slapped. "You vote to not to punish her at all?" he gasped. "Why?"

## Chapter Ten

"You propose that we confine her to her home," Bishop Mast countered. "This method won't work on Maria. Let her come to us in her own time."

Deacon Koblenz had heard enough. His gray eyes glared from under bushy white eyebrows, and his fist clenched in indignation. He coughed loudly to alert everyone that he was about to have another say. The room fell silent.

"I agree with Samuel," he said emphatically. "Giving her a pass will only lead to more trouble. It is not enough to ban her for only one month. In the past we have all witnessed great results with the method of banning rebellious teens from the Singen. I vote that we ban her from all Singens and other gatherings until she fully repents and agrees to become baptized. It is high time that we put our foot down with the Reader family, and we begin by making an example of Maria."

Nobody said a word for a long moment. Downstairs, the Loblied finally ended and the congregation sat silent. A baby squalled and there was a shuffling of feet as the mother left the room with her child. Deacon Koblenz took the silence as an indication to continue.

"I see no need for Maria to wait until next spring when the next group begins baptism classes. She can begin classes immediately and if she seems sincere enough, we will lift the ban and she can attend the Singens again."

Deacon Koblenz glanced around the room, searching for approval to this merciful solution. Samuel Mullet nodded slowly, trying to gauge the mood in the room. "I am in agreement with the Deacon's suggestion," he said.

"I can't agree to that," Raymond Byler said quickly. "It is never a good idea to force someone into baptism. Pressure, yes, but not force."

"Nor will I," Bishop Mast said firmly. "If we start down that path, it will end badly. Baptism must be voluntary."

Everyone stared at Bishop Mast. Never before had he spoken out of turn like this, and never before had he so strongly defied Deacon Koblenz.

Finally, Alvin Keim spoke. The weight of his deciding vote pressed heavily upon him, and his shoulders sagged. "I vote with Deacon Koblenz and Samuel Mullet," he said finally. "We must set firm rules if we wish to keep order in this community."

In this manner the decision was made, by majority vote. The verdict would be delivered by Deacon Rudy Koblenz, and the impact would have lasting consequences for the community of Caroline Creek.

Bishop Mast dismissed the ministers, but just before they started down the stairs, Raymond Byler made a special announcement. Bishop Mast scribbled some names and a date on a piece of paper. He would deliver the news to the congregation after the services were over.

The ministers filed back down the stairs in preparation for the day's services.

Bishop Mast took his spot in the doorway to preach his sermon. The opening was seven feet tall and eight feet long. It was designed so the ministers could stand comfortably and preach to the women in the dining room, and the men in the living room.

What authoritative leadership Bishop Mast may have lacked in the Obrod, he more than made up for when he stood before his congregation. It was as if he was on a stage and the bright lights were on. On this stage, Bishop Mast delivered sermons that forced even the toughest of the men to hide their faces behind trembling hands. When he hit his stride with the high notes and pounded a fist into the palm of his hand for emphasis, many women covered their faces with their aprons, overwhelmed by emotion.

Today Bishop Mast began his sermon with a long slow drawl that described his drive to church. While he drove, he had marveled at all the wonders God had put in his path. There was the clean air to

## Chapter Ten

breathe. That alone was more than many were afforded. And didn't he have a healthy horse to carry him and his family to worship?

Next, he spoke of how blessed was the community that they lived in, in a country that allowed freedom to worship God without malice from a government, or fear of retaliation from other religious organizations. He gave a few examples of the bravery and heroism of Amish members who had been tortured and persecuted for their faith back in the old countries in Europe.

Bishop Mast sensed that a storm of restlessness was brewing within the community. He couldn't quite place a finger on the real issue, but some inner instinct told him he should have taken a stronger stance in the Obrod. Although he had to give Deacon Koblenz credit on one point: ostracizing a church member did have a way of snapping that member back into line in a hurry.

Solitude was strange like that. A person's greatest desire was usually the need for acceptance. In almost all instances, if a member is cut off from the church, and that member senses that acceptance slipping away, they will go to great lengths to make amends. *But would that method work on Maria Reader?* Bishop Mast thought not.

Next, Bishop Mast turned to a topic that was forefront in his mind. "And now as we see and marvel at all these great miracles that God has set before us, verily I say, even in the midst of these very miracles and blessings, we still have wayward children who do not see the love of God." He took a handkerchief from his pocket and wiped his eyes.

From her bench in the kitchen, Ruth Reader caught her breath. She thought she knew exactly where Bishop Mast's sermon was going, and she was right. The back of her neck burned red with shame as Bishop Mast began to openly discuss her children before the congregation.

"It is not enough to simply attend church and put on a public display of worshipping," Bishop Mast continued. "Let your actions speak louder than your words. We must pray for those who are lost to the world, for the bible clearly teaches that all that is of the world is surely sin. Let us also pray for the souls of our lost sheep, that they repent and return to the fold before Jesus comes back to earth again. For on that day, the righteous and the sinners will be separated, and if on that day you are living in sin, it is too late.

"Oh, how hopeless eternity is! The scripture tells us the misery is so unbearable that one loses track of time. One day becomes like a thousand years, and a thousand years are as one day. Verily I say unto you, but our time on earth is so short. Are we to use that time as a plaything, to be toyed with, to gamble with sin, so we may then spend eternity burning in hellfire?"

Bishop Mast's voice cracked, and tears glistened at the corners of his eyes. Aprons moved to wipe teary eyes as the vivid image of hellfire hit home among the rapt congregation. Ruth's head sank lower and lower with the weight of Bishop Mast's words.

Bishop Mast concluded his sermon and the congregation knelt to pray. After the prayer Bishop Mast rose again. He paused sufficiently for full effect, then continued. "I would like to announce that two of our young members have made the decision to join their hands in marriage."

A gasp rippled through the congregation. Amish tradition holds that a couple keep their wedding date a secret from everyone except their immediate family.

Bishop Mast continued. "John Schrock and Sadie Byler have announced their wedding plans. The wedding will be held at Brother Raymond Byler's house one week from this coming Thursday. John and Sadie wish to invite everyone in the community to their wedding."

And then the services were over. The Singen boys were the first to leave the house, and they were hit with a torrent of rain as they ran toward the barn to hitch their horses to the buggies.

# CHAPTER ELEVEN

Bruce poured his third cup of coffee and took a deep drag from his pipe. The smoke curled lazily from the freshly-packed bowl and floated toward the open window. He did his best thinking early in the morning while the rest of the world slept, and the combination of caffeine and tobacco created a soothing balance that calmed a brain already working in overdrive.

Bruce paced the floor of his front office, occasionally stopping to stare through the half-open window. Between the bare branches of the trees he saw the first faint glow of silver as the sun began its ascent.

The window overlooked a vacant lot behind the office. The lot was fenced in, and about twenty yards from the foot of the building, six elm trees sprouted from brown patches of dead crabgrass and crumbling concrete. The elm trees towered to almost three times the height of Bruce's window, their bare branches silent and unmoving in the still of the morning. The branches reached in twisted and misshapen directions, like a child's upward-reaching arms for the parent that is never there. Like his own child, somewhere far away, reaching up for the father it barely knew. Bruce shook his head to clear the depressing image.

At the foot of the trees the empty lot stretched for about a hundred feet until it reached the board fence that ran parallel to the street beyond. Over the years, some street artists had expressed their innermost thoughts in graffiti across some of the patches of concrete. Every spring the ragweed and dandelions grew in fresh and green, but at the first frost they were reduced to a depressing wasteland of shriveled brown patches of tangled grass.

At times Bruce took inspiration from the desolate lot, but this morning it was a distraction. He turned from the window and walked back to his desk.

He had been out of his office for most of the week, and the *Crazy Wall* had suffered because of it.

He had made a few small additions though. The end of the piece of red yarn now taped to a sketch of the Readers' dead dog. Summer's photo had moved in closer to Shug, and since nobody had heard from either her nor Eli in almost two weeks, a large red X now crossed out their photos.

The visit to Caroline Creek had turned up no new evidence. No new fingerprints had been found in the barn, and Bruce had not uncovered any other notes. Nobody had been able to account for the whereabouts of Eli on the night of the murder, so the idea that he could have been a witness could not be ruled out.

The Castleton Police Department had not received a single tip on anyone matching Eli's description, and bringing on the FBI hadn't created any new leads. Or if it had, they weren't sharing.

Bruce took a step back to get a broader view of the wall. When he did, he tripped over a mattress he had thrown onto the floor in the corner of the room. Hot coffee splashed from his mug, across his arm and onto the mattress. "Daggone it," Bruce muttered under his breath. "I keep forgetting about that mattress."

Susan had suggested the idea after she found Bruce asleep at his desk one morning and realized he hadn't gone home the night before. She had reasoned that the five-mile drive to Bruce's house, usually late at night and through dozens of streetlights, was not worth the effort required to get a few hours of sleep. Besides, she reasoned, since Bruce's divorce there was nobody to go home to anyway.

From the front of the closet door above the mattress hung several changes of clothes on hangers. They would have to do

## Chapter Eleven

until the dry cleaner lady came by to exchange them for clean ones. After returning from the Dark Angel several nights earlier, he had tossed his jacket at the foot of the mattress, reasoning that it would be taken to the dry cleaners the same evening. It had not.

Bruce cursed as he picked up the jacket. A large stain spread across the bottom of the jacket where the coffee had spilled. Using paper towels, Bruce tried to soak up the coffee. He did not see the note that fell from one of the jacket pockets and came to rest in the small space between the mattress and the wall.

Bruce gave up on the jacket and tossed it across the back of a chair. Susan would be arriving for work soon, and Bruce wanted to finish his morning ritual before she arrived. First, he ejected the magazine from his Glock. Out of habit, he cleared the chamber. He went through the same routine with the smaller handgun strapped to his ankle.

Since the maneuvers were a regular routine, Bruce worked through them quickly and smoothly. He rolled on the floor and came up on one knee, Glock drawn, the barrel trained on the jacket he had tossed on the back of the chair five feet away.

Other imaginary bodies popped out from random angles of the room, and Bruce spun, ducked, and dove backward and forward. Each time he rose to a stance, his trigger finger was ready to apply the exact amount of pressure required to pull the trigger.

After five minutes he was satisfied.

Next, he took a pair of handcuffs from a desk drawer. He placed a chair in front of the mirror and handcuffed himself to the chair back. He scooted his chair backward until he reached the corner of his desk and, groping at the drawers, felt for the paper clip inside. His fingers closed on an ink pen. He thought of unscrewing it and using the sharp point and the spring inside, but decided that would be too easy. An amateur could do that on a bad day, and he was certainly not an amateur.

The last maneuver took by far the most concentration. Bruce faced the mirror and carefully studied his reflection, searching for the slightest movement in his chest or shoulders.

Before he had been chief of police, Bruce had been a lieutenant. Long before that, he had worked undercover in narcotics. He had watched friends disappear because they weren't prepared, and he had decided he would never be the unprepared one.

His fingers worked along the cuffs of his shirt, feeling for the gadget he had sewn there. Crafted of modified fiber, it was almost exactly the length of a toothpick and rounded to follow the curve of his wrist. It was formed from fiberglass, making it untraceable, even with a metal detector.

The idea had been born during an exercise at the academy when Bruce was the captor, and one of his "prisoners" had effortlessly broken out of a set of handcuffs without raising the slightest suspicion.

The sharp end broke through the stitching of his cuff, and a few seconds later his wrists were free.

Satisfied with his routine, Bruce walked back to the desk in the front room. The stack of paperwork seemed to grow taller every time he looked in its direction, and Bruce glared at it as if to challenge its very existence. The stack did not waver or shrink from his gaze.

Bruce sat down and powered up his computer. He opened the Trontelli file and began to re-read it. Something was missing. It was right beneath his nose, but just out of his reach. How had the Trontelli crime family evaded the law for so long? Sure, there was a time when crime families were a lot more common. But that was back in the early 1900s. Back when they bought the law and paid off the judges.

But this was modern-day America. The internet linked databases internationally. A murder somewhere in the farthest corner of the world could now be quickly connected to another murder

## Chapter Eleven

thousands of miles away. A partial fingerprint found at a crime scene, or a tiny speck of DNA found under a victim's fingernails was enough evidence to convict a suspect. Back when he was a young detective, it had taken weeks or even months to piece together the profile of a suspect. Now, thanks to criminal databases like the FBI's National Crime Information Center (NCIC), worlds of information were only seconds away with just the click of a mouse. And yet, somehow, the Trontellis had thrived.

The fingerprints found on Eli's note still didn't add up. As Bruce saw it, there were two possibilities. The first was that Eli had simply run away with Summer. But if that were the case, why hadn't Summer gone back to work at the Dark Angel by now? There really was no reason to go into hiding with Eli.

*Or was there?*

Bruce glanced at his notes. Eli Reader was only fifteen.

*Would Summer really worry about being prosecuted for having a consensual relationship with a minor?* Stan Prater said that Summer had been booked on multiple prostitution charges. Besides, it was much more difficult to prosecute a woman for having sex with a minor than if the roles were reversed. Would Summer concern herself with such a detail? Bruce knew almost nothing about her, but the love affair seemed like an unlikely scenario.

The second reason was something Summer had said to Passion. She had said that 'a soft touch' was needed? This could only mean that Summer and Eli had not met previously, and that Summer had been sent by someone else to try and draw Eli away from the community without drawing too much attention. It would mean that whomever had sent Summer knew Eli well enough to know that Eli might not leave with someone if that stranger were a man.

So, if the second theory was true, why had Summer left her fingerprints on the note? She had to assume that the prints would be found. She would have known to be careful to leave no clues behind. Unless she had left the prints on purpose. *Had Summer realized that she was putting Eli in danger, and had she wanted to send a message?*

Bruce had told Stan Prater that he would work the case backward—that he would try and prove that the mob wasn't involved in Eli's disappearance. Yet, he found that he couldn't rule the mob out. In fact, the longer he looked at it, the more sense it made. Somehow, Eli must have witnessed the murder and now he was being silenced. Did that mean he was already dead?

Bruce took another pull on his pipe and growled at the smug faces of the photos on the screen. Neither the caffeine nor the nicotine did anything to soften the fact that he, Bruce Ellsworth, had spent much of his life trying to nail these guys to the wall, and had nothing to show for it.

He clicked on Shug's file. There were two addresses listed. The first one was in Kirkwood, a suburb of south St. Louis.

The second address had been more difficult to track because it was listed under a fake corporation that ultimately led to an account in the Bahamas. The address was to a ranch in New Mexico. The ranch sat in the middle of the Navajo Indian Reservation, and because of this, had managed to go undetected for a while. Little was known about the ranch, except that it housed several private airplanes and a landing strip, and several times a month, Old Man Trontelli and his son met Shug there. Occasionally some of the girls from their night clubs accompanied the men to the ranch.

Bruce typed the address of the ranch into Google Maps and zoomed in. The ranch sat about twenty miles south of the Colorado border, and about the same distance from the four corners of Arizona, Utah, Colorado, and New Mexico. Bruce zoomed in and studied the outline of the buildings.

*What goes on in that place? What stories can it tell?*

At precisely eight thirty-five Bruce heard the key turn in the lock, and the front door squeaked open.

## Chapter Eleven

"Good morning." Susan's shrill voice carried up the stairs. "Whatcha doin' up there?"

Bruce walked to the stairway and leaned against the open banisters.

Susan hung her coat on a hook on the wall and set her purse in its usual spot beneath her desk. She was a big-breasted woman with dirty blonde hair that didn't quite reach to her shoulders. She was plump, but not fat. Her blue plaid skirt reached modestly to her knees. She had not taken the time to put on her makeup. No doubt she would finish that job in the bathroom, which would take another forty-five minutes, and would put her actual clock-in time at about nine-thirty.

Susan re-arranged desktop photos of her three children, set her cup of coffee in its usual spot on her desk, then sat down.

"Good morning Susan," Bruce said evenly. "So... how was he?"

Susan swiveled in her chair. She smiled and began to chew intently on a fingernail.

Susan's marriage had ended a year ago when, as a stranger, she had walked into Bruce's office in search of a private investigator. The investigation lasted less than one day and had ended when Bruce followed her husband to a hotel on the outskirts of Troy, Missouri. Bruce had snapped a few photos of the man and his lover having a passionate make-out session in the parking lot before walking arm-in-arm into the hotel lobby and out of sight. The photographs had been evidence enough to convince Susan who, until that moment, had been blindly faithful to the father of her three children.

Through the commotion of the divorce, Susan had somehow ended up working for Bruce. The job turned out to be a pretty good fit for Bruce, largely because business was slow, but also because Susan came at a reasonable price.

The position was likewise a good fit for Susan, who seemed to thrive at a job that didn't require a lot of effort. Her work days consisted of answering the phone and collecting the contact information of would-be new clients, reading and answering the simpler letters, and keeping a fresh pot of coffee brewing at all times. If any clients came through the door, she seated them and rang for Bruce at his desk upstairs.

After her divorce, Susan had re-entered the dating world, with most of her prospects coming from online dating websites. Since her children went to her ex-husband every other weekend, this left Susan free to explore the affections of some of the eligible bachelors in the greater St. Louis area.

Susan leaned back in her chair, lifted a leg, and placed it across her knee. Her painted toenails wiggled from where they hung close to the opposite ankle.

"He was, um, different," she answered.

"Different?" Bruce pried.

"Well let's see," Susan continued. "He picked the restaurant, paid the bill, was polite, cute, but didn't smile much. Heck, come to think of it, he didn't smile at all. I don't even know if he liked me. I have to say, it is a bit disarming to spend an evening with a date who never smiles, especially if you have full intentions of ending that date in bed."

"So… it ended in bed?" asked Bruce with a slow grin.

"Of course," Susan laughed. "You don't actually think I'd put in all that effort, and swipe the dating app that many times, just to come away empty-handed?"

"Naw, I guess not," Bruce said, then continued. "Did this guy engage in conversation, or did he have his nose buried in his phone?"

"Well, besides a few trips to the bathroom, I don't think he checked his phone even once," Susan said proudly.

"And this date—ended in your bed, or his?"

"Mine," Susan said slowly. "Where are you going with this?"

"He's married," Bruce said decidedly.

## Chapter Eleven

Susan looked baffled and a little hurt. "What makes you say that?" she asked.

"If he was single, he would have been more seasoned in the world of online dating. Being single comes with its own sort of vibe. When a single person walks into a bar or restaurant, their singleness reeks from their pores."

Susan pondered this for a moment. "I don't believe I've told you enough for you to make those assumptions yet," she said defensively.

"Sure you have," Bruce continued. "If this man were single, he would have spent a lot more time glancing around for other opportunities in case you didn't interest him. If he were single, he would have been talking to old flames before you and he met at the restaurant. Again, just in case you didn't work out, he'd have a backup plan. Out of habit, he would have been sneaking glances at his cell phone to see if he was missing any come-ons from old girlfriends. Take my word for it, Susan—this guy is new to the world of dating. Probably, it is his first hookup in a long time. Probably, he was having a fight with his wife, and you were his escape. Probably, you won't hear from him again until their next fight."

Susan frowned. "Sometimes I hate working for a detective," she said flatly.

"And I bet going to your house was his idea, right?" Bruce asked.

"Yeah. I guess it was," Susan said thoughtfully. "But he lives somewhere in Effingham, which is over an hour away. So, no thanks, not worth the drive."

"All I'm saying is, he is either seriously dating, or very married," Bruce said. "Take my advice and keep swiping that app."

Susan glared at Bruce as if he were somehow to blame for all of her bad luck with men. Finally, she turned and began to re-arrange the pens in her desk organizer, which was her way of letting Bruce know the conversation was over.

"What's on your agenda for today?" she asked.

"Boring stuff. I'm meeting a guy about a credit card fraud case," Bruce said. "Just once, I'd love to confront these bastards face-to-face, but unfortunately I'm only allowed to do paperwork and let others make the arrests."

"Terribly boring," Susan sniffed. "And after that?"

"I'll have to pay a visit to the FBI office here in town. Report a possible kidnapping."

"Who?" Susan asked, sitting forward.

"Ehh. Just a hunch," Bruce said.

"Who?" Susan repeated.

"Remember the Amish people who stopped by about a week ago?"

Susan nodded.

"I think there is more to that story than a runaway teen."

Susan sniffed again. "And while you are gone, you want me to answer emails and stay close to the phone?" She shot him a smile. "Sound about right, boss?"

"Don't forget your makeup," Bruce fired back. "Oh, and make sure you cover up the bruised area that your married lover sucked on, you know, *riiiggghhhttt* there, peeking out just above your collar. You are in a workplace environment, you know."

Susan's hand moved predictably to touch the spot. She searched for a comeback, but the door to Bruce's office had already closed.

———◆———

Miss Becky Cainbridge preferred to clean offices after all the employees had gone home, so the hour was late when she unlocked the door at 1311 East Fennimore Street. She wiped the desktop down and hung the wet towel over the rim of her bucket, then knelt on the mattress and began to tuck the sheets

## Chapter Eleven

down around the edges. Her hand brushed a piece of paper, which she picked up and held to the light. She frowned and for the thousandth time cursed herself for not getting a better education. It had been at the very top of her goals when she came to America, but the children had come. Mouths had to be fed, and the education had been pushed back. The words on the note were practically meaningless.

But this particular note held Becky's attention because someone had taken great pains to add something to the bottom. Something that even someone who couldn't read could still understand. Whoever had written the note, had carefully sketched a beautiful drawing of a bird. The bird was etched in a shade of darkness, almost like it was hiding in the shadows.

Becky frowned, trying to recall where she had seen such a bird.

*A sparrow*, she finally concluded. *Someone signed the note using a drawing of a sparrow.*

Becky pondered the importance of the note. She had found it on the floor, and as a rule, all scraps of paper found on the floor went straight into the trash. But this note—*someone had gone to great detail to draw a sparrow.*

Finally, drawing a deep breath, she crumpled the note and tossed it into the bag along with the rest of the trash. She carried the trash bag in one hand and the empty bucket in the other, then locked the front door to the office on her way out. Fifteen minutes later she parked behind a grocery store and tossed the trash into a dumpster.

Miss Becky Cainbridge didn't know investigator Bruce Ellsworth. She was just a cleaning lady, after all. So, she had no way of knowing that the deliverer of that note had gone to considerable pains, and risked his life, to slip that note into Bruce's coat pocket in a dimly-lit alley behind the Dark Angel several nights earlier.

## CHAPTER TWELVE

FBI Agent Rick Wright cradled his office phone in the small of his shoulder and tried to focus on the one-way conversation. If the man on the other end of the line had not been his superior, Agent Wright would have hung up five minutes ago. But since the man *was* his superior, he was forced to listen to all the usual bullshit decisions made by people who sat in seats so high above his head that he often didn't even know their names: The numerous efforts to put away the Trontellis were running the bureau way over budget and although he, Agent Wright, couldn't exactly be blamed for the failed efforts, it was time for him to come home. It was an election year, and his services would be better utilized in Washington DC. So, to assure that everyone's ass was covered, he was to write a report of the time spent in St. Louis, then prepare for relocation. The voice on the phone droned on and on.

Agent Wright had heard the same song and dance many times before; at the age of forty-nine, he expected he would hear it many more times in many other offices before retirement finally called him home. He drummed the butt end of his ink pen against his leg and watched the pointy part pop out of the front. Another thrust, and the pointy part disappeared back inside the ink pen again.

Through his open office door, he watched as the girl at the front desk greeted a man who had just walked in the door. The man was tall and broad-shouldered, with a well-groomed mustache and unusual grey eyes. Everything about the man screamed cop. His intercom buzzed.

## Chapter Twelve

"A Bruce Ellsworth to see you," the front desk girl said.

Agent Wright used the buzzer interruption to bow out of the phone call. "My appointment is here, and it's very important that he doesn't wait," he lied to the man on the other end of the phone. Then into the intercom, "Send him on back."

"You a police officer?" he asked, standing to shake Bruce's hand.

"That obvious?" Bruce asked.

"It is to me," Agent Wright said. "Maybe even the chief?"

"I was chief of the Castleton Police Department until about three years ago," Bruce replied.

Agent Wright waved to a chair on the other side of his desk and Bruce sat down.

"What changed?" Agent Wright asked.

"With?"

"Why are you no longer the chief?"

"A woman."

"Was she worth it?"

"No. Unless you count the kid."

Agent Wright nodded and changed the conversation. "What can I do for you this morning?"

"I'm here to report a missing Amish teen. His name is Eli Reader."

Agent Wright crossed his hands behind his head and leaned back in his chair. He studied Bruce's face closely. "By missing, you presume he has been kidnapped, right?" he asked.

"I do."

"And your connection to the kid?"

"His parents hired me to help find him."

"How long ago was this?"

"A week."

"This teen," Agent Wright continued. "He wouldn't happen to be from that Amish community up around Grafton, would he?"

"He would," Bruce replied. "Which is why I'm here. You're working a murder that happened up that way, right?"

Agent Wright nodded slowly. "You could say that."

"Well this kid lived less than five miles from where that murder took place."

"You think there might be a connection?"

"I can't prove there isn't," Bruce said.

"Is there a reason why you haven't come to us sooner?" Agent Wright asked bluntly.

"There is," Bruce said. "It's not that unusual for Amish kids to run away. Why bother you guys if the kid is only busting a rebellious phase?"

"What changed your mind?"

"A hunch," Bruce said. "Well actually. More like five or six hunches."

"If anyone else came to me with hunches, I'd have them thrown out of my office," Wright said. "But you don't get to be chief of police by being wrong on hunches. Tell me more."

Bruce sat back and thought about it for a minute. "Okay," he said. "The kid left a note behind. I had a forensic analyst study it."

"And?"

"We found prints that point to the mob."

"Can you be more specific?" Agent Wright asked.

"The prints belong to a professional dancer," Bruce continued. "She dances at a night club that is owned by the mob."

"That's it?" Agent Wright asked.

"The dancer is missing too."

"And you know this how?"

"I visited the club. I spoke with one of her friends."

"And?"

"The friend remembered the dancer mentioning a trip to coax someone into something. The conversation took place the night before the Amish kid disappeared."

## Chapter Twelve

Agent Wright clicked something on his computer and began to type as Bruce spoke. "That's still pretty flimsy," he said. "Anything else?"

"There was also a dead dog."

"A dead dog?"

"Yes. The kid's dog was found on the back of the property. Kinda like he was trying to protect his master, and got shot for his troubles."

"You got a theory?"

Bruce shook his head reluctantly. "Anything I come up with seems far-fetched."

"Try me," Agent Wright said.

"The kid could have witnessed the murder. So, the mob kidnapped him to keep him from talking."

"That's not really how the mob silences witnesses," Agent Wright said. "A bullet to the head seems more realistic. But then again, you already know that."

Bruce nodded. "Like I said, I don't have much to work with."

"Tell me about the kid," Agent Wright said. "I might be able to shed some light on your theory."

"According to Eli's sister, Eli is about five feet, five inches tall. Slender build, pale skin and blonde hair. Timid, I believe is how the sister described him."

Agent Wright looked up sharply. "Timid?" he asked.

Bruce shrugged. "I haven't met the kid. At least not recently. Worked a few cases in the Amish community way back, but the kid didn't even reach to my knees then."

"Well you had my attention until the 'timid' part," Agent Wright said.

"How's that?"

Agent Wright leaned back in his chair and took a long moment to consider. Finally, he said, "We're talking about two different kids. Your missing kid couldn't have been at the murder."

"You know this, how?"

"You are correct on one thing," Agent Wright said. "There was a witness who saw the murder. I've met him. And he almost resembles your missing boy. Almost."

"Except?"

"Except that the real witness wasn't timid. Matter of fact, he had balls of steel. Matter of fact, he filmed the whole thing, only feet from the actual murder."

"You have a witness, and you have a recording of the murder?" Bruce asked in disbelief.

Agent Wright nodded. "There was a meeting. A deal was made. That's all I can tell you. The rest is top-secret stuff. And we never had this conversation."

"This is the second time I've heard about this meeting. Tell me more about it," Bruce prodded.

"I can't do that," Agent Wright repeated. "If I saw a connection between your missing Amish boy and our murder case, I'd tell you more. In the meantime, I'll file your kid into our missing person's database. If anything comes up, you'll be my first call."

"So, what I'm hearing is that I'm on my own here? That if I don't find Eli Reader, nobody else will? Sound about right?"

"I've got a murder on my hands," Agent Wright said. "It takes priority over your missing kid."

Bruce rose, realizing the conversation was over, then turned and walked out the door.

Agent Wright watched Bruce go, then leaned back in his chair. Perhaps, he thought, he could have divulged more information to the investigator. Besides, what did it matter? He would be re-assigned soon anyway. The case would be shelved, and the murder would most likely remain unsolved. Maybe teaming up with a hungry investigator would be just the thing he needed to break the case. But then a second voice began to tick in the back of Agent Wright's mind. A voice that overrode all others. This voice

## Chapter Twelve

reminded him that the agency simply did not share their secrets with outsiders, regardless how crucial the connection seemed.

Agent Wright glanced around his office and then out the window. The St. Louis arch was so close that it seemed to fill up almost his entire view outside his window. Agent Wright suddenly realized that he hated the idea of relocating. He liked St. Louis. And he had come to love the food. *Write a report*, his superior had said. Well, he would do that. With the new information the investigator had shared, he would write a report so compelling that his superior would have no choice but to let him stay. Perhaps he would weave the missing Amish kid into the report and somehow tie him to the murder as the investigator had suggested.

The connection was strong enough that it could work.

# CHAPTER THIRTEEN

Stan Prater's eleven-year-old son played on a Little League baseball team. His team was down by one run in the bottom of the eighth inning, but there was a runner on first when Stan's son stepped to the plate.

Bruce watched from behind the backstop. He listened with mild interest as Stan, with a voice just loud enough to reach the umpire's ears, cursed the bad calls.

"I swear to God, my grandma could referee a game better than this guy," Stan said. "And she's dead."

"Speaking of the dead," Bruce chuckled, "you're making enough noise to raise them. Maybe if you relaxed a little, your kid could focus on actually hitting the ball."

Stan ignored him and the charade continued. "Watch the damn ball all the way in," Stan yelled through the wire mesh that separated him and home plate.

The pitcher began the wind up, and Stan's cell phone rang. He glanced at it, then answered it impatiently.

The bat connected and the ball bounced slowly toward second. The shortstop scooped it up with his bare hand, bobbled, then threw to first.

The play was close, but the home plate umpire pumped his fist in the 'out' signal, then half-ducked, bracing for the tirade of words that were sure to come. When nothing but silence greeted him, he shot a quick glance over his shoulder, but Stan Prater had his back turned, his phone tucked between his ear and shoulder.

Bruce glanced at his watch and checked the scoreboard. Kid baseball was boring, but Stan had been relentless. Be-

## Chapter Thirteen

sides, he reasoned, Stan had moments where his insight could prove valuable.

Stan came back and joined Bruce behind the backstop.

"Everything alright?" Bruce asked.

"I'm not sure," Stan said, suddenly subdued. "That was Chief Westbritt. Someone just ruined his evening."

"Tell me more," Bruce said.

"Remember how I told you a deal was being made? And you told me to try and find out who was on the receiving end of the deal?"

Bruce nodded.

"Well, turns out you were right. The man on the good end of that deal is Shug."

"No surprise there," Bruce said. "What does this have to do with Chief Westbritt being sour?"

"Well, apparently something has come up. Shug is trying to postpone the agreement."

"Why would he do that?"

"All the chief said is that the case against Joey Trontelli has gotten pretty weak," Stan replied.

The game ended with a double in the bottom of the ninth that brought in the winning run, and the home team swarmed to congratulate the batter. The umpire avoided Stan Prater and disappeared toward the parking lot.

Bruce walked to the parking lot with Stan and his son. Stan put the bat and glove into the bag in the back of his old, rusty station wagon.

"I need a drink," Stan said, turning to Bruce. "Let me run the kid home. I'll be at the Toad in half an hour. Wanna join me?"

"Don't mind if I do," Bruce replied.

The sun set quickly, and Bruce clicked on his headlights as he turned east. A few minutes later he backed into a parking spot behind the Thirsty Toad and waited, watching the entrance. Stan Prater arrived and parked next to him. He got out and started toward the Toad, but when Bruce didn't move, he turned around and got into the passenger side of the Explorer.

"Still watching your tail after all these years?" Stan asked.

Bruce nodded.

"Does it ever end?"

"Does what end?" Bruce asked. "Me trying to stay alive?"

"What would it take for you to stop watching over your shoulder?"

"I hope I never do," Bruce replied.

"I've quit caring," Stan said. "I figure my maker already has the date of my death written in his big old book, and nothing will prolong that date by even one minute."

Bruce, who had long ago gotten used to Stan's long-winded theories, decided not to bite. Instead, he checked his phone. Then they sat in the shadows with the headlights off. Finally, Stan broke the silence.

"There is a drink inside that is clearly calling my name," he said. "Matter of fact, that drink has half a dozen very attractive sisters. Come on, Bruce. Nobody is following you. Let's go inside."

Bruce ignored him.

A Nissan Rogue with dark windows circled the parking lot, hesitated in front of a parking spot, then moved on. When it reached the road, the driver turned right.

Bruce waited until the taillights disappeared, then got out of the Explorer. They crossed the parking lot and entered through the back door. Bruce walked to his usual corner booth and sat with his back to the wall.

Stan motioned to Jen, who smiled and left to get his drink.

"Seriously though, you really can't turn it off?" Stan asked, turning back to Bruce.

"Turn what off?"

## Chapter Thirteen

"You can't stop studying faces."

"I hope I never do," Bruce repeated.

"You need to relax," Stan said, annoyance creeping into his voice. "Put your phone away. C'mon Chief. Enjoy a beer. Nobody is trying to kill you."

Bruce leaned forward and placed his elbows on the table, but his eyes scanned the room warily. Finally, he looked at Stan and asked, "The Nissan Rogue that was circling the parking lot. Did you even notice it?"

Stan rubbed his grizzled jaw and frowned. "I kinda recall an SUV," he said. "What about it?"

"I'm being followed," Bruce said. "That's the third time this week I've noticed that exact vehicle. Heck, if you were paying attention, you'd have seen it at the ball fields earlier tonight."

Stan sat a little straighter, suddenly focused. "You're sure about that?" he asked.

"I'm sure," Bruce said. He held up his hand, revealing a combination of digits written in ink on his palm. "Exact same license plates. If I only saw the vehicle twice in one week, maybe I'd make the argument that it was a coincidence. But three times? Not a chance. I'm being followed, Stan. Why?"

Stan studied him carefully. "I'm guessing you have a theory?" he asked.

"Two days ago, that same vehicle was stolen from a Wal-Mart parking lot in Paducah, Kentucky," Bruce said. "Someone switched the plates to make it harder to trace. These plates," Bruce flashed the digits on his palm. "These plates belong to a similar Nissan that's sitting behind Alan's Auto Body getting the tranny replaced."

Stan took a long swig and wiped his mouth. "Why would someone go to all that trouble just to follow you?"

"They don't want to be identified," Bruce said. "And that makes me very nervous."

Stan thought about that for a moment, then shook his head. "The only thing that's changed recently is that you're looking for a missing Amish kid, right?"

Bruce frowned and nodded. "And that's been a strange case right from the start."

"By the way, how is Hillbilly Harry?" Stan asked.

"What?"

"Well that's who did your homework on the stolen Rogue, right?"

Bruce chuckled. "Didn't take you long to make that connection, did it?"

Harold Travers, the man Stan Prater referred to as Hillbilly Harry, was a retired FBI forensic analyst who now lived in a bunker way off the grid somewhere in the Missouri foothills. Harry's attention to detail, his ability to breach old databases within the bureau, and his insistence on keeping records of every case he had ever touched, had made him an invaluable resource for Bruce during his time at the precinct.

In fact, Bruce thought as he watched the red-faced man across the table gulp his second beer, not counting Stan, Hillbilly Harry was about as close to a real friend as he had had in many years.

Harry had been forced into retirement, replaced by "Some new hotshot straight out of law school," as he had later described it.

After retirement, the FBI stopped caring about Harold Travers and he became Hillbilly Harry. He kept doing forensic work for a select handful of old and trusted acquaintances, but as far as Bruce could tell, he was probably the only person who knew the actual whereabouts of Harold Travers' bunker.

Jen arrived and took Bruce's order, then left.

"Harry seems very… content." Bruce grinned, confirming Stan's hunch.

"You know," Stan said. "Someday my kids will be grown, and my wife will probably move on with some other dude. When

## Chapter Thirteen

that happens, I'm going to live just like Harry. Now there is a man who has it figured out. Live your life, and the rest of society can go screw itself."

"And you're drunk," Bruce stated.

"And you're an uptight ass," Stan said with a good-natured smirk. Bruce shrugged.

A middle-aged man came in and sat down at a table close to the front door. The man was short and wore a grey flannel shirt. Bruce frowned, trying to make the man fit in with the rest of the crowd that usually hung out at the Toad. The man wouldn't fit. There was something wrong about the polished hair, or maybe it was because he seemed too tense.

"Just like old times," Jen interrupted his thoughts. "You two coming in here, sitting at your old booth..."

Bruce glanced up at Jen and smiled, but the uneasy feeling stayed. His eyes darted around the room. *The man in the flannel shirt is leaving? That doesn't fit either. It's too soon. And he doesn't have a takeout dinner in his hand.*

"Jen." Bruce said sharply. "Did that man order food?"

Jen looked in the direction Bruce nodded. "He ordered coffee, but said he wasn't hungry," Jen said. "Why, what's up?"

Something moved. Something glowed where it wasn't supposed to glow. Bruce's eyes followed the movement and stopped at Jen's feet. Black tennis shoes. A red glow. Faint and then gone. *Off. On. Off. On.*

Bruce dropped to the floor and lifted the tablecloth that hung around the table. The movement brought him eye-level with a device secured to the bottom of the table. In the instant before the explosion Bruce was on his feet.

*"BOMB!"* he bellowed at the top of his lungs. *"EVERYONE OUT NOW!"*

It seemed like it took an eternity for Stan to piece together Bruce's words. He rose clumsily from his seat, the effects of the alcohol making him sluggish. He grasped his of beer in his hand, unwilling to part with the foaming prize.

Bruce's right arm shot out and wrapped around Jen's waist. His left hand grabbed a handful of Stan's shirt. With every ounce of his strength, he hurled himself toward the front door, carrying Jen and half-dragging Stan behind.

Only a few seconds had passed since he saw the red glow on Jen's shoes. *There's not enough time.* The first people hadn't even reached the front door.

Bruce was between his fifth and sixth step when there was a white flash, and he was floating.

# CHAPTER FOURTEEN

For what seemed like weeks, Bruce floated. Sometimes he dodged bright stars somewhere in the outer galaxy, other times the stars crushed him with their weight. He tried to draw light out of the darkness that engulfed him, but the darkness was too complete.

Then a faint voice came out of the darkness, and now the stars drilled directly into his eyes. They seemed to grope at the back of his eyeballs like sandpaper. He tried to swallow, but something was lodged in his throat. Perhaps he had swallowed a star.

Gradually a round shape came into focus, shifting and drawing nearer. The shape took the form of a face, which could have belonged to Chief Calvin Westbritt. Bruce tried to focus on the face, to latch on to reality, but the darkness came again.

Then the lighting was different. The shape came into focus quicker than it had before. This time Bruce held on to the vision of Westbritt's face a little longer before the darkness swallowed him.

Then finally, the shape came back. This time it stayed. Through tiny slits that formed the outer walls of his eyelids Bruce studied the face of the man who had replaced him as chief of police.

The next thought Bruce had was not of anger or jealousy, but profound concern. "Stan Prater?" he mouthed feebly.

Chief Westbritt leaned in close over Bruce's face. He answered in a low voice. "Stan's in the Intensive Care Unit. Fighting for his life. Probably won't make it."

Bruce felt a shudder vibrate down the entire length of his body. "Jen?" he asked.

"Dead."

A bolt of guilt shot through Bruce. "Has anyone told their families?"

"Of course," Westbritt said.

"It's my fault," Bruce said. "I sensed the danger but waited too long to act."

"Actually," Chief Westbritt said. "Give yourself some credit. Your quick thinking saved a lot of lives."

"Did anyone else die?" Bruce asked.

Chief Westbritt shook his head. "Five others wounded, but the bomb was designed for close-range impact. Stan was between you and the bomb, and he took the brunt of the impact."

Bruce coughed and then winced as pain stabbed his side. His hand moved to his ribs.

Chief Westbritt nodded. "You broke two," he said.

"Is that it?" Bruce asked.

"You have a severe concussion, a busted ear drum, and they had to reset your left shoulder. You are lucky."

"What day is it?" Bruce asked, glancing around the room.

"This is your third day here," Westbritt said. "It is Monday, November the third."

"Who did it?"

"You sure you're up for all this?" Chief Westbritt asked.

"I'm sure," Bruce said. He groaned as he tried to raise up on one elbow.

"Let's start with this," Westbritt said. "I know Stan brought you the Trontelli files."

Bruce didn't respond.

"And I know he told you about the meeting and the deal we made with Shug."

"Okay," Bruce said. "So, arrest us."

"You're not in trouble," Westbritt said.

"Then why are you here?"

## Chapter Fourteen

"Let's work together, Bruce. Let's share information. One of my best detectives is fighting for his life. Let's find out what's really going on."

Bruce grimaced. Not as much from physical pain as from the image Chief Westbritt standing before the flashing cameras and taking all the credit for Bruce's work. But Westbritt was right about one thing. Egos needed to be put aside. They now shared a common goal, and working with Westbritt couldn't hurt.

"You go first," Bruce said.

Chief Westbritt nodded. "Thought you might say that."

A nurse arrived and adjusted some tubes. She bent over Bruce and took his blood pressure. "How are you feeling?" she asked.

"Like I got hit by a bomb," Bruce said dryly.

The nurse laughed. She adjusted a few bags that hung beside the bed, then left. Just before the door closed, Bruce glimpsed the backside of a figure in a police uniform in the hallway.

"Security," Chief Westbritt said, following Bruce's gaze. "Two officers outside your and Stan's rooms, twenty-four seven."

"Thanks," Bruce said.

"So, you know about the footage, and the eyewitness?" Chief Westbritt continued.

"I've heard bits and pieces," Bruce said. "Bizarre story. Shug had to know the murder was going to take place, which is how he knew when to send his guy to film it, right?"

"Of course," Westbritt said. "But we decided it didn't much matter. The footage would put away Old Man Trontelli and his son. Forever. Without them, Shug collapses. We nail him in less than a year and he follows the Trontellis into oblivion."

"What changed?" Bruce asked.

"The judge set up a date for the deposition, but at the last minute, Shug bailed."

"Why?" Bruce asked. "Shug is a calculated man. He would have thought several steps ahead before ever setting this thing up. Why would he walk away from this?"

"I don't have any answers, but I can tell you that I got real suspicious real fast," Chief Westbritt continued. "That's one of the reasons I'm here."

"What did you stumble upon?" Bruce asked.

"I've never been able to get a warrant to enter Shug's house, but the graphic footage he brought to the meeting changed all that. When he started to get flaky the judge finally gave me the warrant."

"You tapped his phone?"

Westbritt nodded. He took a mini recorder from his pocket. "It's all here," he said, tapping the device. "This is a phone exchange between him and the man he sent to plant the bomb. The call was made fifteen minutes after the bomb detonated. Wanna hear it?"

Bruce nodded and closed his eyes. There was a click as Chief Westbritt pushed the button. For a few seconds there was static, then a voice.

"Okay. I'm on a secure line. Is it done?" The voice was calm and even.

*Shug's voice*, Bruce thought.

"Yes, it's done," the second voice replied.

"Was he alone?"

"No."

"I thought I told you to make sure he was alone. How the hell did you screw this one up?"

"The cop always goes to the restaurant after the game. He always eats in the same booth. So, I put it there before he got there. How was I to know the second guy was going to show up?"

"Who was the second guy?" Shug's voice asked.

"The investigator."

## Chapter Fourteen

"Bruce Ellsworth?"

"Yeah, him. What of it? He's nobody."

Shug's voice interrupted. He did not yell or curse, but the reproach sliced from the speakers of the small recorder all the same.

"I could absorb one drunk cop. But I need the investigator to lead me to someone very important. I need him alive. If he dies, you die. Do you understand?"

"But the investigator found the bomb and I had to do some…" The connection went silent.

There was another click as Chief Westbritt ended the recording.

"The bomb was meant for Stan Prater?" Bruce asked incredulously. "Why?"

Chief Westbritt shook his head. "If he dies, we may never know."

"Who the hell does he want me to lead him to?" Bruce said. "Eli Reader? If so, does that mean the mob doesn't have him after all?"

Chief Westbritt looked puzzled. "Okay, your turn," he said. "What do you know?"

Bruce hesitated. Until recently he had hated the man sitting next to his hospital bed. Now he was expected to divulge everything he had learned over the last week. He decided he wasn't quite ready for that just yet. He glanced at the morphine bag and an idea came to him. He coughed, sending another bolt of pain to his side. He grimaced and reached for his ribs again.

Chief Westbritt nodded and rose. "You'll be out of here in a few days. Come see me at the precinct."

Bruce nodded. This time a surge of morphine really did kick in and the room started to spin. He tried to focus on the bag hanging above his shoulder, but gradually the image clouded, then the darkness returned.

## CHAPTER FIFTEEN

Eli Reader awoke to blinding sunlight. He tried to block the glare, but his arm refused to move. For a few seconds he gazed down at the limp arm, confused. Other objects came slowly into focus. He was sitting on a strip of sand, and about twenty feet in front of him the sand ended and water began. The water formed a large lake of clear blue, undisturbed by wind or rain.

But it wasn't the sand or the water that captured Eli's attention. Rather, it was what held the water in place that startled him out of his half-conscious stupor. On either side of the lake, tall rock walls rose straight up from the water's edge. Eli's eyes moved along the wall, searching for the top. He found it at a height about equal to that of an eight-story building.

For a time, Eli sat on the sand, his brain balanced somewhere between consciousness and disbelief. The logical part of his brain told him he must climb the wall. That such an act was his only chance at escape. That suggestion was followed by a clear image that made Eli shudder. In the image was the tiny figure of a boy, halfway up the rocks, one arm dangling useless by his side as he clung desperately to the face of the wall. At last the boy's strength gave out and he hurtled to his death below.

*There has to be another way out. A wall must have an opening.*

Jagged reddish-orange rocks jutted from the face of the wall, and in some places dead bushes and vines snaked between the rocks, grasping for a foothold in the cracks and crevices.

But there was no break in the wall. At least not that Eli could see. Instead, the wall continued for about the length of

## Chapter Fifteen

three football fields, then abruptly curved around the far end of the lake and continued its return up the other side. The contour continued until the wall came back full circle behind the strip of sand upon which Eli sat, completing the oval-shaped prison.

"A fishbowl," Eli whispered. "I'm trapped inside a fishbowl."

Eli staggered to his feet and walked along the water's edge. A thick, black, velvet blanket seemed to envelop his memory, preventing any logical connection with previous thought.

Eli knelt and splashed cold water on his face. The water didn't help.

*How long have I been in this place?*
*How did I get here?*
*What happened to my arm?*

He reached the point where the sand and water met the wall. He placed a hand upon the wall and leaned back, again calculating his chances of making it to the top. From far above a bird cried out, surprised by the intruder. It flew from its perch, sailed out over the lake, then suddenly folded its wings and dove toward the water. Eli watched, breathless. Just before the darting raptor disappeared beneath the surface of the water, its wings spread out wide and a shiny fish hung from one claw.

The moment was both magnificent and terrible all at once. Eli rubbed his eyes, but the image remained.

*How can it be so real, but at the same time feel like a bad dream?*

The hopelessness of it all hit Eli and he laughed bitterly. When the laughter left his lips, it traveled across the water, bounced off the opposite wall, and returned as an echo. The returning laughter brought a dozen of its friends, and they mocked him together.

Eli's laughter turned to hysteria. And the echoes of hysteria returned as a thousand angry mocking demons.

"I only have one arm," Eli screamed at the wall. "I can't climb out. You win."

The mocking voices came back. *"You win... you win... you win... you win..."*

Eli sat down then, determined not to panic. He placed his back against the wall and closed his eyes, breathing deeply and slowly. For a long time, he pondered the situation. A fleeting dream nudged at the black velvet of his memory. In the dream he struggled inside a dark place. *A cave maybe.* There were seats, and there was water. He swam. Another wall. Then his head broke the surface of the water and there was sand.

Eli opened his eyes and stared at the water. Was the vision real or a dream? If it was real, where was the cave? Nearby?

A branch drifted by and came to rest against the far wall. It took a moment for the significance of the moving branch to hit him.

*Branch moving.*
*Current.*
*Current carries water in from somewhere.*
*An opening in the rock wall.*

Something jolted through the blank black velvet of his mind, a tiny rip in the blackness of a forgotten memory.

*A large shiny object.*
*Airplane.*
*Airplane?*

There *HAD* been an airplane. There had been shouting and flashing lights and someone had pointed a gun at someone else. But the faces in his shifting memory held no meaning.

Eli's vision blurred and he closed his eyes tightly, trying to hang on to the images. He fought to stay awake. "I can't die now," he whispered. "I have to survive. I have to get out of here."

Dizziness came and Eli's head sagged down to rest on his shoulder.

Then there were voices. *They too, must be a dream.*

The voices came closer. They came from somewhere far above.

## Chapter Fifteen

Eli's eyes flew open and he stumbled to his feet. Something splashed in the water ten feet away, and instantly the fishbowl prison flew into focus.

*The voices were real.*

Eli opened his mouth to scream, to tell the voices they had found him. But what came out was only a hoarse croak. He sucked in air to try again but froze when he made out the words coming from above.

"Hey, Jake," a voice yelled. "Get your gun ready. I think I hear something."

On the cliff far above, the second man walked over, and the two men stared down at the water and listened. After a while, the first man picked up another rock and hurled it over the edge. The rock got smaller and smaller as it fell, then there was a tiny glint of water as it splashed into the lake far below.

The splash scared something from about halfway down the wall. The second man raised a gun to his shoulder and stared through the scope. "Just a bird," he said, the scope following the bird's flight as it disappeared over the top of the opposite wall.

The man with the gun studied the water and sand below. Satisfied, he lowered the weapon and lit a cigarette.

"Reckon there ain't nothin' to see down there," he said after a few drags. "There's a storm moving in, let's pitch camp. Tomorrow we head back."

The two men turned to the right in search of a spot to pitch a tent. Had they circled left they would have seen the very thing they had been sent to find. Less than thirty paces from where they had just stood, a large object had crushed a swath of scrub trees and brush. A long, white scrape of scarred rock led to the edge of the cliff. The paint had been left there by one of Shug's private planes as it twisted and nose-dived toward the lake below. One of its wings had caught the edge of the cliff, causing the plane to flip over and over, all the while tossing its inhabitants about like pinballs, before finally crashing into the water far below. Then as the wreckage slowly sank, the momentum of its flight and the current of the water carried it to its final resting place beneath the wall and on into the cave on the opposite side of the lake.

From his hidden spot against the wall far below, Eli waited until the voices faded. Dusk was beginning to set in, and with it came a chill that caused goosebumps to pop out all over his arms. He had to get out of the fishbowl before complete darkness came. The answer lay in the green foliage at the far end of the lake. Surely that was where the current came from.

Eli stepped gingerly into the water, testing it for temperature. He shivered as the freezing blue liquid enveloped his foot. Gritting his teeth, he took a few more steps. He kept one hand on the wall for balance and carefully felt for each foothold in the mud beneath the water. He didn't get far before he was shaking from the bitter coldness of the water. He looked back at the sand and grimaced. He had come less than twenty feet, and already the water was to his waist. At this pace, he would have to swim the last two hundred yards. He would have to do it in freezing water, and with only one arm. He might make it to the trees, but if he was wrong and there was no opening, he would freeze before he made it back to the sandbar.

Miserable and shivering, Eli turned back.

By the time he reached the sandbar a stiff breeze was blowing. Small waves splashed against the far rock wall, and wind whipped up tiny ribbons of froth. Eli pulled his shirt closer to his chest, but it did little to stop the damp air from piercing through the thin fabric.

The harsh truth slowly sank in. He would not survive the night.

The complete and total hopelessness of the situation hit him, and Eli sank to his knees upon the sand. The sand felt warm to the touch, and it gave him a glimmer of hope. He would dig a hole in

## Chapter Fifteen

the sand. He would crawl into the hole and cover himself with as much sand as he could reach. Perhaps he would freeze to death in his sleep, but just maybe, he would not.

*Airplane.*

The word jumped out at him again. There had been an airplane. There had been a cave. There had been shelter.

Eli stopped digging and turned to face the water. The moon was beginning its ascent, casting a pale, yellow path of light across the water. A branch the size of Eli's arm floated into view and bobbed across the path of light. The leaves on the branch fluttered in the breeze.

The branch came to rest in the same spot against the wall that Eli had seen earlier. Something triggered in his mind.

*The current. It works both ways. Water comes from the mouth of the lake, but it must drain out somewhere.*

Eli watched the branch intently.

For a few seconds the branch twisted and spun, then one end dipped beneath the water, as if pulled under by some invisible force. Then it disappeared beneath the wall.

It hit Eli all at once then. The airplane wasn't a dream. The cave wasn't a dream. If he fought and found the cave, he really might live.

Gritting his teeth, Eli carefully pulled his shirt up over his thin shoulders and down his limp arm. He gripped the shirt between his teeth, then using his good hand, tore it in half. He gripped one end between his teeth and wrapped the other end around his waist, then knotted it firmly in place.

While he worked, the temperature dropped, and his fingers began to lose feeling.

*Can't stop now.*

Eli wrapped the loose ends around his limp arm and pulled them snug, then tied and double-tied the knot. He had sacrificed his shirt and the little protection it afforded against the wind, but his useless arm was now tied firmly to his waist where it could no longer flop at will.

He walked to the edge of the water, took a deep breath and dove in. Seconds later his head surfaced, and pulling himself along with the strokes of his good arm, Eli aimed for the spot on the wall where he had seen the branch disappear. The current helped.

When he reached the wall, he kicked around for where the opening should be. His bare foot connected with a sharp metal object and Eli knew he was at the right spot. He sucked in air and let the current pull him under. The tail of the plane was there, torn open by the impact on the cliff above. Eli squeezed through and moments later his head broke above the water inside the plane. The familiarity of his surroundings came back to him as he made his way up the aisle. When a cold, dead, hand brushed his neck, he was ready for it. He ducked and moved on.

The rip in the black velvet blanket of his memory opened a little farther as Eli stepped through the open door of the wrecked plane and into the cave. He took one step toward the rock ledge against the far wall, and his newfound confidence was shattered. Directly in his path, not twenty feet away, were two large orange eyes staring straight at him.

Shock propelled Eli backward. His head hit a sharp piece of metal on the plane's door, and instantly his terror turned to pain. His knees buckled and the cave seemed to shift.

*Dragons live in caves. Dragons blow fiery breaths that obliterate everything in their path.*

But the orange spots weren't eyes. As Eli staggered to regain his balance his nose pieced together the rest of the story, and for the first time in a long time he breathed a shaky sigh of relief. The fire he had stoked before he left the cave was down to a few embers, but with a little coaxing, he could bring it back to life.

Eli waded through the water and sank down upon the rock

## Chapter Fifteen

ledge. He grabbed a few dead branches that were stacked along the wall and fed the flames. In minutes the fire crackled and flickered, illuminating the roof of the cave. The smoke curled and found an opening toward the back of the cave. A draft of air sucked it in the same direction as the water flowed.

But the smoke and the direction of the current went unnoticed. On the rock ledge, fatigue had finally won the battle. A very tired and hungry boy lay sound asleep, one arm under his head for a pillow.

Outside, the wind gathered in strength. A few pellets of sleet began to pelt against the tent on the cliff far above. The two men cursed their miserable fate as they fought to tighten the ropes that anchored the tent.

Far below them, the boy they hunted soaked up the heat from the flames inside the cave. A faint smile crept upon the sleeping lips as dreams came of a forgotten world. In the dream, a woman rocked a baby in her arms and sang.

An image comes of a silver-haired man who lurks in the shadows. Then the man is gone, and the kind woman weeps tears of sorrow.

And Eli slept the sleep of the dead.

## CHAPTER SIXTEEN

To Shug, the concept of luck was a thing so finicky that one simply could not trust one's future to so flimsy a thing. In fact, luck was for the weak and lazy, those unwilling to put in the actual effort required to be successful.

But on this particular rainy night, sitting in the darkness of his basement somewhere in south St. Louis, Shug was finally ready to entertain that voice—the one that insisted that the reason things were not going according to plans was because he was simply on a run of the bad variety of the thing called luck.

Head clasped in his hands, Shug listened to the rain drumming against the outside walls of his house. And in this melancholy state of mind he further contemplated the notion of luck. Until a week ago things had been going quite smoothly. Sparrow had filmed the murder, just like he was supposed to. Sure, the men chasing him had been an unforeseen matter, but Sparrow had managed to evade them. One could chalk up that narrow escape to all of Sparrow's hard training.

Yes, things had been going well. Even the meeting with the judge and the FBI agent had gone well. *Had the meeting been a gamble?* Of course it had. But, as Shug had calculated, when he dangled the tape that placed Joey Trontelli at the murder, the men of law had come around pretty fast. A date for the deposition had been set, with a trial sure to follow. Heck, the way Shug saw it, the Trontellis were as good as in jail. Which left him, Shug, as the lone man to take over the top spot.

Power. That's what made him turn on Old Man Trontelli and his son Joey. Power and money. And, Shug ruefully admitted

## Chapter Sixteen

to himself, women. But if one acquired the first two, didn't the women automatically appear? And could one really be faulted for desiring the three great sins? No, one could not. After all, he was not alone in his desires. As a matter of fact, the country was full of leaders, men and women alike, who had gone to much greater lengths to achieve power, money, and sex.

But the meeting with the men of law was where the bad luck bug had first bitten him. Shug could see that now. Sparrow, the key witness to the murder, had disappeared. And he had taken the tape of the murder with him. Which was something that Shug had never even considered as a possibility.

Bad luck. That's what it all came down to. Simple bad luck. Shug could find no other reason to explain why Sparrow would decide to disappear at such a crucial moment.

Trying to find Sparrow had quickly been ruled out. Simply put, Sparrow was too well-trained to be found. In fact, the main efforts of Sparrow's training had focused on exactly that: the art of disappearing. Of, after a crime was committed, he could simply fade into a crowd, and when witnesses were later prodded for information, they recalled almost nothing about the perpetrator.

So, someone had been needed to replace Sparrow at the deposition. And this had forced Shug to take extreme actions. Sparrow's replacement had needed to be someone who so closely resembled Sparrow that he could pass as Sparrow himself. The replacement had to be someone who, when he disappeared later on, wouldn't create a huge uproar. And the replacement had to be someone whose face had seldom been seen in the outside world. Someone like an Amish kid. And Shug had known exactly such a person. Of course, how he had acquired this information was a secret Shug had guarded with the utmost care. Hell, even the Trontellis didn't know about his connection with the Amish community.

So, on a Saturday afternoon he had made the fateful phone call and, well, things had gone downhill from there. The idea had been to have the Amish kid flown by plane to Shug's ranch in New Mexico. There, the kid would be instructed on what to say and how to act at the deposition. If Sparrow hadn't returned by the time the Trontelli trial began, the Amish kid would get to live. At least until the trial was over.

But here the bad luck bug had bitten him again. The Amish kid hadn't made it to the ranch. Neither, for that matter, had Shug's people who were supposed to accompany him. The airplane had simply vanished. But their disappearance didn't really matter. Not when he thought about the larger picture. Those people could be replaced. The Amish kid could not. There was the matter of Summer, of course. Her absence at the club would be missed. But girls like Summer could be easily replaced as well.

Frowning, Shug rose and walked to Sparrow's room. He unbolted the steel door and flipped on the lights. The room was made of concrete, and there were no windows. The room hadn't been touched since Sparrow left. The bed hadn't been slept in, and most of Sparrow's disguises still hung from hooks in a corner.

But what really caught Shug's attention was the book on Sparrow's study table. The book lay upside down, its two halves fanning out like wings to mark the spot where Sparrow had last been reading. The outspread wings reminded Shug of arms pinned backward as one is shoved into the rear seat of a squad car.

Resentment burned in Shug's throat. How often had he explained to Sparrow the importance of using a bookmark? One simply did not disrespect the works of a Stephen King novel in such a manner. And did it really matter that the book was one of King's more recent novels? That the content within the pages had gone somewhat flat in comparison to King's early works? Did it matter that the main character in the story was

## Chapter Sixteen

an unlikable man who lost so much weight that he eventually floated into outer space and that's how the story ended? No, of course it did not matter. It was the morality of the thing. If one treated a soft-covered novel with respect, a learned discipline like that could have long-term consequences in the shaping of one's future.

The room had belonged to others before Sparrow. Many others. And it would belong to still others now that Sparrow was gone. The room had seen death. They were necessary deaths, of course. But now that Shug thought about it, possibly the deaths were why Sparrow had hated the room. Perhaps it was why he had screamed in his nightmares. They had been muffled screams, barely heard through the concrete walls and ceiling, but they had occasionally woken Shug while he slept one floor above.

Maybe the spirits of the dead still lived in the room. The thought brought with it a measure of peace and Shug smiled. He held out his arms, longing for the cold caress that sometimes brushed against his skin when he was alone in the darkness of his basement.

In the same way that he was comfortable sitting in the darkness of his basement, he eagerly welcomed the restless spirits of the dead. The spirits best matched his mood. Perhaps he would start sleeping in this bed, now that Sparrow was gone.

The trapped wings of the novel needed to be set free. That was a sure thing. Shug started toward Sparrow's desk, then hesitated. Did it really matter? Sparrow was gone. All that training, out the window. And would anyone else care about an improperly positioned book? Besides him, only the spirits of the dead were left to judge the misdeed. And maybe the spirits preferred for the book to be in such an awkward position. Besides, Shug thought. Sparrow had probably placed the novel in that position to prove a point—a final act of defiance.

So, the paperback would remain as it was. If Sparrow ever came back it would be there to remind him of his sinful ways. And Sparrow would come back. Of that Shug was certain. Sooner or later, they always came back. Once they found out how evil and unforgiving the world outside his house was, and once they realized how much they needed him, they always came back.

The hour was late, and the night black. The sound of pounding rain was increasing, which wasn't necessarily a bad thing. For one thing, it meant that the dark car that had been parked across the street wasn't quite as visible on Shug's security monitors. And that was just fine with Shug. It meant that he could almost pretend that the car wasn't there, which was one less reminder of the direction his luck had been going of late.

The car had shown up two nights after Sparrow's disappearance. Shug was pretty sure the car was an FBI surveillance team that had probably been sent by Special Agent Frank Wright after Shug and Sparrow failed to show for the deposition. The fact that the men in the car were men of law was the only reason they were still alive. Killing men of law had a way of raising unwanted questions. It meant that the next dark car to arrive outside his house would do a lot more than park and watch. No, the next car would be accompanied by many more, and there would be search warrants.

Shug walked to his computer desk and sat down. Using a remote control, he zoomed in on the spot across the street where the car was supposed to be. For a moment Shug thought it had gone. Then a cigarette glowed, and the outline of a man's face appeared on the monitor.

Shug wondered how much time he had before the FBI raided his house. He thought probably a week. Search warrants weren't that easy to come by, and strong evidence was needed to obtain one. One week seemed like about the length of time it would take for the judge to issue the warrant.

## Chapter Sixteen

A lot could change in one week. His luck could change, for instance. Either Sparrow, or the Amish kid, could pop up somewhere. And then the deposition would go on. The surveillance team would go away. A bad situation would still be salvaged. With a little luck.

But until his luck turned, Shug decided he could not take any risks. He inserted a blank thumb drive into the computer and clicked on the Trontelli file. To pass the time, he clicked on a few subfolders. There were many files and photos of crimes committed by the mob. True, most had been taken in the dark, and some were blurry and almost unrecognizable, but Shug thought with help from a photo-enhancing software, a strong case could be built. The case wouldn't be nearly as compelling as the video Sparrow had captured, but sometimes one had to work with what one had.

Shug clicked a folder and began to transfer the entire file onto the thumb drive. By the time the men entered his house, the computer would be gone. And the thumb drive would be in a safe place where nobody would ever find it. He could use the thumb drive later, if his luck still hadn't turned.

Shug's eyes moved to the spot on the computer desk where he had placed the tape. He had been foolish to trust Sparrow. He could see that now. He should have left Sparrow bolted inside his room until the trial was over. He could now see that too. But the kid had seemed like he was ready. He had given every sign of being fully capable of being sent on any mission.

The file was large, and the estimated time of transfer was over an hour. Shug leaned back in his chair and closed his eyes. The melancholy mood came back. This time his mind traveled back in time. Back to where it had all started. Sitting in the darkness of his basement, surrounded by the spirits of the dead, had a way of bringing up the past like that. Darkness brought comfort. Darkness brought memories of the blanket his mother would wrap around him when she put him to sleep on cold winter nights. And in the darkness, her calloused finger and thumb had always found Shug's little nose and given it a gentle pinch before she curled up on the dirt floor next to the cot.

But that had been many years ago. Shug very much doubted that the crumpling little stone hut still stood today. Probably, the war had leveled it too, flattened it like it had the rest of the country. Like it had flattened his father early in the war, and then later his mother when the men came to take her away.

His mother had left without a fight, marched away by two uniformed men, one arm held behind her back. Shug had watched from his hiding spot behind the pile of brush in the woods until his mother had faded out of sight.

For days Shug had waited for her to return. The men who took her had promised that if she went peacefully, she could return back home soon.

But his mother had not come back. For days Shug hid and watched men with guns and tanks go by on the road. There were men with arms missing. Men with half of their faces scarred and disfigured. Men who cursed and men who collapsed in the road and were shot. But Shug did not see any men who laughed.

And still Shug had waited. But nobody ever came back for him. Finally, just before his twelfth birthday, freezing and half starved, Shug crawled out of his hiding spot and, struggling to keep up, joined a small group of straggling men. The men barely noticed the new addition.

In his basement, Shug shuddered as the images came. A cold chill brushed his cheek and moved slowly around his neck.

"Is that you, Mother?" Shug asked, his hand moving to his neck and gently touching the cold spot. "Are you finally come back for me?"

For a time, Shug sat like that. He waited. For what, he knew not. But always came the silhouette of his mother, ever fading farther out of sight down the road between the two men.

## Chapter Sixteen

Shug began to massage his temples, and his memory went deeper into the dark place, the place in his mind that he tried desperately not to visit, because it only made the nightmares worse.

But tonight, the memories flooded in unfiltered. Suddenly he was fighting, his gun pointed at shadows that lurked around the camps on the eastern front. At twelve, it was fight or starve. And how he had fought. The more nights he stood guard, the better his night vision became. At first, the enemy had been only fleeting shadows against the pale backdrop of snow in the woods surrounding the camps. But before long, the shadows had taken on the form of real people. And the longer the war dragged on, the more shadowy forms there were. And because of Shug's near perfect night vision eyesight across the open sites of his gun, many of those people had fallen in the snow.

Then one morning there had been no one left to replace him at the guard post. When he searched the tents, all he had found were frozen corpses. Those that could had already fled during the night, leaving the wounded behind. That morning, under the cover of the fading darkness, Shug had finally fled too. Not because he was a coward, and not because he was a quitter. But because he was a survivor. And survivors did whatever it took to survive, even if it meant fleeing and leaving your frozen comrades to the enemy.

He had fought in not one or even two, but three wars. And all three times he had fought for the wrong side. Bad luck? Of course it was.

But when one's country enters a war, how is one to know which side is right and which is wrong? One really can't know for certain until a war has ended, and history has been written. Then one must endure the criticism of those that come along after. Voices who would later have the advantage of siding with the winner, and criticizing the atrocities of those who fought for the losing side.

## Shadows We Remain

But those same monsters had almost won that first war. And what if they had? Would the do-gooders be preaching openly from the streets today? Of course they wouldn't. Probably they would be shivering beneath a single thin blanket inside a crumbling hut that didn't even belong to them. And one morning they would be the ones waking up alone and half frozen. And then they would be the ones forced to fight. Or die.

In the darkness of his basement, Shug shivered. Involuntarily, his hands moved to his cheeks to try and rub some warmth into them.

After the last war, he had chosen America as the country to flee to. Not because he loved America, but because he was tired of losing, and America never lost wars. But America had remained peaceful. And he had never again had the opportunity to fight for the winning side. And now, he was too old to fight a war. Way too old. In fact, as far as he knew, he had outlived all his comrades from the battlefields. But he wasn't done with life yet. Not by a long shot. He expected he still had at least three good decades left. Maybe four.

America had been a good decision. Shug had moved to Chicago, and in his first week there, had been introduced to the Trontelli crime family.

His war skills had served him well on the streets of Chicago, and he had quickly moved up through the ranks in the family. He had been there when Old Man Trontelli's father was buried, and he had been there when Joey Trontelli was born.

Now, he was on the verge of taking over the top spot for himself. At least he had been, until the bad luck bug had bitten him. But he was not defeated yet. Not by a long shot.

The thumb drive showed ten more minutes, so Shug rose and walked across the room. He faced the life-sized portrait that hung on the opposite wall. He tried to hold the man's gaze, but his eyes betrayed him. Like they had betrayed him for many, many decades since that first war.

## Chapter Sixteen

Shug felt his heartbeat quicken and realized the palms of his hands were sweaty. The photo always had the same effect on him. Next would come the shortness of breath, followed by shame. Deep, remorseful shame. Shame that he had devoted his entire first war to fight for the man and his cause. And they had lost. *He* had lost.

But was the cause really dead? Shug didn't think it was. When the man had gripped his hands and told him to fight for his country, to the death if it came to that, Shug, like so many others, had believed him.

No, Shug decided. The man still lived. He had managed to escape the war. That was the only reason his photo still held so much power over Shug. Soon, the man would come back and continue the cause. And when he came, he would need men. Good men like Shug. Men with trained fighters like Sparrow, and the others who worked for Shug. With a little luck, the cause would go on.

*Or would it?*

Shug wavered. The cause had been so long ago.

The shame hit him then, and Shug's knees trembled. In the darkness he stared up at the photo and clutched at his chest, gasping for air.

The man in the photo stared straight ahead. Then slowly, his small square-ended mustache seemed to quiver and come to life.

"Are you still there?" Shug croaked hoarsely. "I am all alone and weak. I need a sign that you are still there."

The face in the photo moved. The eyes softened and the head shifted. Then the eyes met Shug's eyes. They drilled into his very soul. And they judged him for his weakness.

"You live," Shug gasped, his face pale. "The cause must go on."

The eyes seemed to blink, then moved back to a spot on the wall above Shug's head.

Smiling and much calmer from the encounter, Shug walked back to the computer. His run of bad luck was over. Of that he was certain. Besides, he reminded himself, luck was for the weak.

# CHAPTER SEVENTEEN

Firelight flickered on the cave walls, and shadows danced and darted across the water. Eli stood poised on the edge of the rock ledge, his arm raised above his head. Clasped in his fist was a long stick.

The stick had been a surprise. But no more a surprise than the electrical cord that was attached to the end of it.

Eli had pieced the story together a little at a time. The longer he searched the inside of the cave, the more the muffled blanket of his memory was lifted. He still had no recollection of how he had arrived in the fishbowl, but he had remembered some of the events since.

The stick had been sharpened with a knife he found in the pocket of one of the dead bodies floating inside the Pilatus. *Pilatus* was the name he had decided on for the plane, based on logo scrawled across the submerged dash of the plane. The electrical cord came from a damaged wall of the Pilatus, and it served as a leash to draw the stick back after it was speared into the water.

There was a silvery glint. The stick darted from Eli's hand, sliced through the water, and found its mark. The fish darted wildly about, and the cord zigzagged across the water.

Then, as suddenly as it began, the fight was over. Eli knelt and slid two fingers behind the fish's gills, then lifted it out of the water and carried it to the fire. He used the knife to scrape off the scales. The task was tedious, and as he worked, more memories came. Some were nudged along by visual signs, like the thousands of glittering silver diamonds that seemed to cover the

## Chapter Seventeen

ledge around the fire. Diamonds that turned out to be scales from previous fish he had prepared and eaten but did not remember. He gutted the fish and placed it on his makeshift spit over the roaring fire.

Today would be different. Today he would escape the fishbowl. The cold water was definitely an obstacle, but Eli had a plan for that. The walls of the Pilatus held an unlimited amount of electrical cord, and he would have more than enough to tie together a few of the logs that floated in the current. He would sit astride the makeshift raft and simply paddle his way out of the fishbowl. The plan was simple, as long as there was a large opening somewhere in the wall. The reason he hadn't escaped sooner was because every time he lost consciousness, it seemed as if his memory was reset, and upon awakening he had always had to start over with re-discovering his surroundings.

But that had all changed. This morning was the first time he had been able to clearly recall memories of days before. He was quite certain that there was a strip of sand outside upon which he could build a raft, and he was even more certain that escape lay at the far end of the lake.

Eli removed the fish from the fire, and with impatient fingers he devoured the tender meat as fast as he could pull it off the sharp, needlelike bones.

Before he left the cave, Eli took one last look around. He wouldn't be back. Maybe no other person ever would. The only opening to the cave was almost seven feet below water level, and it was only by rare fate that he had been delivered here.

Eli pulled a charred stump of wood from the fire and walked to the wall behind the ledge. He wrote:

*Eli Reader was here.*

Then, almost as an afterthought, he stoked the fire. Today he would escape. Of that he was confident. But on the slim chance something went wrong, he would want a warm fire to come home to.

Eli didn't look back as he waded through the water and entered the Pilatus, which had become his passageway to the outside world. He ran the day's tasks over and over in his mind as he walked down the aisle. His shoulder bumped into one of the floaters and Eli gagged as his nostrils filled with the stench of decaying flesh. With the dull end of his stick, he pushed the floater back between two seats and continued toward the tail end of the Pilatus.

A few seconds later, he was outside the cave. He didn't have long to wait. A log floated into his path and Eli intercepted it. The bigger challenge was to move it to the sandbar, but the job became easier when he discovered that he could use the first log to float upon while collecting the second, then pushing the procession along using his feet against the stone wall.

The sun was directly overhead by the time the two-log raft was completed. Eli straddled the logs and hung a leg into the water on each side, then paddled a few yards out from the sandbar to test it. The raft sank a few inches below the water, then stabilized.

With his hand on the wall, Eli pushed the raft along. As he neared the far end of the fishbowl, the green foliage thinned, revealing a narrow opening that led into a shadowy green tangle of low-hanging branches. Long strands of moss hung from the branches and reached almost to the water's surface.

Underneath this canopy, tree trunks emerged from the water. The tree trunks too, were covered in vines and moss, and the entire canopy was cast in an eerie pale green that resembled a garden of green vines, leaves, and moss. Here and there a rotted log lay half submerged, some held fast by tangled vines, others still partially rooted in the mud.

Eli stared in awe as he paddled through the beautiful green maze. The only sound was an occasional splash as his good hand dipped into the water, first on the right side of the raft, then the left. He paddled in silence, because he couldn't be sure what

## Chapter Seventeen

creatures inhabited this place; it seemed to him that the slightest sound might spook generations of previously undisturbed green ghosts.

Eli rounded a half-rotted tree and came to a sudden stop as the front of the raft bumped into a solid green wall. He had reached the far end of his fishbowl prison. He leaned back and his eyes moved up the wall. Halfway up the wall there was a break, a tiny crack. Eli's eyes followed its jagged pattern as it zigzagged down, like a bolt of lightning, that widened as it neared its target at the base.

The base, as it turned out, was half-hidden among green vines and more moss. By the time the crack reached the water, it was wide enough to allow three of Eli's rafts to pass through side by side. Eli approached it with a surge of confidence. He had been right all along. Now he would pass through the crack and reach freedom.

The current became stronger as Eli approached, but that was to be expected. But when he parted the vines that covered the crack, his face paled. The quick escape he had anticipated was not there. Instead, before him stretched a tunnel of rock. The first twenty feet were partially lit by pale green light, but after that there was nothing but shadows deepening into darkness. High overhead, the walls of the crevice came together, blocking out even the slightest sliver of sunlight.

Horrified, Eli stared into the darkness and considered his options. He could turn back. With the fire and his spear, he could survive in the cave. With time, his arm would heal. He would be better prepared for the tunnel then.

But even as thoughts of doubt crept into Eli's mind, something else began to happen. He felt a tug. An invisible force seemed to pull him toward the tunnel. Somewhere out there, someone searched for him. Someone missed him. And someone wanted him back.

The decision was easier after that. He would not wait. Eli parted the vines and guided the raft into the tunnel. Within minutes he was enveloped in darkness so complete that he couldn't see the wall right beside the raft. Instead, he pushed along by feel.

Without the sunlight for warmth, his teeth were soon chattering. *Keep moving into the current. Keep moving to freedom.*

Eli tried to see images in the darkness ahead, but there were none. For a long time, he pushed along. At times the raft bumped into a rock, forcing him to move to the opposite wall. Here he would have to sit backward on the raft so he could still push with his good arm. He lost track of how many times he had to switch walls to avoid rocks. At one point, when he moved back to the other side, he thought the walls seemed closer together, and a claustrophobic panic set in. He clasped his fingers onto a crack in the wall and held fast, trying to think. His legs were numb from hanging in the water, and his good arm ached so much that he could barely move it.

*Must turn back. Must find fire and cave. Must be warm.*

His grip on the rock started to loosen. It was no use. The current would carry him back to the cave. Besides, he couldn't be quite certain, but he thought his hand was starting to turn blue from the cold.

*My hands. I can see my hands.*
*Daylight.*

With all his strength Eli grasped the rock and pulled against the current. The raft moved a few inches. Then he saw the source of the light. Not so far overhead now, a space began to open at the top of the wall, a narrow crack in the roof that allowed a faint sliver of light.

About half an hour later, the sides of the walls were so low that treetops were visible. Soon after that, Eli reached a point where he thought he could climb out over the edge of the wall.

## Chapter Seventeen

A rock jutted from the wall near the surface of the water and Eli stopped the raft and clawed at a small indention, then pulled himself up onto the rock.

*Woods.*

*Snow.*

Stretched out before him, a gradual slope led away from the edge of the creek. For a creek was what he had followed, Eli realized as his eyes followed the direction the current came from. The creek emerged from between two mountains and disappeared into a crevice at the foot of a third: a crevice that led to the fishbowl.

Eli stood upon the bank and watched as his raft slowly floated out of sight into the crevice beneath the mountain. Maybe the logs would find their way back to the same spot where he had found them earlier. And maybe this time they would make the journey into the cave, and beyond.

Eli was too tired to care where the raft ended up. Darkness would arrive soon, and he had ground to cover. Before him rose a slope that disappeared into trees. High above the treetops at the top of the slope, a snow-capped mountain thrust its majestic peak into a sky bathed in blue.

Eli dodged patches of snow as he climbed. Scraggly thickets of shrubs and brush were scattered across the otherwise wind-blown slope. Before long, the small brush was replaced by much taller evergreen trees. Eli stopped beneath one of these and rested. The mountain peak had disappeared, blocked by the tall trees, but he had to keep climbing, keep trusting his instincts.

Eli lost track of time as he climbed. His stomach rumbled, and his lips, previously blue with cold, became parched with thirst. Eli scooped snow and allowed it to melt in his mouth. He walked on. Dusk came. And then the trees were gone. He straightened. He had reached the top.

Eli stood breathless. Before him stretched an open sky. The bottom half of the golden-orange sun was disappearing over the edge of the world, and Eli reached out his arm to touch it before it disappeared. His outstretched fingers seemed only inches from the giant glowing ball, so Eli moved closer. His bare foot searched for a landing spot but found none. Eli yanked his hand back and glanced down. The mountain ended abruptly before him, the edge cut off sharp, as if sliced with a jagged knife. Eli staggered backward, grasping for a solid foothold at the edge of the cliff.

Far below stretched a vast plain of brown emptiness, broken only by a few tiny twinkling lights glowing from buildings that looked the size of matchboxes.

*Buildings. People live inside buildings. People who could fix my arm.*

Eli Reader had no concept of time as he stood on the top of the world that evening. He had only a few fleeting memories that flashed through his head, then vanished before he could form them into plausible thoughts. So, he had no way of knowing that he had been a captive in the fishbowl for exactly two weeks, or that there were a lot of people searching for him, for a lot of different reasons. And he had no way of knowing that it was Sunday evening, and that over a thousand miles away, in a dimly lit farmhouse, the first married folks were beginning to arrive for the Singen—a Singen he was supposed to be attending for the first time as a member of the Caroline Creek Youngie.

Only a bald eagle, soaring high overhead, could have testified to the solitary figure on the edge of a cliff, a ragged lad in bare feet, soggy button pants covering his lower half, his upper torso bare and sunburned, and a tattered shirt forming a makeshift sling for his useless arm.

And if that proud raptor of the lofty skies were ever to testify to what he saw that night, he might tell of how the lad finally

## Chapter Seventeen

turned and began his descent, winding and climbing, with only one purpose in mind, to draw ever closer to the magnetic force that called from the twinkling lights below.

As darkness descended upon the mountains, a full moon rose, splashing the rough terrain with a pale light and casting shadows here and there across the path as the slender figure crept down the mountainside, scarcely paying heed to the creatures of the wild that hunted the woods all around him.

# CHAPTER EIGHTEEN

Deacon Rudy Koblenz attached one end of the rope to the halter of his horse and looped the other through a worn hole in the manger. He circled to the front and tossed loose hay into the trough so his horse could eat while he was inside enjoying the Singen.

Rudy was in a jovial mood. He glanced around to make sure nobody was watching, then danced a quick little jig.

The actions taken against Maria Reader had been swift and decisive. Sure, they had sent ripples of restlessness throughout the community, but Rudy had turned a deaf ear to the usual undertones of discontent. The Reader girl would not be at the Singen tonight, and in his heart, Rudy knew the right decision had been made.

Rudy had hoped to deliver the news directly to Maria. He had wanted to see the regret on her face, and watch the tears come to her eyes. But instead, her mother had given Maria the news. *Oh well. There will be plenty of future opportunities for all that regret stuff after Maria is baptized.*

Rudy slapped his horse on the rump, then started for the house. With the rebellious Reader girl well under control, there was now the next matter to be dealt with.

A member of the church had brought a complaint. One of his neighbors had used a motorized hay baler. He had driven up and down the rows of loose hay, and he had intentionally chosen a field on the back of his farm where he hadn't expected to be seen.

While hay balers were not forbidden, the rules stated that the baler had to be a stationary piece of farm equipment. The small

## Chapter Eighteen

engine that sat on top worked all the internal gears and even packed and tied the square bales with binder twine, but the loose hay was to be brought in from the fields in wagons, then fed into the baler with a fork. By having a team of horses pull the baler up and down the field, the wayward brother had allowed the baler to do all the work for him. Which was, of course, a grave misdeed.

Rudy thought he had the perfect remedy for the situation. The man would simply be suspended from using a baler altogether. A one-year suspension seemed fair. He could carry the loose hay into the barn one pitchforkful at a time, for all Rudy cared. Yessiree and Jim Dandy he could. Let him feed his livestock by hand instead of with hay bales. It served him right for bending the rules.

Rudy stood on the front porch and scanned the road. There were thirty-seven Youngie. Thirty-eight, if you counted Maria Reader. But tonight, she wouldn't be counted. The thought made Rudy smile again. Smells of the wonderful home-cooked supper wafted from the open door, and Rudy rubbed his plump belly. *The home-cooked food. The best part about the Singens.* Sure, he had home-cooked meals all the time. Actually, home-cooked meals were all he ever had. But the Singens were special. As with weddings, barn-raisings, quiltings, and all the other special events, for the Singens the women usually spent days planning how to prepare the food to perfection. At a normal meal at home, he would get only a few plates, but tonight he would have his choice of dozens of tasty delicacies.

After supper there would be a thirty-minute break while the women washed the dishes. The Singen boys would be in the yard, catching up on the latest news. A few might even sneak behind the barn and smoke a cigarette or drink some homemade corn cider.

Rudy knew all about the mischief and, although he disapproved, he knew that some of the most mischievous boys, once married, turned into the strictest of men. *After all, had he not been one of the wildest when he was with the Youngie? And look at how he had turned out.*

It was during this half-hour period between supper and singing, that Rudy intended to discuss the matter of the hay-baling incident with Bishop Reuben Mast.

Rudy stepped into the kitchen. Through the large opening he saw the setup in the dining room. Wooden tables lined the walls, leaving just enough room for the women to bustle between, trays of steaming food balanced on their arms. Beyond the dining room was the living room, and it too, had the same large opening. A group of married men sat in a circle, their heads close together.

Rudy caught his sister Mattie's eye. No doubt, Mattie was attending the Singen because she did not want to miss out on the humiliation of Maria Reader.

Mattie nodded in his direction and smiled. There was a time when that smile meant so much more. Rudy wondered what the community of Caroline Creek would think if they found out about his and Mattie's teenage years—the secret meetings in the woods on the back of the farm. He hoped they never found out. A thing like that could diminish one's soaring popularity.

Besides, Rudy told himself as he joined the other married men in the living room, they were just kids back then. They hadn't known any better. He put the thought out of his mind and sat down in a rocking chair in the corner.

Unlike church, where everyone is expected to attend, the Singens are for the Youngie, and only a handful of married families are present. Rudy counted eight married men in the circle, with Bishop Mast and himself the only two from the minister bench.

The talk was of the usual boring sort: the weather and the crops, and who was moving to and from what communities.

## Chapter Eighteen

Rudy stared blankly at a gas-burning Coleman lantern that hung from the ceiling. A few flies and moths circled the glass chimney, trying to get closer to the heat inside.

Rudy's mind circled back around to Maria Reader. *What is she doing at this very moment? Is she sorry for the way she talked back to Mattie? Or maybe she is crying into her pillow.*

The thought made Rudy chuckle. He shifted his weight in the narrow rocking chair and tried to suck in his large stomach. He would need a new pair of pants soon, he realized.

"Rudy, Rudy, with the mile-wide booty," the kids in school had mocked him back in the day. *But by George, nobody is calling me that now, are they? No siree, they are not.*

The Coleman lantern had a hole at the bottom of the chimney where a lit match was used to ignite the fumes. A grey moth circled the chimney. Rudy watched, secretly hoping the moth would find the hole and meet its fate.

The moth did exactly that. Once inside, he flew straight for the fragile mantle in the center. The moth fluttered about, ecstatic at his newfound source of heat. The elation was short-lived however, just as Rudy knew it would be. Within seconds, the moth's wings burst into flames. It made a few valiant efforts to remain suspended upon its burning wings, but alas, the flames were too much for it. It crashed toward the bottom of the lantern and disappeared from Rudy's sight.

It was another clear sign. Maria Reader was the moth, and he, Deacon Rudy, had kept her from getting too close to the flames.

Bishop Mast rose and led the way to the table, and the rest followed. After all the men were seated, the women sat down on the opposite side of the table facing them. The Youngie would come next, and they would fill the three remaining tables—the boys with their backs to the outside walls, and the girls on the inside, facing the boys. It was the closest to intimacy the Youngie would have until they started dating.

The married folks waited. The minutes passed, and the silence dragged. And still the benches remained empty. Someone coughed impatiently. Finally, the door opened, and John Schrock entered. Behind him came Marvin Troyer. They filed to the head of the table and sat. After the two boys were seated, the upstairs doorway opened, and two girls filed in.

An awkward silence ensued as the married folks craned their necks and waited for the rest of the Youngie. Reality set in slowly.

*Could it be that nobody else is coming?*

John Schrock cleared the confusion up quickly. "This is all that will be attending tonight. Let's just say the grace and get on with it," he said.

It took a second for his words to sink in, and then the meaning of it hit them all at once. Of the thirty-seven Youngie, only four had come to the Singen. To show their support for Maria Reader, the rest of the Youngie had secretly planned a boycott of the Singen.

John Schrock and Sadie Byler were there because they had to be; their absence would almost certainly mean a postponement of their wedding. Why Marvin Troyer and his sister Edna were there was a question on everyone's minds as Bishop Mast bowed his head to say grace.

Food was passed around the tables in silence. The usual pleasant banter remained a dormant, menacing beast that nobody cared to prod.

Steaming plates of fried chicken, mashed potatoes, sweet corn, and green beans, were passed to the Youngie table, but the food went untouched. Next came the desert. There were bowls and bowls of carrot salad with mounds of whipped cream on top, then more bowls of date pudding, stirred and mixed to a thick sugary brown, and finally, plates of pecan pie, followed closely with bowls homemade vanilla ice cream.

## Chapter Eighteen

The food made the rounds. When it reached the end of the table, the same women who had carried it to the tables, picked up the untouched trays and bowls and walked back to the kitchen.

Deacon Koblenz suddenly wasn't hungry. He glanced at his sister Mattie, but she was staring blankly at her plate of food. Next, he searched for Bishop Mast. The bishop, he quickly realized, was more than willing to meet his gaze. Deacon Koblenz did not at all like what he saw there; Bishop Mast's gaze was steady and defiant. It was holding him accountable for the mess he had made. The look said, "The uneaten food will soon be the least of your worries."

At last dinner mercifully ended, and the women carried the food back to the kitchen. Usually the Singen girls would go upstairs until it was time for the singing part, but tonight the girls joined the married women to help with the dishes.

John Schrock and Marvin Troyer solemnly filed through the kitchen and out the front door. Bishop Mast and Deacon Koblenz followed. Since they were the only two men present from the minister bench, the affair was entirely up to them. The other married men could only speculate as to the nature of the conversation.

John and Marvin were in the middle of a calm discussion when the two ministers joined them in the yard. Completely out of character, Deacon Koblenz stood back and let Bishop Mast take the lead. The light in the front yard was dim, but Deacon Koblenz's formidable gray beard framed the ghastly pale expression on his face. His hands clenched and unclenched, trying to calm the shaking.

"First of all," Bishop Mast began, "I want to thank you boys for coming. I understand how difficult that decision must have been for you."

"Did I have a choice?" John asked flatly.

"No, I don't suppose you did," Bishop Mast answered. He turned to address Marvin. "I'm glad you're here," he said. "But why?"

Marvin cleared his throat. "There is such a big divide between the Youngie and the married folk. Edna and I came because we think common ground can be found."

At last Deacon Koblenz found his voice.

"Aren't you the one that is dating Maria Reader?" he snapped.

Marvin didn't flinch. "It is true that I went on a date with Maria, and I was hoping to make her my wife," he answered. "But the issues in our community are larger than Maria."

Some of the color returned to Deacon Koblenz's face. Suddenly he was angry. Spit flew from his lips as he spoke. "Since you are here, and you wish to be the hero, I have some information that you can pass on to her, and all who didn't show up tonight."

Bishop Mast started to interrupt, but Deacon Koblenz ignored him. "The wedding is off. And it will remain off until the Reader girl agrees to become baptized. I will not have this sort of thing poisoning our community."

Marvin glanced at Bishop Mast. "Is this your will?" he asked.

"It is too soon to make such a hasty decision," Bishop Mast replied. "We will discuss this matter with the rest of the ministers in private. In the meantime, you boys are not required to stick around any longer tonight. Nobody will fault you and the girls if you do not wish to sing at the table by yourselves."

Without another word John and Marvin started for the barn to hitch up their horses. A few minutes later the two buggies disappeared down the driveway.

When he was sure they were alone, Bishop Mast cleared his throat, but Deacon Koblenz was quicker in having his say.

"This thing is completely out of control," he said. "And it's

## Chapter Eighteen

all Maria Reader's fault. Not only do we cancel the wedding, but we also cancel all future Singens until Maria repents."

Bishop Mast waited patiently for Deacon Koblenz to finish. Years of experience had taught him that a heated discussion with the deacon would not work to his advantage.

When Deacon Koblenz was finished, Bishop Mast began. "You have been in this community for a long time. I was just a kid when you were ordained to the minister bench. And because of your longstanding service to the community, I have let you do things your way, but..."

Deacon Koblenz started to interrupt, but Bishop Mast ignored him. He spoke with a firmness that Deacon Koblenz found unsettling. The only other time he had heard it was in the Obrod when they had first voted on what to do with Maria Reader.

"I'm not sure the old ways are working anymore," Bishop Mast said. "I talk to other communities, and their bishops are saying the same thing. We are losing our youth."

Deacon Rudy stared at him in disbelief. Was he hearing right? Was Bishop Mast suggesting a new and altered method of control?

Bishop Mast continued. "Perhaps Marvin Troyer had a point tonight. We could do more to bridge the gap that divides the Elders and the Youngie. I was chosen to lead this community in the best way that I know how. Right now, I feel like I'm failing."

"We have gotten careless," Deacon Koblenz snapped. "Discipline is the only way. Clearly, we need to set a stronger example. We must postpone the wedding."

"I will not vote for a postponement," Bishop Mast said sharply. "If we postpone, have you considered the fallout?"

"You forget one thing," Deacon Rudy spat. "I was ordained to the minister bench as well. My vote counts as much as yours. I am telling you right now that I will never allow one rebellious girl to control this community."

"Let's talk about that," Bishop Mast said abruptly. "Yes, you were ordained to the minister bench. And as I said, I was only a kid when the book was drawn that held your name. But I was not so young that I don't remember the controversy surrounding your ordination. At the time, you were the only married man in this community who was not already on the minister bench, and you pushed really hard to get that vote in before more families moved to Caroline Creek. In doing so, you assured yourself the final spot on the minister bench. Perhaps you were not chosen by God at all. Perhaps by forcing your way onto the minister bench, you brought a curse upon this community."

For what seemed like an eternity, Deacon Koblenz stood speechless. His jaw worked, and his yellow teeth gnawed and flashed, but no words came.

Bishop Mast took the silence as an opportunity to continue. "I'm going to allow the vote, but like I said, I will be against it. If the vote falls in your favor, I will have no choice but to support it. But you need to hear one thing."

"What's that?" Deacon Koblenz managed weakly.

"This is your last chance to run this community your way. If the rebellion continues, there will be decisive action taken against you, and you will not like the outcome."

The fact that this was the first time Bishop Mast had openly stood up against him, was completely lost on Deacon Rudy Koblenz. He felt a deep sense of relief that Bishop Mast had agreed to the vote. There was no doubt in his mind that he still held enough influence with the other three ministers to achieve an outcome in his favor. There was also absolutely no doubt that postponing the wedding was exactly what the community needed to pull the Caroline Creek Youngie back into shape.

Deacon Rudy Koblenz was halfway home before he finally admitted to himself that he had drastically underestimated Maria Reader.

# CHAPTER NINETEEN

Ivan Totsoni parked at the edge of the field and got out. He lit a cigarette and opened the tailgate to his rusty Ford. Wolf, his German shepherd, jumped to the ground and began to race in circles, excited to be free from the truck bed.

Ivan took a canister of cyanide gas from his truck and attached a hose. He strapped the canister to his back and started across the twenty-acre field. He counted twenty-seven groundhogs. That number would be at zero in a few hours if he had his way.

The owner of the ranch was a Navajo Indian, and like Ivan, had ties to the land that went back many generations. Ivan had been to the ranch before. The previous spring the rancher had hired him to exterminate the groundhogs, and Ivan had done a remarkable job of it. But the success was short-lived. Groundhogs were a pesky bunch, and with the return of fall, a whole new village had moved back in.

Ivan opened the gate and started across the field. He stopped at the first burrow and kicked dirt into the hole until it was full, then stomped it down with his boots. When he had closed all the other holes in the vicinity of that burrow, he shoved the gas hose into the last one and packed the dirt firmly around it. He turned the knob on the canister and gas hissed into the underground labyrinth. When the time on his watch reached thirty seconds, Ivan turned the valve off, pulled the hose from the dirt, and packed the hole firmly shut. The groundhogs inside would be dead in less than a minute.

Ivan started toward the next hole. He figured he would be done by early afternoon, then he would move on to the next farm.

## Shadows We Remain

Wolf scampered about the field, excited at the prospect of chasing any groundhogs that remained. Ivan had never actually seen him catch one, but it was a game Wolf never tired of.

The dog stopped suddenly and froze, his nose pointing in the direction of the woods several hundred yards away.

"What is it boy?" Ivan asked.

Wolf gave a deep, throaty growl and moved closer to the woods. Ivan followed cautiously behind.

Wolf circled a clump of trees and as Ivan drew closer, the outline of a small grey hut came into view. From its outside appearance, the hut had long ago been abandoned. The walls consisted of old weathered boards, and a tree protruded from an opening at one end of the collapsed roof.

The hair on Wolf's back bristled. He sniffed at the front door of the hut and pointed again. Ivan approached cautiously. The door hung crooked on one rusty hinge, leaving a triangle-shaped opening on one side. Ivan moved silently so as not to disturb the beast inside. When no sound came, he picked up a rock and threw it at the door.

"Hello," he called out. "Who's in there?"

Silence.

Wolf's behavior left no doubt that someone or something was inside the hut. Ivan stepped to the opening and peered inside. His eyes adjusted slowly to the shadows. He was startled by what he saw. Just inside the opening, a pair of bare feet protruded from the darkness. The feet led to a pair of loose-fitting trousers, and beyond that, a naked torso.

The figure was that of a boy no older than twelve, Ivan thought. Curly blonde hair was matted all about and stuck to the face and neck. A closer look told a story of hardship. Ribs protruded from beneath pale skin, and scratches and bruises covered most of his shoulders and back, and one arm was in a makeshift sling. Ivan knelt and brushed the boy's hair from his face to get a

## Chapter Nineteen

closer look. A ragged breath startled him.

Wolf snarled and leapt through the doorway, fangs bared.

"Wolf. No," Ivan said sternly. He grabbed at Wolf's collar and pulled him back. "Down. Sit."

Wolf whimpered and reluctantly moved aside, but his eyes stayed on the boy.

Ivan's fingers moved to the boy's neck. The pulse was strong, and the breathing even. For a few minutes he tried to wake the boy; when he didn't stir, Ivan unstrapped the canister of gas from his back and scooped the limp body up in his arms.

"What in the world is your story?" he muttered aloud.

He carried the boy to his truck. Wolf stayed close by his side, occasionally sniffing at the boy's feet.

"Wolf," Ivan said sternly. "You get to ride up front this time." He carefully placed the boy in the bed of the pickup and closed the tailgate.

Twenty minutes later Ivan stopped in front of the Navajo Regional Medical Center, a two-story hospital in the small town of Shamrock, New Mexico. The hospital employed some of the best nurses and doctors in all of the reservation.

Ivan carried the boy inside, and Wolf followed.

"Found him out on Buck's Ranch," Ivan said to the first nurse. "From the appearance of things, the kid hasn't eaten in weeks."

A gurney appeared, and the boy was lifted onto it. He was quickly moved down a hallway and then disappeared into an elevator.

Ivan left his name and phone number at the front desk. "Let's go, Wolf," he said. "The boy is in good hands now. We'll stop in and check on him later tonight on our way back through town."

# CHAPTER TWENTY

The time was eleven fifteen on a Tuesday morning, and at the exact moment that the nurses at the Navajo Regional Medical Center were working to get an IV into the frail arm of Eli Reader, Bruce Ellsworth was signing his release papers at a different hospital in St. Louis.

Susan, his secretary, had arrived an hour earlier with a fresh set of clothes. She waited as Bruce pulled his belt through the loops on his jeans. His movements were awkward, his hands clumsy.

"One of the first things on my to-do list," he said as he rubbed the four-day growth on his jaw, "is to shave this horrible nightmare from my face."

"You got me until five p.m.," Susan replied. "After that, it's back to my kids."

Bruce finished buttoning his shirt and reached for the shoulder holster on the bed stand. "Where is my gun?" he asked sharply.

"They won't let you have guns in a hospital," Susan said. "You know that. I took it back to the office the first night."

Susan removed Bruce's cell phone from her purse.

"This thing hasn't stopped ringing," she said. "I had no idea you were so popular."

"Neither did I," Bruce said. He shoved the phone into his pocket. He didn't look at the screen. It could wait until later.

"Where first?" Susan asked.

"Let's stop by and see Stan," Bruce said.

Susan went quiet.

"What is it?" Bruce demanded.

## Chapter Twenty

"Boss," Susan said, avoiding his eyes. Her voice had lost its boisterous tone. "Stan lost both of his legs."

Bruce's fingers froze on the stubborn shoelaces.

"I'm so sorry to be the one to break this to you, but I could not allow you to see him unprepared," Susan said, almost in a whisper.

Bruce stared at her, struggling to comprehend the words.

"He is still in a coma, Bruce. They have no idea when, or if, he will recover. There was so much trauma to the back of his head that even if he does recover, the doctors are saying there may be brain damage."

Bruce sat on the edge of the bed and stared at the floor, the little color in his face gone.

"Bruce," Susan said. "Are you sure you are up to this?"

"I'm sure," Bruce said, shakily getting to his feet.

They rode the elevator down to the fourth floor. Susan chattered on about random events that had occurred in Bruce's absence, but he didn't hear any of it.

The elevator door opened, and they walked down another hallway. Bruce's mind raced. He tried to recall the events leading up to the bomb explosion. He got as far as the Nissan Rogue circling the parking lot, and then they were at the doorway to Stan's room.

Rebekah Prater, Stan's wife, met them at the door. Behind her, the two youngest of their children played on the floor. Coloring books were scattered all about, and a half-eaten bag of chips hung from a dirty hand. The children barely noticed the new visitors. No doubt they had seen hundreds come and go over the last few days.

"The children haven't been told," Rebekah whispered softly as she gave Bruce a quick hug.

Bruce nodded and walked to the bed. The man he had last seen on the other side of the booth at the Thirsty Toad now lay frail beneath white sheets. The only sign that he was alive was the slight rise and fall of the linens across his chest with each breath. Stan's head was wrapped in bandages, with only a small opening in front where tubes passed through.

A lump formed in Bruce's throat as he stared at his former partner. He sat down in a chair next to Stan's bed and fumbled for his hand. Susan recognized the moment and nodded at Mrs. Prater. They silently slipped out of the room, children in tow.

For a while Bruce sat in silence. He searched for words of wisdom he might bestow, but none came. The lump in his throat grew. Maybe it was the overload of too much information hitting him all at once, or maybe it was the guilt at allowing such a gruesome injury to happen to his friend, but for the first time in many years Bruce cried.

Anger, guilt, shame, and frustration washed over him all at once. Anger at the senseless injustice done to his friend, guilt that he had been unable to stop it before the explosion happened, shame for letting down his partner, and frustration at his incompetence in not suspecting the bomb sooner.

Twenty minutes and a handful of tissues later, Bruce finally reached his breaking point. Sitting in Stan Prater's room, holding the feeble hand with the needles and tubes, and staring at the stumps, half-hidden beneath the hospital sheets, Bruce's emotions turned into stone-cold resolve. The game had changed. Until now, he had played by the rules. But that had resulted in a near-death encounter.

It was at Stan's bedside that Bruce silently vowed his vengeance. The stakes had been raised to a payout of life or death, and he, Bruce Ellsworth, regardless of the laws he would have to break, could play that game as well as anyone. He squeezed Stan's hand and rose to leave.

## Chapter Twenty

Neither Bruce nor Susan talked much as they walked out of the hospital and got into Susan's car.

"Where to now?" Susan asked.

Bruce looked bewildered. "You know," he said. "I just realized I haven't given any thought to what I would do when I finally got out of that godforsaken hospital."

"Why don't I take you home?" Susan said. "I'll fix you a cup of coffee, clean your house up a bit, you know, try and get you comfortable."

"No." Bruce said, remembering.

"No?"

"Take me to Castleton," Bruce said. "I have an open invitation to sit down with Chief Westbritt. I think I'll start there."

A feeling of nostalgia washed over Bruce as they pulled up in front of the old precinct. For a few moments he and Susan sat and watched as squad cars moved in and out of the parking lot.

"Did I ever tell you why I left this place?" Bruce broke the silence.

"You were fired for having an affair with an employee," Susan laughed. "I've done my research."

Bruce nodded. "Seemed like the end of the world at the time, but I'm happier on my own. That's for damn sure. When the mayor called to deliver the news, I vowed I would never set foot in this place again."

"And yet here you are," Susan stated.

"And yet here I am," Bruce repeated.

## CHAPTER TWENTY-ONE

Eli stared at the tube connected to the back of his hand. A nurse hovered over him and said something he didn't understand. Eli stared at her face, trying to make sense of the strange words and features. The nurse had raven-black hair that was pulled back into a tight bun, and shiny black eyes glowed from somewhere in a deep, wrinkled brow. She had broad cheeks and a wide, square chin. Against her pale blue uniform, her dark skin was so prominent that Eli couldn't focus on anything else.

The nurse still spoke in the strange language, and when Eli continued to stare blankly, she finally seemed to understand. She nodded, patted his shoulder, and disappeared through the door. A few minutes later she returned with a man.

The man had the same strange, dark features. Over the next few days however, he would meet many others that looked very similar to the nurse and the man who came back with her.

The man was holding a chart, and he sat down in a chair beside Eli's bed. "I'm Doctor Allen Toshibi," he said. "But you can call me Doctor Al."

Eli managed a feeble smile. Finally, someone who spoke in a language he understood.

Doctor Al returned the smile, and Eli breathed easier.

"How are you feeling?" Doctor Al asked.

"I... I'm good," Eli said. "I feel fine."

Doctor Al nodded and flipped through his chart. He seemed to be in deep thought.

"There wasn't any identification on you when they brought you in, so we haven't contacted anyone to let them know where you are."

## Chapter Twenty-One

"Okay," Eli said slowly, not sure how to respond.

"Let's start with this," Doctor Al said. "What is your name?"

"I... I'm Eli Reader," Eli said. The sound of his own name suddenly sounded foreign to him.

"Eli Reader," Doctor Al repeated. "Can you spell that for me?"

Eli spelled his name and Doctor Al scribbled some notes.

"Do you have parents, or legal guardians?"

Eli shook his head, trying to think. He glanced down.

Doctor Al followed his gaze and smiled again. "We had our work cut out with you," he said, studying his chart. "Wanna tell me what you got tangled up with?"

"I... I don't know," Eli said. He scanned the room, suddenly aware that he had no idea where he was.

"You are in a hospital in Shamrock, New Mexico," Doctor Al said. In his chart he scribbled, *memory loss,* then continued.

"A local brought you in. Do you remember that?"

Eli shook his head. Things were beginning to move too fast again. Bits and pieces of memory flashed and vanished. The room suddenly felt too small.

"Well, we had to do surgery on your shoulder," Doctor Al said. "Your left humerus was dislocated from the scapula, and the clavicle was broken. I screwed it all back together."

Eli looked blank. "Wha... what?" he stammered.

Doctor Al smiled. "I'll simplify it for you," he said. "Your left arm was popped right out of its socket. Actually, the top of the socket was busted completely off. And your left collarbone is broken. From the look of things, it's been in that shape for a while. So, I put the arm back into the socket and screwed a plate on top to hold it in place."

"I... I didn't feel anything at all," Eli said.

Doctor Al tapped his pen on Eli's plastered arm. It made a hollow sound.

"A shoulder and neck cast," he said. "You will need to wear it for some time."

"Okay," Eli said, staring down at the contraption that covered his left arm and shoulder.

Doctor Al continued. "If you feel like you are up for it, I want to ask you a few more questions. Mainly I want to let your family know where you are."

Eli frowned and closed his eyes. A faint image came of water. A log.

"I think I was under water," he said out loud. "I swam out. No, I think I walked."

Doctor Al made more notes on his chart.

"We did a CAT scan," he said, looking up. "You're lucky to be alive."

"What?" Eli asked, confused.

"You've had serious trauma to the back of your head."

Instinctively Eli's hand moved to his head.

"I'm afraid you won't find much," Doctor Al said. "The wound is healed, but I did find something really strange."

He waited for Eli to ask. When he didn't, the doctor pulled a loose page from his chart and held it up for Eli to see.

"See that dark spot right there below the base of your skull bone?" he asked, pointing with his pen.

Eli nodded.

"That is a fragment of something. Could be a bullet, but I don't think so. Could be a piece of shrapnel. Any idea how it got there?"

Eli shook his head.

"Well I guess I'm not surprised. We're dealing with a brain injury, and unfortunately, this hospital isn't set up to operate on something like that. If we could track down your parents, I would contact them and try and set up an appointment with another hospital that specializes in this kind of trauma."

## Chapter Twenty-One

Eli tried to comprehend Doctor Al's words, but suddenly the room was spinning.

"Eli...?"

Eli snapped back to the present.

"I've reported this matter to our authorities," Doctor Al was saying. "But we work at our own pace out here. Nobody gets into too big of a hurry. I expect our tribal police department will be stopping by to ask more questions sometime tomorrow morning."

Eli nodded groggily.

Doctor Al continued. "Due to the location and severity of your injury, intense stress or prolonged fatigue can cause you to lose consciousness, sometimes for long periods at a time."

"Will I ever be normal again?" Eli asked. He closed his eyes, not sure if he wanted to hear the answer.

"In some cases the memory comes back in sections. What you pick up this time may disappear the next time you lose consciousness. Try to avoid excitement. Remain calm and conscious, if that makes sense?"

Eli nodded. He closed his eyes again to stop the spinning. An image came of a giant crack in a reddish-orange wall. A tiny figure passed into the dark shadows within the wall and Eli shuddered as the memory of the coldness came. He opened his eyes to describe the memory, but Doctor Al had left the room.

---

Doctor Allen Toshibi walked to his office and sat down at his computer. He opened his browser and typed the name *Eli Reader* into the search bar. A single profile appeared, but it was of a female somewhere in South America.

Doctor Al tried a few popular social media sites with similar results. Finally, he clicked a link that connected him to a website for missing persons. It required him to enter an email address, so he entered his personal email. The results were the same. Nothing. No missing person named Eli Reader.

After ten minutes of research, Doctor Al logged out of the website. He began to type his notes on Eli into the hospital's registry database. At the bottom of his computer screen an alert popped up. Doctor Al clicked on it and an email opened. The subject line was blank, and the body of the email was brief.

The message simply said: *Do you have a patient by the name of Eli Reader at your location?*

Doctor Al responded. *I have someone claiming to be Eli Reader. Who am I speaking with?*

Doctor Allen Toshibi waited for a few minutes, but when no response came back, he closed the screen. *Probably some automated spam response.*

Doctor Al stopped at Eli's room, intending to mention the email, to see if it would trigger any memories. But when he stuck his head into the room, Eli was sound asleep, a pale cheek resting against his new cast.

"I would pay a pretty nickel to know what your story is, son," Doctor Al muttered as he quietly closed the door to Eli's room.

Doctor Allen Toshibi's search into the missing person's database created a much bigger stir than he could have ever imagined. The entry created a code-red alert that was instantaneously sent to FBI headquarters in Washington D. C.

Within minutes, Eli Reader's name was circulated to all FBI field offices, and five minutes after Doctor Al entered the name, Special Agent Rick Wright from St. Louis was staring at Eli's information and trying to connect the dots.

## Chapter Twenty-One

Bruce sat on the wrong side of his old desk, which was now occupied by Chief Calvin Westbritt. They had forgone the formalities of coffee and small talk. Instead, Bruce got right down to business.

"I'm not gonna sugar-coat it," he said, a dark scowl on his face. "You don't want me here any more than I want to be here. I'm here for a copy of the recording between Shug and the guy he sent to plant the bomb. Give me that, and I'll be on my way."

Chief Westbritt nodded. He opened a desk drawer and took out a tiny black device. He placed it on top of the desk and slid it toward Bruce. "The recording," he said. "I thought you might ask."

Bruce slid the device into a coat pocket.

"I have to say," Westbritt continued, studying Bruce with a keen eye. "You've recovered well. Did you drive here by yourself?"

"My secretary brought me," Bruce said flatly.

"How are you holding up?" Westbritt asked.

"I'm ready to do whatever it takes to nail the bad guys," Bruce said. "But since you ask, I feel a bit jumpy. Could be because I feel like I'm a ticking time bomb. I've never been the guy that had to check under his vehicle every time before he got in, but I guess that'll change."

"Want my guys to follow you for a few weeks?" Chief Westbritt asked.

Bruce shook his head. "I'll be all right," he said. He stood to leave. "Thanks for the recording," he said flatly.

The phone on Westbritt's desk rang. "I told you to hold my calls," he spat into the receiver.

He started to replace the phone but stopped the motion in midair. Bruce was halfway out the door when Westbritt called him back.

Westbritt scribbled something on a notepad.

"Okay. You're sure? In New Mexico?"

There was a short pause, then Westbritt continued. "Hold on, I'll look it up. Just a moment. Uhum. Report says he went missing on Sunday, October 19."

Another pause, then Westbritt read from his computer screen. "Parents are Andy and Ruth. Address is N1723 Caroline Creek Road."

Bruce stared, dumbfounded. "Is he dead?" he asked.

"Nope. Very much alive," Westbritt said, hanging up the phone. "Turned up at a hospital in New Mexico earlier today."

"New Mexico?" Bruce asked in a husky voice. "What the dickens is he doing in New Mexico?"

"Don't know. But apparently, he just popped up on a lot of radars. FBI called me because Eli seems to be tied to a case they're working. They are going to bring him in for questioning."

"Where in New Mexico?" Bruce asked.

"You're not thinking…"

"Right now, I don't trust anyone," Bruce snapped. "Not the FBI, not this… hospital in New Mexico. I'll go get Eli myself."

Westbritt tapped his keyboard for a few seconds, as if weighing his options. Then he scribbled an address on a sticky note and handed it to Bruce.

"Okay," he said, turning back to his computer and reading from the screen. "The FBI has a branch called the Safe Trails Task Force, or STTF. It is located in Albuquerque, New Mexico. It was formed as a coalition between them and the Navajos to fight crime on the reservations."

"And?" Bruce asked.

"They're your closest competition. It's a three-hour drive from Albuquerque to Eli's location, and I seriously doubt the Fibbies will make the drive tonight. Too much paperwork. They'll leave their offices in Albuquerque at eight o' clock tomorrow morning,

## Chapter Twenty-One

which puts them at the hospital at about eleven."

"What are you getting at?" Bruce asked.

"Like you, I trust the FBI about as far as I can see them," Westbritt said. "Eli didn't get to New Mexico on his own. Probably it was Shug, or someone else from the mob. But who's to say what branches of the law the mob has in their back pockets."

Bruce only half listened. His mind calculated routes, fuel stops, and whether he could pull an all-night run without sleep.

"One more thing," Westbritt said.

"Yes Chief?" Bruce asked, distracted.

"You are on your own out there. I don't want any of this shit coming back to bite me in the ass. You were never here. And you and I never had this conversation."

Susan was waiting when Bruce opened the passenger door and slid into the seat.

"Where to now, boss?" she asked.

"Is my Explorer still at the Toad?" Bruce asked.

"No. I had it dropped off at the office," Susan replied.

"Take me there," Bruce said. "I'm going to New Mexico."

# CHAPTER TWENTY-TWO

Eli sat up suddenly. Bright sunlight poured in through the window behind him, splashing radiant colors of light across the bed.

"Good morning." The soft voice came from almost under Eli's arm and he jumped. A nurse was leaning in close, and Eli wondered why he had not heard her enter.

"Sorry I scared you," she said. "How are you feeling? Do you think you can walk?"

The nurse did not smile, and Eli pulled his blanket close to his chin, suddenly uncomfortable.

"I… I think I can."

Eli's eyes moved to the nurse's name tag. *Benesha Mitshun.*

"You can call me Nurse Beth," the nurse said, following his eyes. "And I'm here to help you get out of this hospital. We don't have much time."

"Okay," Eli said hesitantly.

Suddenly the room didn't feel so safe anymore. He eyed the nurse uneasily, half expecting her to draw a weapon from somewhere under her uniform. A knife maybe, to slash him in half where he lay. His eyes went to the window. He could make a run for it. He might make it before the knife got him too bad.

"You must go now," Nurse Beth said emphatically. "Some bad men are coming to take you away. I can't let that happen."

Eli's mouth went dry. "Bad men?"

"There isn't time to explain," Nurse Beth said. Her fingers moved swiftly as she removed the drip needle from the back of Eli's hand. She pointed to a stack of folded clothes at Eli's feet.

## Chapter Twenty-Two

"Change into these," she said. "Hurry." She grabbed Eli's arm and helped him to sit up.

Eli's movements were slow and awkward. His legs refused to obey. Working quickly, the nurse untied his gown and slid it off. She swiveled his feet to the floor and helped him pull on a pair of pants, then wrapped a coat around him and guided his good arm into the sleeve.

"Go," she said, pointing toward the door. "At the end of the hall are some stairs. Go down one flight until you reach the door at the bottom. Go through that door and turn right. If anyone tries to talk to you, ignore them. Walk across the lobby and out the front door."

Eli tried to swallow, but something seemed stuck. Suddenly he couldn't breathe, and his knees wobbled. "I don't know anyone outside," he managed to whisper. "I don't know where to go."

"When you reach the street, turn right again. Walk two blocks until you get to a red Conoco gas station. Someone is waiting behind the gas station for you. You can trust her."

"It's a girl?" Eli asked.

"Yes. She is about your age and has a black ponytail."

"I don't even know who I am."

"You are Amish," Nurse Beth said. "The girl can explain better."

Nurse Beth shoved Eli firmly toward the door, and he found himself in a hallway. He started toward the stairs, then hesitated. He glanced back. Nurse Beth had tears in her eyes.

Eli continued down the hallway toward the stairs, but something clicked in his mind as he walked. Nurse Beth had used the word *Amish*. Suddenly there were images of black buggies. Then a man with a black beard and hot, stinky breath. A strong arm pinning him by the neck, and a searing pain surging through him as a leather belt came down across his back and thighs. Now the man's face had a horrible smile, and between the strikes, he was panting out words. "You are not good enough to be a Reader. You will never be good enough to be a Reader."

Then an image of a woman. He had seen her before. She was running toward him, screaming for the man to stop. Then she was tumbling into a corner of a barn with blood streaming from her mouth. A dog appeared, and the leather strap went away.

Eli's shook his head. The stairs seemed to swim. He grasped at a doorknob and then he was in another hallway. He turned right, just like Nurse Beth had said. He stumbled along in a daze, images flashing like lightning bolts from all directions.

His knees buckled, and Eli braced against the wall for balance.

A tall, shadowy figure appeared from a side door. A man with broad shoulders and dressed in a hospital uniform. As he drew closer, he came into focus. Something was out of balance. The man didn't have a name tag, and his hair was disheveled. Now his face was streaked with dirt.

Was the man real, or part of the jumbled images flashing through his mind?

The man was almost upon him when another side door opened. Someone about Eli's size darted from the door and the two men collided. There were two soft thuds, and the big man slid to the floor.

*What is happening?*

Nurse Beth had said to ignore anyone who tried to speak to him, so Eli moved past the two men. The small man rose and faced Eli. Eli stared into the man's eyes. *Where have I seen them before?*

The man's mouth was moving. "Hi Eli. I'm Sparrow."

"You… you know my name?" Eli stammered.

"Go quickly," Sparrow said. "The girl is waiting for you."

Yet Eli stared. *Those eyes.* Where had he seen them before? Sparrow shoved him gently.

## Chapter Twenty-Two

Confused, Eli ran. He reached the end of the hallway and sprinted across the lobby. In a few bounds, he was out the front door and in the street. From somewhere behind him an alarm sounded, and through the glass doors, Eli saw a security guard running in his direction.

Eli ran. He had no idea in which direction, but he knew he had to put as much distance between himself and the hospital as possible. Ahead he saw a red gas station. A large sign read *Conoco*. Eli started down a side street, aiming for the rear of the building.

A dark station wagon was parked in an alley behind the gas station, and a slender girl with a black ponytail was waiting. She waved toward the open passenger door. "Come on," she said. "We don't have much time."

Eli approached warily.

The girl noticed his hesitancy and smiled. She opened her mouth to speak, but her gaze dropped to Eli's chest.

Eli looked down and gasped in horror. Two thick stripes of blood were smeared across the front of his coat.

The girl pressed her fingers against Eli's chest. "It's not yours," she said, relief on her face.

Eli reeled. The girl's words were faint. Then she slapped him hard across his face.

"I need you to focus," the girl said.

"Wha... what?"

"I asked if that blood came from the big man or the little one? If it's from the little one, I have to go back."

"I think it was the big one," Eli stammered. "Yes... yes. The big man was asleep, and the little man talked to me."

The girl smiled. "Let's go," she said, again pointing at the passenger door.

The girl drove the station wagon down an alley behind the gas station, then turned onto a gravel road. Fatigue swept over

## Shadows We Remain

Eli and he leaned his head back against the seat. He was vaguely aware that the girl was talking on a phone.

"Yes. Yes. He's with me. Yes, I will set it up."

After a while they turned into a dirt driveway and parked behind a dark ranch house. The girl cut the engine and turned to the boy in the passenger seat.

"You poor thing," she said softly. She reached and brushed the blonde curls from the sleeping boy's forehead. "It has been a rough stretch for you, but it's almost over."

---

Bruce Ellsworth pulled up in front of the Shamrock Hospital. He was greeted by a dozen squad cars with flashing lights and the words "Shamrock Tribal Security" on their sides. Yellow police tape sectioned off the entire block, and an officer led a dog around the side of the hospital.

Bruce's heart sank. He was too late. He started to open his door, when his cell phone rang. The caller ID was from a private number.

"Oh, why the hell not," Bruce thought as he hit the "answer" button on his phone. "How much worse can it get?"

"Detective Bruce Ellsworth?"

Bruce instantly recognized the sound of a voice-altering device.

"Speaking," Bruce replied.

"I have the person you are looking for."

"And who might that be?" asked Bruce. He glanced into his rearview mirror.

"I have Eli," the voice said. "And I'm willing to turn him over to you, but only under one condition."

Bruce decided to play along. "What condition is that?" he asked.

## Chapter Twenty-Two

"You have to keep him safe," the robotic voice said.

"Who the hell is this?" Bruce asked sharply.

"My name isn't important. What is important is that we both want to help Eli."

"Then why suggest I wouldn't keep him safe?" Bruce asked shortly.

"Don't trust the law," the voice said. "The mob owns some of them. That's why."

"I think we speak the same language," Bruce said. "Go on."

"I've been watching you," the voice continued.

"And?"

"I think you can be trusted. That's why I am giving Eli to you."

Bruce rubbed his temples and checked his rearview mirror again. "Tell me when and where," he said finally.

"Drive west on Highway 121," the voice said. "Exactly 7.2 miles outside of Shamrock you will come to a deserted ranch. You will recognize it by the rusty windmill in the front yard. Eli is inside the house."

"How do I know this is not a set-up," Bruce asked.

"You don't," the voice replied. The line went dead.

Bruce sat behind his steering wheel and weighed his options. Instinct, born from years of fighting crime, told him to call for backup. But he wasn't a cop anymore. He was easily a thousand miles from the closest cop he knew. Stan Prater could normally be depended upon, but he was unconscious. And Chief Westbritt had made it clear that he wouldn't be sticking his neck out for him.

"The hell with it," Bruce finally said out loud. He took his Glock from its holster and chambered a round, then turned onto Highway 121 and headed west.

Ten minutes later he parked in front of the deserted ranch house with the rusty windmill in the front yard. When he stepped out of his Explorer, he half-expected to be met by bullets.

Nothing.

The front door was unlocked, and Bruce entered. He moved quickly, scanning the empty rooms. Eli Reader was on a mattress in the second bedroom. He was covered in a blanket, and Bruce knelt to check for a pulse. It was strong.

Bruce drew back the blanket and stared at the plastered cast. As he considered the person on the mattress, Bruce's mind traveled back to a night about ten years earlier.

The night was dark, and a steady drizzle of rain made it difficult to see the bumpy road. The light bar on top of his squad car carved beams of red and blue into the dense fog. From the passenger seat, Stan Prater worked the radio, communicating directions to the fire department that followed close behind. As they approached Caroline Creek Road, the darkness lifted. Overhead, a bright light circled lower and lower as a helicopter descended, its blades slashing the air.

There had been three people in the creek. The first two were carried out on stretchers, and a few minutes later they left in the helicopter.

The third person had been responsible for the horrible collision that smashed the horse and buggy into the creek. Bruce shuddered as he recalled the man hunched over the steering wheel of the pickup truck that had plowed into the buggy. Unhurt and defiant, the face of an intoxicated Andy Reader still angered Bruce.

The next image was that of an Amish woman and her two children, awoken in the early hours of the morning. Ruth Reader, her eyes red and sleepless, the worried wife awaiting the return of her husband. Maria, a child of perhaps eight years, squinting suspiciously at the two officers from behind her mother's nightgown.

## Chapter Twenty-Two

But the clearest image of that night was of Eli. An innocent child of about seven, an expression of sheer terror on his face as the two officers delivered the news that his father was in trouble with the law again.

The face on the mattress in the ranch house had changed, but it was Eli Reader. Of that, Bruce was certain. He lifted Eli and carefully carried him out to the Explorer.

Two hundred yards beyond the ranch house, the girl with the black ponytail watched from behind a clump of bushes. She waited until the Explorer was out of sight, then withdrew her rifle from the opening between two branches. She began to break the rifle down, carefully placing each piece into the case at her feet. Last of all, she placed the voice-changer into a slot in the corner of the gun case.

"This plan better work," she said out loud. "Otherwise a lot more people are going to die."

# CHAPTER TWENTY-THREE

After Bruce left the ranch house, he suddenly felt overwhelmed with questions. He still had no idea how Eli had ended up in New Mexico. Then there was the confusion of squad cars outside the hospital. Everything indicated that someone had been murdered. *Is that all connected to Eli?*

Finally, there was the person with the voice-changer. That person had suggested mob connections within the law. Bruce decided it wouldn't be wise to put too much emphasis on accusations from an anonymous caller. But the information from that call made just enough sense to give Bruce pause. Until he was certain who he could trust, he would have to hide Eli. He would start by putting as much distance between himself and the hospital as possible.

Bruce followed Highway 121 west until he crossed into Arizona, then circled south toward I-40. He passed through several small Navajo villages. Children played in the dirt streets, and they stared at the strange man in the large brown vehicle.

When he reached I-40, Bruce turned east. He glanced over his shoulder at the quilt in the back. For the first time, he thought about the consequences if Eli were found in his vehicle. Eli was a minor, so Bruce would be charged with kidnapping. By crossing the state line, the kidnapping would instantly fall under federal jurisdiction, which carried a much harsher penalty.

Then Bruce remembered Stan Prater. The rules had changed. He would get Eli to safety, or he would die trying.

## Chapter Twenty-Three

The sun was beginning its descent when they crossed into Texas. The lights of Amarillo came into sight and Bruce turned south on 27. He had a plan, and no matter how tired he was, he would execute it.

On Amarillo's south side he found a dozen dingy motels sprawled behind a shopping mall a block off the main street. Bruce circled the area three times, taking mental notes. He checked off each component he would need for his plan to succeed.

The motels were close to a busy highway, in case they needed to move quickly. And there were multiple motels so he would see anyone coming before they saw him. Finally, several blocks from the motel, he found a perfect spot to park the Explorer.

The figure under the quilt was still asleep, so Bruce locked the doors to the Explorer and walked inside to check in.

"I'll take room 117 for one night," he told the girl behind the desk.

The girl stared at him, puzzled by the specifics. "Will that be for one or two?" she asked, typing away on her keyboard.

"Two," Bruce replied. "My fourteen-year-old son and I."

Bruce gave the girl a fake name and a fake description of his vehicle. He paid in cash, took the room key, and left. Two blocks down the street he pulled up next to a girl he had spotted earlier. The girl had long, bony legs that looked like they would snap if she stepped on a pebble. She had on a short purple mini-skirt, and her hair was dyed green.

Bruce rolled down his window, and the girl eyed him suspiciously. Her long, painted fingernails closed firmly around her shiny black purse.

"Excuse me, miss," Bruce said. "Can I talk to you please?"

The girl walked slowly to his window and leaned close. "Whatcha want?" she asked.

"A favor," Bruce said.

The girl sniffed loudly. "Not for you I ain't," she said. "You got 'pig' written all over you." She turned to walk away, her high heels clicking against the pavement.

"Hold up," Bruce yelled after her. He waved several one-hundred-dollar bills. The girl came back.

"I'm looking to get a motel room," Bruce said, jerking a thumb over his shoulder in the direction of the motels. "But I can't leave a trail. Wife issues, you understand?"

"How much?" the girl asked.

"More than you make on your best night," Bruce said.

"Maybe you underestimate my skills," the girl said, leaning closer.

"All I need is for you to go to that motel right there," Bruce said, pointing at the one he had picked out. "They recognize you there, right?"

"Sure," the girl said. She rubbed her nose to wipe away something that Bruce couldn't see.

"Check into room 232. If it isn't available, take the one next to it, and so on. Sign in under your usual name, then bring me the room key."

"What's in it for me?" the girl sniffed suspiciously.

"I'll give you an extra two hundred when you get back," Bruce said. "But there's a catch."

"There always is," the girl said dryly.

"You are going to take the rest of the night off."

The girl pondered this for a moment. "That'll cost you five hundred," she said finally.

"Five hundred dollars?" Bruce sucked in air.

"Five hundred," the girl repeated. "For that price…" She pinched her index finger and thumb together and slid them across her lips, indicating they were sealed. "I'll disappear for the night."

"Alright," Bruce said wearily. He counted out the money for the room and handed it to the girl. She shot him a sidelong

## Chapter Twenty-Three

glance and disappeared. She was back in ten minutes with the room key. Bruce handed her five one-hundred-dollar bills. The money disappeared into her purse. Bruce shifted the Explorer into drive.

"Say, Mr. Pig," the girl said. "You sure you don't want some company, you know, after your lady friend leaves? I can do you better than she can."

"I'm good," Bruce said. He snapped his fingers at her. "Now disappear."

The girl walked toward a dark alley, her high heels clicking defiantly at the man who had rejected her, her defiance punctuated by a bony middle finger stuck high into the air, a parting shot at the lawman she had so cleverly sniffed out.

Bruce backed his Explorer up to room 232. If anyone were following him, they would be close, so he moved quickly. He picked up the figure, quilt and all, then carried him inside and placed him on the bed. He scribbled a quick note in case Eli woke up while he was gone.

Bruce drove his Explorer five blocks further back off the main street. He pulled in behind an auto repair shop and parked between two used vehicles. Moving swiftly, he switched plates with a Ford pickup truck. If someone found his Explorer during the night, the plates would throw them off.

Bruce walked the five blocks back to the motel. While he walked, he searched his phone for any news out of New Mexico. The Shamrock Daily carried the headlines in a blinking red banner that announced the breaking news across the top of the page.

**Murder at Navajo Hospital**
*On Tuesday, November 4th at 8:30 a.m., authorities were called to the Navajo Regional Medical Center where the body of an unidentified male subject was found with multiple stab wounds.*

Bruce clicked again and found a more recent link.

*The victim of the gruesome murder that took place at the Navajo Regional Medical Center earlier today has been identified. Authorities are withholding the man's name but have said that he is a local with Navajo ties. The main investigation hinges on what the man was doing at the hospital. Further information will be forthcoming.*

Below the article was an image of someone in a hospital uniform. The face was hidden from the camera angle by a baseball cap pulled low. The story continued.

*Authorities are asking for your help in identifying this person. This image was taken from a security camera at the hospital, and authorities believe this person may be linked to the murder.*

Bruce was relieved that no mention was made of a vehicle with out-of-state license plates.

The time on his phone showed 9:30 p.m. Bruce locked the motel door and slid a chair under the door latch. It would buy him a few extra seconds if needed.

———•———

Forty-five minutes after Bruce parked his Explorer behind the auto repair shop, a gray Dodge truck circled and parked. Two of Shug's men got out and quickly closed in on the vehicle. The first man pointed a gun, and the second shined a flashlight in through the Explorer's window.

"They can't be far," the first man said. "Let's start checking motels." He stooped and checked the GPS tracking device that

## Chapter Twenty-Three

was fastened inside the rear bumper of the Explorer, then the two men got back into the Dodge and left.

# CHAPTER TWENTY-FOUR

Bruce moved the window curtain an inch and studied the parking lot outside the motel. The motel was a large three-building complex laid out in a U-shaped design. Their room was on one of the outside legs of the U, and the vehicles of tenants filled the cavity between the three buildings.

Bruce saw nothing suspicious.

He had watched his rearview mirror all the way from Shamrock, and was pretty sure nobody was following him, but he simply couldn't shake the uneasy feeling that danger was close by. He drew his Glock from its shoulder holster and, raising it to eye level, lined the sights at the doorknob barely visible in the dark. If the door came down, he wouldn't have time to use the sights, but all the same, he wanted to get comfortable with the movement.

There was a movement from the bed, and Bruce snapped awake, not realizing he had dozed off.

"Where am I?" the voice came from the darkness.

Bruce rose and walked to the bed.

Eli studied him carefully.

"You don't know me," Bruce said. "But I'm helping you. I'm taking you somewhere safe."

"Where?" Eli asked.

"Back to St. Louis. I have a friend who can help you."

"Where is the girl that was helping me?" Eli asked.

"What girl?"

"There was a nurse," Eli said slowly. "Nurse Beth. She's the one who told me to go to the girl in the car."

*The person with the voice-changer is a girl?*

## Chapter Twenty-Four

Bruce walked back to the window and scanned the parking lot again.

"What are you doing?" Eli asked. "Are we in trouble?"

*If you only knew,* Bruce thought. Out loud he said, "I want you to tell me what you remember so far."

"There isn't much," Eli replied. "There are bits of memories that come and go, but they are almost never the same, so I don't know what is true."

"What happened at the hospital?" Bruce asked. "Do you remember that?"

"I know someone died," Eli said.

A gray pickup truck pulled into the parking lot. It stopped at the motel lobby and two men got out and went inside. A minute later they came back outside. One was carrying a sheet of paper in his hand.

*They got the motel registry*, Bruce thought. He was so intent on watching their movements that he jumped when Eli spoke.

"Why are we sitting in the dark?" Eli asked. "Why don't you turn the lights on?"

"Come here and I'll show you," Bruce said, without taking his eyes from the men outside.

Eli followed Bruce's instructions and opened the curtain a crack on his side of the window.

"Do you see those two men?" Bruce asked, pointing.

The men walked toward a door on the first floor of the motel opposite Bruce and Eli's room.

"I see them," Eli replied, bewildered.

"Those men are looking for us," Bruce said matter-of-factly. "I rented two rooms for the night. They're outside the wrong room. That one is empty."

They watched the first man press an ear to the door. He removed something from his pocket, then stepped back. His foot came up and he kicked hard at the latch. The door flew open and the men disappeared inside. Beams of light darted across the window as the men searched the room. Then the men charged back outside, nervously glancing around as if expecting some sort of a trap.

"They have guns," Eli croaked hoarsely.

Bruce held up his finger for silence.

"Who are they?" Eli asked.

"They aren't cops," Bruce answered. "That's for damn sure."

The men seemed to be discussing what to do next. Finally, they got into the truck and sped away.

Bruce dragged the mattress from his bed and placed it on the floor next to the front door. Placing his Glock on the floor next to the mattress, he lay back and folded his hands behind his head and took a deep breath. He tried to count how many hours total he had slept in the last two days but fell asleep before he had accounted for the first one.

# CHAPTER TWENTY-FIVE

Maria had just finished drying the last plate in the sink when she saw them coming. The single kerosene lamp on the kitchen countertop flickered as if to predict a bad omen.

It had been a week since the ministers' last visit, and Mam had spent much of that time begging Maria to change her mind about the baptism. Maria, who still stung from the last visit, had countered every one of Mam's reasons with one of her own as to why she would, in fact, not be forced or bribed into such a huge decision.

Unlike a week ago, when the ministers had made their first trip to the Reader farm, this visit was anticipated. What was not anticipated, though, was that they were arriving in three buggies instead of the usual two.

The buggies stopped in front of the hitching post, but nobody got out. Without a word, Mam dried her hands on her apron and started for the front door.

"Mam, I'm coming with you," Maria stated firmly. "I will not sit back and watch you face them alone again."

Mam started to protest, then gave a sigh of resignation.

The double buggy carried Bishop Mast and Deacon Koblenz in the front. Samuel Mullet rode alone in the back.

The second buggy carried ministers Alvin Keim and Raymond Byler, father of the soon-to-be bride. The third buggy was parked farthest away, but in the gathering dusk, Maria made out the faces of John Schrock and Sadie Byler, the newly engaged couple.

Maria's heart leapt at the sight of her friend, but then she quickly sobered. *Just what in the world are John and Sadie doing here?*

"Is Andy home?" Bishop Mast's voice came from the buggy.

"No. He is not home yet," Mam replied, omitting half the truth. She did not tell them that Andy hadn't been home all week, and nobody asked.

Bishop Mast nodded at Maria, who returned a weak smile.

"I'll get right to the point," Bishop Mast began. "Maria, you are an not a baptized member of the church, so you are excused."

Maria's back stiffened. "I'll stay," she said decidedly.

Bishop Mast frowned and glanced at Deacon Koblenz, who avoided his gaze. His eyes were firmly fixed on the Reader girl, and resentment burned in his heart at her brazenness. Without taking his glare off Maria, he nodded for Bishop Mast to continue.

"Well I suppose it is as well that you hear it straight from us then," Bishop Mast went on. He spoke slowly, carefully feeling for his words. There was an awkward pause before he continued.

"The minister bench has voted, and the decision has been made to cancel the wedding until things are back under control."

Mam gasped, then began to cry softly.

"And what things are out of control?" The words flew from Maria's mouth before she had time to weigh them.

"Well for starters, we can't have people from other communities coming to our wedding and seeing us divided," Bishop Mast said. "It's a bad look for Caroline Creek."

For a moment Maria was unable to speak. How could she change the minds of five ministers? How could she convince them that the wedding was not theirs to cancel? That the community of Caroline Creek had much deeper problems than one girl who, in the heat of the moment, had defied the sister of a deacon?

Deacon Koblenz took Maria's silence as a sign of weakness.

"This could all have been avoided," he said, his voice rising loudly above the crunch of the horses' hooves on the gravel driveway. "If you had agreed to be baptized."

## Chapter Twenty-Five

Maria ignored him. She walked to John and Sadie's buggy. She searched Sadie's troubled face. Sadie, whom all the Youngie looked up to as the perfect role model. Sadie, who had never once made any trouble for the ministers.

Maria recognized the presence of John and Sadie for what it was. The ministers were using them as a tool to manipulate her. There was still a way for the wedding to happen, but it would come with a cost. She turned back to Bishop Mast.

"If I promise to become baptized, the wedding will go on as scheduled, correct?"

As one, the ministers nodded.

Bishop Mast went on, "But you must agree to start baptism classes this Sunday, not wait until next spring when the next class begins."

Maria stood before the buggies and studied the faces that looked down at her from their lofty heights. She fought to hide the turmoil that raged within her. She would not let them see that she was weakening.

Ruth finally broke the silence. "Maria. Please just do it," she said softly, wiping her eyes with her apron. "Don't make any more trouble for the ministers than you already have."

Maria stared at the ground and kicked at a rock that had the misfortune of being in the wrong place. Among the many things that bothered her, one reared up above the rest, and finally Maria decided to voice her thoughts. She turned to face Deacon Koblenz and locked eyes with him.

"Do you realize that this whole thing started because your sister Mattie was speaking evil against my brother, when she really had no idea where he is or what he is doing?" she asked. "Do you realize I'm being punished for defending my brother?"

"You were out of line," Deacon Koblenz snapped.

"And what of your sister?" Maria shouted angrily. "She was out of line too. She made up terrible lies about Eli. What will her punishment be?"

In that very crucial moment when Deacon Rudy Koblenz might have done well to bite his tongue, he readily took the bait. Had he been able to curb his tongue, there might have been some hope for him, but, like Maria secretly knew he would, he willingly caved in to one of his biggest weaknesses: that of lashing out when he was confronted.

"First of all," he spat. "Mattie did nothing wrong. Eli is playing with fire out there with the English people. The scripture clearly tells us to 'Be ye not of the world.' Eli is damned to hell in the outside world, and you or anyone else who dares to defend him will surely find a seat in hell beside him."

A faint whoosh sounded as the air went out of her mother. She stumbled blindly toward the hitching post, grasping for anything to cling to for support.

Maria did not flinch. "And what if you're wrong?" she asked defiantly. "I don't know much about the scripture, but doesn't it clearly state that 'thou shalt not judge'? Do you think you might be judging Eli, Rudy Koblenz?"

The accusation hit its mark, and the fact that Maria addressed him by his first name instead of the rightful title of deacon seemed to stagger him in his buggy seat.

"God chose me to interpret the bible to the members of my church," he hissed. "Not have it preached to me by some spoiled girl who plays with hellfire!"

Maria's plan was working to perfection. "How long have you been a deacon?" She asked.

"Twenty-nine years. Why?"

"You've just condemned Eli to hell. How many other ex-Amish have you discouraged from believing in God, simply because they chose to try life in the outside world?"

"Hundreds," Deacon Koblenz stated proudly. "That is my duty as an Amish minister."

Maria turned to the other faces in the dark shadows of the

## Chapter Twenty-Five

buggies. When her eyes found Bishop Mast, he cringed. Even the horses seemed to sense the tension, and for once stood completely silent, ears pointed forward. Finally, Maria turned back to Deacon Koblenz.

"What if you are wrong?" she asked flatly.

"Wrong?" Deacon Koblenz stammered.

"What does the scripture say about the father who, when his son asks him for a loaf of bread, gives him a stone? Does not the scripture state that such a father is worthy of hellfire, and that it would be best if a stone is hung around his neck and he was drowned? You can't just pluck verses out of scripture that support your personal whims and ignore all the rest, Rudy Koblenz."

Koblenz stuttered his reply. "That's talking about a loaf of bread, my child. I would gladly give anyone a loaf of bread if they're hungry."

Maria turned back to Bishop Mast. "Do you believe the parable is talking about an actual loaf of bread, or the word of God?" she asked.

Bishop Mast suddenly seemed preoccupied with something on the floor of his buggy. He did not respond, but a smile played at the corners of his lips.

"You are dead wrong," Deacon Koblenz snapped at Maria. "There is absolutely no hope for the ex-Amish, and every one of the ministers here will agree with me."

Maria pressed the matter a bit further.

"But let's just say there is a one percent chance that you are wrong. Are you actually prepared to stand before God on judgment day, knowing that you have openly discouraged people from following him?"

Deacon Koblenz sat back in his buggy seat, the blood draining from his face. His mouth worked, and finally, with little conviction, he managed to croak the words out.

"Since I know that there is not even a one percent chance that I am wrong, then I have nothing to fear," he whispered hoarsely.

Bishop Mast looked like he had just seen a ghost. In all of his years on the minister bench, he had never seen anything that even remotely resembled the exchange he had just witnessed between Maria and Deacon Koblenz.

Maria interrupted Bishop Mast's thoughts. "I'd like to speak to John and Sadie alone," she said.

Bishop Mast nodded his assent.

John helped Sadie from her side of the buggy and together they followed Maria across the yard toward the house. When they were a safe distance from the buggies, Maria paused.

"Sadie," she said. "I'm so sorry that I dragged you into all of this."

Sadie smiled wearily and squeezed Maria's hand. "I was there, remember? Mattie was out of line, and she deserved everything she got. Everybody knows it."

"But at the cost of cancelling your wedding?"

"Maria," John spoke for the first time. "Whether we get married in two days, or two months, isn't that important. The point is, sooner or later we will be married folks. We will be one of them." John nodded his head in the direction of the buggies.

"Don't ever be like them," Maria said shortly. "You don't have to be like that."

"Well, we aren't married yet," John laughed. "At least for now we are on your side. You have managed to raise awareness about the divide between the married folks and the Youngie. That is a worthy cause to fight for. I think I speak for both of us when I say that we won't hold it against you if you decide to continue taking a stand."

John looked at Sadie, who nodded.

Maria softened. Maybe it was the tender way that John looked at Sadie. It reminded Maria of someone who had recently

## Chapter Twenty-Five

looked into her eyes in the same way. She caught her breath at the thought of Marvin. He would be at the wedding, and he would ask her to the table for the wedding Singen. *I could do it. I could get baptized, and all these problems go away. I could do it. No for the ministers, but for John and Sadie. And for Marvin.*

She turned back to John and Sadie who waited anxiously. "Okay," she said. "I'll do it."

"Are you sure you are doing this for the right reason?" John asked.

"Probably not," Maria said. "I will never be the obedient little church mouse they want me to be, but I can fake it. I can live by their silly little church rules."

"If that is your decision then we are forever grateful," Sadie said.

The three retraced their footsteps back to the buggies. The air was static with anticipation. There were no illusions among the preachers. The next words that came out of Maria's mouth would have a lasting impact on the future of the Amish community of Caroline Creek.

Maria ignored Deacon Koblenz. She walked to the other side of the buggy and faced Bishop Mast.

"I'll do it," she said simply. "I'll become baptized into your Amish church, and I'll try to follow your Amish man-made rules and I will do my best to believe your Amish God. But I want to be completely clear on something." She paused.

"Go on," Bishop Mast said.

"I am not agreeing to this because I suddenly see the holy light of the Amish church. I am doing it because I respect John and Sadie, and I will not stand in the way of them getting married."

Bishop Mast winced but forced a smile. "It will be good to have you back in the Singen," he said simply.

Deacon Koblenz cleared his throat to speak, but Maria didn't wait. Instead, she turned and walked toward the barn, her back rigid.

The ministers watched her go, and a huge sigh of relief escaped from the buggies.

———◆———

Maria closed the barn door from the inside and stood in the darkness. She tried to control the shaking in her knees. There was solace in the barn that she could not find anywhere else. It was here, among the gentle barnyard creatures who accepted her without judgment, that she could always come when her heart was troubled.

Maria felt her way to the wooden ladder in front of the horse stalls and climbed up to the hayloft. She collapsed onto a pile of loose straw and buried her face in its dusty comfort.

Here, there were no ministers to watch her weakness, and the tears finally came. They were hot tears of anger, confusion, and bitterness. Deep in her soul, she had felt like she was doing the right thing when she stood up to Deacon Koblenz. She had even felt at peace when she told John and Sadie that she would agree to become baptized. But now, in the silence of the hayloft, a cloud of doubt crept into her mind, penetrating, torturing, and forcing its will upon her.

And then from somewhere amidst all the self-doubt and confusion, there came one more doubt to add to her misery.

"I'm sorry Eli," she sobbed. "I promise I haven't forgotten about you."

Maria clenched her fists and pounded the pile of straw, punching up billows of dust. The sharp stems clawed at the soft skin of her hands, and hot tears of anger and confusion penetrated the dry stack of straw.

Gradually the fists lost their zeal, and finally she lay silent, her body trembling in the darkness as the dust slowly settled back down upon the straw around her.

## Chapter Twenty-Five

The hour was after midnight when another figure stepped from the porch and moved noiselessly toward the barn. Ruth opened the barn door, the light from the lantern casting enlarged shadows of the animals that slept on the floor.

Ruth climbed the ladder to the hayloft and found Maria curled up in the corner, sound asleep. She tapped her gently on a thin shoulder, then helped her to her feet.

Fog was beginning to drift in off of the Mississippi River as mother and daughter made their way toward the house.

While the rest of Caroline Creek slept, Ruth sat on the edge of her daughter's bed and stroked her sleeping child's hair. With the tender touch that can only come from a mother grieving for her troubled child, she smoothed the dusty, tear-stained cheeks and wiped the closed eyelids.

# CHAPTER TWENTY-SIX

Someone was shaking him by the shoulder, and Bruce's hand flew for his Glock. His fingers clawed frantically at the spot on the carpet where it should have been.

The Glock wasn't there.

Only half awake, Bruce's fist shot out, trying to connect with something.

"It's only me." The sound of Eli's voice cut through the layers of exhaustion.

"What... why are you waking me up for?" Bruce asked, rubbing his eyes.

"It's daylight," Eli said.

Bruce glanced at the window. Sunlight poured through the small opening at the edge of the window curtain. "Where is my gun?" he asked.

Eli handed him the gun. "I moved it a little," he admitted sheepishly. "I was afraid when I woke you up, you might start shooting."

Bruce walked to the bathroom and leaned over the sink. He splashed cold water on his face and over the top of his head. It worked. The fog around his brain disappeared.

"We have to be careful when we leave this place," Bruce said, coming out of the bathroom. "Those guys from last night are probably still in the area. They must have put a tracking device on my vehicle. That's the only way they found us."

"Do you have a plan?" Eli asked.

"Follow me," Bruce said.

Instead of crossing the parking lot, Bruce stayed under the low-hanging roof that ran along the outside wall of the motel.

## Chapter Twenty-Six

About five paces later he ducked into another side door and started down a dimly lit hallway that led to the lobby. Others were beginning to stir in their rooms, and stale cigarette smoke wafted into the hallway. Somewhere someone began violently coughing.

Bruce led Eli through the motel lobby and out the back door, away from the direction of the men in the Dodge truck.

Outside, they were greeted by rush hour traffic.

Bruce pointed at a McDonalds across the street.

"First we eat breakfast," Bruce said. "Then you will wait there while I go get my vehicle."

Eli nodded.

Five minutes later they were sitting at a table in a back corner of McDonald's. Eli devoured his biscuits and gravy, while Bruce sipped coffee and worked on a plate of hotcakes.

Bruce watched the customers carefully and studied the traffic on the street outside. Seemed like just another normal working day. The air felt right. No extra tension; no strangers walking the sidewalks looking for a missing teen in an arm and shoulder cast.

"Okay, Eli," Bruce said, standing up. "I'll be back soon. And I'll come inside and get you."

"What if you don't come back?" Eli asked.

"Those guys are amateurs," Bruce said. "Believe me, I'll be back in fifteen minutes."

Eli nodded and slid lower in his seat.

Bruce crossed the street and walked toward the auto repair shop. All around him horns blared. A jacked-up truck with a loud exhaust thundered through the light where, only the night before, the girl with the long slender legs had stood. Bruce wondered where the girl went during the daylight hours.

A block to the south, Mexican construction workers were climbing around on a half-finished roof, those above loudly yelling instructions to the workers on the ground.

Bruce rounded the corner of the auto repair shop and quickly got into the Explorer. He had meant to switch the plates back, but since he was now sure he was being watched, he changed his mind. The men would have expected him and Eli to come back together, and they probably had orders to shoot him and take Eli alive. But if he came back alone, their plans would have to change, because if they killed him, they might never find Eli.

Bruce fought the urge to glance around and see if he could find the men. It was crucial that they not suspect he knew he was being followed. Even so, as he turned the key in the ignition, he caught a sudden movement in his rearview mirror. A figure darted from behind a tree and disappeared, no doubt running toward the Dodge parked close by.

Bruce smiled. *Seriously though*, he thought as he gunned the Explorer. *They send amateurs to do a man's job these days.*

Twelve minutes after he left the McDonald's, Bruce pulled up outside Eli's window. Fifteen seconds later Eli lay in the back of the Explorer, the blanket pulled up over his head.

Bruce merged into traffic and turned north. He turned onto I-44 and headed east toward St. Louis. Fifteen miles into the trip, he suddenly switched lanes and turned onto an exit ramp. He watched his rearview mirror closely to see if anyone behind him made the same maneuver. Nobody did. He pulled into a gas station and drove around behind the building where he was hidden from the highway. He got out of the Explorer, walked around the side, and slid his hand under the rear bumper. He found the tracking device all the way on the left side. It was held in place by magnets. Bruce removed it and walked quickly toward a white Suburban at the pumps. The owner was fueling and had his back turned. Bruce stooped low on the passenger side and attached the device to the inside frame of the Suburban.

They passed through Rolla, Missouri late in the afternoon, and fifteen minutes later Bruce left the highway and turned north.

## Chapter Twenty-Six

Almost immediately they were climbing the rolling hills and winding roads through the back country of the Missouri Ozarks. For the first time in days, Bruce breathed easy. Finally, he was in familiar territory. If anyone decided to follow him now, Bruce welcomed the challenge. They would have to face him on his own turf, and even though he was tired and a little banged up from the bomb explosion, anyone following him would regret it.

The safe house Bruce had chosen was located somewhere south of Hermann. Only a handful of people knew where Harold Travers, former forensic analyst for the FBI, now called home.

It was dark when Bruce turned off the main road and started down a winding dirt path. Several hundred yards later he pulled up to a rusty gate. Bruce parked and got out. He spun the dial on the padlock, passed the Explorer through, then looped the chain around and snapped the lock back into place.

Arrangements had been made earlier that afternoon. Bruce had explained the circumstances, and Hillbilly Harry had reluctantly agreed to take Eli in for a few days. "Heck, this thing is busting wide open," Bruce had said. "It shouldn't take more than a day or so to get to the bottom of this, make the necessary arrests, and I'll take the kid off your hands again."

The truck crawled along a narrow path, winding in and out among the trees. Had the tracking device still been attached to the bumper, it would have marked its progress as it crossed a dry creek bed, followed the same creek for another mile, and finally came to a stop beneath a grove of tall pine trees.

But the Dodge truck was not following them. Instead, as Bruce was arriving at the home of Hillbilly Harry, the truck carrying Shug's two men was passing through Nashville, Tennessee. The men had been careful. They had stayed several miles behind the tracking device, and when the driver of the Suburban finally stopped for dinner, only then, would the men learn of their mistake.

"Wait here," Bruce said to Eli. "Harry is expecting us, but just to be safe, I'm going to check things out before I take you inside."

Bruce followed a footpath beneath the pine trees. It was dark, but his eyes adjusted easily. Seconds later he stood at the foot of a high hill that rose sharply before him. Half-hidden among a cluster of thick firs, painted in camouflage colors to blend in with the trees, was the front door to Hillbilly Harry's hidden underground bunker.

Bruce's knock was interrupted by a rustle and the soft thud of a footfall from somewhere right behind him. Bruce went for his Glock, but his recently injured shoulder made the draw a fraction of a second too late. Just before it cleared the holster, cold steel pressed against the back of his neck. From the shadows a few paces away, three more clicks sounded as other revolvers were cocked.

Bruce froze, his hands moving slowly above his head.

The camouflage door in front of him opened and the barrel of another gun moved out from the shadows. The man on the other end of the gun leaned close and removed the Glock from Bruce's holster.

"Follow me," the man said simply.

Bruce hesitated, his mind racing. The man didn't give him time to weigh his options.

"You can follow me voluntarily," the man said, "Or we will carry your unconscious body. Your call."

Bruce followed the man inside.

They walked down an unlit hallway. The air had a cold and damp mustiness that Bruce remembered from previous visits to the bunker. Mixed in with the usual fragrances now came another: one that Bruce hadn't inhaled in many years, but which, identified once, etches itself in one's mind permanently. It was the unmistakable presence of freshly discharged gunpowder. And

## Chapter Twenty-Six

right on the heels of that came the scent of warm copper.

Bruce's heart sank as the truth hit him. The stench of warm copper equated to recent bloodshed. Which probably equated to death. Hillbilly Harry had been expecting Bruce, but instead was met by gunpowder and bullets.

The hallway led into the main room. The room, usually well lit, now had only a single battery-operated light suspended from a long wire hanging from the ceiling. Probably the power had been cut before the men entered the bunker, so Hillbilly Harry couldn't contact help on the outside.

The room was about thirty feet square. The ceiling consisted of jagged, uneven rock that was the inside of the bunker Harry had somehow carved out of the hill. To the left was the kitchen, separated from the living area by only a kitchen island that was also made out of stone.

A single table stood in the center of the room, and Bruce sensed the presence of the man before he saw him. But the man could wait until Bruce had assessed the rest of his surroundings.

To the right, at the far end of the room, a small fire burned in a fireplace, creating shadows that danced and bounced across the concrete floor. Above the fireplace the stuffed head of a moose stared down at the visitors in the room below.

The wall behind the table stretched from the kitchen to the fireplace, broken up by two doors, evenly spaced. If Bruce remembered correctly, the first door led to Hillbilly Harry's bedroom, and the second to his working quarters.

Bruce took in the entire room in one careful sweep. Only then, did his eyes move back to the figure at the table. The overhead light illuminated a head of silvery-white hair and eyes that seemed to gleam from beneath thick, white eyebrows.

Behind him, the men who had escorted him into the bunker faded back into the shadows.

The man seated across the table nodded at Bruce, then pointed to a chair. "Sit down," he said firmly.

Bruce sat down.

One of the men re-appeared and handcuffed his hands behind his back.

The man across the table looked to be in his mid-sixties and had a small and wiry build. He wore a dark shirt and an even darker winter coat that was buttoned all the way up to his clean-shaven jawline.

The man was someone who Bruce had never met, but instantly recognized, for his photo hung front and center on Bruce's *Crazy Wall*. For the past two weeks Bruce had studied that cold face and silvery-white hair hundreds of times as he paced the back room of his office sipping coffee and smoking his pipe.

"Hello, Shug," Bruce said, fighting to remain calm.

Shug's face showed no emotion, and his words came out in a soft, silky half-murmur. "You wanted to play with the big boys, Bruce. Well, you lost, and now you die."

# CHAPTER TWENTY-SEVEN

The copper smell of warm blood, accompanied by the sensation that death was near, did not escape Bruce as he gazed steadily at Shug from across the table.

Shug seemed to be enjoying himself. His face held a mocking smile, almost as if he held some secret yet to be revealed. A secret he would only divulge when the time was right.

"I want to personally thank you for bringing Eli directly to my feet," Shug said, smiling. "And just in time."

"Just in time?" Bruce asked.

"The deposition. The deadline for that is tomorrow."

"Deposition?"

"Hell, Bruce." Shug frowned. "You must have heard about the meeting at Judge Major's place a few weeks ago?"

Bruce stalled, trying to buy time. "Why don't you tell me about that?" he asked.

"I had an airtight case against the Trontellis. A tape that would hang the whole group."

"So, what went wrong?"

"My witness disappeared."

"Who was your witness?"

"If I told you that, I'd have to kill you," Shug said. Then he slapped the table with his open palm. "Oh wait!" He laughed. "I'm going to kill you anyway."

"What do you want with Eli?" Bruce asked.

"If I told you that I'd have to kill you a second time." Shug laughed again.

Bruce eyed the room. He counted four men, all with weapons drawn. The closest was behind the kitchen island, his gun leveled at Bruce's head. He grinned at Bruce and nodded. The second man guarded the hallway that led to the front door, and the third and fourth flanked Shug, but were careful to remain in the shadows.

"Eeny, Meeny, Miny, and Moe," Bruce said, trying to feign bravery. He turned back to Shug. "Which one of them will be the first to go?"

Shug smiled. "You wag a mighty big tail for a puppy that is handcuffed to a chair," he said.

"How did you know I was bringing Eli here?"

"We tracked you."

"You're lying," Bruce said. "I ditched the device your men installed on my vehicle."

"Yes, you did," Shug said.

"So, there was a second device?" Bruce asked, stalling for time. He furrowed his brow, pretending to be in deep thought, but his focus was on the handcuffs. He knew something that Shug did not know. Sewn inside the cuff of his shirt was a tiny tool that he had placed there for an occasion exactly like the one he currently faced. His destination was the kitchen island, which was made of stone. If he made it behind there, he stood a chance.

Shug watched Bruce's face and waited patiently.

Bruce noticed that Shug's right hand remained beneath the table and suspected the barrel of a fifth gun was pointing in his direction.

The tool in his cuff came free, and Bruce switched it to his right hand. *Ten seconds,* he thought. *Just buy another ten seconds.*

"Or did you pay off Hillbilly Harry?" Bruce asked, knowing that this was not even close to the truth.

Shug nodded at the man behind the kitchen island. The man moved from his spot and walked over to Bruce.

## Chapter Twenty-Seven

Bruce slipped the tool between his index and middle finger and squeezed them tight to keep from dropping the tool. If the man searched him and found the tool, he was dead.

"Bruce's phone is in the front pocket of his jeans," Shug said. "Take it out and show him what you did to it."

The man seemed happy to oblige. He found Bruce's cell and took out the battery. He lifted his hand up to the light and Bruce saw a tiny gold chip held between his thumb and index finger.

"You bugged my phone?" Bruce asked, incredulous.

Shug smiled and nodded. He breathed deep, soaking in the moment of power.

The man beside Bruce slipped the gold chip into one of his pockets. He returned to the counter, but this time he stayed in front, leaning his large body comfortably back, his gun pointing casually at Bruce.

The tool was back between his thumb and forefinger. Bruce felt for the hole, but the handcuffs kept slipping beyond his grasp. He needed just a little more time.

"Why did you try to kill Stan Prater?" he asked.

"Try to keep up," Shug said.

Bruce stared blankly across the table.

Shug yawned. "When my people didn't make it to my ranch in New Mexico with Eli, I thought the whole bunch was dead. Then you popped up asking questions about Summer. I decided to have you followed. Maybe you would lead me to Eli, maybe not. It doesn't really matter. What mattered is, working alone, you were perfect. But when you and Stan Prater started working together, you became a threat. I couldn't risk you guys uncovering things that needed to remain buried. The fact is, one of you needed to be eliminated, but not both."

"What needs to stay buried?" Bruce asked. "What are you afraid of, Shug?"

Shug shook his head. "I answered your question. Your turn. Who was helping Eli?"

"Besides me?" Bruce asked.

"Am I to be convinced that an unarmed Amish kid single-handedly killed four of my people?" Shug asked, his voice rising.

Bruce had a story halfway fabricated in his mind. It was a story that would take up just enough time to get the cuffs free. But as he opened his mouth to speak, Shug's cell rang. Shug lifted a hand for silence and removed the phone from his coat pocket. He glanced at the message on the screen and frowned. He looked up and his eyes met Bruce's. A look of curious approval crossed his face.

"Well done," he said, dropping the phone back into its original pocket. "I'm not sure how you knew I'd be waiting for you here, but that was a magnificent move, Bruce."

Bruce frowned, trying to follow Shug's words.

Shug rose quickly from his chair. He slipped the handgun in his left hand into his other front jacket pocket.

"I really wanted to kill you myself," he said, moving around the table and starting for the front door. "But we have company."

Bruce's mind raced as he tried to follow the sudden change in plans. From the corner of his eye he watched Shug carefully, waiting for the bullet that was sure to come. The tool was in place, and the first link fell silently from his wrist.

"Kill this man and get out," Shug said as he glided soundlessly toward the front door. "And there is a second gun on his ankle that you would have found if you had searched him properly."

The front door made no sound as it opened and closed, a breath of air on the back of Bruce's neck the only indication that Shug was gone.

There was a slight hesitation that followed Shug's departure, but it was the break Bruce needed. The second hand came free and the cuff clattered to the floor. Bruce rolled from his chair and

## Chapter Twenty-Seven

dove toward the kitchen. In mid-lunge, his hand came up with the much smaller handgun from his ankle holster. The Ruger LCP 380 only held six rounds and was designed for close-combat action. He would have to make each shot count.

Bullets splattered the chair where he had just sat, and splinters flew from the tabletop. Bruce rolled, aimed and rapidly fired two rounds at the man near the kitchen counter.

The man's gun clattered to the floor, then he slowly sank down on top of it.

Bruce pivoted and fired twice more in the direction of the man in the hallway. He heard the air go out of the man.

The sound of exploding gun shots inside the close quarters of the bunker were deafening. Bruce's ears screamed, and he stumbled, for a moment disoriented by the thundering noise.

Bullets whizzed over his head and thudded into the rock counter.

Bruce regained his composure quickly. He spun instinctively, first to the right, then to the left, trying to make himself a harder target to hit. A searing pain shot through his recently injured shoulder as he hit the floor again. From his back, he fired his last two rounds into the nearest corner. He heard a gun clatter to the floor. Several bullets discharged and ripped through the front wall of the house.

One man to go. But his gun was now empty.

Bruce's momentum carried him into the kitchen. He had to get behind the island. He rolled twice, then lunged. His foot slipped on something wet and sticky, and he sprawled flat on the floor. The scent of warm blood was right under his nose.

*Hillbilly Harry's blood.*

Bruce lunged toward the island again, but his foot caught on something heavy sprawled on the kitchen floor.

*Hillbilly Harry's body.*

Bruce sprang over the body and lost his footing in another puddle of blood. He slid head-first against the island. He sat up and gingerly rubbed the top of his skull. In the dark, he fumbled in Harry's pockets for a gun. Bullets. All he needed was one more bullet. He was pretty sure three of the four men were dead, or too seriously wounded to be a threat.

There was no gun. And he found no bullets.

Slipping and sliding, Bruce inched across the floor until he reached the corner of the island. If he was lucky, he could sneak a gun from one of the dead men.

Bruce tried to listen for the sound of approaching footsteps, but his ears were still ringing from the volley of gunfire.

A hail of bullets pelted the front of the island. Bruce didn't move. He barely breathed. The man was trying to flush him out. Maybe he thought Bruce was already dead. Either way, he would have to give up the idea of retrieving the other gun. He was trapped behind the counter, but he had one thing working in his favor. The man would have to come close in order to kill him. Real close.

And when he did, Bruce would have the element of surprise. Maybe he wouldn't be able to overpower a man with a gun, but the odds were much closer to even now.

Bruce held his breath, waiting for the man to make another move so he could get a fix on his position. His ears were still ringing, but not so loud now. Then he heard it. The sound was faint, but it came again. The soft rustle of clothes as the man slid along the wall, moving in his direction.

The man was quiet, but not quiet enough. Bruce dropped silently onto the floor behind Hillbilly Harry's body and waited. *Come to me, you son-of-a-bitch. I'll break your neck before you know where I am.*

He raised his head a fraction of an inch above Harry's body and watched the spot along the wall where the man would appear.

## Chapter Twenty-Seven

*Three seconds.*

*Two.*

Then the front door burst open and a dozen blazing lights swept the room. Lasers bounced off the floor, trained on the dead bodies, and moved on.

Then a single gunshot reverberated through the room.

In an instant all the lasers were trained on the man, but it was too late. Bruce recognized the muffled report of the gunshot for what it was. Rather than be taken alive, the man had put the gun into his mouth and pulled the trigger.

"Don't shoot," Bruce said. "I'm a friendly." He raised his hands above the island and waved. Lights swept across the island, and men swarmed him.

"Stand down," a familiar voice commanded.

At the sound of the voice, Bruce stood up, his hands still high above his head.

"Put your hands down," Chief Calvin Westbritt said. "Nobody is going to arrest you tonight."

"Did you get him?" Bruce asked.

"Get who?" Westbritt asked, his eyes darting around the room.

"Shug. He left through that door less than thirty seconds ago," Bruce said.

Westbritt motioned, and half the men disappeared in the direction Bruce pointed.

"Where is your Amish kid?" Westbritt asked. He shined his flashlight across the bodies and grimaced.

"I don't know," Bruce said. "I walked him right into a trap."

"I'll put an APB out for the entire St. Louis area," Westbritt said. "Do you wanna tell me what the hell happened in here?"

Bruce gave Chief Westbritt a brief account of the events.

When he was finished, Westbritt remarked, "I'd like to know who tipped Shug off."

"That should be easy to narrow down," Bruce said. "Who knew you were coming here?"

"I've suspected for some time that Shug has a source inside the FBI," Westbritt said. He stooped and picked up the handcuffs, dangling them from a finger.

"Close call, huh?" He grinned.

"Never been closer," Bruce said. He took a towel from the kitchen countertop and began to wipe the blood from his hands. "How did you know where to find me?"

"I guess you haven't heard," Westbritt replied, picking up Bruce's bloody cell phone from the floor next to the chair where Bruce had been handcuffed.

"Heard what?"

"Stan Prater woke up this afternoon. I brought him up to date, told him where you went. Convinced him that you and Eli were in serious danger. It took a while, but he spilled the beans on this hideout."

Westbritt spoke into his radio. "Anything on Shug?"

"Negative."

"I have to get out there and find Eli," Bruce said. "I'll stop by your office tomorrow and give a full statement."

Bruce started for the door, but Westbritt stopped him.

"Bruce. You realize that you are now the only man alive that can testify to seeing Shug commit murder, correct?"

"What of it?" Bruce asked. "You think I'm scared of Shug?"

"No. I don't think you are scared," Westbritt said. "But you should be. You look terrible. A blind man can see that you need sleep. And you're really favoring that right shoulder, which is the side you shoot from. Should I send a few men with you to watch your back for a few days?"

"I can hold my own," Bruce said shortly. "But thanks for the offer."

## Chapter Twenty-Seven

More than a dozen squad cars were parked outside Hillbilly Harry's bunker. Someone was running yellow tape in a wide arcing circle between the trees.

The scene was all too familiar to Bruce. For the first time in a long time, he was glad he was no longer on the force. Inside the bunker, Westbritt was just starting to write a report on the mess. The report would grow and expand for months, and Westbritt would be questioned and re-questioned about the circumstances surrounding the hideout. Fingers would be pointed. Someone would be held accountable for the lives lost, and Bruce knew from experience that it would not be the FBI.

Bruce headed north, and fifteen minutes later turned onto I-70 and started toward St. Louis. He put the battery back into his phone and pressed the power button. He held his breath. The phone had been through a bombing, and more recently a bloodbath.

The screen turned blue, and his cell phone provider's icon popped up. Less than a minute later it rang. Bruce glanced at the familiar "private number" notification on the screen. He answered without hesitation.

"Good evening, Bruce," the voice-changer said.

"Hello, girl with the black ponytail," Bruce replied.

There was a brief pause on the other end of the line, then the voice continued. "You only have that information because we wanted you to have it."

"And who are 'we'?" Bruce asked.

"That is not important right now," the voice said. "I called to thank you, Bruce."

"For what?"

"You played your role perfectly. The only thing that went wrong is that Shug got away."

"I had a role?" Bruce asked.

"You did. And now it is time for you to walk away."

"Walk away from what?" Bruce asked.

"All of it, Bruce. Get back to cheating spouses and solving credit card fraud. You will live longer."

"Just tell me one thing," Bruce said. "Where can I find Eli?"

"Eli is with me," the voice-changer said. "You never had him."

Bruce frowned as the words sank in. He glanced at the screen on his phone, but the call had been disconnected.

# CHAPTER TWENTY-EIGHT

Shug had spent the better part of his life running away when things got too intense, and although fleeing Hillbilly Harry's bunker didn't rank near the top of all the narrow escapes he had encountered in his life, he fled anyway. He fled, not because he was a coward, but because he was a survivor. And he fled because he was on the verge of realizing a lot of his dreams. And, Shug reminded himself as he sprinted toward his car, none of those dreams involved spending the rest of his life in jail.

It wasn't until Shug had put a safe distance between himself and the bunker that he began to contemplate those dreams, and the impact that tonight's encounter with Bruce Ellsworth might have on them. All of the previous times he had fled, there had been no witnesses. All of the times before he had simply reappeared back into society and, although people pointed fingers and whispered, never once had he been arrested. Even after the wars he had fought in, he had always managed to vanish and dodge the questions.

But this time was different. This time he had left a witness behind, and if his men were unsuccessful in killing Bruce, well, the image of the inside of a jail cell suddenly became a lot clearer.

Not that Bruce could possibly escape the armed men inside the bunker. Literally nobody Shug had ever met was fast enough to pick a pair of handcuffs, draw a gun from an ankle holster, and kill four men who had the advantage of already having guns pointed at the prisoner in the middle.

So why was he worried?

Shug considered this as he ran. Was he worried because he had followed Bruce's movements and listened to his phone calls for the better part of two weeks, and because of this he had come to realize that Bruce simply didn't waste any movements? Or was it because Bruce approached each situation without emotion, and his calculated decisions seldom allowed him to make a mistake?

The engine purred to life just as Shug heard the first bursts of gunfire from inside the bunker.

With only seconds to put as much distance between himself and the bunker as possible, Shug hesitated. He simply had to know. He rolled down the driver's side window and counted the shots.

Three shots, execution style, were all that were needed.

But the shot pattern was wrong. There was an initial volley of shots, a short pause, and then a handful of more deliberate, well-placed shots.

Shug cursed as he floored the accelerator and the car sped down the dirt path toward the highway. He didn't turn on the car headlights; he could see better without them, and besides, they would only draw attention to his whereabouts.

As he drove, Shug watched for oncoming headlights through the trees ahead. They always came with their high beams on and their blue and red light bars flashing.

Shug sped his car across the creek and up the bank on the other side. The speedometer nudged fifty-five miles per hour.

He was almost halfway to the rusty gate when he saw the first lights. He had hoped to make it to the highway, but when you're on the run, you take whatever little advantages you can find. In this case, his advantage was the cover of darkness.

He picked an opening between two trees and whipped his car off the path. His headlights picked out an overgrowth of spruce trees, and he aimed straight for them. He almost made it, but the front bumper caught the edge of a fallen log hidden in the tall

## Chapter Twenty-Eight

grass. The car spun sideways and veered sharply, then crashed into a tree.

Shug cut the engine. The car was less than thirty feet from the path, but they might not see it. He would know in a few seconds. He jumped out of the car and sprinted across the path, then ducked into the trees on the other side.

Seconds later, the flashing lights were right in front of him, but whoever was in the lead was not looking for a vehicle in a thicket of spruce trees. Squad cars flashed by, the men inside oblivious to the man watching them from behind a tree only a few feet away.

Shug waited until the last car had disappeared, then crept back to his car. A strong smell of anti-freeze filled the inside. He turned the key in the ignition, but the engine refused to turn over. If he was going to escape, it would have to be on foot.

---

Trucker Joe was winding through the hills of Hermann, Missouri when he glanced at his fuel gauge and frowned. He would need to refill before he reached St. Louis.

At the intersection he shifted down and turned in to the truck stop. When he finished fueling, he went inside, refilled his coffee mug, and picked up his fuel receipt. A few minutes later, he nosed his big rig back onto Highway 50 and headed east.

The night was dark, and Trucker Joe's only scenery was the asphalt within the range of his headlights. He searched his CB radio for another trucker to chat with, but soon gave up. He tuned his AM/FM radio and sang along to some country music.

Two hours later he stopped at a warehouse and went to check in. When he got back into his truck, he noticed something strange. The curtains that separated the cab from his sleeper were standing open. He flipped on the bunk light and surveyed the space.

He checked the top and the bottom bunks, but they were both empty. Puzzled, he started his truck and backed toward the dock door to unload.

---

Shug walked down a dark alley behind the warehouse. During the ride, he had removed the battery from his cell phone. Using a rock, he crushed the cell phone and the battery and threw the remains into a dumpster.

He was now a wanted man. The list of people he could trust for help had shrunk to a handful.

For over an hour he walked the back streets of East St. Louis, but finally he reached his destination. It was one of about a thousand deserted houses in the government projects area. Plywood covered the doors and windows, and a blue tarp covered half of the roof.

Using a key, Shug unlocked the front door and stepped inside. The electricity to the building had been disconnected, but he had a rough idea where the basement door was. He moved silently down the stairs and when he reached the bottom, fumbled for the flashlight he had left above a ceiling beam.

The hideout was one of about a dozen secret locations scattered in and around St. Louis. The only reason he had picked this particular one was because it happened to be closest to where the trucker had stopped at the warehouse.

The flashlight was still there, exactly where he had left it. Gripping it between his teeth, Shug worked on a rock in the basement wall. It came away, and he withdrew a black leather briefcase. He took it into the bathroom and placed it on the vanity. The mirror above the sink was clouded over from lack of use, and spider webs hung from the ceiling. Shug wiped the mirror down and went to work on altering his appearance.

## Chapter Twenty-Eight

An hour later, a man in his mid-thirties, with the same height and build as Shug checked into a nearby motel. He wore designer glasses, a St. Louis Cardinals baseball cap, and had thick, dark hair. The young woman who booked his room smiled pleasantly as she handed him the key.

"Mr. Rutledge," she said, handing back his ID. "If you need anything, and I mean anything at all, please feel free to come see me at the front desk."

Mr. Rutledge nodded, smiled, and walked down the hallway to his room. He placed his briefcase on the bed and opened the lid, then took out a new burner phone and powered it on. He would use it for three days, then destroy it and move on to the next one.

The many IDs in the briefcase were all fake, and most had never been used. There were two unregistered and untraceable handguns, an assortment of wigs, with matching sideburns and mustaches, and a variety of knives. A hard, plastic liner formed the outer wall of the briefcase, and when removed, revealed over a dozen thin stacks of one-hundred-dollar bills.

Shug picked up the burner phone and placed the first and most important call.

"Hello, boss," the driver from the getaway vehicle said when he answered his phone. "It... it couldn't be helped."

Shug's smile vanished. Not because of the choice of words, but because of the tone with which the words were delivered. The voice was high-pitched, and the driver, who was usually calm and calculated, was clearly disoriented.

"Please tell me you have Eli with you."

The voice on the other end of the line was rambling on hysterically, ignoring Shug.

"He... he got away," the driver's voice was frantic. "Eli broke out of his handcuffs."

Shug's head swam as he listened to the excuses and explanations. He pinched the bridge of his nose and took a deep breath.

"Listen to me. LISTEN TO ME!" he shouted. His fingers gripped the cheap burner phone so tightly that his knuckles turned white. With every ounce of strength in those crushing fingers, he wished the driver were in the room at that moment so he could choke the life out of his inferior throat.

The driver went silent, except for heavy, ragged breathing.

"Tell me exactly how a feeble Amish boy in a plaster cast managed to break out of his handcuffs and escape from you *and* the two men sitting on either side of him?"

"He... he slashed their throats, sir," the man replied, his voice returning to its hysterical pitch. "Then he held the knife to my throat and made me pull over and he..."

"Stop!" Shug screamed into his phone.

The voice on the other end went silent, only panicked gasps of breath indicating he was still there.

"I will give you one chance to calm down and talk to me like an adult instead of a blabbering baby. How did Eli break out of his handcuffs, and where did the knife come from?"

There was a long pause as the man gulped deeply. Finally, his voice came back.

"He seemed prepared," the driver stammered. "I think he hid a handcuff key and the knife inside his cast. It's like he knew he was going to be caught."

Shug sat up abruptly in his bed. He glared at the blinking red numbers on his bedside table that told the digital time.

"Where exactly did this happen?" he asked with renewed patience.

"We were almost to Hermann," the driver said. "It happened so fast! One second I was pulling up to a stop sign, and the next thing I knew the entire car was covered in blood. The windshield..." The voice paused, struggling for composure as he relived the memory. "Blood squirted all across the windshield. It's in my hair, and it's all over my clothes."

## Chapter Twenty-Eight

"And then?" Shug asked. A puzzled expression playing at the corner of his mouth.

"He had a knife against my throat. He told me he was leaving, and that if I even flinched, I would be next."

"What happened next?" Shug asked, sudden admiration creeping into his voice.

"He opened the car door and walked away."

"And why do you suppose he didn't kill you too?" Shug asked.

"I don't know." The driver sounded confused, as if considering this possibility for the first time.

"Did he say or do anything else before he disappeared?"

"Yes," the driver said uncertainly. "When he got to the trees, he took the bloody knife and cut off his cast. He threw the cast at my car. Then he... he... *smiled* at me."

"He smiled at you?" Shug asked.

"Yes. He stood there, all covered in blood, and he just smiled at me."

"Describe the knife he used."

The driver hesitated. "It was a very large knife. Maybe... a dagger."

Shug smiled to himself, his suspicions confirmed.

"How long did he stand there before you got out of the car and chased him?" Shug asked, deliberately prolonging the driver's misery.

"I couldn't move," the man replied. "He was so... so in control. He took off his shirt and wiped the blood from his face. Then he wiped the blood off the... the knife and put it into a pocket somewhere. Then he just walked into the woods."

"Sparrow," Shug murmured. "That son-of-a-bitch! The whole thing was a set-up from the start."

"What?" the driver asked, confused.

Shug cut the call. He lay back on the bed and carefully revisited the events from earlier.

*How did I not see this coming? It was never Eli in the Explorer with Bruce Ellsworth. And of course, Bruce had been in on it the entire time. But Bruce would have needed help. So, who was helping him?*

"Hell of a good thing I had a guy inside the FBI to warn me," Shug said aloud.

Shug glanced at the blinking clock on his bedside table and frowned. It was over. He was done for. Thoroughly outmaneuvered. And that meant he would have to make the most difficult phone call of all. Not tonight, because Old Man Trontelli was a real bear if someone woke him from his sleep. But sometime very soon that call would have to be made.

Instead, Shug turned off the lights. He lay back on the bed and folded an arm under his head. A slow and deliberate migraine headache began to inch its way into the forefront of his head. With it came the voices. The ones he wanted so desperately to drown out but could not.

"I told you joining the fight was a bad idea." The small, thin face appeared at the very edge of Shug's vision. The face seemed to hover just above the side of the bed, floating closer and closer.

"It was… join the fight or starve," Shug replied defensively, a tremor coming to his voice. He lifted his hand to touch the face. "You came back, Momma."

The expression on the floating face turned to one of distrust. It shrank back, just out of reach, then the figure slowly faded into a blend of shadows between the men who had her arm pinned behind her back. Just like so many years ago.

# CHAPTER TWENTY-NINE

The morning of Thursday, November 6, started much like any other late fall day in St. Louis, Missouri. While the hunters were sighting in their rifles for the upcoming deer season, while the St. Louis Blues were riding a hot six-game winning streak, and while CEOs of multi-million dollar companies were grumbling about the size of their early Christmas bonuses, thirty miles to the north a long procession of buggies was arriving at the home of Raymond and Alma Byler.

The atmosphere was euphoric, and as relatives from other Amish communities began to arrive, they too felt the energy that filled the crisp morning air.

By nine-thirty a.m., the large barnyard at the Byler home was filled with buggies and vans. Those that arrived at the last minute parked on the narrow shoulder of Caroline Creek Road. The English drivers, that is to say, the non-Amish people who chauffeur Amish to events in their vans, gathered in the grassy pasture at the end of the driveway, speculating from afar.

As the farmhouse filled, those who were not as closely related to the couple began filling the haymow above the barn.

At exactly ten o'clock a silence descended upon the gathering, and Bishop Reuben Mast took his place before the congregation in the main house. At the same time, Uriah Miller, an uncle by marriage, who had traveled from Lancaster County Pennsylvania, began the services in the haymow.

John Schrock and Sadie Byler sat on two hard wooden chairs facing each other. Their heads were bowed in the solemn posture that is expected of those who are about to make the most important decision of their lives: a decision that, once finalized, could never in their lifetimes be undone.

Bishop Mast began his sermon with the story of King David and his successful reign, how he stumbled along the way, allowing his eyes to lust after a woman that was not his, and how he eventually had her husband killed so he could marry the woman.

The congregation pretended to listen to the story, but it was an oft-told one, and minds drifted. People who hadn't seen each other for many years searched for familiar faces among those who had traveled from afar.

Here and there a married mother glanced up from a baby she was rocking to meet the eyes of some long-lost love who had slipped through her fingers and married another, and who now just happened to be looking in her direction and wondering how different his life might have been with her instead of with his current wife.

Maria Reader sat on the back bench and observed the traditional rituals that were so sacred to the Amish communities. She wondered if she had made a mistake by committing to be a part of it for the rest of her life. She had never felt like she belonged, but every time she tried to imagine life on the outside, she had hit dead ends.

Who did she know that would take her in? How would she earn money? Get a car? Maybe if she managed to find Eli, things would be simpler. Maybe they could live together. She supposed that would be a lot more fun than the stuffy church with all the bad breath and barnyard smells.

Her eyes fell on Marvin Troyer. Marvin was leaning forward and listening intently to Bishop Mast. Maria's stomach instantly tied up in knots.

Throughout the sermon, a battle raged war inside her. By the time Bishop Mast got to the marrying part, Maria had reached a

## Chapter Twenty-Nine

decision. Her heart belonged to Marvin, and no amount of turmoil could change that. She wanted what she saw on her friend Sadie's face as she and John stood before Bishop Mast and sealed their vows of love.

The newlyweds walked solemnly back to their chairs and took their seats as husband and wife. Sadie was now a married woman, thereby forever removing herself as one of the Caroline Creek Youngie.

The wedding ceremony ended with a German hymn.

*Gelobt sei Gott im höchsten Thron,* which translated roughly to *Praised be to God in the highest throne.*

After the ceremony was over, the girls broke off into groups. Some went upstairs to visit with friends, while others volunteered to help the married women in the kitchen. With lunch still an hour away, Maria's group decided to go for a walk on the back of the farm.

The boys also broke into groups. Those that were dating remained in the front yard and caught up with old friends and relatives they hadn't seen in many years.

Marvin Troyer joined a group that consisted of baptized members not currently dating. They set up a volleyball net in the pasture next to the barn. While they swatted the ball back and forth across the net, they would be able to see the girls as they carried the food from the house to the haymow.

The third group of boys ranged in age from sixteen to twenty and consisted mostly of non-baptized members. This last group was led by Henry Schrock, younger brother of the groom. At sixteen, Henry had only recently joined the Singen. During the week, Henry had managed to sneak a barrel of corn cider into an old, abandoned barn in the river bottoms about a mile to the west. As soon as the third group of boys was out of sight of the house, black wool hats came off, shirt collars flew open, sleeves were rolled up, and suspenders disappeared. For most of them it would be an afternoon they would not soon forget. For some, it was their first go at the homemade liquor, and it would be an afternoon they would not fondly remember.

Maria, Edna and a group of twelve girls walked to the one-room schoolhouse bordering the back of the Byler farm. School was closed for the wedding, but the doors were never locked.

The day had warmed, and the girls took off their bonnets. Maria threw open a few windows to allow the wind to warm the inside. Some of the other girls found their old desks and squeezed into the seats, giggling at how small the desks now seemed. Maria and Edna stood behind the teacher's desk and frowned at the unruly pupils before them.

Through the open window came the faint sound of hooting and laughing. Maria's eyes met Edna's, and they smiled knowingly at each other. The two strict teachers forgot their roles as they turned to the window and in the direction of the commotion. Already the corn cider was having its effect.

Back at the wedding, the married men arranged the benches along the outer walls of the room. After the tables were set up in a large square, the men arranged the remaining benches inside the square to face the main corner where the newlyweds would be seated.

The newlyweds filed in and sat down. John Schrock on the right side of the corner, with Sadie right around the corner to his left. The wedding party would remain in their respective positions all afternoon with the exception of a two-hour break while the women washed dishes and prepared the food for the Wedding Singen.

The married folks were served first. Then tables were cleaned and dishes washed, a process that would be completed at least a dozen times until the ceremonies ended sometime around midnight.

While the women washed dishes, the married men settled in for an afternoon of singing. Musical instruments were considered too worldly, so they were not allowed in the community. The men sang

## Chapter Twenty-Nine

while the women set the tables with food for the Youngie. They sang while the Youngie were eating, with a brief pause while Bishop Mast led a prayer of thanks for the food, then they continued to sing.

At dusk the married folks hitched up the horses and buggies and made the trip home to do the farm chores. Those closely related would be back for the Singen, but most would remain home, where the events of the wedding would be discussed for weeks to come.

———◆———

In the same way that the afternoon was designed for the married, the evening belonged to the Youngie. The thirty-some Youngie that usually fit into one room at a normal Singen now expanded through the living room and into the dining room.

Unlike the regular Singens, where the boys and girls are segregated to opposite sides of the table, at a wedding all the boys and girls are paired up. The first to take their seats at the table were the newlyweds John and Sadie Schrock.

As is commonplace in many Amish farmhouses, the upstairs of the Byler house was divided into two large bedrooms, with a narrow hallway separating the boys' bedroom from the girls' bedroom. The beds had been removed, and the two rooms were now filled with Youngie.

The girls gathered and waited nervously as, in order of age, the Singen boys came down the hallway. The steady-dating couples went first. Junior Yoder, who was the oldest of the boys, stopped at the doorway and beckoned to Rosemary Schwartz, who was waiting close to the front. She walked quickly to meet Junior, and the couple walked to the end of the hallway and started down the stairs.

The door from the stairwell could be seen by all the married folks that waited downstairs. The most anticipated part of the wedding celebration had arrived.

Junior and Rosemary made their grand entrance. They walked across the room and sat down side-by-side next to the wedding party. One by one the other steady couples entered and seated themselves. The row of couples expanding outward from the main corner in both directions until finally the last of them were seated.

Then, a hush fell upon those gathered downstairs. Upstairs a stir could be heard as the boys jostled and elbowed, arguing about who was oldest and therefore should go first. Finally, it was decided that Albert Zook, who hailed from a community in Kentucky, and a second cousin to the groom, was the oldest single boy at twenty-three.

The other boys nudged and bantered with the bashful newcomer until he reluctantly made his way down the hall and stopped at the doorway. Albert, who didn't know any of the girls from Caroline Creek, nervously observed the remaining girls. He knew that the girls who already had admirers, but weren't dating steady yet, usually hid toward the back of the room, reluctant to be paired with anyone but their chosen admirer.

Albert chose a comely girl close to the front. She joined him and, hearts pounding at the sudden touch of a stranger's hand, the two walked down the stairs. In the kitchen the married women craned their necks to see the matchmaking that had just occurred. Whispers flew as they pieced together who Albert was, and the possibilities of a relationship that stretched across several states.

Maria Reader stood against the back wall and ducked low, trying to hide behind the rest of the girls. Edna Troyer stood on her right, and Alma Yoder, Caroline Creek's newest member of the Youngie, on her left. Edna was hiding in the back because Eli, although absent, might eventually come back, and Edna wanted to wait for him. Maria was not sure whom Alma was waiting for.

The time for Marvin's appearance drew closer. Maria's palms became sweaty and her breath came out in nervous gasps.

## Chapter Twenty-Nine

Together she and Marvin would walk down the stairs and all eyes would follow them.

It was not lost on Maria that they were the most talked-about couple at the Singen. They would steal the spotlight when they entered the room below. Everything she had endured would be worth it when she placed her hand in Marvin's. Much of her decision to bow under the authority of the ministers and become baptized had been in anticipation of this very moment. She could do it. With Marvin at her side, she could be whomever they needed her to be. Perhaps she would even smile at Deacon Koblenz and Mattie Borntrager. Not a wicked smile, but a sincere one. A smile of scorn that would portray that she had defied them, come through unscathed, and in the end, was the winner.

Maria breathed deep, trying to calm the butterflies in her stomach.

Then, Marvin's tall frame filled the doorway. His eyes scanned the room searching for her. Maria's heart skipped and she started forward. But Marvin was not beckoning to her.

Could he be mistaken? Could the dim light have caused him to miss her way in the back?

There was a rustle as a figure moved from the wall, and Alma Yoder started for the door, a shy smile covering her face. As if in slow motion, the other girls parted to let her pass through.

Maria's mouth went dry and her knees went weak. She tried to pry her eyes from the impending disaster, but could not. She watched in horror as Alma placed her small, pale hand in Marvin's and together they disappeared from the doorway. As their footsteps faded, reality hit Maria like an avalanche, and the world as she knew it came crashing down around her.

Her first instinct was to run—to simply vanish from this house full of fake people with their fake religion and ancient beliefs. With all her heart, she longed to be at home in the safety of the barn, among the gentle creatures that had never betrayed her. How could she have been so stupid? How had she not seen the warning signs? She had heard that Marvin and Edna had taken Alma home from the Singen the previous Sunday night, but thought nothing more of it.

"I'm so sorry," Edna whispered at Maria's elbow. "I hadn't the heart to tell you."

Maria turned bitterly toward her best friend. "You… You knew about this and didn't tell me," she blurted. "All afternoon we were together, and you never said anything."

Edna's face turned ashen. "I tried to talk him out of it Maria, I promise I did. He wouldn't listen to me."

"You are my best friend," Maria spat hotly. "You could have warned me!"

Edna reached to squeeze Maria's arm, a gesture of sympathy the two girls had become comfortable with in times of distress, but Maria yanked her arm away, her elbow smacking the wall with a hollow thump.

Perhaps she had known all along that she wasn't good enough for Marvin, that her rebellion against the ministers was more than any Amish man could be expected to endure. Hot tears of frustration and embarrassment stung her eyes and rolled down her cheeks.

Someone nudged her and Maria turned. Her name was being called. The boy who had chosen her was standing patiently in the doorway. Even from across the room, Maria could see that he was shorter than her by several inches. She quickly recognized Henry Schrock, a gangly pale-faced kid with pimples and an untamed cowlick that protruded from the right side of his forehead. She knew Henry to be a younger brother to John Schrock, the newlywed, but had never thought him in the least attractive. In fact, he was about as opposite from the tanned and athletic Marvin as anyone could be, and for an instant Maria wondered at her chances of escaping through a window.

## Chapter Twenty-Nine

Bitterly brushing the tears from her eyes with the heel of her hand, Maria moved through the girls and took Henry's hand.

Henry stopped halfway down the stairs and cleared his throat. "I've got a handkerchief," he said, producing a folded white piece of fabric from a pocket. "Here."

Maria took Henry's handkerchief and wiped her red and swollen eyes. Henry stood awkwardly by and waited, not sure what to say.

"Thank you," Maria finally said, handing the handkerchief back. "I'm sorry that I am such a bad date."

"No problem." Henry smiled, his eyes lighting up. "I'll be as strong as I can for you tonight."

They waited in the empty stairwell until the next couple appeared at the top of the stairs.

"We can wait," Henry said. "Let a few couples go around us. Nobody will care."

"No," Maria said quickly. "It won't make a difference."

For weeks Maria had been dreaming of her entrance at the Wedding Singen. Marvin was the clear catch of Caroline Creek, and even married women would secretly envy her as they marched across the floor hand in hand. Perhaps she would even sway her hips just a little. Not much, but a subtle twirl that would cause her dress to swirl and float just above her knees before settling back to her ankles.

But instead here she was, towering over a pale-faced boy who looked to be about fourteen.

They made their entrance and the whispering stopped. From the kitchen Mam watched with an agonized expression on her face as her daughter followed a gangly kid.

Henry led Maria to their spot at the table and they sat down. Maria did not look around the room to meet everyone's eyes as she had dreamt she would. Instead, she fastened her eyes on the door leading from the stairs and did her best to pretend that she was happy for the rest of the paired couples. During a break, she caught sight of one man sitting all alone on the very back bench.

Andy Reader sat hunched over, hair unkempt, a permanent scowl on his face—an outcast by choice. Maria felt a stab of sympathy for her father. She could not remember a time when she felt any emotion for Andy, but now, for the first time, she realized that perhaps they had more in common than she had thought.

The girls outnumbered the boys, and after the last couples were seated, one by one, seven more girls entered the room, minus the companionship of a boy. Theirs was the walk of shame, for they were the rejects—the leftovers after the prettier girls had all been spoken for.

Dinner was a blur for Maria, who had lost her appetite. Henry tried to make conversation, but Maria, still numb, mostly ignored him. Once, she glanced in the direction of Marvin and Alma. Their arms were looped, and Alma smiled innocently up into his face as she fed him a bite from her plate. Maria gagged and almost vomited.

"If you look around," Henry spoke quietly so only Maria could hear. "You will see that there are a lot of people here tonight that support the stand you made."

Maria turned and for the first time, actually looked at Henry. Eli and Henry had been friends, she remembered. Eli had often spoken highly of Henry, so perhaps there was something there after all.

Henry smiled back at her with grey eyes that held more confidence than Maria thought possible for a child his age. Maybe he even had a certain appeal about him, she thought. Henry would not have a problem finding a girl that would fall for those eyes, and he could lavish her with his weak attempts at polite charm, but for Maria, the very thought of love was now galaxies away.

Henry's undoing came during dessert. In another world—one

## Chapter Twenty-Nine

where the interaction between boys and girls is a lot more common, where teenagers with raging hormones have been educated from an early age—Henry's advance might not have been so awkward and uncertain. But now, with his fork poised in midair, precariously balancing a rich piece of pecan pie that looked like it could crush his toe if it fell, his left hand slid into Maria's lap, seeking the warmth of the hand he had held during their journey down the stairs.

Maria's face flushed and she yanked her hand away.

Henry, of strong character despite his frail appearance, took it in stride, grinning sheepishly at the gawkers on the other side of the table.

Edna's partner wasn't having much better luck. He was a burly boy with large hands and thick lips. His beard was much longer than the length required for the unmarried. Maria thought it made him look old enough to be Edna's father. Edna, usually so beautiful and graceful, now sat with downcast eyes, her fork picking at tiny particles of food that weren't finding their way to her mouth.

Maria realized that in her anger, she had crushed her best friend, wanting her to feel what she had felt.

As if reading her thoughts, Edna looked up, seeking Maria's eyes.

"I'm sorry," Maria mouthed, her face flushing.

Edna returned a weak smile and nodded at Henry. Making sure Henry wasn't watching, Maria wrinkled her nose in disapproval. She raised an eyebrow at Edna's partner and nodded approvingly in return. Edna snorted before she could catch herself, then red-faced, quickly coughed into a closed napkin.

*She has already forgiven me*, Maria thought to herself. *How can I ever be such a good person?*

Dinner ended and the women came from the kitchen, clearing and wiping down the tables. Before the tablecloth was dry, the men began passing out the hymnbooks.

Someone led off in a song. Maria willed herself to sing. The evening, she decided, was not about her. She would try and celebrate the night for the sake of John and Sadie.

Maria poured her soul into the words, the melody of each syllable tugging at her heart. As the joyful voices of Youngie soared, Maria almost forgot the stabbing pain in her heart over Marvin's betrayal.

The song ended, and when Maria lifted her eyes, she found Deacon Koblenz staring at her. His cold, mocking gaze chilled Maria, even from across the room. His lips curled up at the corners, revealing a smile so evil that Maria shuddered. Red-hot resentment burned in her chest. Her well-planned evening had turned into a disaster, and the entire blame lay upon Deacon Rudy Koblenz's shoulders. By using his power and influence, he had forced her to stay home from the Singen, thereby missing her date with Marvin, and in her absence, Marvin had chosen another.

Maria fought off a strong temptation to walk over and wring Deacon Koblenz's fat neck in front of everyone. She would wipe that evil smile from his lips.

Henry also caught the evil grin from Deacon Koblenz and his back went rigid. He turned to Maria, his grey eyes suddenly cold. Gone was the pale-faced boy who had tried to sneak her hand under the table.

"Whatever you do, we will support you," he said, his voice tense. "If you stand up and walk out right now, everyone will understand. Many of us will walk out with you. This oppression has gone on for too long and everyone is tired of it."

"It's o... okay," Maria stammered. "I will suffer through this for Sadie. This wedding is about her and John."

She could see that Henry wasn't satisfied, but he nodded.

The next song started. Maria opened her mouth to sing, but her throat choked. She swallowed hard and fought to keep the

## Chapter Twenty-Nine

tears back. She fixed her eyes on the hymnbook, avoiding the other faces at the table.

"I... I can't sing," she whispered to Henry. "I'm so sorry."

Without a word, Henry closed the hymnbook and slid it several inches across the table. He leaned back and sat, stoic and unsmiling, looking straight ahead, his eyes burning holes into Deacon Koblenz.

The couple next to him saw the book close. They looked at the expression on Henry's face, saw his cold anger directed at Deacon Koblenz, and understood that the line had finally been crossed. They closed their hymnbook and slid it to the middle of the table. Then, they stopped singing.

Slowly, like a silent, invisible messenger, the signal went around the tables. One by one, all the hymnbooks closed and were rejected. The song came to an embarrassing and uncomfortable pause in the middle of the second line.

Maria's cheeks flamed with shame. "No. No," she whispered. "Let's not ruin the Wedding Singen. It is John and Sadie's special day."

Nobody moved.

Burning hot with shame, Maria leaned forward and searched the main corner, expecting a look of disapproval from the newlyweds. But their hymnbooks were closed as well. Sadie smiled warmly in her direction, and John gave her a weak nod of approval.

Suddenly Maria understood. The marriage was final, and it could never be undone. Tomorrow John and Sadie would be married folks, but for one more evening, they were Youngie. To them what happened next was not important. They had, much like her and the rest of the Youngie in Caroline Creek, played the role that was required to allow the wedding ceremonies to proceed, but their resentment toward the elders had not changed.

Marvin Troyer tried to pick up the song where it had ended, and a few married men joined in. The feeble effort was abandoned after only a few syllables.

Maria's eyes darted across the room, scanning the married men. Half of them sat with their hymnbooks closed, unmoving. Deacon Koblenz's face was beet red, and his chest heaved. He seemed to be trying to physically shrink into the floor beneath the wooden bench; the effort left shiny beads of sweat on his forehead.

Bishop Mast sat with his hymnbook closed, head bowed, eyes shut. He suddenly looked much older than his thirty-six years.

How much longer this uncomfortable scenario would have continued would be discussed for years to come, but suddenly the silence was interrupted by the sound of a loud engine. Bright headlights illuminated the entire house, bouncing and dancing patterns across the room and glowing brightly against the opposite wall. Necks craned to the windows to see who had rudely interrupted the Singen.

Raymond Byler walked outside. A few minutes later he reentered the house. He walked to the back of the room and knelt beside Andy Reader. He whispered something in his ear, and Andy's face changed. Andy rose, walked to the kitchen and beckoned to Mam who followed him out the door.

"Eli," Maria gasped. She sprang from her seat and darted out the door.

Outside, Bruce Ellsworth stood beside his Explorer. He was not smiling.

"Eli." Mam's voice trembled as she moved toward the open door of the Explorer, leaning to see inside. "Where is he?"

Bruce stepped between Ruth and the Explorer and raised both hands, palms outward, to stop her. "Eli is not with me," he said solemnly. "I had him and I lost him."

Andy Reader stepped close. "What has Eli gotten into?" he asked, his face emotionless in the soft moonlight.

## Chapter Twenty-Nine

"At this point I really have absolutely no idea what to believe," Bruce replied. "I drove all the way to New Mexico to pick him up, and now I know less than I did before I left. Honestly, I'm not even sure it was Eli that I brought back with me."

As Bruce relayed the events from the previous two days, others gathered around. The Singen was over, broken by the news.

In Caroline Creek's weekly addition of *The Budget*, Mattie Borntrager's take on the incident read as follows:

*The otherwise perfect wedding of John and Sadie Schrock was dampened by the re-emergence of Eli Reader, long thought to have run away from home. While reports have it that Eli may have been taken involuntarily, one must not be too quick to jump to conclusions on such matters. The lesson to be taken from this unfortunate incident is that one can never watch one's children too carefully. Had Eli been an obedient child of God, there is little doubt that he would have been passed over for another, but Satan will seek out those who are weak in their faith.*

Mattie Borntrager, *Disciple of good, Soldier against evil.*

# CHAPTER THIRTY

Joey Trontelli picked up on the second ring. He glanced at the clock. 2:30 a.m.

"Who died?" he growled into the receiver.

"It's Shug," came the voice on the other end. "I'm calling you from a burner."

"This better be important," Joey growled.

"It is. I have been compromised."

Joey closed his eyes and took a deep breath. He swung his legs over the edge of his bed and slid his feet into slippers, then walked outside onto his balcony. He lit a cigarette, took a deep drag, then exhaled. "You are the guy everyone is searching for?" he asked finally.

"You already heard?"

"I have my sources. What happened?"

"It was a set-up," Shug replied. "I'm going to have to disappear."

Joey frowned. "What are you saying?"

"I might need connections to get out of the country?"

Joey was silent for a long moment. "I've known you for over thirty years," he said finally. "You've never asked me for help."

Shug said nothing.

Joey took another drag on his cigarette and blew the smoke out through his nose. He scanned the calm waters of Lake Michigan that stretched below. To his right the Chicago skyline loomed into the dark night sky, its reflection cast perfectly in the water.

"Okay," Joey finally replied. "I will help you get out, but someone will need to clean up after you?"

## Chapter Thirty

"I have four names. Possibly a fifth."

"A fifth?"

"I believe there is someone working behind the scenes, but I have no idea who it is."

Joey interrupted. "Let's not do names over the phone. Let's meet at the usual place Wednesday, alright?"

"Yeah, sure," Shug replied. "Wednesday. I'll be there."

After he hung up the phone, Joey placed a call to the most important man in the crime family—"Old Man" Ralphie Trontelli, the head of the family. The reason Joey made the call without fear of retaliation was because Ralphie was his father, and after he was gone Joey, the only remaining son, would inherit the business.

The old man did not take the call well. "What is it?" he hissed into the phone.

"Shug's luck has run out," Joey said, getting straight to the point. "We will need to replace him, effective immediately."

"Make some damn sense," the old man growled.

"Let's just say that he narrowly missed getting caught in the middle of a double homicide. He is on the run and asking for help."

"Shug," Old Man Trontelli replied, his voice slowly becoming calmer. "He's still running our strip clubs and casinos in the St. Louis area, right?"

"That's right," Joey replied.

"How much money are those clubs making the family?"

"Just north of thirty million a month."

"Thirty-plus years Shug served this family," Old Man Trontelli said, as if talking to himself. "Even before I was a made guy, Shug was one of my father's most trusted men."

"Make the call," Joey said.

Old Man Trontelli hesitated, as if the decision was painful. "It's gotta be done before he hangs all of us," he finally said.

"Make it look like he left the country, you know, to throw off anyone who is looking for him."

"Okay," Joey replied. "Anything else?"

"Thirty-some years of faithful service," Old Man Trontelli muttered on the other end of the line. "Heck, it could even be forty. I've lost track."

Joey grimaced and hung up the phone. The old man's mind was going. That was for sure. But he was right about one thing. Shug was now a liability that had to be eliminated.

———◆———

Back in his motel room Shug took the battery out of the burner phone he had just used. He knew something that the Trontellis did not know. The FBI had tapped their phones, and his call had just been recorded. With a little luck, they would use that phone call in the Trontelli trials. It wasn't as good as the tape and Sparrow's testimony would have been, but it might be just the thing that was needed to hang the old man and his son.

Shug suddenly wasn't tired. Something bothered him, but he couldn't pinpoint it. Joey Trontelli had taken the news a little too well. He had agreed just a little too readily to help him disappear. Something about that didn't feel right. Did the Trontellis know about the tape and Sparrow? Shug thought they probably did not.

The red lights on the digital clock glared menacingly back at him, judging him, making it difficult to concentrate. Finally, Shug yanked the cord from the wall, and carrying the hated clock into the bathroom, shoved it into the trash basket beneath the sink. That cleared his head a little. His mind went back to Joey Trontelli. Perhaps it wasn't anything Joey had said, but rather some deep instinct that convinced Shug he would do well to miss the meeting with Joey on Wednesday.

## Chapter Thirty

By the time the first rays of sun began to pry in around the edges of the window curtains, Shug had become convinced that his instincts were exactly on point. He was on his own.

With the important phone calls out of the way, there remained one last call. The desire for a girl's touch had not diminished, and Shug had the perfect solution to the matter. He dialed the number.

"Darla's Massage Parlor," the familiar voice answered.

"Good morning Darla," Shug said. "I need your best girl."

---

The voices were back. Shug tossed and turned. Finally, he powered on the new burner phone. He typed in a website and searched for the video. He placed the phone on his chest and lay back on his pillow, then closed his eyes and sighed.

The voice was that of an Evangelistic preacher, and before long, the hypnotic voice began to soothe Shug's troubled spirit. "There are no sins so great that God Almighty can't forgive them," the voice said. "Just ask and it will be done unto you."

Little by little the tossing stopped and gradually a peaceful expression crept across Shug's face. Finally, his body relaxed.

And the preacher's voice droned on.

Outside, a black Pontiac pulled up to the curb and a girl named Belle got out. She walked around to the passenger side and reached inside for her handbag. Using the sideview mirror, she began to touch up her makeup. Something in the mirror caught her eye and she straightened quickly. A figure was rapidly approaching from behind, and Belle's hand reached for the pepper spray in her bag. She relaxed when she saw that it was only a girl. The girl's nose and chin were pointed, and her black hair was tied up in a neat ponytail. She approached and held out her hand. Belle glanced down and saw a wad of one-hundred-dollar bills.

"There are ten of them," the girl said.

"What do you want from me?" Belle asked.

"Disappear," the girl said.

Belle looked at the money, back at the girl, understood, and took the money.

A few seconds later Belle and the Pontiac disappeared around the corner and only the new girl remained. She turned and walked confidently toward the motel, Belle's bag in hand.

# CHAPTER THIRTY-ONE

The voices are getting louder and louder, and now the yelling is much closer. A grenade lands on the dirt several yards away and Shug dives behind a log. The grenade explodes, filling Shug's eyes with dirt and the bark from a nearby tree.

Another loud pop sounds right next to Shug. This pop is different from the others, and Shug turns to see what made it. The man next to him is slumped over the log and his brains are strewn across the ground.

Shug has never seen the man before. Where did he come from? Are they fighting for the same side?

Another pop, and this time Shug sees what's making the noise. A bullet enters a comrade's forehead, and the pop happens as the back of the skull is separated from the rest of the head.

Shug has lost the will to fight. He slumps behind the log and, holding the gun over his head, squeezes round after round in the direction of the enemy.

He will die now. And it won't even matter. There won't be anyone to send his body home to anyway. He will become another senseless statistic, and in a few days, nobody will even remember his name.

The enemy is closer now, the voices directly on the other side of the log. Someone is pounding against the log, and Shug squeezes his eyes tightly shut and waits for the end. Maybe if he lies really still, they won't find him.

*Thump. Thump. Thump.* The pounding continues.

There is a small crevice beneath the log. Shug might fit. He rolls aside the man with the missing brain and squeezes into the crevice. Then he pulls the body in tight to close the opening.

A face hovers just on the edge of his vision.

"Mother?" Shug gasps. "This time you really came back."

Shug reaches a feeble hand out and tries to touch the weathered cheek, but the vision begins to fade.

"No," Shug sobs. "Come back. You promised."

His mother opens her mouth to speak and Shug strains to hear the words. But the voice is not the voice of his mother. It is the voice of another woman, and Shug shrinks away. A million times he's seen her face in his visions, and a million times she's faded out of sight before he can reach her. In agony now, Shug claws at his head.

*Thump. Thump. Thump.*

Shug crawls further beneath the log. Another grenade explodes right on top of him, and now he is covered in dirt. Bodies are collapsing all around him, sheltering him beneath the log. Hiding him.

Now the lighting is changing. Somebody has lifted the log. The thumping is louder and the strange woman's voice is clearer.

And then Shug is standing in the middle of a motel room. And he is gasping for air. He looks down at his hands but all he finds are a few strands of silvery hair clutched there.

Shug's eyes dart around the room, searching for the source of the pounding. His eyes fasten on a spot in the middle of the bed that is soaked in his own sweat.

"I don't even remember which war it was when I hid under a log," Shug muttered to himself. "It's been so long they all blend together." He gulped deep breaths of oxygen and listened as his heart rate began to slow back to normal.

The thumping came again, and the voice is back. Someone is pounding on the motel door.

## Chapter Thirty-One

"Who is it?" Shug asked, leaping for his briefcase.

"I'm here for Shug," a female voice replied.

The demand was followed by another series of thumps.

*Of course*, Shug thought. *The girl has arrived. No telling how long I would have been on that nightmare trip if she hadn't interrupted.*

Shug grabbed a handgun from the briefcase and tucked it into the back of his jeans. He opened the door a crack and carefully studied the girl in the hallway. He hadn't seen her before, which didn't bother him. Darla went through new girls all the time.

When he was certain the girl was alone, Shug opened the door all the way and let her in, then walked to the bathroom and checked himself in the mirror.

The girl dropped her bag onto a chair and began to unbutton her shirt. She tossed it across the back of the chair, then stooped and removed her shoes. These she carefully placed beside each other on the floor.

Instinct had carried Shug for many years, and he decided to act on it now. "Toss me your purse," he demanded sternly.

"Wha... Excuse me?" the girl said, turning to face him.

"You heard me," Shug snapped. "I don't trust anyone. Nothing personal doll, but toss me the damn bag."

The girl obeyed.

"Now sit on that bed while I have a look inside," Shug commanded.

The girl took two steps backward and sat down on the bed across from him. Keeping his eyes fastened on her, Shug sifted through the contents of the bag.

The girl held his gaze, expressionless, unmoved.

"You don't look or act like one of them," Shug finally said.

"Do you always treat your girls this way?" the girl asked, still expressionless. Her folded hands in her lap pushed the skirt down between her legs, cutting off the point of view about midway up her thighs. She was not particularly beautiful, but her dark features commanded attention.

Shug studied her carefully, then tossed the bag onto the bed.

"Are we gonna do this or are we gonna play undress all day?" the girl pressed.

"Not so fast," Shug said. "Take off the skirt and let me see you."

The girl rose and unzipped the skirt. It dropped to the floor, revealing green, silk panties. She stepped out of the skirt and moved closer.

"Hair up, or down?" she asked.

"Down."

The girl's fingers moved, and the hair came free. She tossed her head and flung the hair over her shoulders.

Shug watched every move, a slow smile creeping across his lips.

"Well you definitely have more sass than the others," he said. "Come here for a minute. I want to talk to you before we get cozy." He patted the bed.

The girl walked over and sat down next to him. Shug slid a hand up her back, caressing the soft, pale skin. With nimble fingers he unhooked her bra. The bra fell to the floor.

Shug's hand tugged at a strand of hair. He lifted it to his nose and breathed deeply.

The girl remained expressionless, her eyes fixed on the opposite wall.

Shug's hand moved to her chin. He pulled it toward him until her eyes were looking directly into his. The eyes remained void of emotion.

Shug lifted one of her hands and studied it carefully. He checked each of her feet and even looked between her toes. There were no needle marks.

## Chapter Thirty-One

"I think I will call you *The Black Fox*," he said, tugging at the pointy chin. He watched carefully for a change in her expression, but none came.

"After we are finished here, I am going to need an even bigger favor from you," Shug continued. "And I've decided that you are the perfect fit for the job."

"What is the job?" the girl asked.

"I have a house not too far from here," Shug replied, carefully weighing his words. "It is being watched by the FBI, so I can't get to it. But they won't stop a girl. So, I need for you to get into that house and bring me back an important item."

The girl nodded.

Shug took a pen and a piece of paper from his briefcase and began to sketch a diagram of the inside of his house. He marked the hidden location where the thumb drive was located. When he was finished, he wrote seven numbers across the top of the paper. "The combination lock to the front door," he said.

The girl walked to her bag and dropped the paper inside, then got back into the bed. She lay down on her stomach with her head on the pillow. Her hair fell down, covering her face and most of the pillow. She lay silent and waited.

Shug lifted a hand and ran it slowly up one of her legs. "When can I expect you back with the item?" he asked.

"Figure about two hours," the girl replied from under her hair.

"Okay, deal," Shug said. He lay down next to her on his back and brushed her hair from her face.

The girl stared at him but didn't move.

"Come here, *Black Fox*," Shug said. "Kiss me."

The girl straddled his stomach. She leaned in slowly, her hair falling around Shug's face.

Shug's hand moved behind her head and his fingers entwined in her hair. He pulled her down gently until her cheek rested against his own, then whispered into her ear.

"I never told you how to get to my house, *Black Fox*. So, how do you know how long it will take to get there and back?"

The girl's body tensed. She hesitated for just an instant, then one of her hands flashed up. The needle brushed an artery in Shug's neck before he could react. The numbness was instant. He threw both arms up, fighting for space. At the same time, he rolled and bucked his hips, trying to throw her off balance.

The maneuver was a mistake. As soon as his hips lifted from the bed, the girl's legs easily moved in underneath, locking his lower body into submission.

Shug punched with his fists, trying to connect with her face, but strong hands clasped his wrists and pinned them to his chest.

"Did you really think you would be lucky enough to screw me, you disgusting old pervert?" she hissed into his ear.

"Who… are… you?" Shug's lips were beginning to lose feeling.

The girl released his hands and they fell limp. "How many lives do you have, you lucky old fool?" she asked, sitting back.

She slid off the bed and left him lying there, gasping for air as the poison coursed through his veins.

"Who… are… you…?" Shug rasped again.

The girl laughed scornfully. With nimble fingers, she pried the cash from the walls of his briefcase.

"It's a shame you don't remember me," she said. "You ordered me killed as an infant.

Shug rolled his eyes to get a closer look at the girl. She was moving swiftly about the room, wiping away fingerprints. When she was satisfied, she stooped, pulled on her skirt, shoes, and last of all, her shirt. She tossed the bra into her bag, then walked over to the bed and stooped low over Shug's face.

"Remember me now?" she demanded.

Shug nodded slowly. "You were a mistake," he slurred. "You were supposed to be a boy."

## Chapter Thirty-One

"Who are my parents?" the girl demanded.

"I don't remember," Shug said, his eyes turning glassy.

"It's okay," the girl said. "I'm sure it will all be on the thumb drive at your house. You know, the one I was supposed to bring back to you." She straightened from the bed and started for the door, then paused.

"You have just used up your last life, you rotten, slimy scum," she said. "Now go burn in fucking hell, you filthy bastard!"

The door closed and she was gone.

Shug rolled off the bed and onto the floor. His limbs felt numb, which made it difficult to crawl, but he managed to reach his briefcase.

*I should be dead by now,* he thought. *Why am I not dead?*

He dragged the briefcase off the chair, spilling its contents onto the floor. The girl was right. He would probably die, but before he did, he had one last, flimsy hope. The briefcase was one of over a dozen he had hidden around East St. Louis. Each carried one key ingredient. Maybe all the rest of the experiments that had been performed on human test subjects during the war had been a waste of time, and lives. But the antidote had proven itself quite trustworthy on several occasions. Maybe it was not the correct antidote for the poison the girl had given him, but it gave him a slim chance.

Shug fumbled with the handle on the briefcase and one end popped free. He shook the handle and the capsule rolled out onto the floor. Numb fingers grasped at the capsule but refused to close on it. He dropped face-down onto the carpet and tried with his mouth instead. By the time he managed to pick the capsule up with his lips, his mouth was filling with thick blood. He coughed and blood spewed across the carpet. He rolled over onto his back, and using every ounce of his remaining strength, he tried again to swallow. He thought he felt the capsule pass down his throat but couldn't be sure. Exhausted, he closed his eyes and the darkness came.

———— ♦ ————

When Bruce Ellsworth awoke it was early afternoon. He stretched and got out of bed, then walked to the counter and started a pot of coffee. The desk he had pushed against his office door in the front room was undisturbed, and the whole building seemed strangely quiet for the middle of a workday. Then he remembered he had given Susan the day off.

Bruce walked to the window facing Fennimore Street. A squad car was parked against the opposite curb, and Bruce frowned. Despite his insistence that he could take care of himself, Chief Westbritt had sent security.

Bruce sipped his coffee and checked his voicemail. There was a message from the person with the voice-changer. The message had been left a little over an hour ago.

"The man you are searching for is at the Riverside Motel. You will find him in room thirty-seven. I killed him because he didn't deserve to live."

There was a short pause before the voice continued. "You won't be hearing from me again, Bruce. I know you want to find me, but don't waste your time. I've told you before, I'm a shadow, and I wish to remain that way."

———— ♦ ————

Thirteen minutes after Bruce listened to the message, a tactical team stormed room thirty-seven at the Riverside Motel. It was empty. The only signs that anyone had been there were traces of blood splattered across the floor, and a few specks of blood in the bathroom sink.

# CHAPTER THIRTY-TWO

The second line of the hymn ended and the third began. The ministers in the Obrod sat silent, awaiting the footfall on the stairs that would announce Maria's arrival.

Seconds turned into minutes, and still the footfalls didn't come. With the beginning of each new line to the hymn, Deacon Rudy Koblenz's head sank lower.

Finally, Bishop Mast reached into a jacket pocket and pulled out a silver-plated watch. He popped the lid and carefully studied the time. "We will give it another five minutes," he said, returning the watch to its pocket.

The song ended, followed by the thumping of hymnals as they were placed on the benches between the members.

Bishop Mast cleared his throat and spoke the dreaded words: "It is obvious that Maria will not be joining us for baptism classes."

Heads nodded in agreement.

Bishop Mast continued. "This thing has gone on for way too long, but it ends now. Already two families have purchased homes in other communities, and on my way to church this morning I counted **For Sale** signs in front of four others. We take necessary actions now, or we will lose the entire community."

None of the other ministers spoke, so Bishop Mast continued. "Deacon Koblenz. I gave you one last chance to prove that your methods still work, and they did not. I warned you to sit back and let Maria come to us in her own time. You did not listen. Now you will face the consequences. The charges I bring against you are these: You have become so obsessed with your hatred for Maria Reader that you neglected your other duties as Deacon of Caroline Creek. In your blind pursuit for revenge you have come dangerously close to fracturing this community right down the middle. In short, you chose hate over love."

The other three ministers sat speechless and stared at the floor. Bishop Mast's decision didn't come as a surprise, but Deacon Koblenz was a powerful man. Would the punishment further damage the morale of the community?

"You will be asked to leave this Obrod," Bishop Mast continued. "But before you go, I will give you a final chance to defend yourself."

Deacon Koblenz, who had a reputation for flying into fits of rage in moments like these, quickly recognized that he was out of options. Bishop Mast had the authority to ex-communicate him on the spot if he chose to do so.

Given these circumstances, Deacon Koblenz decided to take a more humble approach. He hunched over, portraying the posture of a beaten dog. He folded his hands, closed his eyes, and in a soft and submissive voice began to speak.

"I only did what I thought was best for the community," he said. A tear trickled down his cheek. "But now I can see clearly that I was mistaken. I am but a humble servant of God who seeks forgiveness for my many sins. I apologize for those sins. My biggest regret is that I can't go back and do things differently."

A second tear followed the first, and he wiped at it with a handkerchief.

"Your apology has been heard," Bishop Mast replied. "But I think we can all agree that it is too late for apologies. However, there may come a time when you will be called upon to repeat that apology where it is most needed, and that is directly to Maria."

Deacon Koblenz grimaced inwardly but nodded his head enthusiastically.

## Chapter Thirty-Two

"Deacon Rudy Koblenz," Bishop Mast continued. "Do you clearly understand the charges brought against you by the minister bench?"

"I do," Deacon Koblenz said.

"Then at this time you are excused from the Obrod. You may go downstairs and sit with the rest of the congregation. The rest of us will reach a verdict."

For a long moment Deacon Koblenz sat frozen, trying to fathom the words. He had expected a tongue-lashing, yes. Maybe not as intense as the one he had received, but a strong reprimand for sure. But to be excused... he shot a helpless glance at the other three ministers, silently pleading for someone to come to his defense, but their eyes were cold and unforgiving. Finally he rose and, shoulders slumped, left the room.

After the door closed, Bishop Mast continued. "As the Bishop of Caroline Creek, I will make a case to ex-communicate Deacon Koblenz indefinitely. While this may seem a little drastic, given the morale within the community, I feel it is our only choice."

Bishop Mast's words were met with enthusiastic nods.

Bishop Mast continued. "And I will now hear the rest of your cases."

Raymond Byler's vote was short and to the point. "My vote is with you," he said. "The Wedding Singen was a disaster, and Deacon Koblenz is to blame."

Without the usual menacing presence of Deacon Koblenz at his own hearing, the decision was finalized in less than five minutes, with all four ministers casting their votes with Bishop Mast.

While the rest of the ministers were deciding his fate, Deacon Koblenz sat by himself on the minister bench downstairs. The congregation continued to sing, but it felt like every eye in the room was on him. He slumped low and his cheeks burned red.

He pondered what punishment he would be given. The Amish church had two methods of punishment for someone who is found to be living in sin, and Deacon Koblenz fervently hoped for the lesser of the two.

That first method is simply referred to as "confessing one's sins." The wayward member is excused, while the rest of the congregation is asked to vote on whether that member's sins can be forgiven on the spot. If three or more members are opposed, then the wayward member remains in unfortunate standing with the church until two weeks later, when the process is repeated. When the opposed members feel like the wayward member has sufficiently repented, they give their vote of confidence. The wayward member is then called back inside the house and asked to kneel before the congregation. The member is required to repeat his baptism vows, apologize for his sins, and promise not to repeat the same mistakes.

The second form of punishment is ex-communication, which can only be executed if the person is baptized and a part of the Amish church. Ex-communication isolates a member from the rest of the community, and very quickly forces a wayward member to beg forgiveness for his sins. Ex-communication forbids one from leaving one's home, except for the sole purpose of attending church. It forbids eating at the same table with other members of the church, or even working side by side with them. Finally, it forbids intimacy with one's spouse for the duration of the ex-communication.

The ministers returned from the Obrod and the services commenced. When the final song ended, Bishop Mast stated that all members of the congregation were to remain seated, while the young and un-baptized were excused. Then he stood and addressed the congregation.

"Today we have a fallen brother sitting among us. Deacon Rudy Koblenz has admitted to taking things too far in his stance against Maria Reader and the rest of the Youngie. His stance has greatly divided the community of Caroline Creek.

## Chapter Thirty-Two

His methods have worked for many generations, but times are changing. Many of the old methods no longer work, and as Bishop of this community, I will seek to find new methods to adapt to the changing times."

The silence was electric as all members clung to Bishop Mast's words.

Bishop Mast continued. "The four remaining ministers have unanimously voted to ex-communicate Deacon Koblenz from the Caroline Creek congregation."

Bishop Mast turned and faced Deacon Koblenz. "Deacon Koblenz," he said, speaking without emotion. "You are excused from this congregation until further notice."

Stunned, Deacon Koblenz rose. With head hanging, he took the dreaded walk of shame. Every eye followed him as he exited the house.

After he was gone, Bishop Mast continued. "The rules forbid you to visit or speak to Deacon Koblenz until he is accepted back as a member. In his absence, Raymond Byler will fill the role of deacon. After six months, if Deacon Koblenz is still not accepted back, I will move to have his spot permanently filled by someone else."

Bishop Mast's statement left no doubt as to his intentions. His actions had made it clear that he welcomed any and all votes that would assure Deacon Koblenz remained an outcast for a long time. A huge sigh of relief swept through the congregation as Bishop Mast dismissed the rest of the members.

---

Ruth Reader kept her outward emotions in check, but inside she rejoiced for the justice shown to her daughter. Any attempts at getting Maria to attend church had been met with stoic resistance. When her husband had demanded that she drop the topic Ruth had reluctantly obeyed.

Ruth tried to engage her husband in conversation during the buggy ride home, but Andy remained sullen and refused to speak.

As soon as the buggy stopped in front of the house, Ruth practically ran up the porch steps and started for the stairs. She burst into Maria's room, excited to tell her daughter the good news, but the room was empty.

Then she saw the note. It was folded in half to make it stand upright on top of Maria's dresser. With trembling fingers Ruth unfolded the note and read.

*Mam. I am so sorry, but I was never meant to be Amish. It has always felt like a lie. I will write in a few days.*

Across the bottom was scrawled, *Your rebellious daughter, Maria.*

The air went out of Ruth and a sob escaped her lips as she collapsed to the floor.

When Andy Reader entered the room fifteen minutes later, he found his wife sitting on the floor, her face as white as the note she clasped to her bosom. In her other hand she held one of Maria's dresses. As Andy watched she buried her nose in the fabric and breathed deeply, sobs shaking her body.

Andy watched from the doorway. His wife was weak, and he resented that. He clenched and unclenched his fists. He desperately wanted to beat her for her weakness, but he had a strong hunch she wouldn't even care. Maybe she would even welcome it right now. There were a million things he wanted to say, but he finally settled on, "You deserved this, you know. You taught her to be independent and stubborn, so don't sit there like a hypocrite and act all sad about how she turned out."

When his wife didn't respond, Andy shook his head in disgust, then turned away and left her sobbing on the floor.

# CHAPTER THIRTY-THREE

The rain spattered on the sidewalk in a relentless torrent, determined to dissuade those who would jog on such a miserable December evening.

Bruce had picked out a thin, black raincoat, and the hood was pulled close over his head. His sneakers pounded a steady rhythm on the sidewalk. A mile later, the pavement ended, and Bruce turned on to a path that followed the river. He ran with his head down and his shoulders forward, but his eyes scanned the path ahead.

Normally, Bruce did his best thinking in his office, but that always changed when it was raining. Staying indoors on a rainy day made him feel like a caged animal. Besides, there was something mystical about running in the rain. Nobody else ran in the rain, which meant that he had the world all to himself.

A heavy fog rolled in off the Missouri River. Bruce welcomed the extra blanket of coverage. In an hour it would be dark, which was even better. He was familiar with the route and preferred the darkness.

Bruce's mind turned to Eli Reader. What could he have done differently? Why hadn't he asked Eli more questions when he had the opportunity?

The person with the voice-changer had claimed that Bruce never had Eli, but that wasn't true. He had seen Eli himself. He had recognized Eli's face. He had talked to him.

Or had he? Had he asked Eli a single question that proved he was who he claimed to be?

Bruce didn't think he had. He had simply assumed the girl with the voice-changer was telling the truth when she directed him to the ranch house in New Mexico where he had picked up someone that he thought was Eli.

It had been two weeks since he had last heard from the voice-changer. Until now, Bruce had worked under the assumption that the girl was lying—that she was working for Shug, and that she had helped Shug get Eli back.

But those assumptions had gotten him nowhere. Shug had vanished from the Riverside Motel, and nobody knew if he was alive or dead.

He was nowhere closer to finding Eli. In fact, Bruce realized, since the incident at Hillbilly Harry's bunker, he had not made a single significant connection.

The path narrowed and curved sharply to the right. Twenty feet off the path was a fallen tree. If someone were waiting to ambush, the tree would be the perfect spot to hide behind.

Bruce left the path and veered left, passing the tree on the side. Nobody was behind the tree.

Bruce glanced at his watch. Twenty minutes to the office. He turned from the river and started up a muddy hill toward a connecting path.

*One way or another, the person using the voice-changer was lying*, he decided. First, she had told him he would find Eli on the mattress at the ranch house outside Shamrock. Then later, she had told him that he had never had Eli.

So, which was the truth? If he never had Eli, that meant he had brought a lookalike all the way back from New Mexico. And if that were true, that meant that the girl with the voice-changer and the lookalike were working together.

Bruce stopped running and leaned against a tree, suddenly overwhelmed with questions. *She, the girl with the voice-changer, and the lookalike, were trying to find Shug.* They must have

## Chapter Thirty-Three

suspected that Shug was following Bruce, and that Bruce would lead them to Shug.

*And now they have Eli.*

*Why? Are they protecting him?*

Once again, the answer jumped out.

*Shug wants Eli, and they are protecting Eli from Shug.*

Bruce stalled. He couldn't think of a single reason why two strangers from New Mexico would protect an Amish boy.

1311 East Fennimore Street loomed in front of him and Bruce reached into a pocket for his office key.

Something bothered him and he hesitated, his hand moving to his hidden holster.

Something that didn't belong.

His eyes moved to a white van parked across the street.

Where had he seen it before?

Bruce spun and crouched, the Glock flashing up in his hand. If they came for him now, they were making a mistake. He was ready.

# CHAPTER THIRTY-FOUR

Without taking his eyes off the van across the street, Bruce fumbled with his keys and tried to find the keyhole in the door behind him.

Someone got out of the passenger side of the van. The person didn't appear to be in a hurry, and certainly wasn't trying to hide their movements.

Bruce slowly rose from his crouching position and replaced the Glock. He waited warily.

The van pulled away from the curb and merged into traffic. The person now stood alone on the other side of the street, barely a silhouette in the gathering darkness. A gust of wind caught the black shawl and Bruce relaxed. That was it. It was the same van that had parked on the curb less than three weeks ago. It was the van that had brought the Readers to his office.

The traffic broke and the person crossed the street.

"Ruth," Bruce said, confused. "How long have you been waiting?"

"Maybe a half hour," Ruth smiled. "May I come in?"

Bruce held the door and she passed through. She shivered as she removed her coat and bonnet and hung them on the hooks behind the front door. The shawl stayed.

"You know that you are welcome to stop by anytime," Bruce said. "But why the late hour?"

Ruth nodded, but seemed uncertain how to respond.

Bruce flipped on the light and removed his raincoat. He took off his soaked sneakers and put them on the floor behind the door.

Ruth watched in silence.

## Chapter Thirty-Four

"Well come on, let's go upstairs," he said, waving his hand.

Ruth followed him up the stairs and sat down when Bruce pointed to a chair.

"What's going on?" Bruce asked, facing her.

Ruth's lip quivered. She scanned the room, as if searching for something.

"Where is she, Bruce?" she finally asked. "I have to see her."

"Who?" Bruce asked, knowing exactly who Ruth was referring to.

"My daughter. I miss her terribly," Ruth replied. "I know she has been here. I can feel it." Her dark brown eyes pleaded for answers.

Bruce wasn't sure how to answer the blunt question, so he said nothing.

"When Eli left," Ruth continued, "I kept setting the table for him. I would go to the door and call out for my lost child. I guess I thought maybe he could feel me calling, from wherever he was."

Ruth paused and her eyes moved to the floor. "Now Maria is gone, and I set the table for two empty seats."

Bruce felt a wave of sympathy for Ruth Reader. He walked to where she sat and gently patted her shoulder, although he still didn't know what to say.

"I just want to make sure Maria is alright," Ruth said. "Can I talk to her?"

Bruce could feel Ruth leaning against his leg and worried that she might start crying soon. Crying women made him uncomfortable, largely because he had never quite figured out how to react.

He quickly changed the topic. "Can I get you anything? Coffee? Water?"

"Do you have a bathroom?" Ruth asked, wiping at her face. "I'd like to freshen up a little."

Bruce pointed toward the bathroom. As soon as the door

closed behind her, he took out his cell phone and hastily sent a text message. While he waited for the response, he glanced around the office. The room was a mess.

When Ruth stepped out of the bathroom a few minutes later Bruce was sitting at his desk, pretending to be busy on the computer. The office was strangely quiet, except for some Fleetwood Mac music coming from the speakers of his computer.

Bruce expected the questions about Maria to continue but Ruth remained strangely quiet. After a while Bruce glanced around the edge of his computer monitor. The sight across the room made him catch his breath.

Ruth was moving silently to the music. Her arms were outstretched, and her eyes closed. She smiled as she swayed.

Fascinated, Bruce watched as Ruth transformed. The meek woman who had entered the bathroom a few minutes earlier now floated, her head tilted back, a look of pure joy spreading across her face.

Bruce felt like he was catching a glimpse into the most vulnerable of souls—a soul that had found complete peace within itself, a soul that, when left undisturbed and without judgment, had finally been set free in the words of a song.

Bruce suddenly felt guilty. He withdrew his head to its rightful position behind the computer monitor, but it refused to remain there. Unconsciously, it moved back out from that safe location and watched in awe as the magical transformation continued across the room.

A pale hand moved and undid the cap strings, and the cap fluttered to the floor. A few flicks from the same hand and rich, brown hair fell to the waist. Ruth's lips began to move softly with the music, and Bruce caught his breath. As she sang, it seemed like years of worry and sadness vanished from her face.

Bruce knew, in that moment, that he had never seen anything

## Chapter Thirty-Four

as beautiful or as graceful as the delicate figure gliding silently across the floor. His heart, long dead to the charms of a female, suddenly flooded with desire for the soft caress of a woman's touch. But as quickly as the thought came, Bruce tried to push it away. Sure, he admitted to himself, he had always felt strangely drawn to Ruth. And at times he had even thought she felt the same way about him.

Bruce found himself wondering how different life could have been. What if Ruth and he had acted on their instincts back when they first met; back when he had been investigating a strange story about a midwife who performed a C-section on Ruth at her home. Way back then when her husband was never around.

Well, Bruce decided, they would never know what could have been. Ruth belonged to someone else, and that settled that.

The chorus came, and Ruth stretched out her arms. She grasped the edges of her black shawl in each hand and extended it like outstretched wings. Slowly she spun to the music, floating, dipping, and gliding. The shawl rose and fell with her movements, now enveloping her, now spreading like wings again.

Ruth's lips moved and the words came alive.

*Lovers forever, face to face*
*My city your mountains, stay with me stay*

Bruce sat unmoving, completely entranced.

Then Ruth was gliding toward him. Her cheeks were flushed, and her lips were full. She leaned across the desk, inches from Bruce's face, and her warm, dark eyes drew him in further.

"Come dance with me," she whispered. "I haven't danced in such a long time."

Powerless, Bruce rose and took her hand.

Ruth wrapped an arm around his neck and placed a cheek

against his chest. Together they moved across the room, dipping and floating with the words. Outside the rain beat against the windows, keeping a rhythm to the swaying of their bodies. As if drawn by some invisible force, they moved through the open doorway and into the back room.

The song ended and a fast-talking salesman began to talk about used cars. With his foot Bruce pushed the door shut, and the salesman went away.

Ruth entwined a hand in Bruce's hair and pulled his head down until their lips met. Bruce found it impossible to resist. He placed an arm under her arched back and leaned her weight back against his strength. Bending over her flushed face he gently kissed her. Ruth leaned back and a soft purr escaped her lips.

Then as suddenly as the moment had begun, it ended. It ended because Ruth's body went rigid as she stared at something behind him.

Bruce turned to follow her eyes. They were frozen to his *Crazy Wall*.

"What is it?" Bruce asked, drawing his hand from her waist.

"That man," Ruth replied, her face pale with terror.

"Which one?"

"The one with the silvery hair," she gasped. "How do you know him?"

"Shug?" Bruce asked. He got up and walked to the wall. With his finger he tapped on Shug's photo.

Ruth nodded.

"This is the man that kidnapped Eli," Bruce said.

Ruth stared at Shug's photo, but struggled to find words to speak.

"How do you know Shug?" Bruce prodded.

"That man and my husband are friends," Ruth whispered, her eyes still fixed on Shug's face.

# CHAPTER THIRTY-FIVE

Susan answered on the first ring.

"'Sup, boss?" she asked.

"You're sure she wants to talk to her mother?" Bruce asked.

"Absolutely certain," Susan responded. "She wants to know if we can meet for dinner."

The arrangements were made, and Bruce hung up the phone. He had been surprised when Maria first called. He had tried to convince her to stay in the community, but Maria's arguments were persuasive. She had convinced him she would leave the community, whether he picked her up or not, so Bruce had reluctantly agreed.

He had discussed it with Susan, and the decision became easier. Susan had reasoned that St. Louis was no place for a young, vulnerable Amish girl to try and start a new life on her own, so Maria would move in with her and her children for a while.

Bruce had picked Maria up while her parents were in church. He had found it odd that Maria's biggest concern was that no one from the community could find out where she was going to stay. He smiled as he remembered the ride to St. Louis. Maria had insisted on listening to the radio. Country music was her choice. He was more of a Classic Rock guy, but he reluctantly changed the station.

By the time they arrived at Susan's house though, Bruce had a much better understanding of the suppressive authority the community had been forcing on Maria.

The place was a quiet pizza joint on the outskirts of Fairview Heights Illinois.

Bruce parked the Explorer and got out. When Ruth didn't move, he walked around and opened the passenger door. "Coming?" he asked.

Ruth remained in her seat, unmoving. Her hands clasped and unclasped in her lap.

"What's bothering you?" Bruce asked.

"I am so afraid I will say something wrong," Ruth replied.

"She is your daughter," Bruce said. "You will do fine."

Ruth shuddered. "But what if she hates me?"

"Look at me, Ruth." Bruce's voice was stern. "You are going to get out your seat and follow me through that door."

And with eyes downcast, Ruth obeyed.

---

Susan was seated at a table in the back of the room. Her three children were scattered between the table and the playroom area in the back.

Bruce did a double take when he saw Maria. He hadn't seen her since the day he dropped her off at Susan's place, and he hardly recognized her now.

Maria was wearing a new pair of blue jeans, a white button shirt, and black sneakers. The head covering was gone, and apparently her hair had been cut, because it barely reached her shoulders.

Maria sprang from her seat, a huge smile radiating her face. In a few bounds she crossed the room and threw her arms around her mother's neck.

Mother and daughter embraced inside the front door. Bruce stood awkwardly by and waited for them to finish, but when the

## Chapter Thirty-Five

women began to speak in German, he decided it best to leave them alone. He joined Susan at the table.

Susan nodded at the emotional scene. She picked up a napkin and wiped a tear. "Give them all the privacy they want," she said.

When Maria finally led her mother back to the table, Susan pretended to be wiping a child's mouth. She acted surprised when Maria spoke.

"Is… is it okay if we get our own table?" Maria asked hesitantly.

"Why, of course," Susan said quickly. She opened her purse and handed Maria a fifty-dollar bill. "Dinner is on me," she said.

Maria thanked her, then led her mother toward the counter to order food.

Bruce and Susan watched them go.

"How are you doing on money?" Bruce asked.

"Better than ever," Susan said proudly. "Maria is a wonderful babysitter, and she is much cheaper than the day-care center."

"Has Maria told you what her plans are once she gets a vehicle?" Bruce asked.

"She talks of cleaning houses."

Susan lifted a large slice of pizza to her mouth. She tried to act inconspicuous behind the slice but took a long look at Ruth and Maria at their table. "What I wouldn't give to listen in on that conversation right about now," she smiled.

Across the room Maria took a sip from her fountain drink and watched as Mam tried hers.

"Have you heard from Eli?" her mother asked.

Maria shook her head. "I have no idea where to start looking. St. Louis is so big."

"Do you need money?" Mam asked, reaching for her purse. "I don't have much, but…"

"Mam," Maria insisted. "Stop worrying about me. I'm doing fine. Really. Susan pays me money for watching her children."

Ruth nodded, a serious expression on her face.

"What is it?" Maria asked.

"I think you should know that Deacon Koblenz has been ex-communicated for how he treated you."

Maria nodded. "It doesn't matter anymore, Mam. I'm not going back," she replied. "I don't belong with the Amish. I belong here, where I don't have to feel guilty for who I am."

Her mother sighed deeply. "Actually," she said, choosing her words carefully, "I didn't come here to try and make you come home."

"You didn't?" Maria asked.

Ruth shook her head. "There is something I have to tell you," she said. "Something that I should have told you a long time ago."

"What?" Maria asked, putting her slice of pizza down and leaning forward.

Ruth's hand moved to her face, suddenly self-conscious. "Promise you will never repeat a word I tell you tonight?" she asked.

"I... I promise," Maria replied hesitantly.

Her mother lowered her voice. "Remember when I told you that I believe my children are being punished for my sins?"

Maria nodded, her appetite disappearing. "What did you do?" she asked.

"It was during Rumspringa," she began.

"You went on Rumspringa?" Maria asked incredulously.

Ruth nodded. "My parents didn't approve, but most of the Youngie went on Rumspringa back then, so they let me go."

Maria stared. "You ran away when you were with the Youngie?" she asked.

Ruth nodded. "Things were different back then. The community understood that teenagers needed to sow their wild oats before they can be expected to settle down and be good members of the church."

"Is that all?" Maria asked, a little relieved.

## Chapter Thirty-Five

Ruth shook her head.

"Tell me," Maria demanded.

"I took a job as a waitress," her mother said. "I met a man and we started dating."

"Andy?" Maria asked.

"No. Andy came later."

"Why are you telling me this?" Maria demanded.

"Because I got pregnant," Ruth said simply. "You are that man's child, Maria. Andy is not your father."

Maria stared, horrified.

Her mother didn't seem to notice. Her expression transformed from one of embarrassment to something more dreamy. "I loved him, Maria," she said. "I have often wondered what happened to him."

"What was his name?" Maria whispered hoarsely.

"I went through his wallet once," Ruth continued. "And I found his real name."

Ruth took a worn piece of paper from her purse. She studied it carefully, as if she might regret parting with the last piece of the man's existence. Then with a sigh she slid it across the table. "I want you to have it," she said. "Maybe one day you will want to meet your real father."

Maria stared at the note in shocked disbelief. "What happened to him?" she managed to ask.

"When I told him I was pregnant, he left me. He went back to his wife and children. I never saw him again."

"Did… did you know he had a family?" Maria asked, not sure she wanted to know the answer.

Ruth shook her head, but the dreamy expression stayed. "I thought we'd be together forever," she said. "I was so naïve back then."

Maria swallowed hard and tried to concentrate on the cold slice of pizza on the plate before her. She lost the battle and bolted for the bathroom. She found the toilet stall and, gripping the sides for support, vomited.

A calm peace seemed to have settled upon her mother when Maria came back to the table. The burden of a secret she had carried for so many years was finally lifted.

"Tell me the rest," Maria said. "Where does Andy fit in?"

"Andy and I left the Amish at about the same time," Ruth continued. "Andy had asked me out, but I wasn't interested in him. Then, around the same time that I got pregnant, Andy ran into some trouble with the law. The only way for him to stay out of jail was to go back to the community. The timing worked out well for us. If you think about it, we deserved each other, really."

"Andy has never loved you," Maria snapped. "Why did you ever agree to marry him?"

The accusations brought Ruth back to the present. "I had no choice," she said softly. "I had tried life in the outside world and failed miserably. I was done with Rumspringa. But imagine the scandal if I came home single and pregnant. So, Andy agreed to marry me and keep my secret. In exchange, I would never tell the community that the law was looking for him."

"Was I born Amish?" Maria asked.

"You were," her mother answered. "Andy and I joined the Amish church and got married. You were born six months later."

"And Eli?" Maria asked tensely.

"My husband is Eli's father," Ruth said, a little too defensively.

"How?" Maria asked. "You and Andy didn't love each other."

Ruth thought about the question for a moment.

"For the first few years of our marriage I worked really hard to make Andy love me," she said. "I wanted a happy marriage. I wanted to move on from my past. And despite what you may think, I actually love him."

"That's why Andy never wanted me to call him father," Maria stated.

## Chapter Thirty-Five

Ruth nodded shamefully. "I'm so sorry, Maria," she said. "But you had to know."

From their table, Bruce and Susan watched the conversation in the corner. Not long after Maria's return from the bathroom, mother and daughter rose and walked back to Bruce and Susan's table.

It was after eleven o'clock when everyone said their goodbyes. The two youngest children were asleep, and Susan and Maria carried them to the car and buckled them into their car seats.

Mother and daughter shared another long hug before Maria got into Susan's car and they drove off.

"Where to now?" Bruce asked, turning back to Ruth.

"Take me home," Ruth said. "It's been a very difficult evening."

The ride to Caroline Creek would take forty-five minutes, so Bruce decided he would revisit the earlier conversation about Shug. Ruth seemed to be in deep thought, so he approached the topic carefully.

"How often does Shug come out to your place?" he asked.

"Who?"

"Shug. The man you recognized on my wall."

"Oh. Him," Ruth said, suddenly drawn back to the present moment. "He doesn't come around anymore. Actually, it's been many years."

"Well, you had a strong reaction to his photo," Bruce persisted.

Ruth pondered this for a moment. "Do you remember how you and I first met?" she asked.

"Of course," Bruce said. "At the hospital right after Eli was born."

"That's right. Your police department was called because things went wrong with the delivery at home."

Bruce nodded. Go on.

"That man on your wall," Ruth continued. "He is the one that brought the midwife."

"Shug?" Bruce asked in disbelief.

Ruth nodded. "Some memories came back to me when I saw his photo. Memories that could have been dreams, but I don't think so. I think they are memories of when I was under the anesthesia."

"Like what?" Bruce pried.

"I remember the midwife was crying and saying that she didn't want to do it, but he threatened her with a gun."

"Why?" Bruce asked. "What was so important about Eli's birth that Shug needed to be there?"

Ruth shrugged. "Eli was such a beautiful baby, and I just kinda pushed that night out of my mind. But I have always wondered what happened with that midwife. She never came back to check on me."

"Why would a man like Shug possibly want to be involved in the birth of your child?" Bruce asked.

Ruth shrugged. "I have no idea," she said. "I only know that I want my son back."

Bruce's mind flashed to several possible scenarios. *What terrible things could a man like Shug do to a newborn baby while the mother was under anesthesia? Was he involved in some larger government operation—one where they implanted chips into newborns—or where they performed any number of other tests that could never be traced?*

*Or was it possible that Shug had an interest in Eli for some other reason?* Bruce knew he had to approach the topic carefully.

They drove in silence for a few miles, then Bruce cleared his throat. "Ruth," he said, "I have to ask a difficult question."

Ruth nodded, but seemed to be only half listening.

"Did you and Shug ever… did you ever, you know…"

"Sleep together?" Ruth asked, turning back from the passenger window.

## Chapter Thirty-Five

Bruce nodded. "It could make sense. Maybe he thinks he is Eli's father…"

"Absolutely not," Ruth said, the color coming back into her face.

"Okay," Bruce said. "I had to ask."

Ruth shrugged. "My husband is Eli's father," she said, for the second time that night.

"Speaking of your husband," Bruce said, happy to change the subject. "Will he be mad when you get home?"

"My husband tells me I disgust him," Ruth responded matter-of-factly. "Once you hear those words from a spouse's mouth, something inside of you dies. You stop caring about details, like what kind of mood he is in."

They drove the rest of the way in silence.

———— ♦ ————

It was just after midnight when Bruce turned onto Caroline Creek Road and started back toward St. Louis. He glanced at the time on his watch. It would be two hours earlier on the west coast. He decided he had to try. He picked up his cell phone and scrolled through the contacts.

"Hello," the voice on the other end answered.

"Hello to you," Bruce said.

"Why are you calling this number?" the woman asked angrily.

"Is she still awake?" Bruce asked. "I am really missing her tonight."

"She has been asleep for over an hour," the woman said, fighting to keep her voice low. "She has school tomorrow."

"Can you wake her up, please?" Bruce asked, suddenly feeling very tired. He pinched the bridge of his nose and waited for the answer he knew would come.

"She doesn't remember you anymore," the woman stated flatly. "She calls someone else father now."

"Please?" Bruce said. "I just want to hear her voice one more time."

"Do not call this number again," the woman hissed.

There was a click and the connection went dead.

# CHAPTER THIRTY-SIX

Bruce took a drag from his pipe and flipped to the sports section of the newspaper. Footsteps sounded on the stairs, and he reached for the gun holstered beneath his desk drawer. The door opened and Maria Reader marched confidently into his office and sat down in a chair across from Bruce's desk.

"Good morning," Bruce said. "What can I do for you?"

"I'm here to help find my brother," Maria stated firmly.

"You don't say," Bruce replied, removing his legs from the desktop. He waved at Susan, who had followed Maria up the stairs and was now mouthing apologies from the doorway. Susan nodded and disappeared back down the stairs.

"I know Eli better than anyone else," Maria insisted. "If we work together, we will find him."

"I think I'm beginning to understand why you ran into some problems in the Amish community," Bruce chuckled. He folded the newspaper and placed it on his desk, took another long pull from his pipe and studied Maria carefully.

"This particular investigation comes with a certain amount of risk," he said. "It seems like everyone who gets involved either disappears or dies."

"Show me," Maria demanded.

Bruce nodded thoughtfully. "Okay," he said. "I believe I could use a fresh perspective. Follow me."

They walked to the back room and Bruce pointed to the *Crazy Wall*. "Well, let's see," he said. "Missing are Eli and Summer. Dead? We don't know yet. Then there was a guy at the hospital in Shamrock who was knifed to death. And let's not forget Hillbilly

Harry, who was murdered in his own bunker. And later that night, two more men died up around Hermann."

Maria stared at the *Crazy Wall* in disbelief as Bruce pointed and connected scenes and events.

"Do you want me to continue?" Bruce asked.

Maria nodded, but she seemed a little less certain.

"Then there was the bombing at the *Thirsty Toad,*" Bruce said, pointing to a newspaper clipping that had a photo of the restaurant. "One dead."

Bruce traced a piece of yarn from the newspaper clipping to the photo of Shug. "Have you ever seen this man?" he asked.

Maria shook her head.

"Well, all of the murders are connected to him in some way or another. Do you want to hear more?"

Maria nodded.

"Shug is still at large," Bruce continued. "And at this very moment he could easily be sitting across the street with a gun pointed right at the front door of this building."

"But… I just came through that door," Maria said, horrified.

"Exactly," Bruce said. "So, now that you know the stakes, do you still want to help me look for your brother?"

"Do you think he has Eli?" Maria asked, pointing at Shug's photo.

"I really don't know," Bruce said. "But if he doesn't, he's made it clear that he intends to find him."

"Then I want to help," Maria stated firmly. "Where do we start?"

Bruce chuckled. "I like your style," he said. "Pull up that chair, I'll fill you in."

Maria brought the chair and sat down.

Bruce started over, explaining each connection on the *Crazy Wall* in detail. The presentation lasted for almost an hour.

When Bruce finished, Maria walked to the wall. She waved

## Chapter Thirty-Six

her hand across the photos and newspaper clippings. "Okay," she said. "So how does it all connect?"

Bruce took a deep breath and began. "I'll start with the 'why'," he said. "It starts with power. History tells us that anyone with any amount of ego, wants power. All you have to do is look at the Amish preachers in Caroline Creek to figure out I'm telling the truth."

Maria nodded but didn't speak.

"And Shug is no exception," Bruce continued. "Shug is one of the Trontelli mob's top guys. But I don't think that's good enough for him. He wants to be number one. In fact, he will go to any length to get there, even if it means murdering anyone who stands in his way."

Maria nodded. "I know a few people like that," she said.

Bruce continued. "Now let's focus on the 'how.' How will Shug get to that top spot? Well, Old Man Trontelli is going die of old age one of these days, so that leaves Joey, his only son. But Joey isn't going anywhere fast. He's too reckless. He's been in jail once, and with any amount of luck, will go back again real soon. So, what does Shug do? He decides to speed up the process by double-crossing Joey. The idea is to catch Joey committing a serious crime, then when Joey goes to jail, Shug is the only one left."

"Why not just kill Joey?" Maria asked.

"That would raise too many questions," Bruce responded. "The Trontellis have casinos and night clubs that stretch all the way to the Gulf of Mexico. And they have a guy like Shug that runs operations in each town along the way. If the old man or Joey gets murdered, those guys will come to St. Louis asking a lot of questions. But if Joey goes back to jail, nobody will ask too many questions. Shug moves into the top spot and inherits the wealth and power."

Maria nodded and Bruce continued.

"Two months ago, Joey Trontelli murdered an FBI informant. The murder was secretly filmed by one of Shug's men. That same evening Shug and the witness held a meeting with a judge, an FBI agent, and a cop. I have an inside source that says everyone in that room actually saw the recording of the murder."

"Two months ago?" Maria asked. "And Joey is still not in jail?"

"Nobody seems to know the answer to that," Bruce replied. "But I think it starts with Shug's witness. I think he disappeared."

"So how does all this connect to my brother?" Maria asked.

Bruce continued. "Well, so far I've been giving you facts. I've been giving you bits and pieces of information I figured out on my own, or information that came through my source. Now, I will run a few ideas by you that are completely speculative."

Maria leaned back and waited.

"So, check this out," Bruce continued. "The murder happened less than five miles from your farm. Two days after the murder your brother Eli gets kidnapped. By Shug, or by his people. Shug only admitted that to me in the bunker because he thought I was going to die anyway."

Maria shook her head. "You're hinting that my brother was somehow involved in the murder of the FBI informant. But I will never believe it. Not even for a minute. I can see how the evidence points in that direction, but you don't know Eli. He is way too timid to get involved in anything like that."

"I'm not saying Eli was the person who filmed the murder for Shug," Bruce said. "But could Eli have accidently witnessed the murder? Like, is it possible that Eli was in town that day and was simply in the wrong place at the wrong time?"

Maria pondered this for a long minute. Finally, she spoke. "My brother isn't the witness," she said. "I can be sure of that only because I probably know Eli better than he knows himself. Eli was at home on the farm for two more days after the murder

## Chapter Thirty-Six

happened and before he was kidnapped. I remember having a dozen conversations with Eli in those two days. He would have told me if he saw something that terrible. At the very least, I would have been able to tell that something was wrong."

Bruce nodded slowly, his rationale slowly unraveling.

Maria continued. "You've worked this from the angle that Eli must have been there, right?"

Bruce nodded again.

"Now let's work it from a different angle," Maria said. "Let's assume that there wasn't even a witness at all. Let's assume that the only other person at the murder was the person doing the filming. Let's assume that after he got done filming, he disappeared with the film. Don't people in gangs cross each other like that all the time?"

Bruce nodded. "Go on," he said.

"What if Shug panicked when the filmer disappeared? Didn't you say that Shug needed that guy and the video evidence for the trial? So, maybe Shug sent his men back to the area to search for the missing man and the film?"

"I don't think I'm following," Bruce said.

"What if Eli and the filmer looked alike? Don't you see, Bruce? What if my brother is simply a case of misidentification?"

Bruce nodded slowly. "Only one problem though," he said. "How would Shug and his men know whether or not Eli looks like the filmer?"

Maria shrugged helplessly, then changed the subject. "Your old partner?" she asked, pointing at the photo of Stan Prater on the *Crazy Wall*.

Bruce nodded, making the connection slowly. "That's right. Stan came out to Caroline Creek with me a few times. That's how you know he is my old partner?"

"Do you visit him much at the hospital?" Maria asked.

"Not often enough," Bruce said. "I've been twice since he regained consciousness."

"Can we go today?" Maria asked. "I want to see him."

"Something on your mind?"

"You guys worked together for years, right?"

Bruce nodded.

"Do you still trust him?"

Bruce nodded again.

"Maybe he will think of something we missed."

Bruce nodded for the third time. "Am I going to have to listen to country music on the way there?" he asked.

"Of course," Maria laughed.

"I hate country music," Bruce replied. "With time, I'll teach you about real music. Bruce Springsteen. Pink Floyd. The real stuff that resurrects the soul."

"Never," Maria stated flatly.

# CHAPTER THIRTY-SEVEN

The two officers posted outside Stan Prater's room were clearly bored with their assignments. The first was lounging in the waiting room across the hallway. He had his back turned to Stan's room and was watching a sports channel on TV.

The second sat in a chair in the hallway outside Stan's room. He glanced up from his cell phone and acknowledged Bruce, then waved them into the room.

Stan was sitting up in bed. He had a tray of food in his lap. Bruce stooped and gave him a quick hug. "I brought company," he said. "Meet Maria Reader."

Stan stuck out his hand.

"Stan Prater," he said. "But you can call me Stumpy." He laughed and waved a hand at the flat spots where his legs should have been. "See?" he said.

"I'm sorry about your accident," Maria said, not laughing.

"Aww hell," Stan joked. "The good news is, I finally managed to lose some weight. About ten pounds per leg, actually."

"That joke is getting old," Bruce chuckled. "Stan, do you remember Maria?"

Stan studied Maria's face for a long moment, frowning.

"Well I'll be god dammed," he finally exclaimed. "You are the little Reader girl." He shot a glance in Bruce's direction. "You recruiting them out of the community now?" he joked.

Bruce shook his head and smiled at Stan's attempt at humor. "Maria and I have a few new ideas. Wanna hear them?"

Stan picked up his tray of food and took a bite. "Please. Fill me in," he said.

Bruce recounted the conversation he and Maria had had earlier.

Stan listened intently until Bruce finished. "You know what your next step is, right?" he asked.

"Actually, I'm kinda stuck," Bruce admitted. "That's the reason we're here. Maria thought you might have some ideas."

"I can only think of one thing," Stan said. "And it seems pretty flimsy."

Bruce nodded for Stan to continue.

"Go back to Shamrock and talk to the nurse at the hospital. The one that told Eli to get out. Obviously, she knows something."

"I've considered that," Bruce began. "But there is a lot of confusion around that hospital. And the person I brought back. Who knows if there even was a nurse?"

"All the same, you have to follow up on it," Stan repeated. "Right now, it's all you have."

Bruce nodded reluctantly and shot a glance in Maria's direction. "Ever been to New Mexico?" he asked.

"No."

"Wanna go?"

"Sure."

A nurse entered the room and stated that it was time for Stan's daily sponge bath.

Bruce and Maria bid Stan farewell with promises to return soon. They left the room to the sound of Stan making some lame joke about the nurse saving time because at least she didn't have to wash his legs.

———•◆•———

After Bruce and Maria left, Stan Prater lay back on the hospital bed and closed his eyes. He tried to connect a few of

## Chapter Thirty-Seven

the details Bruce had told him, but his mind kept drifting, and he found it more and more difficult to focus. For two days he had managed to resist the liquid temptation his wife had slipped into the hospital for him.

But ever since Rebekah had finally caved, a battle of wills raged within him. It was almost as if two little demons were sitting on the headboard above him, each making their own personal cases for why he should open the bottle and have a taste.

For a while Stan fought the good fight. He tried to ignore the little demons, and he silently questioned where Jesus was in all this mess. *Wasn't Jesus supposed to be one of the two men on the headboard? Wasn't Jesus supposed to be the voice of reason that counter-balanced the voice of sin?*

Stan's hands shook as he reached for the bedside drawer. He held the object up to the light and studied the dark liquid inside the glass bottle. His mouth went dry and his breath began to come out in short, choppy gasps. His fingers trembled as he untwisted the cap.

*"If you hadn't been drunk you might have noticed the bomb,"* said the demon on the right.

"Yeah," said the other demon. *"And you'd still have your legs. But it's too late now. You're damaged for life. You're no good to anyone. Not even your family. Go on, drink it. It's what anyone else in your... uhum... stumps would do."*

Both demons cackled together.

Stan tried to block out the voices. He lifted the bottle to his nose and sniffed. His mouth, previously as dry as a plastic bag of cotton balls, instantly salivated.

*"Do it,"* said the demon on the left.

Stan tilted the bottle and counted as two tiny drops of the precious liquid fell into the bottle cap.

The demons went silent. Possibly because they realized the battle had already been won.

Stan stuck his tongue into the bottle cap. The intense flavor of liquor hit his taste glands and in one second his entire body went nauseous.

*"Atta boy,"* both demons praised him.

This time both voices were so clear that Stan jolted and glanced up at the headboard. But the demons had vanished, their work done.

The moment of hesitation gave Stan the strength he needed. Quickly, before he could change his mind, he screwed the bottle cap back on. He rolled over onto his stomach and leaned over the edge of the bed. For a moment he pondered his next move. If he shoved the bottle across the room, toward the farthest point from the bed, he would have to see it every time he looked toward the door. Maybe he could resist the temptation of the liquid for a few hours, but sometime after midnight, about the time the rest of the world was sound asleep, his resolve would weaken. He would crawl out of bed, dragging his new bandaged leg stumps, and he would crawl to the bottle. He would finish it in a few swigs. And the numbness would come. For a few hours at least, he would be able to drown out the demons and the questions he had about his future. For a few hours he could avoid the issue of how he would support his wife and children without legs.

But what then? What came after the first bottle of alcohol was consumed? Was it back to the same drunk he had been before the bomb exploded? Or worse, would he eventually drink himself to death?

No, he would not leave the bottle where he could see it. Shuddering, Stan flipped his wrist and the bottle flew back beneath the bed. He breathed easy when he heard it smack against the back wall. Now, even if he desperately wanted to reach it, he would never be able to drag himself in underneath the narrow space.

Stan rolled over and faced the wall. Silent tears trickled into the soft pillow as slowly the light in the room faded to dusk, and then complete darkness.

# CHAPTER THIRTY-EIGHT

The ambulance backed up to the emergency doors of the Navajo Regional Medical Clinic. The rear door opened, and two paramedics rolled a stretcher out onto the asphalt. They moved through the double doors and started across the lobby.

The patient on the stretcher didn't move.

The procession entered an elevator and climbed one floor. Then the doors of the elevator opened, and the stretcher was wheeled into a room. Very carefully, the new patient was lifted from the stretcher and placed onto the bed.

A nurse entered the room, was updated on the injuries, and the paramedics left. The nurse took the patient's blood pressure and wrote something on a chart.

Twenty minutes later Doctor Alan Toshibi entered. The nurse handed him the chart and he mumbled to himself as he read the report. "Subject found unresponsive in the parking lot behind the Shamrock Public Library. Vital signs okay. Paramedics managed to revive subject, who claimed to have received blunt force trauma to the back of the head. Paramedics were unable to locate any external damage but can't rule out an internal brain injury."

Dr Al leaned in close and checked the patient's pulse. He turned to the nurse. "What's her name? It's not listed on the chart."

"There was no identification," the nurse explained.

Dr Al scratched his head, puzzled. He turned to leave the room. "Keep a close eye on her," he said over his shoulder. The nurse nodded, then followed him out the door and closed it softly behind her.

After the nurse left, a slow smile spread across Maria Reader's face. She opened her eyes and sat up in bed, her hand going to the back of her head. There was no injury, of course, but after all the prodding the paramedics had done, she had almost begun to imagine one existed.

Maria glanced at the clock on the bedside table. The time showed 11:17 a.m., which coincided almost exactly with the time Eli had been admitted to this very same hospital.

Like Eli, Maria was brought in with an unexplained head injury. An injury that almost guaranteed that she would be placed in the same unit as Eli had been, and that she would meet the same doctors and nurses Eli had met.

The plan hadn't taken much effort. During the drive to New Mexico, Bruce and Maria had discussed the best possibility of meeting Nurse Beth. Bruce had quickly ruled out the idea of entering the hospital and simply asking for her. Without a badge or search warrant, he thought the possibility of garnering unwanted suspicion was pretty high. Especially since there had recently been a murder at the hospital.

They had moved on to the next plan. Since Bruce had only a vague idea of how the nurse looked, they had to rule out the possibility of waiting outside the hospital for her to get off work.

The idea of faking a head injury that placed her in Nurse Beth's unit had been Maria's.

———— ♦ ————

While Maria lay in the hospital bed and played her part, Bruce sat in the hotel room and waited. This, he knew, would be the most difficult part. He flipped through the local channels on cable TV and wondered how Maria's plan was working. *Had he put too much faith in her?*

## Chapter Thirty-Eight

At eleven o' clock Bruce began to nod off. He flipped off the lights and turned off the TV.

He had been dozing for only a few moments when a light tap sounded at the door. Bruce reached for his Glock, but before he could get out of bed, he heard the spare key card slide in its slot. The door swung open and Maria entered the room. She was followed by a woman in a nurse's uniform.

The woman appeared to be in her mid-fifties. She had broad shoulders and thick arms, and her hair was put up in a tight bun. She seemed startled to see Bruce.

"Nurse Beth?" Bruce asked, rising from the bed.

The nurse hesitated and took a distrusting step backward toward the door.

"What is this?" she demanded. "Maria, you didn't tell me there was a second person."

Maria moved between the nurse and the door, then pointed to the bed opposite Bruce. "Please sit there," she said firmly.

The nurse glanced at the door and seemed to weigh the odds of escaping.

Bruce took a slow step toward the nurse and extended his hand. "It's okay, you can trust me," he said. "I'm Detective Bruce Ellsworth."

"Benesha Mitshun," the nurse said, reluctantly shaking Bruce's hand.

"You are not a hostage here," Bruce continued. "You are free to leave anytime you want, okay?"

The nurse nodded. "What do you want with me?" she asked hesitantly.

"We have some questions about a boy whom you recently helped to escape from your hospital," Bruce said.

"Eli?" the nurse asked.

Bruce nodded. "Who warned you that Eli was in danger?"

"Someone called my cell phone," the nurse said. "They told me I must get Eli out fast."

"Who called you?" Bruce asked.

The nurse shook her head and looked at the floor. "I don't know," she said.

"I don't believe you," Bruce said decidedly. "How often do you scare your patients into running from the hospital because some stranger called your phone and told you to?"

The nurse shrugged. "Is Eli alive?" she asked cautiously.

"I don't know the answer to that," Bruce replied, his frustration rising. "Eli is missing, and we drove a long way because we hoped you might help us find him."

The nurse shuddered but didn't answer.

"Was the voice on the phone a man or a woman?" Bruce asked.

"A woman."

"A girl with a black ponytail?" Bruce muttered under his breath.

The nurse nodded cautiously, then caught herself and stopped abruptly.

"Where can I find that girl?" Bruce asked.

"I don't think she wants to be found," the nurse replied. "If she wants something from me, she calls. That's all I can tell you."

"We are on the same side here," Bruce said, stepping closer. "We are here to help Eli, just the same way you tried to help him. Where is he?"

The nurse shrank back and turned toward the door. She stopped when she saw Maria still blocking her escape. "Can I go now?" she asked shakily. "You promised."

Bruce nodded reluctantly. "Can you do me one favor before you leave?" he asked.

The nurse nodded.

"Take my phone number. Please call me if you remember anything else."

## Chapter Thirty-Eight

The nurse took her phone from her purse and Bruce recited his number. She keyed it into her cell. Then she stepped gingerly past Maria, avoiding eye contact. The door closed behind her.

"I can't believe you let her just walk out that door," Maria snapped. "She was lying, and we both know it."

For a long time, Bruce and Maria sat silent and defeated, too exhausted to speak. Neither felt like going to bed. There was unfinished business, but they didn't know how to finish it. Then Bruce's cell phone rang, startling them both.

Bruce didn't have to check the caller ID. Somehow, he knew without checking, who would be on the other end.

"Didn't I tell you to walk away?" the voice-changer asked.

"As long as Eli Reader is missing, I will keep looking for him," Bruce replied firmly.

"I can help you with that."

"What's the catch?" Bruce asked.

"No catch. I tried to kill Shug, but failed, and now he's disappeared. If we are to find him again, we need to work together."

"I agree," Bruce said. "Let's meet. Just tell me when and where."

"You're in room 210. Step into the hallway and knock on door 212. There you will find what you've been looking for. And Bruce?"

"Yes," Bruce replied, rubbing his temple with his left thumb.

"You and I, and the people in 212, are all on the same side, okay?"

"What does that even mean?" Bruce asked.

"It means you need to keep your guns holstered," the voice said.

The phone went dead.

Bruce rose and moved quickly toward the door.

Maria watched expectantly, waiting for an explanation.

"Stay here," Bruce said firmly.

"Where are you…?" Maria started.

"I have to check on something," Bruce replied. "And it might not be safe for you to come with me."

Maria stared uncertainly at him, but Bruce avoided her eyes. Silently he stepped into the hallway and the door to 210 clicked as it locked behind him.

# CHAPTER THIRTY-NINE

The man who opened the door to 212 appeared to be in his late thirties. The man wore a pair of designer glasses and had dark brown hair and a well-trimmed beard of the same color. He was much shorter and slighter than Bruce.

Bruce relaxed, but kept the Glock inside his coat pocket trained on the man's chest. There was something familiar about the man, and it took a moment for Bruce to remember.

"You were at the *Dark Angel*," Bruce said. "You bumped into me as I was leaving the café."

"That's right," the man said with a nod of acknowledgment. "I'm Sparrow, and you can put your gun away. We're all on the same side here."

"Sparrow," Bruce said, a hint of irritation creeping into his voice. "I'll tell you what, Sparrow. I'm really tired right now. Mostly, I'm tired of fake names. First it was 'Shug', then it was 'the girl with the black ponytail', and now... 'Sparrow'? Let's cut the bullshit, shall we? What's your real name?"

"Call me what you'd like," Sparrow replied calmly. "But Sparrow is the only name I've ever had."

"Have it your way," Bruce said. "My name is Bruce Ellsworth."

Sparrow extended his hand and Bruce shook it.

"We've actually met twice," Sparrow said, taking a step back so Bruce could pass.

Bruce hesitated. His eyes moved past Sparrow and stopped at a second man who sat on a couch in the corner. For a second, he thought he was seeing ghosts. His brain was just beginning to make the connection when he heard a rustling noise in the hallway behind him. Maria ducked under his arm and sprang into the room.

"Eli," she cried, flinging her arms wide open.

Sparrow stepped aside and let her pass.

In a few bounds Maria was at the couch. She flung her arms tightly around her brother in a warm embrace.

Eli recoiled at Maria's touch and a bewildered expression came over his face. Bruce caught the confused look, and so did Sparrow.

"It's okay, Eli," Sparrow said. "She is a good person."

"What do you mean?" Maria demanded, taking a big step back. "What have you done to my brother?"

"It's the head injury," Sparrow explained patiently. "His memory comes and goes. Give him time, he might remember you."

Sparrow turned back to Bruce. "He needs surgery, and I need your help in scheduling it," he said.

Bruce stared but didn't move. Things were moving at a speed that was too fast for his brain to process.

"You coming in?" Sparrow asked.

Bruce nodded and stepped into the room.

Sparrow pointed to an empty chair at the table and Bruce sat down. He noted that the chair was warm and wondered who sat in it before he got there.

Sparrow closed and locked the door, then walked to the table and sat down facing Bruce.

"Who do you work for?" Bruce asked.

"I was one of Shug's men before," Sparrow replied.

"And now?"

"I am working with the person who uses the voice-changer."

"Is she here?" Bruce asked.

"She doesn't want to be found."

Bruce nodded, but his eyes scanned the room. Maria now sat on the couch next to Eli, and Bruce listened as she pleaded with

## Chapter Thirty-Nine

her brother to try and remember something. The happy reunion Maria had so long anticipated was joyless because her brother was unable to comprehend who the talkative stranger was who sat beside him.

Bruce turned back to Sparrow. "I have questions," he said.

"I'll answer a few," Sparrow replied. "But this meeting isn't going to turn into a history lesson. Shug is alive and free, which means none of us are safe."

Bruce ignored him. "Where else have we met?" he asked.

"I was the man you picked up at the ranch house a few miles outside Shamrock. You thought you were picking up Eli, but I swapped places with Eli before you got to the farmhouse. And I was the man you drove all the way back to Missouri and into Shug's trap."

Bruce laughed dryly. "You think I'm a fool?" he asked. "I remember faces. It's a gift. And believe me, you're not that person."

"I am exactly that man," Sparrow stated flatly.

"Impossible," Bruce said. "That person was half your age."

"I have a gift as well," Sparrow replied evenly. "Mine is deceit. Or misdirection, if you like that word better. You needed to see a young person in a cast, so that's what I showed you."

Bruce stared at Sparrow's face. He tried to recall the details of the person on the mattress in the ranch house. He thought Sparrow's figure was about the same size, but there the similarities ended.

"You are a professional disguise artist?" Bruce asked.

"I'll make it easy for you," Sparrow said. "Ask me something about the return trip that only you and the person in the cast would know."

Bruce sat back in his chair and took a deep breath. In his mind, he retraced the trip. He had been exhausted in Amarillo, but could he possibly have been that careless?

"In the motel room in Amarillo," Bruce said out loud. "Which bed did I sleep in?"

"You didn't," Sparrow said. "You slept on the floor, fully dressed."

Bruce stared.

Sparrow nodded. He removed his glasses and with his thumb and index finger, began to remove the contact lenses. In two seconds the dull, black eyes changed back into the eyes of the person Bruce remembered.

With trained hands that had gone through the motions thousands of times, Sparrow's fingers moved across his face. The facial hair came off next, and as if pulled by some invisible force, his middle-aged appearance disappeared. Finally, he removed the wig, followed by eyebrows and sideburns. Maria was the first to see it, and she gasped.

"It's him," she said weakly.

"Who?" Bruce asked.

"It's the man that looks like Eli," Maria said. "Remember my theory about a lookalike?"

Bruce's eyes moved from Sparrow's face to Eli, ten feet away on the couch. Maria was correct: the features were exactly identical.

"What is the meaning of this?" Bruce asked sharply, turning back to Sparrow.

"We are identical twins," Sparrow said simply. "Separated at birth by an evil man named Shug."

Bruce stared open-mouthed, unable to speak. Even as Sparrow's words began to sink in, Bruce knew them to be true. Somewhere beside him he heard a faint rustle as Maria sank weakly to the floor.

Without emotion, Sparrow glanced down at the ghostly face staring up at him from the floor. "Hello sister," he said. "I never expected our first meeting to be in a hotel room in New Mexico."

## CHAPTER FORTY

Maria sat on the hotel bed, her back against the headboard for support. Her face was pale and tight with tension. Finally, she found her voice. "How did this happen?" she managed weakly.

"I first learned the truth about a month ago," Sparrow replied. "Right after I filmed the murder."

"That's why you ran?" Bruce, who had been quicker to recover than Maria, asked. "You knew that after you testified at Joey Trontelli's trial, Shug would have you killed to tie up loose ends."

Sparrow nodded.

"So, when you ran…?" Bruce continued.

"When I ran, Shug became desperate. He had to replace me and there was only one other person on earth that could pass as me."

Bruce turned to Maria. "Do you believe this?" he asked.

Maria shook her head, dazed.

"There is one more thing that you should know," Sparrow continued.

"What?" Bruce asked.

"Someone inside the Amish community is helping Shug."

"Who?" Maria interrupted, suddenly coming to life.

"I'm not sure," Sparrow said. "Shug never meets him in person, but they have some secret method of communication that I haven't figured out."

"That's how Shug knew Mam was having twins," Maria stated. "Someone within the community told him."

"That brings up an even bigger question," Bruce said. "How did the accomplice know your mother was expecting twins, but your mother didn't?"

Maria pondered the question for a long moment. "The Amish bring in English midwives," she said finally. "The midwives use battery-operated ultrasound machines. And since the Amish aren't allowed to know the gender of their baby until it's born, the midwife would have discovered the twins, but never told Mam. That's also why they performed the C-section, instead of waiting for the natural birth. Mam never knew, because they knocked her out during the operation."

"So, your mother's midwife worked for Shug?" Bruce speculated.

For a while nobody spoke, each consumed with their own thoughts. Then Sparrow said. "We need to make sure this never happens again."

"You have a plan?" Bruce asked.

Sparrow nodded. "It begins with finding Shug. He does not deserve to live anymore."

"What's your plan?" Maria insisted.

"What does Shug want more than anything else right now?" Sparrow asked.

"Revenge," Bruce and Maria said at the same time.

Sparrow nodded in Eli's direction. "Exactly," he said. "Between Eli and me, we have ruined every single one of Shug's plans. Shug knows he will never find me, so that leaves Eli."

"We're not using Eli as bait," Maria snapped. "Can't you see that he's been through more than he can handle?"

"We won't use Eli," Sparrow said. "I'll go in his place."

# CHAPTER FORTY-ONE

A week after Bruce and Maria returned from New Mexico, a lone figure appeared at the south end of the Amish community. He walked north on the gravel shoulder of Caroline Creek Road, then hesitated at the end of the Reader driveway.

The figure wore a pair of faded denim pants, a blue button shirt, and a pair of boots. His left side was covered in a clumsy cast, and from a distance one might have noticed the blonde curls that protruded from beneath the tattered straw hat perched on top of his head.

The figure turned and walked up the Reader driveway. As soon as his feet touched the wood floor of the front porch, the screen door flew open and Ruth Reader rushed outside. She threw her arms around her long-lost son and they shared a long embrace.

Within hours the story spread to the far corners of Caroline Creek. The search for Eli Reader was over; the son many had wrongly accused of running away, had returned.

By noon, media outlets were picking up the story, and by the time people tuned in to the evening news, it was a national sensation.

What the media did not know was that a plan had been put in place to try and capture Shug, so the story they had received was only a variation of the actual truth.

Bruce Ellsworth, former Chief of Police, was credited as the hero in the story. The headlines broadcasted a story of a shootout that had left over a dozen dead. Ellsworth had single-handedly snatched the boy from the claws of the mob and had safely returned him home.

News anchors were quick to point out that the criminal responsible for Eli Reader's kidnapping was still on the loose. Shug was thought to be critically wounded, and the concerned news anchors warned that he was expected to be armed and extremely dangerous.

Bruce Ellsworth received two important phone calls before noon on Saturday. The first was from the mayor of Castleton. The mayor seemed uncomfortable in his attempts at small talk. Before long though, he got down to the real reason for his phone call. After a half-hearted apology about being too hasty when he fired Bruce several years earlier, the mayor offered Bruce his old job back as chief of police.

Bruce prolonged the mayor's misery by telling him that he would think on it. Then he hung up abruptly.

The second call came twenty minutes later. A TV show called *The Facts in 50 Minutes* wanted to do a segment on the bizarre events. The ratings on the story were high, and the network wanted to capitalize while it was hot. After dancing around the obvious for a while, it became apparent that the network was only interested in interviewing Eli Reader, and that anyone else involved was of only small interest.

Bruce said he would get back to them, then turned off his cell phone.

In Caroline Creek, Bishop Mast confirmed what everyone already knew: Eli Reader had made it safely home. He went on to explain that the man who had kidnapped Eli was still out there, and that until he was caught it was assumed that nobody in Caroline Creek was safe. The Amish religion, he explained, was under attack from the evils of the outside world.

Bishop Mast recited a telephone number that was to be called in case Shug was spotted in the community. When called, the number would activate an emergency alarm that would connect to both the Castleton Police Department and to Bruce Ellsworth.

## Chapter Forty-One

Fear swept through the congregation as Bishop Mast laid out the details. Parents hugged their children close and prayed that they would be spared from the clutches of such an evil man.

In closing, Bishop Mast forbade anyone from visiting Eli Reader, who was seriously injured and in need of rest and recovery.

After he finished the first part of the meeting, Bishop Mast excused the children. Since Deacon Koblenz was still ex-communicated, he rose to leave with the children, but Bishop Mast motioned for him to sit back down.

"An inexcusable thing has happened to our community," Bishop Mast began. "While we were focused on Maria Reader and a trifling disagreement she had with several of our elders, we allowed ourselves to become vulnerable to a much larger issue."

Deacon Koblenz squirmed and his neck turned red.

"I will accept most of the blame," Bishop Mast continued. "I was ordained to lead this church, and I failed. I allowed myself to be swayed by man instead of listening to the voice of God. But that will change, starting today. While it may be too late to bring Maria back, it is not too late to learn an important lesson in where we failed her."

The story Bishop Mast gave the congregation was a watered-down version of the truth. What he did not tell them was that the person at the Reader home was not Eli at all, but his twin. And he did not tell them about the abduction at birth, because such a thing could create a panic so horrific that the community might never recover.

Finally, Bishop Mast chose not to tell his congregation that he had spent much of the previous week in secret meetings with Bruce Ellsworth, Stan Prater, Chief Calvin Westbritt, and Ruth and Maria Reader.

The same watered-down story that Bishop Mast told his congregation was also intentionally leaked to the press. No one was told that Bruce Ellsworth had hired a retired Navy Seal, and that the armed agent was secreted somewhere on the Reader farm to provide protection, should the plan to draw out Shug work.

On Monday Bishop Mast called Bruce Ellsworth from a private line. He reported that he had fulfilled his part of the plan and that the entire community was now on the lookout for Shug. At the end of the brief conversation Bishop Mast asked the simple question.

"What more can we do?"

"Nothing," Bruce Ellsworth replied before hanging up the phone. "Now… the waiting begins."

# CHAPTER FORTY-TWO

The story of Eli's kidnapping was told and retold throughout the community. And with each telling, its legend grew. Somewhere around the middle of the first week, a particularly nasty rumor emerged; Shug was kidnapping children and eating them as a delicacy. He kept them in a cage and fatted them like a calf. And he skinned them alive before eating them.

The story quickly blossomed, and within a few days was being discussed as fact. Overnight, Caroline Creek found itself facing a terror completely foreign to them. Shug's name was whispered in undertones, as if saying it out loud might call him from the shadows.

Children began to have nightmares and parents dashed to their rooms, terror filling their sleepless eyes, fully expecting to see the madman disappearing through a window with a child under each arm.

School-aged children, who had previously walked to and from school alone, now had to be accompanied by an adult.

In her weekly article for *The Budget*, Mattie Borntrager gave her account of the events. She had personally visited Eli Reader, she lied, and she would readily testify that he had gone mad; that for over an hour she had tried to carry on a conversation with him, but the entire time he had looked right through her as if she were a glass window.

Mattie still held to the opinion that it was all the drugs and loose women that had ruined him, but softened her story a little by suggesting that Shug might have somehow taken Eli's soul, which would explain why he seemed like an empty shell.

An ambitious reporter from St. Louis found Mattie's article and suddenly the quiet Amish community became the hub of media frenzy. Dozens of reporters arrived daily, clamoring for a peek of Eli Reader. All were greeted by a burly security guard that magically appeared and denied them access.

Gradually, the reporters moved on to other stories, and the throngs of curious English passers-by diminished.

But the terror inside the community remained.

That winter cold and gloomy winds blew in off the Mississippi River. For much of the season a heavy fog hung over Caroline Creek, as if cloaking them and reminding them that a dark sin was being atoned for.

One day in early March, before the first rays of light were beginning to penetrate the early morning fog, a long, dark car crept up the Reader driveway. Bruce Ellsworth got out, opened the rear door, and Ruth Reader got in. With headlights off, the car crept back down the driveway, turned onto Caroline Creek Road and disappeared in the direction of St. Louis.

The same car came back three days later under the same cover of darkness. When Ruth Reader re-entered the farmhouse, the agent noted an extra spring to her step and a joyful smile on her face.

Eli's surgery had been a success. Before the surgery, he had not recognized his mother as she sat and held his hand. For hours she and Bruce had waited for the doctors to finish.

When Eli finally opened his eyes and latched his gaze on his mother's face, his words were slurred and almost incoherent, but they were words that would make his mother smile for a long time.

"You are the woman I see in my dreams," he had said. And for just a moment his mother saw a glimmer of recognition in her son's face, and she had broken down and sobbed for joy.

## Chapter Forty-Two

By late March it was apparent that the plan to lure Shug out of hiding wasn't going to work. The Navy Seal had other assignments but could stay for a few more weeks.

The agent occupied a room on the second floor of the farmhouse and spent much of his day reading newspapers and drinking coffee. He kept a detailed log of all activities and reported back to Bruce Ellsworth at his office.

His report on March 22nd went as follows:

*Feet on the floor at 0513.*

*Subject had coffee with Ruth while I cleared the barn.*

*Chores in barn completed by 0742, and subject re-entered house, where Ruth and subject had breakfast together.*

*At 1157 Maria Reader arrived in her new car and Ruth, Maria and subject had lunch.*

*Topics of discussion involved farm activities, Maria's life in St. Louis and the classes she is taking to try and get her GED.*

*At 1335 Maria left the house but stopped at the barn and visited with the animals before heading back to St. Louis. After she departed, subject announced he would begin plowing the north field.*

*Subject returned from field at 1737 and chores in barn commenced.*

*Subject turned in at 2115.*

---

That spring, the congregation voted on the matter of accepting Rudy Koblenz back into the church. The ministers made their rounds and bent down so they could clearly hear the whispered responses from the members. If the "nays" numbered more than three, Rudy Koblenz would not eligible for a new vote for another month.

As he stood before his congregation to announce the results, Bishop Mast was startled to see that the membership had shrunk by almost one third. The families that had moved out had stated various concerns. Some had reservations about the division on the minister bench and wished to live in a community with less conflict. Others were still miffed over the past treatment toward Maria. Mostly though, the families had moved out because of the terror they felt over the madman called Shug.

None of which helped Deacon Koblenz. When the votes were tallied, the "nays" reached forty-three.

———◆———

But finally, the snowscape of winter gave way to the blossoming green fields of spring, and the restlessness in Caroline Creek began to stabilize.

The school year ended, and the children worked side by side with their fathers in the fields and their mothers in the houses. The threat of the lurking madman was not forgotten, but other topics took prominence, and the subject was discussed less and less.

Spring in western Illinois brought rains and high winds. Caroline Creek swelled to the top of its banks and for a while there was concern that some of the lower farmlands would be flooded. With time however, the waters began to recede, and life in Caroline Creek returned to normal. Until one day it didn't.

# CHAPTER FORTY-THREE

The meeting was held in an old metal cow shed on the back of Bishop Mast's property. In one corner of the building was an old, dusty office with a single window that overlooked the Illinois River less than a quarter mile away.

Bishop Mast had arranged chairs around an old oak table. An oil lantern burned on the floor and a plastic five-gallon bucket was placed upside down over the lantern to curb the light, should any unwelcome eyes look on from the river.

When Bruce parked the Explorer, Sparrow slipped out of a side door and disappeared into the woods. From there he would guard the meeting against surprise intruders.

Stan Prater arrived next. His truck had been modified to accommodate a wheelchair.

Bruce and Maria watched from the window as Stan parked the truck and opened the driver door.

"Should we go help him?" Maria asked.

Bruce shook his head. "Stan is pretty serious about getting around on his own," he replied.

They watched as Stan pushed a button on the dash. A lift raised the wheelchair from the truck bed and placed it on the ground next to the driver's door. Stan easily slid from the driver's seat and into the wheelchair. He closed the truck door, then rolled the wheelchair toward the shed.

After everyone was inside, Bishop Mast locked the door. He pointed to the table and everyone sat down. Bruce opened the conversation.

"This meeting is to be kept secret. We were never here. Does everyone understand the conditions?"

Heads nodded around the table.

Bruce nodded at Stan.

Stan withdrew a yellow folder from a pouch on the side of his wheelchair. He removed two sheets of paper and placed them on the table. He smoothed them out and scanned each of them in turn, to make sure he had them arranged in the correct order.

"What I'm about to say won't be easy for any of you to hear," he said.

Nobody spoke, so he continued. "We found out who is feeding information to Shug, and as suspected, the source comes from inside your community."

Bishop Mast flinched.

Stan picked up the first sheet of paper and tapped it with his index finger. "Andy Reader," he said without looking up.

Ruth gasped. Her head sank into her hands. But as Stan continued to speak, she began to nod, as if somehow, she had suspected the awful truth all along.

Maria, who had been updated during the drive to the meeting, sat with fists clenched.

"We still don't know how Andy is communicating with Shug," Stan said. "We know he has a cell phone, but we've had it bugged for months, and we haven't intercepted a single phone call or text message between Shug and him."

Bishop Mast was a little slower to accept the truth. "Then how do you know it's him?" he managed to whisper.

"We fed him some false information," Stan said. "Then we waited to see if it would have a ripple effect. It did."

Bishop Mast and Ruth looked confused.

"We've had the Trontellis under surveillance for years. We know they are running a money laundering scam through some of their clubs, so we created a fake raid. One of our undercover agents met Andy at his favorite casino. Over drinks, our agent

## Chapter Forty-Three

befriended him. The agent pretended to be drunk and spilled all our plans."

"And it worked?" Bishop Mast asked.

"The nightclub closed its doors an hour before the raid was to happen. Of course, in order to keep our cover intact, we raided it anyway. But believe me, Andy tipped them off. The place was so clean we could have been looking at the inside of a church."

Bishop Mast nodded solemnly, satisfied. "But why is he helping them now?" he asked.

"Andy has a serious gambling problem," Stan said. "He owed a lot of money to a Trontelli casino that's run by Shug. Andy was given a choice; betray the community in order to even his debt, or die."

"You mean betray one of his own children?" Bishop Mast asked incredulously.

"It certainly looks that way," Prater said.

"But what does Shug want with an Amish baby?" Bishop Mast asked.

"Think about it," Prater said. "The mob is always looking for new members. Can you think of a better fit than someone who never existed? No records. No fingerprints. No DNA. Nothing. Shug can train the person to be whatever he wants him to be. And if he ever gets tired of him, he can kill him. And since he never existed... well, you get the picture."

Stan paused to catch his breath and Bruce continued. "Sparrow disappeared before the Trontelli trial could begin, and Shug was forced to kidnap Eli to replace him. The weird thing is, if Sparrow hadn't run, we might never have learned about any of this."

Nobody spoke, so Stan continued. "Sparrow is trained in deception and disguise. He can easily vanish, and even Shug has no idea how to find him. We have uncovered a plan where, after the Trontelli trial, Shug was going to send Sparrow into a top security facility to assassinate a very prominent government official."

"My son," Ruth gasped. "A murderer?"

"We are pretty sure that Shug is not working alone," Stan continued. "He is answering to someone who sits a lot higher than the Trontellis. Someone who would pay good money for a trained assassin who can't be traced."

"Who?" Bishop Mast asked.

"Let's just say that I ran out of clearance levels," Stan replied.

"Government?"

"That makes the most sense," Bruce interjected. "Political assassinations that can't be traced. Shug is the little man way down the line who trains and produces the assassin. The man at the top looks the other way."

There was complete silence around the table as the news was processed. Ruth's shoulders shook, and Maria put an arm around her and squeezed to try and calm her mother.

Stan Prater put the sheets of paper back into his folder and nodded at Bruce.

"I'm pulling my agent tomorrow," Bruce said. "We're going to try a new plan."

Bishop Mast nodded. "What's the plan?" he asked.

Bruce took the long way around to answer the question. "Well, we've tried to draw Shug out by dangling vengeance in front of him. That didn't work."

"You scared him off?" Bishop Mast asked.

"I don't think that's what happened," Bruce said. "Shug doesn't scare easily. I think we've been looking at this thing wrong from the start. I think there is something that Shug wants even more than revenge."

Nobody spoke, so Bruce continued. "Shug went to a lot of risk to kidnap an Amish baby, raise it, and train it. That took care-

## Chapter Forty-Three

ful planning and patience. But just about the time that baby was a highly trained assassin, he disappeared, which ruined everything for Shug."

"What are you suggesting?" Bishop Mast asked.

"I think Shug would go to great lengths to repeat the process all over again," Bruce said. "He got away with it the first time, so what's to stop him from bringing in a midwife and going through another baby kidnapping?"

Bishop Mast nodded, following Bruce's words slowly. "How can we help?" he asked hesitantly.

"We are going to use Andy to get to Shug," Bruce replied.

Bishop Mast thought about this for a moment. "It won't work," he said finally.

"Go on," Bruce prodded.

"Well," Bishop Mast said, "you guys are cops. So Andy knows you won't kill him. But Shug certainly will if Andy doesn't do exactly what he wants."

"You are correct," Bruce replied. "Andy definitely fears Shug more than he fears any of us. But I'm going to change all that."

"What will happen to him?" Ruth whispered.

"We will need your help," Bruce replied, looking directly into Ruth's eyes. "That's why you are here."

Ruth cringed. "I don't think I can do it," she said. "My husband and I have been through too much together."

"Mam," Maria said, speaking gently. "If this plan works, it will bring Eli home for good."

Ruth's face was pale and drawn. "What do I have to do?" she asked.

Bruce nodded for Maria to continue. "This part was your idea," he said.

"Sadie and John are expecting their baby soon, right?" Maria asked.

Ruth nodded.

"You are going to tell Andy that John and Sadie are expecting twins," Maria said. "Bruce and Stan will take care of the rest."

# CHAPTER FORTY-FOUR

Andy Reader tapped the shaver against the edge of the stainless-steel bowl and swirled it in the warm water, trying to remove the last of the stubble from the blades. Through the window he scanned the front yard. He frowned. The English driver was late. He picked up a hand towel and dried his face.

Bishop Mast could have his community, for all Andy cared. Bishop Mast could have the strict rules, and he could have the hypocritical churchgoers. Heck, he could have the Reader farm, his wife, and even Sparrow, the son he barely knew.

The Amish way of life, which Andy had loathed ever since he could remember, was over. Andy's luck had changed less than two weeks ago when Shug first heard about the young mother who was expecting twins. If Andy could deliver, Shug had promised that old transgressions would be buried. The judge's order to have Andy arrested if he ever again set foot outside the Amish community was going to be lifted. And Andy had only Shug to thank for having friends in such high places.

Andy reflected back on the decision he had faced twenty years earlier while he was on Rumspringa. He had made the right choice, he now realized. He really had gotten off pretty easy, all things considered. After all, it had been his third drug trafficking conviction, and the other choice had been an eternity in prison.

Andy listened to the sound of his wife washing the dirty dishes left over from breakfast. He wondered why she wasn't singing. Back when they were first married, she had always sung while she washed the dishes. But now that Andy thought about it, he couldn't remember when he had last heard her sing. But it didn't matter anyway. Today was his last day as an Amish man. Whether or not his wife ever opened her mouth again was the least of his concerns.

Andy slicked back his thinning hair. He checked the front yard again, then smiled. A van was slowly making its way up the gravel driveway. Escape lay only feet beyond the walls of his house, and Andy felt quite certain that the slot machines were about to finally turn in his favor.

The van stopped at its usual spot in the front yard. Andy waited until he heard his wife move into the living room to get more dirty dishes from the table, then he slipped out the front door.

"Good morning," Andy greeted the driver cheerily. "Point her toward St. Louis. I'm thinking I'll try my luck at Blackjack today."

Too late, Andy heard a noise coming from the back of the van. He started to turn around, but his vision went dark as a gunnysack was yanked down over his head and strings were tightly drawn shut. A second pair of hands locked on to his arms, pinning them against his sides. Andy fought against the strong grip, but the fight was over in seconds.

"Hello, Andy," a voice said into his ear.

Andy hesitated, trying to remember the voice. Then he felt himself being dragged backward out of his seat. He landed clumsily on the floor of the van and a heavy figure pinned him down, while strong hands tied his arms firmly behind his back. He found himself being rolled over and over until he bumped into the back corner of the van.

"How are you enjoying your new freedom?" the voice hissed.

"Don't kill me," Andy begged in a high-pitched, panicky voice. "I'll do whatever you want. Just don't kill me. Please."

"Too late for that," the voice said. "Do you know what the mob does to rats?"

"Please," Andy begged. "I have a family. They need me."

## Chapter Forty-Four

A second voice sounded. "Let's go," the voice commanded. "If we hurry, we can have him buried before anyone finds out he's missing."

The engine revved, and the van lurched.

The second voice leaned low to Andy's ear and Andy could feel hot breath coming through the gunnysack. He strained to make out a face through the coarse fabric, but only saw the outline of a large silhouette.

"My name is Joey Trontelli," the voice hissed. "And I want Shug. If you don't help me find him, you die."

Andy froze. "Shug?"

"Shug," the voice repeated. "He is the filthy rat that squealed on us, and you know where to find him."

Andy shrank back. "I'll do… do anything," he stammered.

Something sharp pricked the soft skin beneath his chin, and Andy thought he felt a trickle of blood run down his neck.

"I would love to slit your goddamn throat," the voice continued. "Maybe I will, maybe I won't. Your life depends entirely on you."

"Please," Andy begged. "I'll do anything."

"You will lead us to Shug," the voice hissed. "And if you try any funny business, I will hunt you down and torture you to death."

"Okay, okay," Andy sobbed. "I will help you."

"That's a good little Amish rat," the voice replied. "I thought you'd do the smart thing."

The van turned onto a gravel road, rocks crunching under the wheels.

Bruce Ellsworth's Explorer followed closely behind the van. From the passenger seat Maria watched without much emotion. They passed a dead-end sign in the ditch next to the road, then Bruce brought the van to a stop.

"Do you think Andy fell for it?" Maria asked.

"I do," Bruce replied. "These guys are pretty good."

"And you're sure they're not going to hurt him?"

Bruce shook his head. "From here on out, it's all mind games. Convince a man like Andy that he is on the brink of death, and he will do anything for you."

Bruce and Maria watched until the van disappeared into the trees, then turned back toward St. Louis.

# CHAPTER FORTY-FIVE

The narrow slat at the bottom of the door opened, letting in a tiny sliver of light. A plate of food slid through the opening and rattled to the floor. A baked potato spilled from the plate and rolled toward Andy. Andy sprang to his feet and sprinted for the slat, but he was too late. The slat closed and the darkness returned.

Andy pounded his fists against the solid steel door. "Help me," he yelled. "Just tell me what you want. I'll do anything."

Nobody came back, and the darkness stayed. Andy thought he felt blood running down his arm. He held it up in front of his face, but the darkness was so complete that he couldn't even see the outline of his fist. He slumped against the door and slid to the floor. His hands searched for the plate of food. His fingers closed on some warm noodles, and Andy began to stuff them into his mouth.

*How long have I been a prisoner?*

For a while he had tried to keep track of time, but now everything was blurred together.

When they first put him into the room there had been lights. He had searched the walls and ceiling and quickly realized how hopeless escape was. Concrete closed in from all sides, the only exception the one break in the wall where the steel door was.

Never once had anyone tried talking to him. Andy had listened for sounds—anything that would give him some clue as to where he was. There had been nothing. The only highlight was when the food arrived, not because he was hungry, but because for a few seconds there was a precious glimpse of daylight.

Isolation can have a strange effect on people. The Amish used isolation to draw wayward members back into line. The men who held Andy were applying the same principles, and hoping for the same results.

Andy leaned his head against the concrete wall. The wall was as cold and unforgiving as his situation. Did it really matter where he was, or who was holding him prisoner? He was going to die anyway.

Andy held his breath and listened again. He heard a clicking noise coming from somewhere nearby. It moved closer and Andy shuddered. The sound was like tiny claws clicking against a concrete floor.

*Rats?*

A scream froze in his throat and Andy sprang backward, trying to avoid the claws. He bumped into the wall and pain shot down his spine. He went limp on the floor.

The sound moved closer. The rat was bringing company. Andy lay, half conscious, and listened. Something was breathing in his ear. *Do rats breathe loud enough that I can hear them?*

Panic welled up from somewhere deep inside. Now the warm breath was on his cheek. Andy screamed and swatted wildly at the invisible creature. He sprang to his feet and lunged across the room. He ran headfirst into the opposite wall and teetered, trying to keep his balance. Then he began to pound the wall with his fists.

From a soundproof room one floor up, one of Andy's captors turned up the volume. He zoomed in on the footage of the half-crazed man inside the concrete room. The night vision camera cast Andy as an eerie blue-white spectacle.

"How much longer?" the man asked, glancing at the second man whose eyes were also glued to the footage.

"Five minutes, maybe less," the second man said. "Get ready for extraction."

In the room below, Andy stood still and listened, his head leaning against the wall. The cold concrete felt good, and he

## Chapter Forty-Five

suddenly had a crazy thought. *I'll simply crawl through the concrete and escape out the other side. Why didn't I think of that before? No wonder I'm still a prisoner. I deserve to be one, failing to recognize such a simple escape.*

Drawing back, Andy smashed his forehead into the concrete. *The pain isn't so bad, really. And did the concrete wall give a little?* He couldn't be sure, so he drew back and tried again. This time it seemed as if stars exploded inside his head. Which, now that Andy thought about it, was hysterical.

"You don't want to talk to me?" he screamed at the wall. "No problem. I'll just kill myself."

Then he had another hysterical thought: He was in a castle. If he broke through the wall he would fly. Finally fly. His bloody knuckles would turn into feathered wings and like a bird he would soar all the way to the ground far below.

With newfound determination, Andy took two steps back and leaned into the next charge. This one was the one that would crack the concrete wall. There was no doubt about it anymore. No doubt at all.

Andy took one giant step and suddenly the door burst open and two men entered.

Andy spun, wild-eyed. He blinked hard, trying to adjust to the blinding light.

The men wore masks and one was pointing a gun. The gunnysack came from nowhere, and then he was being dragged through the door and down what felt like a hallway.

The time had come. He was going to die. Someone would shoot him in the back of the head, and he would be buried where he would never be found. *But that's better than being eaten alive by rats.*

But the bullet didn't come. Instead, Andy was shoved into a chair, and his hands were tied behind his back. The gunnysack was removed, and as Andy's eyes adjusted to the light, he was able to focus on a dark window in the wall before him. He squinted, trying to see what was beyond. A man with a haggard, pale face stared back at him. The face was covered in blood and the top was bald, except for a few strands of dark hair, matted with blood. It took Andy a full minute to realize that he was seeing his own reflection.

A voice sounded from somewhere above his head.

"You have one chance to help us," the voice said

"Okay," Andy said, his mouth trembling. His voice sounded hollow, as if the words were being spoken by someone else.

"How do you communicate with Shug?"

"I… I…" Andy stalled, unprepared for the question. From somewhere in the back of his mind something clicked. *If these are Trontelli's men, they would have killed me by now.*

"Time's running out," the voice said.

Yet Andy hesitated. If he turned on Shug, he would be stuck as Amish forever. Or at least until Shug decided to kill him.

From nearby came a thin squeak, then tiny claws clicked somewhere behind his neck.

Andy's spine turned to ice and a terrified scream came from his throat. He hurled his weight forward, trying to escape from the creature. He sprawled face first onto the floor.

A man in a mask entered the room. With a few easy motions he lifted Andy and the chair back up and sat Andy back down in the chair. The man leaned down close to Andy's ear. "Don't do that again," he said. "It won't end well for you."

The man disappeared and the second voice came back.

"Shug. How are you doing it?" the voice asked.

"My phone," Andy said feebly, the blood slowly returning to his face.

"We've checked your phone. You're lying."

"It's a gaming app," Andy sobbed.

"Which one?"

## Chapter Forty-Five

"Chess," Andy said.

His confession was met with silence. Andy rocked in his chair and waited for the next question. He no longer cared who was on the other side of the window. He would answer their questions. It was that or be eaten alive by rats. He had no doubt about that.

"There is no chess app on your phone," the voice was back on the speaker.

"I delete the app after every conversation," Andy said. "That way it deletes all the messages in our private chat room."

"What was the last conversation you had with Shug?"

Andy hesitated, then said, "We set up a meeting place for a package."

"Was this package a baby?"

Andy nodded. "I had no choice," he said defensively.

"You're still going to deliver that package," the voice said.

"It'll never work," Andy said.

"Why not?"

"Shug is too smart to be caught," Andy said, laughing hysterically. "He knew it was Sparrow on our farm the whole time."

"I don't think I made myself clear," the voice interrupted. "So, I'm going to speak slower. You. Are. Going. To. Help. Us. Catch. Shug."

"Oh yeah," Andy said. "I remember that now."

The voice continued. "You are going to keep messaging Shug through your chess app. And we will monitor every single message. If you try to secretly warn him, you will die a slow and painful death. Do you believe me?"

Andy nodded distractedly. He stared at his reflection and wondered where the blood on top of his head came from. Was it even blood? His head really didn't hurt that badly, and now that he looked closer, the blood was a lighter color red than he thought blood was supposed to be.

"Do you understand me clearly?" the voice snapped.

Andy jolted back to the present. "I do," he said, sobering quickly. "I do."

# CHAPTER FORTY-SIX

The van bounced over the muddy dirt path along the river's edge. Rain spattered against the windshield, and Andy Reader flipped on the wipers. His fingers trembled as he held up the piece of paper and studied the instructions on the hand-drawn map.

At the fork Andy turned left. The road led away from the river, and in the rearview mirror Andy watched the riverbank fade out of sight. His eyes moved to the floor of the van.

"Keep your eyes on the road," the voice snarled from somewhere in the back.

Andy gulped and gripped the steering wheel tighter. Although he still hadn't seen any of his captor's faces, he now knew they couldn't be Trontelli's men. That assumption should have made him feel more at ease, but it had the opposite effect. A glance at his reflection in the rearview mirror made Andy shudder. The face that stared back at him was barely recognizable. Gone was the handsome man who had been shaving at his kitchen sink not so long ago. What he wouldn't give to be back there right now. Forget about the freedom that almost was. Given another chance, he could keep up the charade within the Amish community. Especially if his life depended on it, which it now seemingly did.

Andy approached an old homestead and glanced at his map. The place had been abandoned after the last flood, and the buildings now sat vacant and crumbling. Andy drove past a weathered farmhouse, and his eyes scanned the front of the building. Most of the windows were broken, and the porch roof sagged in the middle.

Next came a shed, and then a few silos. Andy barely noticed the buildings as he passed. His gaze was fixed on the barn, which was about two hundred yards beyond the silos. Shug's last message had told him to meet inside the barn.

Until now, Andy had not questioned the orders his captors had given him, but suddenly he felt torn between two forces. The first force was Shug who, if he suspected a trap, would kill him instantly.

The second was the men hiding in the back of the van. Andy held no illusions. They too, would kill him if he didn't follow their instructions to the minutest detail.

Andy parked in front of the barn and checked his cell phone. There was a new message from Shug. It read:

*Open all the doors on the van and drive around in a circle three times.*

Shug's message was instantly mirrored onto a dozen other nearby cell phones. Hidden men began to whisper to each other through tiny microphones.

Stan Prater's voice reached Bruce Ellsworth, who sat in his Explorer less than a quarter of a mile away. "Shug wants to see the inside of the van," Stan said. "Can we risk it?"

"We don't have a choice," Bruce replied. "If Andy doesn't complete those circles, Shug will suspect a trap."

Stan's voice came back. "Boys. Prepare to get your chopper in the air. We're gonna need that surveillance."

At a remote site fifteen miles away, the blades of a chopper began to whir as the crew prepared for takeoff.

Back in the van, Andy was shaken. "What should I do?" he asked nervously.

"You're going to do exactly what the message says," the voice from the back of the van replied.

Andy's hands trembled, but he got out and opened the doors to the van. He tried to avoid looking at the area beneath the two rear

## Chapter Forty-Six

seats where he knew the men were hidden. His hands shook as he shifted the van into drive and pressed the accelerator. The baby carrier in the passenger seat shifted and Andy held his breath. If the carrier rolled out onto the ground, he was as good as dead. The baby under the pale blue blanket was only a plastic doll and when it didn't cry out Shug would immediately realize the ambush, and then Andy would die.

In his Explorer, Bruce stared at the screen on his cell phone and waited for the next message.

"He's going into round three," a voice in his earpiece said.

"Copy that."

"Bruce, I'm not sure your boy has what it takes to pull this off. I can see him sweating from here."

"All he has to do is carry the package into the barn and identify the subject," Bruce said. "After that I really don't care what happens to him."

Maria silently observed Bruce's movements from the passenger seat of the Explorer. The debate about whether she would join Bruce on this mission had been heated. The matter had been settled when Maria argued that she knew Andy better than any of the trained men, and that if Andy panicked, she could be the one voice he trusted to calm his nerves.

"Circles completed," the voice came in. "Please advise."

"Were you seen?" Bruce asked.

"I don't think so," the voice came back.

"Then wait for the next message," Bruce said.

"Copy that."

Ten seconds later the next message flashed up on Bruce's screen. It read: *Take the package out of the passenger seat and meet me in the barn.*

Stan Prater's voice crackled with excitement. "We're a go, boys. I need that chopper in the air now."

"It seems too easy," Maria replied. "This guy has evaded the law for so many years, but suddenly he is willing to risk it all because Andy agreed to bring him a baby?"

Bruce held up his hand for silence as he listened. The agent in the back of the van spoke sharply to Andy. "Remember. Don't fuck this up," his voice snapped.

A microphone inside Andy's shirt collar picked up Andy's response.

"I… I… can't do it."

"Just focus on the goddamn drill," the voice snapped. "It's raining, so keep the doll covered. Once you have eyes on Shug, set the car seat down and say the code words. Your microphone will pick up the words and we will be there in seconds."

"I… I can't remember the code words," Andy stuttered.

"*Package delivered*," the voice spat. "Even a fool can remember two simple words."

There was a long pause, then the creaking of the van door. A few seconds later the man's voice came back.

"Andy is entering the barn." The voice crackled with adrenaline. "Does everyone copy?"

"Copy," Bruce replied.

"Copy," came a dozen other responses.

Every man tensed, waiting for Andy's code words.

One minute passed. Then two. Nobody spoke.

The silence was interrupted by the sound of the van door opening and closing.

"What happened?" the voice in the back of the van demanded.

"He wasn't there," came Andy's voice. "I told you he is too smart to be caught."

The man spoke into his microphone. "The subject wasn't in the barn. Please advise."

Stan Prater's voice cut in. "We know Shug has eyes on the van. I'm ready to storm that barn."

## Chapter Forty-Six

"Negative," Bruce retorted sharply. "Shug could have hidden cameras set up. Heck, he could be watching the live feed from another country. If we storm the barn, Andy's cover is blown."

"Copy," came the responses.

"Stan," Bruce continued, "how much longer do I have the police department?"

"Half hour tops," Stan Prater replied.

"Copy that. Let's wait."

Bruce and Maria listened as Stan called off the chopper.

"What now?" came the voice of the agent in the back of the van.

"Have Andy send another message," Bruce replied.

The rain started to pick up, and with it came darkness. With the reduced visibility, Maria felt her patience waver. She opened the glove compartment and thumbed through some old receipts. Her hand touched something cold and hard. "What's this?" she asked, pulling the object from under the receipts.

Bruce glanced at the knife. "Every redneck in the Midwest carries one," he said distractedly.

Maria started to replace the knife, but when Bruce turned his head, she slipped it into her back pocket. *Just in case.*

"It's one of the hardest things to adjust to," Bruce said.

"What is?" Maria asked.

"The waiting."

Maria looked out at the darkening sky. When she spoke her voice quivered.

"Bruce can I ask you something?"

"Go ahead."

"What happens to Sparrow when this is all over?"

"He has murdered people," Bruce replied. "He will be arrested tomorrow."

"You are just going to let him go to jail?" Maria asked pointedly.

"I can try and soften the blow," Bruce said. "Find him a good lawyer."

"Who knows his whole story?" Maria asked.

"Only a handful of us," Bruce replied.

"Who?" Maria repeated.

"Well, let's see," Bruce said. "Your mother and Bishop Mast are the only people within the community that know the truth. Everyone else still thinks the person at your farm is Eli."

"So, outside the community, the only people who know the real story are Stan, yourself, and me, correct?"

"Almost," Bruce said.

"So, it's always been Eli. Sparrow never existed," Maria said hopefully. "If Sparrow disappears, and we never tell the real story, nobody will ever know to look for him, right?"

"Like I said, almost," Bruce repeated.

"Who else knows?"

"Chief Westbritt," Bruce replied. "I had to pull a huge favor to get Castleton's police force out here tonight," Bruce replied. "Stan and I had to tell Westbritt everything."

"Five minutes," Stan Prater's voice interrupted in Maria's ear.

Maria stared out the window and frowned. She only half listened to the transmissions going through the earpiece Bruce had given her. Instead, she found herself thinking about Sparrow, and how little anyone knew about him.

Sparrow had silently followed the plan to try and catch Shug, a man he openly resented. Shug had held Sparrow captive for almost his entire life and would do so again if given the opportunity. So, should Sparrow be held responsible for crimes he had committed while under Shug's power? After all, it was quite literally the only world he had ever known.

Maria sighed at the injustice of it all. She decided that as soon as she had the opportunity, she would warn Sparrow about the arrest. Sparrow could easily disappear, and probably would.

## Chapter Forty-Six

It wasn't the solution Maria wanted, and certainly Mam would be very upset, but what about Sparrow? What did he want?

The window fogged and Maria traced the outline of a tree with her finger. She wondered where Shug was at that very moment. Maybe he was watching her from the woods only feet away. *Maybe he is directly behind the tree I just outlined.* Maria shivered and shrank lower in her seat.

The thought grew larger in her mind. If Shug was nearby and still hadn't shown himself, did that mean he knew about the trap? Or was he waiting for something? What? The cover of darkness? Or was he simply waiting to meet Andy until the last possible moment, knowing that if there was a trap, eventually the men would show themselves?

Bruce's voice startled her. "Boys, I think this was a dry run," he said into his microphone. "Let's search the barn and get out of here."

"Agreed," came the agent's voice in the back of the van. "What do you want me to do with Andy?"

"Take him back to the compound," Bruce replied. "Let's meet tomorrow and re-evaluate."

"Bruce?" Maria interrupted suddenly.

"Yes Maria."

"I have an idea," Maria said. She removed the earpiece to stop the sound of the crackling voices. Bruce waited.

"If Shug is here, but he hasn't shown, that means he suspects a trap, right?"

"Go on." Bruce nodded.

"He knows your men will eventually show themselves, right?"

Bruce nodded slowly.

"Run a simple test," Maria said. "Have Andy send one last message to Shug explaining that he is done waiting. He doesn't know what to do with the baby, so he will take it back to its parents."

Bruce picked up the wire that held his microphone. "Hold on, boys," he said.

Maria continued. "After Andy sends the message, have him drive away. If Shug is watching, he'll stop him."

Bruce nodded thoughtfully. "It's worth a shot."

"What's going on, boss?" came Stan Prater's voice.

"Change in plans," Bruce replied.

Bruce gave the instructions, and they listened as the agent in the back of the van relayed the words to Andy.

For a few moments there was silence as the message was sent, then came the sound of the van engine.

"We're moving," the agent in the back of the van announced.

The screen on Bruce's phone lit up with an incoming call.

"It's working," Maria whispered.

"Have Andy answer that call," Bruce barked into his microphone.

There was a moment of hesitation, then Andy's voice.

"Shug?" he said, his voice trembling.

"You've passed the test," came a voice Maria had never heard before.

In the driver's seat, Bruce stiffened.

"Okay," came Andy's voice. "Wha… what do you want me to do?"

"Bring the baby to me. I'm waiting in the farmhouse you passed earlier."

"Ok… kay…" Andy replied.

Bruce's screen went blank.

The air was charged with electricity as the men waited.

A minute passed, then a voice came back. "Andy is entering the front door to the house now. Be prepared to move."

Maria stared through the windshield and into the darkness beyond. The rain made visibility impossible. "Perfect timing," she muttered.

## Chapter Forty-Six

"What?" Bruce asked.

"Shug wanted the cover of darkness to escape."

"It won't matter," Bruce said. "If he's in there, we're getting him."

A long minute ticked by. Nothing.

"What the fuck is he doing in there?" Bruce muttered. "Something is wrong. I can feel it."

"Did you hear that?" Maria asked, breathless.

It came again, a soft whooshing pop of air in her ear.

"What the hell?" Prater's voice demanded sharply.

Instantly, Bruce came alive. "Shots fired," he yelled into his microphone. "Cover that house now!"

Bruce keyed up the Explorer and flipped on the headlights. He floored the accelerator and the Explorer shot out of the woods and onto the road.

"What was that?" Maria asked, her voice sharp with excitement.

"A gun with a silencer," Bruce yelled above the roar of the engine.

At the intersection, Bruce spun the steering wheel and sped down the gravel road. "I'm a fool," he yelled. "Nobody suspected the farmhouse. Our focus was on the barn."

Seconds later they were in front of the farmhouse.

Men were running from all directions. Flashlights bobbed across the broken windows of the house.

Bruce threw the Explorer into park and kicked the door open. "Do not leave this vehicle," he yelled at Maria.

Maria stared, dumbfounded. She nodded that she understood, but then pushed the passenger door open and ran after Bruce.

In a few bounds, Bruce crossed the porch and disappeared through the front door. Maria was right behind him. The first thing she noticed was the baby carrier. It sat on the floor in the middle of the room, and the blanket had been yanked back to reveal the doll.

Several men knelt around an open doorway on the other side of the room, and as Maria approached, she saw a dark red pool of blood forming around their knees. A man lay on the floor in front of them.

Bruce Ellsworth stopped next to the huddle, his gun drawn. He glanced down and yelled something, but Maria couldn't understand the words. Then suddenly, Maria realized what she was seeing. The man lying on the floor was Andy Reader. The puffs of wind she had heard through her earpiece were meant for him.

Horrified, she knelt and stared at Andy's pale, blood-covered face.

"Maria," Andy mouthed weakly. "Why?"

Maria couldn't take her eyes off Andy's face. She leaned closer, trying to read his lips.

"Da… daramore."

"What?" Maria asked.

"Daramore," Andy mouthed. Blood spurted from the corner of his mouth and oozed down his neck.

Maria's eyes followed the blood and stopped at Andy's chest. Two tiny bullet holes, not more than three inches apart, made neat little circles on each side of the row of buttons that ran up the front of his shirt.

Something else caught Maria's eyes, and she looked lower. Written across Andy's front were scrawled the letters:

## *TRAP*

The blotched red letters seemed to explode from the backdrop of Andy's white shirt. Maria's eyes moved on to Andy's hand. Then she understood. Andy's hand was bruised and bloody from battering the concrete wall in his holding cell. The wounds on the hand had scabbed over, but Andy had torn a scab loose enough to draw blood. Realizing that the microphone hidden on him would alert the men outside, he had used the bloody knuckle to write out a message of

## Chapter Forty-Six

warning to Shug.

Suddenly, Maria felt an overwhelming urge to touch Andy's face, to find meaning in the haggard features there. To somehow make sense of the terrible mistake he had made. But when she reached out a trembling hand, only lifeless eyes greeted her.

As Maria stared and tried to comprehend, she became aware of the sound of whirring chopper blades somewhere overhead. Then strong arms, Bruce's arms, were dragging her away from the body and out of the room.

---

Several hundred yards from the house, Shug climbed up the muddy riverbank. He crested the top and turned to scan the vast expanse of flowing dark water. *It should be here somewhere.*

A dark form slid out of a clump of bushes next to Shug. Shug's hand flew for the revolver in his coat pocket, but a hand flashed forward and the revolver sailed through the air. It made a splashing sound when it hit the dark water below.

Shug turned to face the intruder. "*Sparrow.*"

"Looking for the boat?" Sparrow asked.

"I knew you would come back to help me," Shug said. "The well-trained ones always come back home."

"Not this time," Sparrow said evenly.

"But you are here to help me?" Shug asked, taking a step closer. "If you don't, they'll get us both."

"No, they won't," Sparrow said. "They'll only get you."

"What?" Shug asked, incredulity in his voice. "But you..."

Sparrow's leg shot out and connected with Shug's knee. There was a sharp snapping sound and then Shug was writhing on the ground. As the lights from the chopper in the sky drew nearer, Sparrow quickly faded back into the of bushes at the edge of the river.

# CHAPTER FORTY-SEVEN

Back at the farmhouse, Bruce and Maria ran toward the Explorer. Bruce mouthed something to Maria, but his words were drowned out by the roar of the chopper blades. Maria stared numbly up at the massive machine, which seemed to be suspended only feet above her head. Bruce grabbed her wrist, threw open the passenger door and shoved her inside, then slammed the door and ran to the driver's side. The engine roared to life.

Bruce pointed through the windshield. "The river," he mouthed. "Someone said he's at the river."

Men were now running everywhere in the yard. More squad cars were arriving. As if to lead the way, the chopper hovered above the trees ahead of them. Bruce followed the floodlights.

The riverbank suddenly loomed right in front of them, and Bruce slammed the brakes. The Explorer skidded sideways and stopped inches from a squad car. Bruce's gun was in his hand as he leapt from his seat.

"This time you stay in the car," Bruce yelled.

Maria shrank away from the order.

"I mean it, Maria. This man is a killer."

Maria nodded numbly.

Bruce slammed the door and sprinted toward the river.

Men appeared from all directions and dark silhouettes quickly lined the top of the riverbank. Maria tried to comprehend what was happening, but things were moving too fast.

The men were forming a circle, their guns drawn. Then Maria saw him. In the middle of the circle of drawn guns, one figure stood all alone, silhouetted against the dark night

## Chapter Forty-Seven

sky. The figure was hunched over, and one leg stuck out at an unnatural angle.

The voices in her earpiece snapped Maria back to reality.

"Get down!" Bruce Ellsworth shouted.

The figure didn't move. He stood rigid, back turned, and stared down at the river below.

"He's gonna jump," someone else yelled.

The sound of the chopper blades thundered in Maria's ears and suddenly the entire riverbank was flooded in bright lights as the chopper found its target.

The figure on the bank stood still, arms crossed defiantly. Rain beat against his wet shirt and a gust of wind ruffled his long silvery hair. But the man didn't seem to notice the rain or the men that surrounded him. Instead, he stared out at the river, an expression of disbelief on his face.

Then, something struck the man in the back. He lurched forward and almost fell, but then regained his balance. Something else hit him in the thigh, and his legs buckled.

"They're shooting him," Maria mouthed as she stared through the windshield at the scene on the riverbank. She threw her door open and ran. Her shoes slipped in the mud as she sprang up the steep bank. More thuds sounded as she neared the scene.

The man sank to his knees, then fell forward onto his face.

Bruce was the first to get there, and he dropped to one knee, pinning the man to the ground.

"What happened to your leg, Shug?" Bruce yelled, leaning down to hear.

"I tripped and fell," Shug sputtered.

Bruce straightened. "Someone toss me a pair of handcuffs," he yelled.

Maria reached Bruce's side just in time to see handcuffs close around the man's wrists. Bruce's knee forced the man's face into the mud. Mud covered the silvery hair, and tiny white bubbles began to appear in a puddle beside his mouth.

"Charles Schlugen," Bruce said. "You are under arrest for the murder of…" Bruce paused for a moment. "Oh hell," he said. "For at least a dozen people."

"But he's already dead," Maria interrupted, confused.

Bruce glanced up at the sound of Maria's voice. He grinned. "Beanie bags," he said.

"What?"

"We shot him with beanie bags," Bruce repeated. "They hurt like hell, but they don't kill."

Maria nodded slowly. She stared at Shug's face, then knelt down and studied him more carefully. "You really aren't all that tough now," she said softly.

Shug ignored her. He gasped, trying to draw air into his lungs. His lips moved.

"What?" Maria asked.

"The boat. There was supposed to be a boat."

"What's he trying to say?" one of the other men asked.

"Who the fuck cares?" Bruce said. "Get this worthless scum out of my sight before he 'accidently' suffocates on mud."

Two men knelt, one on each side of Shug. They helped him to his feet and turned to lead him away.

"Come on, Maria, let's get out of here," Bruce said. He turned and started down the riverbank.

Maria didn't move. She watched intently as Shug drew abreast. He hopped along on one leg and dragged the other in the mud. His muddy hair clung to his face, and his eyes locked on hers. Recognition flashed across his face, and his lips curled back in a contemptuous grin. He pulled against the handcuffs and stopped, inches away. The men yanked on his arms, but he didn't flinch. His face was so close that Maria felt his breath move her hair.

## Chapter Forty-Seven

"The girl who wants to play cop," Shug snarled. "You're nothing but a two-bit whore, just like your motha." Shug tried to draw up saliva to spit in Maria's face, but the effort dribbled down his chin.

Maria trembled. Then, as suddenly as it hit her, the weakness was replaced by a surge of anger. "You," she hissed, taking a step closer. "You have ruined our family. My mother is a widow. Sparrow is going to jail. Eli may never recover."

"What are you gonna do about it?" Shug sneered.

Something inside Maria snapped. All the pain and resentment that had built up over the last year bubbled over in one dark second. As if guided by an invisible force, her hand moved to her pocket. The blade of the knife flashed open as she lunged forward and buried it in Shug's stomach.

The air went out of Shug in a loud gasp. In disbelief his eyes moved from her face to his stomach.

"Jail is too good for you," Maria screamed.

She yanked hard on the knife. It came out much easier than she had imagined. The momentum carried her backward, and she struggled to regain her balance. She lunged again. This time she aimed higher, determined to cut down the life of the evil man.

The blade was inches from Shug's throat when strong arms grabbed her from behind and forced her to the ground. Above, chopper blades drowned out the noises around her, but Maria recognized Bruce's voice. "Get him to a hospital. Now."

The shock of what she had just done was too much. The last thing Maria remembered before the darkness closed in was someone prying the bloody knife from her fingers.

---

One time zone to the west, where the last fingers of daylight were finally fading between the two buildings at the end of the street, a man in a dark suit ended a phone call and replaced the cell phone back into one of the pockets of his tactical uniform. He moved from the shadows where he had stood to guard the room, stepped across the opening, then stopped outside a door. He knocked softly.

*Three quick knocks. Pause for two seconds, then, one final knock.*

The muffled sound of a television came from inside the room. The door opened just wide enough to reveal a thin face encompassed by a shock of curly blond hair. The face gazed hesitantly up at the agent.

"Pack your things, Eli." The agent smiled. "You are going home."

A smile of sheer joy crossed Eli's face. He nodded that he understood, then the door silently closed again.

# CHAPTER FORTY-EIGHT

Maria's head hurt, and she opened her eyes slowly. She took a deep breath and her nose filled with the smells of her mother's cooking. She glanced at her surroundings and wondered why she was back in her old room.

For a few precious seconds the events from the previous evening evaded her memory, then all at once, everything came rushing back. Maria shuddered and pulled the blanket up over her head. She squeezed her eyes shut, hoping it would all go away.

Gradually she became aware of the sound of muffled voices in the living room below. Curious, Maria sat up and swung her legs over the edge of the bed. Her clothes were waiting for her, hanging from the hook on the back of her door. Maria silently got dressed, then tiptoed across the floor and into the hallway. The door to Eli's empty room stood open and Maria caught her breath. "Eli," she gasped, suddenly remembering. She turned and started down the stairs.

The warm sense of nostalgia vanished as soon as Maria stepped into the living room. She saw Bishop Mast first, and her eyes shot around the table, evaluating the other men. Bruce Ellsworth sat across from Bishop Mast, and next to him, Stan Prater. The man at the end of the table was a black man whom Maria didn't recognize.

The man rose and extended his hand. "Chief Calvin Westbritt," he said.

"I'm Maria," Maria said timidly, shaking the hand.

The sound of Maria's voice brought Ruth from the kitchen. She smiled and set a pot of coffee on the table. Maria sat down and poured a cup for herself.

Nobody spoke.

"Where is Eli?" Maria asked.

Bruce glanced at his watch. "Eli is arriving at Lambert International Airport in St. Louis at 2:40 this afternoon."

Maria smiled and nodded. She studied the faces around the table. Nobody else was smiling. Her mind flashed back to the events from the night before, and she sobered. The memory of Andy's bloody body sprawled in the open doorway made her nauseated, and her hands shook. "Is Andy… dead?" she asked reluctantly.

"He is," Bruce replied.

Ruth moved from the table and hurried toward the kitchen, her hands drawing her apron to her eyes as she walked, the conversation about her dead husband too much to bear.

Maria glanced curiously around the table. "Where's Sparrow?" she asked, suddenly not sure she was ready for the answer.

"Disappeared," Bruce replied. "And he's not answering his phone."

Maria took a deep breath and smiled again.

Chief Westbritt cleared his throat. "Sparrow was a big help in catching Shug," he said. "But the fact is, he is a murderer. As such, if he is ever found, he will stand trial."

"But he is a good person, and you know it," Maria said defensively.

"I didn't say that we are going to go out of our way to find him," Chief Westbritt replied. "Actually, the way I see it the Castleton Police Department will be busy with more important matters for a very long time."

"You mean…?" Maria began.

Chief Westbritt held up his hand for silence. "The only people who know that Sparrow ever existed are in this room right now. I think it's better if it stayed that way, don't you?"

Chief Westbritt looked slowly around the table and everyone nodded.

## Chapter Forty-Eight

"That being said," Chief Westbritt continued. "If Sparrow makes trouble for us in the future, my memory will come back really fast. Understand?"

Everyone nodded again.

Maria took a careful sip from her cup. "Shug?" she asked hesitantly.

"He's going to make it," Bruce replied.

Chief Westbritt tapped the table with his fingers. "Do you want to tell her?" he asked, glancing at Bruce.

Bruce nodded uncomfortably. "Maria," he said, carefully weighing each word. "I understand why you attacked Shug, but you have to understand that there must be consequences."

Maria hesitated, studying Bruce's face to make sure he was serious. "Why?" she asked sharply. "He is a murderer."

"All the same," Bruce insisted. "Shug was in handcuffs. The law says he deserves a fair trial."

Maria stared dumbfounded, trying to comprehend Bruce's meaning.

Chief Westbritt spoke. "We're all thankful Shug is behind bars," he said. "The world is a safer place because of it. And, according to Bruce, you played a large role in capturing him."

"But I'm still in trouble?" Maria asked, confused.

"Maria," Bruce said, his voice cracking with emotion. "Chief Westbritt is here to arrest you. You are being booked on charges of attempted murder."

Maria stared at Bruce, betrayal written all over her face. From the kitchen, she heard her mother sobbing loudly.

Chief Westbritt slowly removed a pair of handcuffs from his belt.

Maria's eyes darted wildly around the table, searching for a friendly face. "You have to help me," she pleaded, reaching for Bruce's arm.

Bishop Mast spoke for the first time. "Maria," he said calmly. "We've been talking while you were sleeping. We think there might be another way."

"What is it?" Maria stammered. "I can't go to jail."

Bishop Mast nodded at Chief Westbritt. "You can explain it better than I can," he said.

Chief Westbritt took a long breath. "Well, you see," he began, "the Amish have a very solid reputation of handling the problems within their community privately. Quite often, the outside law doesn't even get involved at all."

"I don't understand," Maria said tensely.

"For generations, the Amish have lived under the protection of the First Amendment," Chief Westbritt continued. "This amendment guarantees them the freedom to practice any religion they like. If you think about it, that amendment could potentially protect someone who commits a crime within the community. It has protected many Amish from outside prosecution in the past."

"What does that have to do with me?" Maria asked.

"Well you are not currently living under that protective umbrella," Chief Westbritt said. "But let's just say that you were."

Maria turned to Bruce, disbelief and shock written on her face. "You want me to go back to the Amish?" she asked.

"The choice is yours," Bruce said.

"You will be put on supervised probation," Chief Westbritt continued. "If you ever leave the Amish community again, you will be arrested."

Maria sat frozen. Her eyes came to rest on Bishop Mast. "Rudy Koblenz?" she managed weakly. "Will he be the deacon again?"

Bishop Mast shook his head. "Rudy Koblenz is actually here today," he said. "I believe he has something he wants to tell you."

Maria's face flushed with anger. "I don't want his apology," she spat defiantly. "I don't want any of it. I choose jail." She

## Chapter Forty-Eight

jumped to her feet and extended her hands. "Handcuff me," she said. "I'm ready."

"Let's not make any hasty decisions," Bruce interrupted quickly.

Maria's eyes flashed angrily. "What?" she snapped.

Bruce stood and walked to the window. He motioned for Maria to follow.

Still indignant, Maria joined him at the window.

Bruce pointed, and Maria gasped.

Outside, dozens of horses and buggies were parked along both sides of the Reader driveway. Amish people, dressed in black and white, were gathered in the front yard and gazing expectantly at the house.

"What are they doing here?" Maria whispered.

"They're here to welcome you home," Bruce said.

"I don't understand," Maria said, a lump forming in her throat. "I thought they hated me."

Bishop Mast joined them at the window. "Everyone is pulling for you, Maria," he said. "You are more loved than you will ever know."

Maria's eyes scanned the crowd. She was surprised to see that the Youngie and the married folks were mingling. *Could it be that the divide was narrowing?* Close to the front, Edna Troyer's eager face was upturned, a sincere smile radiating at the sight of the friend she hadn't seen for so long. Next to Edna stood her brother Marvin, and Maria caught her breath.

Bishop Mast seemed to read her thoughts. "Alma's family is one of those that moved out," he said. "I believe Marvin is back on the hunt for a wife."

Maria shook her head and ignored the comment. She noticed Mattie Borntrager watching her. It seemed like Mattie's lips were moving, and Maria thought she was probably visualizing the words for her next article in *The Budget*.

"Is this all that is left?" Maria asked, addressing Bishop Mast.

"We're down to seventeen families," Bishop Mast replied sadly. "We need you, Maria. With both you and Eli home, the community has a chance."

Maria nodded numbly.

"You know I wanted the best for you in the outside world," Bruce said. "But what you did last night changed everything. I'm sorry, Maria. I really am."

Tears stung Maria's eyes as she scanned the crowd.

"You have two options," Bruce continued. "You can walk out that door in handcuffs and get stuffed into the back of Chief Westbritt's squad car, or you can walk out in your Amish get-up and start shaking hands as if you belong."

Hot tears of frustration and confusion ran down Maria's cheeks and she brushed them away. "It's all so sudden," she sobbed.

"You will make the right decision," Bruce said, putting a strong arm around her shoulders. "And I support you regardless of what that decision is."

Too filled with emotion, Maria couldn't speak.

Bruce continued, "I was thinking we could stop by the office and you can say goodbye to Susan. While there, you guys can decide what to do with your 'English' things that are still at her house."

"What about them?" Maria asked, pointing at the growing crowd in front of the house.

Bruce laughed. "They've been waiting for you for six months," he said. "I'm pretty sure they can wait for a few more hours. We'll sneak out the back way. Deal?"

Maria struggled for words but nodded.

Bruce held out his hand and she took it.

They walked back to the table and sat down.

Maria faced Bishop Mast. "Why do you even want me back?" she asked. "You know I can never be the person the church expects of me."

## Chapter Forty-Eight

Bishop Mast nodded. "You are good for this community," he said. "And besides..." He paused and smiled ruefully. "The Singens have been really boring without you."

"Will the church still try to force me to be baptized?" Maria asked.

"As long as I'm bishop, there will never again be forced baptism," Bishop Mast said decidedly.

Maria closed her eyes and rubbed her temples with her thumbs. She tried to think clearly, but gruesome images from the night before began to flash through her mind and fog her brain.

Everyone waited. The silence was deafening.

Finally, Maria opened her eyes and fixed a firm gaze on Bishop Mast. "I can't think here," she said. "Can you give me ten minutes alone please."

Chief Westbritt interrupted. "Don't try to run," he said sternly.

"I'm not going to run," Maria said evenly. She pushed her chair back and stood up from the table. Heads turned and followed her movements as she walked to the back door of the house. The door opened and closed silently.

Maria took the back route to the barn, careful to avoid the curious eyes in the front yard. She closed the barn door and stood for a minute, allowing her eyes to adjust to the darkness.

Eli's horse neighed from her stall, and Maria smiled. She walked to Trish and stroked her nose. Trish rubbed her head against Maria's shoulder and nuzzled at her pocket, seeking the usual snack.

In the darkness of the barn, without judgmental eyes upon her, Maria was finally able to think clearly. Here, when she opened her soul, nobody laughed at her. Here, in this barn, she had laughed, and she had cried. She had cursed God and then begged his forgiveness. And it was here that she had finally committed to abandoning the Amish way of life.

But what had been her main reason for leaving? Had it been because she couldn't abide by their strict rules, or was it because she wanted to find Eli?

Maria made the rounds, stopping at every stall. Betsy had recently given birth to a calf, and absent-mindedly Maria stuck her hand into the calf's pen. The calf didn't need any coaxing. Maria's fingers resembled the teats on Betsy's udder, and the calf began to suck on them. Slobber dripped from Maria's hand and she laughed out loud.

"Maria." A familiar voice spoke from a few feet away.

Maria flinched and spun. "Marvin," she gasped. "How… how did you know I was here?"

Marvin inched closer, his handsome features becoming more prominent with each step.

"I've missed you," Marvin said softly. There was a sad expression on his face.

"Don't come closer," Maria snapped.

Marvin stopped, and his expression changed. "Maria." He said again. "I made a terrible mistake."

"You're just saying that because your new girlfriend moved away."

"I don't expect you to forgive me," Marvin said. "But I want you to know that I have never stopped loving you. I think about you all the time."

Maria felt her knees go weak. She raised a hand to slap Marvin, to keep him from coming closer, but she felt suddenly powerless. Without meaning to, her hand brushed Marvin's cheek, then fell weakly to her side. The touch sent shock waves through her arm.

Marvin hesitated for only a moment, then stepped closer.

Maria felt her resolve waver. She started to close her eyes, to lean in and allow Marvin's strong arms to draw her close. To let him pick her up and hold her. Suddenly she wanted to inhale the

## Chapter Forty-Eight

wonderful smells she hadn't even realized she had been missing.

The calf broke the spell. Its warm tongue reached out from between the paneling and licked Maria's arm. Maria jerked sideways and took a wide step around Marvin, suddenly embarrassed.

"I'm not ready to love you," she whispered hoarsely. Then she turned and bolted for the front barn door.

# CHAPTER FORTY-NINE

As one, the faces in the front yard were upturned, nervous anticipation showing in their features. Finally, the door opened, and Bruce Ellsworth stepped out onto the porch.

Everyone held their breath. Would Maria follow in handcuffs, or would she be in her Amish dress and cap?

Maria stepped out onto the porch. She was wearing a black dress and a black cap, and a sigh of relief passed through the crowd as everyone exhaled.

Bruce walked to the edge of the porch. "Good morning," he began.

He was greeted by a rustle of shawls and denim.

"As many of you know," Bruce continued, "the man who had infiltrated your community is now safely behind bars. Andy Reader was helping that man, and he paid for it with his life."

Bruce paused, but when nobody spoke, he continued. "Ruth wanted me to thank you for coming, and she wanted me to tell you that the funeral will be Friday."

Silence.

Bruce cleared his throat. "Maria and I are going to pick Eli up this afternoon. Eli is coming home to stay."

There was a rustle as Mattie Borntrager pushed forward. Her lips moved and dry spit projectiles seemed to clear her path to the front of the crowd. She avoided Maria's eyes, but addressed Bruce instead. "Ptuh, ptuh," she sputtered. "So, is Maria coming back with Eli, or…"

Mattie's voice trailed off.

## Chapter Forty-Nine

"I think that question is for you," Bruce said, motioning to Maria.

Maria took a deep breath and stepped forward. She glanced down at her clasped hands and hesitated. Her hands still had flecks of Shug's dried blood on them from the night before. Like a bad omen of things to come, the blood represented all that Maria had endured, and all that she would endure. Maria slowly moved the hands out of sight behind her back. She lifted her chin proudly to address the familiar faces.

"I have decided to come back home with my brother Eli," she said simply.

She hesitated. It really sounded so simple once she said the words out loud. Like she needed to say more. As if she was expected to say more.

"Thank you to those of you who have tried to understand me," she said. "It is not too late to make this a strong community, and together, we can pull together and make it."

The words were what everyone had been waiting for, and warm smiles broke out as the crowd moved in closer.

Maria nudged Bruce to let him know she was finished speaking. They walked down the steps and started for the Explorer. The sea of black and white parted and let them pass through.

# CHAPTER FIFTY

Only a few clouds remained as a gentle reminder of the storms that had passed through the night before. Steam, caused by the heavy rains, rose from the fields, and Maria rolled down the passenger window to catch some of the fresh, clean air. She reached for the radio and tuned the station to country music.

Bruce waited until the community was out of sight before he spoke. "You going to be alright with all that?" he asked, jerking his thumb backward.

When there was no response, Bruce glanced in Maria's direction. Maria was sitting back in the seat, eyes closed, seemingly in deep thought.

They drove on in silence.

As they neared the airport, Bruce glanced at his watch. "We have a couple of hours before Eli's plane lands," he said. "You wanna stop by and talk to Susan?"

"I don't think I can face Susan and the children right now," Maria said. "I will call her next week. We can make arrangements for my car over the phone."

Bruce nodded. "Anything else?"

Maria thought about the question for a beat. "I've always wanted to go to the arch," she said finally. "Is it true that they have little cars that take you all the way to the top?"

Bruce laughed. "You know, my entire life I've lived in St. Louis, and I've never been inside the arch either. Why don't we go check it out?"

They parked at a spot overlooking the Mississippi River, then walked down some concrete stairs that led through a gift shop.

## Chapter Fifty

Aisles of souvenirs lined the main floor and Maria stopped when one caught her attention. She picked up a glass replica of the arch and held it carefully to the light. She rocked it back and forth in her hand and watched as the little car swam inside the glass. "It's the perfect souvenir," she said.

"It is?"

"The car is me. See?" Maria laughed, a touch of bitterness in her voice. She tilted the replica to one side and the car started its journey from the base of the arch. It swam all the way to the top, then as Maria tilted the replica the other way, floated down the other side until it reached the bottom.

"My life for the last year," Maria said. "I started at the bottom, climbed to the top, and now I'm going to end up at the bottom again."

"Maria," Bruce said, not laughing. "I'm sorry. I really am. I wish there was another way."

"Well, I'm going to buy it," Maria said, not taking her eyes off the souvenir. "And the church must never know. It will be the only thing I have that reminds me of my time in St. Louis."

Maria paid for the souvenir and they left the gift shop.

The ride to the top of the arch took almost four minutes and Maria sat with fists clenched, face drawn.

Her fear vanished when they stepped out of the tiny elevator and into the room at the top. Narrow windows lined the walls on each side, and Maria stared breathlessly at the mighty Mississippi River below. Barges lined the banks, and tiny men crawled on top of their flat surfaces. The height was dizzying.

Beyond the river stretched East St. Louis, flat and crumbling, and barely a shadow of its prospering neighbor on the west side.

Maria watched a tiny sliver of a boat slowly working against the current. Shug's face suddenly appeared in her mind.

*Boat.*

*Boat.*

*What was it Shug had said?*

"There was supposed to be a boat," Maria said out loud, the words coming to her as she spoke.

"What did you say?" Bruce asked, half listening.

"Shug said there was supposed to be a boat," Maria repeated.

"What are you talking about?"

"When he was on the ground," Maria said. "I heard him say it."

"Are you sure?" Bruce asked.

Maria nodded slowly. "You didn't hear it?" she asked.

Bruce shook his head. "A boat?" he asked again.

"I think he meant that a boat was supposed to be there to pick him up," Maria said. "That's why he ran to the river."

Bruce thought about Maria's claim for a few seconds, then took out a notepad and scribbled something. "Well hell," he said. "I was going to start removing things from the *Crazy Wall* and get ready for the next case, but now you gave me something new to add."

Maria walked to the other side of the room and leaned her elbows on the window ledge. Breathless, she stared at the city below. Skyscrapers that towered to intimidating heights when viewed from below now looked like tiny toys. The view was a jungle of highways, train tracks, and concrete buildings.

Then, in the middle of it all, Maria's eyes fastened on something strange. Plopped down right in the middle of all the concrete was a green field. Tiny red walls rose on all sides.

"Busch Stadium," Bruce said, following her gaze. "Some of the world's best baseball is played there."

Maria stared for a long time, lost in thought. Her eyes scanned the thousands of square miles of buildings, and silently she wondered about her real father. She settled on a tiny brown brick house with a red roof. Was that the one where he lived with his other family, the one she might have grown up in had things worked out between him and her mother? It could be the

## Chapter Fifty

one. Did he ever wonder what became of the waitress he met at a restaurant? And did he ever wonder about the child, his child, that he would never meet?

The thoughts cast a dark shadow on Maria's mood and she straightened. "You know what I regret the most?" she asked, taking a step back from the window.

"What's that?" Bruce asked.

"I lived in St. Louis for almost six months, and I accomplished so little," Maria said. "I mean, look at all that." Maria waved her arms in a broad arc. "There is so much, but I was so busy working and studying, that I missed all of it."

A blue and silver passenger plane appeared from somewhere overhead. It flew low and silent over the city. Maria traced it with her finger, watching its descent. "Just think," she said. "Eli could be on that one."

"He better not be," Bruce laughed. "The airport is twenty miles away, so he will be waiting on us for a while."

The thought snapped them both back to the present.

"I'm ready to go get my brother," Maria said.

"Let's go," Bruce replied.

# CHAPTER FIFTY-ONE

Traffic was light as they drove west on I-70. Suddenly giddy with anticipation, Maria watched the planes descending into the airport.

The moment wasn't lost on Bruce. For the last six months the two most important people in Maria's life had been Susan and himself. Maria had grown on him. Yes, she wore her emotions on her sleeve, and yes, her impulsive outbursts of anger got her into trouble, but all the same, he would miss her. But Bruce held no illusions. From the moment Maria and Eli reunited, Bruce's role in Maria's life would fade. He would become the private investigator from the big city once again.

Someone was touching his arm, and Bruce snapped out of the depressing image.

"What?" he asked, glancing at Maria.

"I asked what you were going to do now that Shug is caught?" Maria repeated the question.

"I, uh. I guess I haven't really given it that much thought," Bruce replied. "Maybe I will take a vacation."

"And go where?" Maria asked.

"You know," Bruce said thoughtfully. "I think I'll go west. I have a good friend who moved out there a few years ago. I miss her very much."

"An old girlfriend?" Maria pried.

"Not exactly," Bruce replied.

"Tell me," Maria insisted.

Bruce thought about it for a moment. "Okay," he said reluctantly. "Not many people know this, but I have a daughter."

"What?" Maria asked, shocked. "Where?"

## Chapter Fifty-One

"Her mother moved to the west coast a few years ago," Bruce replied.

"How old is she?" Maria inquired.

"She just turned five," Bruce replied.

"This is the first time I'm hearing about this," Maria exclaimed. "Why so secretive?"

Bruce pondered the question for a moment. "If I'm being honest," he said, "I guess I feel like I'm a shitty father. I put a child on this earth, and I wouldn't know her face from any number of other preschoolers."

"Have you tried to see her?" Maria asked.

Bruce nodded. "When things didn't work out between her mother and I, she gave me a choice. Her and my daughter came as a package deal. I get both or I get neither."

They drove in silence for a few miles, then Bruce continued. "I guess that's why I like you, Maria. You remind me of the daughter I neglected."

"Well I think if your daughter ever gets to know you, she will be proud to call you Daddy," Maria said. "I know I would be."

"Thank you," Bruce replied, his hand suddenly moving up to smooth his hair, a move that prevented Maria from seeing the moisture that had formed at the corners of his eyes.

"I wish I could go with you," Maria continued. "I like traveling with you. You make me feel safe."

"I would like that very much," Bruce replied.

———◆———

Ten minutes after they walked into the waiting area, flight 317 from Albuquerque International Airport landed, right on schedule.

The weary passengers poured into the terminal, luggage in tow. Maria fidgeted from her left foot to the right, then back again. The crowd thinned down to a few stragglers.

Bruce suddenly felt a pang of anxiety. He checked his cell phone to see if he had any missed calls.

Nothing.

Then, at the very end of the line, Eli Reader appeared in the doorway.

Bruce stared, uncertain if his eyes were playing tricks on him. The cast was gone. The pale, sickly boy he had last seen coming out of surgery had somehow been transformed into a brawny teen. The jawline was more profound. And Eli had apparently spent some time working in the sun, because the thicker muscles and dark tan added to the image of a young boy coming into manhood.

Beside him, Maria completely transformed at the sight of her brother. It was as if the rest of the airport and all the churning faces faded. Suddenly nothing else in the whole world mattered. The distance between brother and sister closed, and the two embraced.

"Eli," Maria said, throwing her arms around her brother's neck. "Do you know who I am?"

"Maria," Eli said softly.

"Oh, thank God," Marla laughed happily. She took a step back and surveyed her brother. Questions flew from her lips.

Bruce stood back and waited patiently. He studied the crowd. He noticed someone that seemed to be hovering and taking a particular interest in the meeting between Eli and Maria. It was a middle-aged man with short, dark hair. The man wore a dark blue suit and tie, and a pair of glasses were perched comfortably on his nose.

Bruce watched the man closely. He thought he saw a glint of sadness cross his face. Then the man turned and disappeared into the crowd.

"Sparrow," Bruce muttered, half aloud. Of course, Sparrow would have made the flight with Eli, if for no other reason than to ensure that Eli landed safely.

Bruce smiled with satisfaction. It was over. Shug was in jail. A year ago, he, Bruce Ellsworth, had been hired to find Eli and return

## Chapter Fifty-One

him safely home. And while that feat had been a lot more complicated than it had at first appeared, nevertheless, he was about to deliver on his end of that promise. There were still many unanswered questions, but they could wait. Let Eli get settled back into the community first.

As if reading his mind, Maria nudged his elbow. "We're ready, Mr. Detective Man," she joked.

Bruce nodded and led the way back to his Explorer. Maria sat in her usual spot in the passenger seat and Eli sat in the middle. The two chatted in their Amish language, seemingly oblivious to Bruce's existence.

---

When Bruce turned north onto Caroline Creek Road, he had to brake hard. Vehicles were lined up on both sides, and dozens of reporters had their cameras set up at the end of the Reader driveway.

"You've got to be kidding me," Bruce said. "Nobody here is capable of dealing with the media?"

A few quick questions and it became apparent that Chief Westbritt and Stan Prater were gone. All that remained of the group that had gathered at the Reader living room table earlier that morning were Ruth Reader and Bishop Mast.

Bruce parked as close as he could and got out of his Explorer. He had one more task to complete before his time in Caroline Creek was done.

"All right everyone," he shouted. "Party's over. Pack it up and move on."

Behind him, the passenger door to the Explorer opened and Maria and Eli emerged. Cameras spun on tripods as the reporters fought to get the best shots. A thousand questions were hurled as the two started up the driveway.

The crowd in the front yard had their backs turned to prevent their faces from being filmed, but someone must have kept a lookout, because there was a shift as Eli and Maria approached. Black hats and bonnets became faces, and faces turned into smiles as the sea of black and white opened to absorb Eli and Maria into their midst.

For a few moments Bruce Ellsworth watched from the end of the driveway. There would be a funeral for Andy Reader. Then life in Caroline Creek would go back to normal.

Bruce turned back to the road.

The reporters had gotten their footage and camera gear was disappearing into the backs of vehicles. A girl struggled with her camera case and Bruce stopped to offer his help. She refused.

Bruce walked to his Explorer with his head down. He took a deep breath, and the smell of green fields and horse manure filled his nostrils.

As he drove away, something began to fester in the back of his mind, and Bruce fought to draw it to the forefront. It hung there, just outside the edge of his subconscious, but he couldn't quite place it.

Bruce made the connection twenty minutes later as he was passing through Grafton Illinois.

*The female reporter. The one who was struggling with her camera case.* He had seen her before, but where?

The pointy chin and nose convinced him his hunch was correct. The Thirsty Toad. Almost a year ago. A college girl working all alone on her laptop. A girl with a distinctive black ponytail.

Bruce pulled over on the shoulder of the road and glanced in his rearview mirror. He could go back, but the girl would be gone.

The girl had called herself a shadow, Bruce reminded himself as he pulled back out onto the highway. *Well by golly, who am I to try and force her out into the daylight?*

## Chapter Fifty-One

Bruce stepped on the accelerator and reached for the radio. He inhaled deeply and smiled as country music flooded from the speakers.

"For you, Maria," he said.

## Shadows We Remain

# EPILOGUE

*Daramore.* The last words uttered by Andy Reader before he died. I listened through my earpiece as Andy mouthed the confusing phrase. And I held my breath and silently hoped the words would not be understood by anyone.

They weren't.

Perhaps one can credit the chaos that followed Andy's death, but his dying confession evaded Maria's memory, and she never told Bruce what she had heard.

Had Andy's dying phrase been repeated to Bruce, this story might have ended very differently. Bruce might have written the word *Daramore* on his *Crazy Wall*, and quite possibly, during one of his long nights, pipe clamped in the corner of his mouth, he might have stumbled upon its true meaning.

But it was not to be, therefore I am the only one who knows.

*Daramore. Dar a more. There. Are. More.*

I am *the girl with the black ponytail*, and I am one of the sins Andy was trying to confess to Maria. In the above pages, I have given a true and accurate account of the events that unfolded in Caroline Creek, leading up to Shug's arrest. In the following pages, I will now give a brief account of my own story. I will do so, but not because I wish to draw attention to myself.

Actually, quite the opposite is true.

The reason I am divulging a small part of myself is that I am in danger. If I am discovered and killed, my true desire is that another shadow, in following the crumbs I have left behind, will find these written records, and only then, after my death, can the shadows be revealed.

I, like Sparrow, was never given a real name. We were subjects, to be used and, once our value diminished, to be tossed aside.

For the first sixteen years of my life, I lived among the Navajos in Shamrock, New Mexico. It was there that I discovered my entire life had been a lie. The more of the truth I uncovered, the more horrified and devastated I felt. I had been brought to the reservation as a baby. The man who brought me had been told to kill me. There had been a mix-up. Twin boys had been expected, but what they got was one boy and one girl. Me.

Upon learning of the mistake, Shug flew into a terrible rage. The midwife was killed and, since it was too late to switch me back for my twin brother, I was ordered to be killed.

I may never learn why the man didn't follow orders. Nurse Beth and I were unable to find him and, as far as I know, he never came back to check on me.

Maybe he was a shadow. Like me.

Regardless, with time I became the invisible force that would become Shug's undoing. I convinced Sparrow that his life was in danger, which is why he stole the tape and fled Shug's house, thereby foiling Shug's plans to head the mob.

The steel plates in the headrests of the airplane were my first experiment with explosives. But when the time came, I couldn't bring myself to flip the switch. If I was off on the detonation force, even by a few ounces, Eli would be seriously injured. Or even killed. Instead, I watched from my hiding spot beside the runway as the plane took flight with Eli inside. I'm not sure what detonated the headrests. Possibly a lightning strike created an electrical current. Either way, Eli survived, albeit with injury.

The game I intend to play is a dangerous one. After the encounter at the Riverside Motel, I went to Shug's house in

## Epilogue

St. Louis. I found the thumb drive exactly where he told me it would be. The thumb drive holds hundreds of files of crimes committed by the Trontelli crime family.

In one encrypted file I found what I had hoped wasn't true or possible. There are more shadows than just Sparrow and me. Shug's experimental operation encompassed multiple Amish communities.

But perhaps the identities of the other shadows are best left untold. Perhaps, like Sparrow and myself, they wish to live a life of non-existence. Perhaps Shug's original plan was not so absurd after all. For we were taken in the shadows, and *shadows we remain*.

Shadows We Remain

# AUTHOR'S NOTE:

When I started writing this manuscript, I had one clear goal in mind. I wanted to tell the tale of an Amish teenager who is kidnapped, and his journey to reconnect with a twin he never knew existed.

I thought I identified with Eli Reader, like I was living inside his soul.

At first, Eli's sister Maria was a mere afterthought. However, she kept rearing her head up, demanding to be acknowledged. I, like the Amish ministers, kept trying to silence her, but Maria would not be denied.

I can compare Maria to a garden full of red roses. The gardener waters and cares for the beauty, giving them every opportunity to develop into the magnificent works of art they are created to be. Then one day, among the sea of red, he discovers a single black rose.

At first the gardener resents the black rose. Her brazen beauty makes him feel uncomfortable, like his gardening skills have betrayed him.

Before long however, he comes to appreciate her for her individuality, even in the face of all that is good and evil.

By the end of this novel, I realized that I wasn't Eli Reader at all. I was Maria.

Therefore, I dedicate this book to all the Maria's—the black roses who are miserable with their current life as a misfit in society. Know that there is a brighter dawn tomorrow. And know that rain will only make you bloom the mightier.

Don't ever let the red roses around you crush your dream. Nobody knows better—the dream that burns within you, than yourself.

Reach for that dream. If you are eighty years old, and you feel like your dream has passed you by, reach for it anyway. If the red roses of society try and conform you to better fit into their garden of comfort, reach higher. And may your black rose blossom.

# AUTHOR'S BIO

Mose J Gingerich was born and raised in the Old Order Amish community of Greenwood, Wisconsin. During his 22 years among the Amish, Mose lived in over a dozen Amish communities, teaching school in several of them. Mose is best known for his roles on television shows like UPN's *Amish in the City,* 2004, and *Amish: Out of Order*—National Geographic Channel, 2012. When Mose is not blogging on his website at www.amishinthecitymose.com, he might be found hunched over a laptop, meticulously punching away one key at a time (blame the lack of technology during his childhood) and finishing book two of the Caroline Creek Series.

*Shadows We Remain* is Mose's debut novel and was written at night in the sleeper of his big rig while trucking coast to coast. You can contact Mose through his website, or send mail to P.O. Box 701, Holts Summit, Missouri 65043.

Made in the USA
Coppell, TX
22 January 2022

72082849R00218